BEY
THE MARRIAGE
VOWS

A Novel of Love, Loss, and Dementia

Jill Butcher

To my Laurie.

CONTENTS

ACKNOWLEDGMENTS

The Rare Dementia Support Group:
www.raredementiasupportgroup.org

The Alzheimer's Society:
www.alzheimers.org.uk

The Al-Anon Family Group:
www.al-anonuk.org.uk

Extract from YES, MINISTER © Jonathan Lynn & The Estate of Sir Antony Jay by kind permission of Alan Brodie Representation Ltd. – www.alanbrodie.com

PROLOGUE

The Beginning

In the beginning there were words.

Lots and lots of words.

Words were used for all sorts of things — negotiating, flirting, joking, arguing, explaining. They were even used for telling lies. Most of all, words were used for thinking. Words were used for all the things that make us human.

In the beginning there was a handsome man called Lionel. He had a lively personality, a clever brain, and a wicked sense of humour. He liked cricket, he liked playing cards, and he liked girls. He liked amateur dramatics too, and in those days he had no trouble learning the words. And because he was so good-looking he always got the romantic leads, but really he'd have preferred to play the villains. Villains have more interesting words.

Lionel was in his late twenties. He'd embarked on a promising career and had just been promoted. He had the gift of the gab and used words to wheel and deal and think on his feet. He worked in a big department on the sixth floor of an office overlooking the Thames. He had six people under him and he was very pleased with the way life was going.

One day there was a new girl in the office. She wasn't in his department but she was on the same floor. He found out that her name was Frances but that people called her Effie. He watched her for a while and contrived reasons to talk to her. Whenever he saw her he'd make a light-hearted remark, and she'd smile shyly but look away.

Effie was a bit nervous of Lionel. But intrigued. The other girls in the office told her he was a 'bit of a lad'. She didn't know whether that was a warning or a challenge.

One Friday afternoon, Lionel timed things so that he got into the lift with Effie. "Where are you going now?" he asked her as he pressed the button for the ground floor.

"Home," she said.

"And how will you get home?"

"I'll get a train at Waterloo," she said.

Then he pressed the emergency button to stop the lift. In those days you could do that. "What happens if you miss it?" he asked.

"Nothing," she said.

He saw the anxiety in her eyes as the lift juddered to a halt. So he laughed and switched it on again. "Only joking!" he said.

They walked across Waterloo Bridge and they used words to discuss the weather and the office and how the River Thames sparkled in the early evening sunlight. And Lionel suggested a drink in the bar of the National Theatre. He bought a gin and tonic for Effie and whisky and water for himself. They talked, amongst other things, about drama, and while they were there, they booked tickets for a play.

And they fell in love.

Later they used words to make promises. Promises about keeping each other *in sickness and in health,* and *as long as ye both shall live.* Neither of them thought, really thought, about what those words might mean. Those promises were to be kept be *until death us do part.* That all seemed okay at the time.

Neither of them knew that, with all the love in the world, you could be parted long before death. You could be parted by sickness itself.

One day there will be no words at all.

CHAPTER 1

A Visit to the Leisure Centre

Lionel checks his watch. It has an expandable gold strap that he wears stretched on top of the cuff of his shirt which he pulls below the sleeve of his jumper. That's the way he likes to wear it and he wouldn't have it any other way. It is always ten minutes fast. That's the way he likes it. The watch tells him that it's half past five which is time for his afternoon walk. It is a nice day in early summer, and on nice days in summer he goes for an afternoon walk. That's after he has woken up from his afternoon nap. The heart nurse told him he should go for a walk every day. The sun is shining and the sky is blue, and he is looking forward to his afternoon walk.

He goes to the front door and puts on his coat. He doesn't do it up because the bottom bits of the zip are hard to link together. It doesn't matter. Nothing matters very much. He checks that his cigarettes, his lighter and his blue puffer are in his coat pocket. He has a brown puffer too but that stays at home. That doesn't go in his coat pocket. His credit cards are in the top pocket of his shirt beneath his jumper, and he has money in the back pocket of his trousers. Those are the places where they are supposed to be. He picks up his house keys which are hanging on the furthest right of the hooks by the front door in the hall, and puts them in his trouser pocket. He is ready.

The steps from the front door lead down to the drive where his green X-Type Jag is parked. He goes out every morning in his green X-Type Jag. Today he went to Boots to collect his pills. He's not allowed to go to Ratigans Chemist any more. He doesn't know why, but there was a letter after that stupid woman had a go at him. It said he was excluded from entering the premises. He hasn't told Effie about the letter because she'll question him. "Why? When? What?" she'll ask. And she'll go on and on and on even though he doesn't know the answer. Effie takes stuff so seriously. The letter said a whole load of stupid fucking nonsense about 'inappropriate behaviour'. It didn't make any sense to him. But he doesn't mind going to Boots. It's in the High Street. That's further but it doesn't matter.

If you cross the road and go down the twitten between the garden fences you come to the park. Lionel likes to peer over the left-hand fence because there are chickens in the garden and he likes to look at chickens. His mum and dad kept chickens and he used to like running down to the hen house every morning to collect the eggs. There are four chickens here and they are different colours. They live at the house which is number fourteen. It belongs to his old friend, Richard, and his wife, Harriet. Harriet is a nice chiropodist who cuts his toenails sometimes. She told him the names of the chickens, but he can't be bothered to remember them. It's not important. Every so often he phones Harriet and makes an appointment and he pays her fifteen pounds to cut his toenails. She got a bit upset once about something he said to her, but it doesn't matter. It's not important. People are so sensitive about swearing and stuff.

It's a nice park with trees and grass. It's where the Leisure Centre is. He used to play squash there when he was young, but he's not young anymore. And the man he played squash with has gone away.

Maybe he died. People walk their dogs in the park and pick up the dog shit in plastic bags. There is a special bin for the dog shit. There is a children's playground with a fence and a gate to keep out dogs who are not allowed in. Quite right too, thinks Lionel. That's one of the modern ideas that's okay. He can remember Effie being furious when Nigel used to come home with dog shit on his shoes.

Lionel opens the gate into the children's playground and sits down on one of the benches there. He feels a bit breathless. He lights a cigarette and inhales deeply. That's better. He coughs. On the other bench are young mums, chattering like chatterboxes while their kids play. There are kids on the climbing frame, kids on the swings and kids on the slide. They are shrieking with laughter. Lionel winces at the noise. Noise makes his ears hurt.

One of the mums on the other bench is a big fat slob and she is wearing yellow leggings and a black bra that is visible underneath an orange top that looks like a vest. One strap of the black bra has slipped down and lies loosely on her horrible fat arm. He stares at her. Her boobs are huge, but her belly is bigger. She is a saggy sort of woman.

"What's up, Grandad?" says the big fat slob. "What yer starin' at?"

He points. "Your bra strap's slipped down," he says.

She starts pulling up the bra strap.

"Want a hand?" he asks. He laughs to show he is making a joke. "Say yes or no," he adds.

"You filthy old..." she begins.

"That was a joke," he says. Why don't people get his jokes? Doesn't she realise he wouldn't touch a fat slob like that with a barge pole? Somebody must have done to get her pregnant though. More than touched her. Poor bloke must have been desperate. How could you get it in past all that flab?

He turns away and looks at the children. Children are much nicer.

They have smooth skin and shiny hair and he likes to look at them running and jumping and laughing and climbing. One little girl has climbed to the top of the slide and is perched up there, not daring to go down it. She waves down to the fat slob who must be her mother and is watching her carefully. The little girl is wearing a frilly sundress and she has golden curls that hang down her back. You can see that she is wearing matching knickers, which is a nice idea. How could that fat slob have given birth to a beautiful child like that?

"Go on!" he shouts to her. "Go for it!"

And she lets go and slides down to the bottom of the slide.

"Whee!" he calls to her as she whizzes past. Then, "Well done!" he shouts when she gets to the bottom. He claps.

The little girl beams at him, and he feels a warm glow. He smiles at her and winks. He likes children. It's a pity his grandchildren don't live nearer. He'd like to bring them here.

"Sally, you come 'ere this minute!" calls the fat slob. He doesn't quite hear what's said next but it's something about keeping away from horrible dirty old men. The girl runs off to play on the roundabout.

He isn't horrible or dirty, he thinks. But he is feeling his age these days. It was that spell in hospital that did it. Things haven't been the same since.

He finishes his cigarette, drops the end on the ground, and grinds it out with his shoe. He looks at his watch. It is ten to six now and it's time to visit the Leisure Centre.

He goes up the steps and in through the glass doors. He likes to see what's going on. You can sit at a table and watch the children having lessons in the little swimming pool. It's called the training pool. Other people are sitting at tables and some of them are drinking cups of tea and eating stuff from the café here. Why are people always eating? No wonder so many of them are fat. That's the pool where he and Effie used to take Suzie and Nigel when they were little. There is a teacher standing at the edge of the pool instructing a class of children who are splashing across with bright orange floats.

"Can I help you?" comes a voice.

A girl in a red polo shirt with a Lansdown Leisure motif is standing expectantly at his table.

Help him? What she could possibly help him with? How fucking stupid!

"Course you can't!" he reacts. He glares at her.

"It's just that this is the cafeteria. These tables are for people who want to eat. Maybe I could you get you a cup of tea?"

He pushes back his chair. "I was just watching," he says as he stands up. He shuffles off and heads for the stairs. He pants with effort to get to the viewing area of the main pool. That's where Suzie and Nigel competed when they were teenagers. Suzie was good. Used to win races sometimes. The pool is roped off into lanes and people are swimming up and down as fast they can. He sits on the front row but stands up to cheer the winner. The lifeguard down there gives him a funny look. A couple of spectators glare at him too.

"What are you staring at?" he says. They look away.

Then he makes his way to the gym. You can look through the glass and see the machines and all the stupid sweaty people who are using them. He went there for a while after he came out of hospital. It was supposed to be good for his heart. That's what Dr Andrews said. But he didn't like it much. Then he fell off one of the machines and hurt his wrist. Effie was furious that he wasn't being looked after properly so she went to complain to the manager. But she returned even more furious. "I've never been so embarrassed in my whole life!" she'd shouted at him.

"It wasn't my fault the machine broke," he'd said.

"Yes, it was. You adjusted the wrong clip. And it was definitely your fault that you were just wandering in there without paying."

His wrist got better and it didn't matter. It wasn't important.

He heads along the corridor which looks down on the main hall. People are playing table tennis there. He used to be good at table tennis. He played in that business league when he first worked in London. And then he played here with the oldies. Until that other row about him not paying. He likes to watch.

He leans over the barrier. "Your grip's not right," he calls to a young girl who's messed up her serve. "You want to turn your wrist this way."

"Give it a break!" says her partner, looking up at him crossly.

Lionel shrugs and shuffles off. He was only trying to be helpful. People are so aggressive these days. He could do with a cigarette.

He goes back down the stairs. It's easier but he grips the handrails tightly, all the way down.

A whole lot of children are running in through the main doors. What a rabble! They are shouting and laughing and none of them are looking where they are going. Why doesn't someone keep them under control? If he'd behaved like that when he was young he'd have got a right clip round the ear. A young lad crashes into him. Almost makes him lose his balance. "Careful!" shouts Lionel. He pushes the child roughly aside. "Look where you're fucking going."

The child falls to the floor and begins to cry.

"Don't cry," sneers Lionel. "You're not hurt."

The fat mum in the yellow leggings is waddling forwards, black bra strap hanging down again. God, she's revolting, thinks Lionel.

She helps the child up and puts her arms around him. "Come to Mummy," she says, but she is glaring at Lionel. "You filthy old man!"

she snarls. "How dare you lay your hands on my Timmy!"

Lionel growls, raises his arm and clenches his fist at her. He's not going to hit the stupid bitch. He just wants to scare her.

There is a crowd of people all milling around, and the girl in the Lansdown Leisure polo shirt is speaking into a walkie-talkie. "Duty manager, duty manager," she is saying. "Please come to reception. It's urgent."

"Call the police!" yells the fat slob.

The manager pushes his way through the crowd. "Calm down," he says. "Now, what's upset everyone?"

"That man!" cries the fat slob. "He's just attacked my Timmy and he raised his fist at me. Threatened me! He's a nutter. He's a paedophile." She looks around at the other mothers for support. "We've all seen him. 'Aven't we? Every afternoon he's down the playground, lookin' up girls' knickers. Our children aren't safe. He should be locked up. Call the police!"

"Please, madam, calm down," says the manager. "Let me deal with this." Then he addresses Lionel. "Would you come this way please, Mr Butler, sir? We need to have a chat in private."

"You need to call the police," yells the fat slob. "He's attacked my Timmy. If you don't call the police, I will. And I'll call the local paper an' all, and tell them our kids aren't safe here."

In the manager's office, things are quieter. Lionel is puzzled — how does the manager know his name? What a dreadful woman! he thinks. Why don't they arrest her? Women like that shouldn't be allowed to have children.

"I'm sorry, sir, but we do have to call the police. You did hit that child and the matter must be followed up."

"Oh, for fuck's sake! I didn't hit the little monster. I pushed him out of the way. He was out of control. He wasn't looking. Haven't you got anything better to do than picking on me? Say yes or no."

"Yes, I have," said the manager, evenly, "but I have had complaints about you before, Mr Butler, about you watching children in the playground. Some of the mothers have indicated their concern."

"It's a public place. What's wrong with me going there?"

"Maybe nothing. In any case, the playground is not my responsibility. The Lansdown Leisure Centre is."

CHAPTER 2

A Car Mechanic's Diagnosis

Effie scanned the row of cars. There it was – her little lime green number, bright and shiny in the afternoon sunlight, standing out from the all the silvers and whites and beiges that filled the car park. She smiled. That car was the one thing in her life that could be relied upon to brighten her mood. She clicked her key as she approached, opened the driver's door and slid into the driver's seat. She undid the roof clips, turned on the ignition, and pressed the button behind the handbrake. In the driver's mirror, she watched the boot begin to open. Above her, the roof of her oh-so-cool convertible slid back to reveal a widening strip of pale blue sky. She watched it fold ready to disappear from view. She always loved this moment, especially if someone was watching.

Nobody was.

And nothing happened.

There was an electronic buzz and everything stopped. The roof half open, the boot half open. She frowned. What was stopping it? She pressed the button again. A buzz, but no action. She turned the ignition off, then on, then tried again. Nothing. She got out and walked round the car. There didn't appear to be anything stopping the mechanism. She jiggled the half-open boot lid a little. Not too much. She didn't want to force anything. Nothing. She looked around. There was no one she could ask to help, and even if there had been, what could she have asked them to do?

She got back into the car to consider her options.

Option one: she could call Lionel. That's what most married women do in a car crisis – call their husbands. But she wasn't a normal married woman. She didn't have a normal husband or a normal marriage. And anyway, Lionel had never had been much use with cars, not even when he'd been normal. Whenever that was.

Option two: she could call the AA. They might be able to fix it, but she'd have to wait for someone to come, and this was not like changing a wheel. They mightn't be able to solve the problem there and then.

Option three: She could drive it home. Was it still drivable? She started up, put it in gear and lifted the clutch. Yes, it went forwards. The rear view through the driver's mirror was of the open boot sloping up to the sky, but it's easy enough to drive on wing mirrors, she thought. If she went slowly it would be ok. But what was the point of going home? That wasn't going to solve the problem.

Option four: She could drive it straight to Barton's Garage. She and Lionel had been getting their cars serviced at Barton's Garage for over thirty years. She could leave it there and walk home. That was the best option. And if Gary were there, she'd be able to talk to him. Yes, that was what she'd do.

It was seven miles back to Dalton Heath. It must be illegal, she thought, to drive a car with a half-open boot and a half-open roof. It felt weird, but at least it wasn't raining. She didn't dare go faster than twenty miles an hour and didn't come out of third gear once. Every time someone overtook her she felt herself cringe with embarrassment. But no one stopped her and she made it into town and pulled up outside Barton's Garage.

She headed for the office and opened the door. "Hello Gary," she said. She was glad he was there. It was always more difficult if she had to talk to one of the younger mechanics. Gary had been a trainee when Lionel had first taken his car there. They'd only had one car in those days. Now Gary was running the business, but he was still a hands-on manager and he knew both her car and Lionel's. They had watched him grow from a skinny young lad with a mass of dark curls into a middle-aged, thick-set manager with thinning hair. His smile and the sparkle in his eye were just the same. Sometimes he seemed like an old friend.

She explained about the car.

"Let's take a look," said Gary. Then, "I see what you mean!" he laughed when he saw it. "How far have you driven like that? You were pushing your luck!"

He checked a couple of things, then went to get his diagnostic gear.

"That looks like a computer," she remarked.

"Yeah. It is," he said. "Things weren't like this when I started this job."

He was pressing buttons and checking figures on the screen. "You enjoying the car?" he asked.

Effie nodded. "I have so far this summer," she said.

"Mmmm. The weather's picked up now," he said. "And how's Lionel's new Jag?"

Effie gave a resigned smile. "Just like the other one," she said.

Lionel had written off his first second-hand green X-Type that he adored. They'd been on the A23. They'd pulled into the left-hand lane to turn off onto the M25, slowed down to join the heavy queue for the exit, and a van had driven straight into the back of them. It had been a cold winter's morning and Lionel had told the van driver he was 'a fucking idiot'. He'd also been rude to the AA man, who wanted them to get out of the car to stand behind the barriers for safety. The colour had drained from Lionel's face. He was shivering, looking most unwell. "No, I'm not going out in that fucking cold," he'd said.

The incident wasn't Lionel's fault, though Effie did think he should have pulled over somewhat earlier. The damage wasn't that bad, but an old Jag isn't worth a lot and the insurance company had written it off. Lionel replaced it with a newer, but still second-hand model that looked exactly the same.

"Wouldn't you like the red one?" she'd suggested when they'd looked at the two possibilities on a garage forecourt. "Just for a change."

But no. He'd wanted another green one.

Effie had realised afterwards that he was trying to pretend to himself that the accident had never happened. Much later, she was clearing out a drawer when she found some paperwork about changing car numbers. Lionel would have liked the replacement car to have the same car number as the write-off, but he must have found the form filling required too confusing. Even then.

"Same scratches on it?" remarked Gary.

"He said they've happened in car parks," said Effie.

"Hmmm!" said Gary. "Maybe."

He leaned forward, making an adjustment to her car roof. "You do realise," he said, his eyes on the job in front of him, "that Lionel is in the early stages of dementia?"

Effie stared at his back, her eyes wide, her mouth open in disbelief. Surely not? Then a slow understanding crept through her system. Is that what this was about? Did that account for the weird behaviour, the extraordinary things that were happening? The sheer nastiness of Lionel's attitude to people? Was all that to do with his brain? There was a long silence as Gary worked.

Finally, Gary closed the roof, clicked the clips into place, and turned to look at her. "It's not his fault," he added.

"I... I know he's difficult," she said. "I know some people find him impossible, but..." Her voice faded. She found him impossible. A dozen incidents flashed through her mind. "But I never thought..."

"I recognise the symptoms," said Gary. He turned to close the boot. "We went through it with my father-in-law. He was a nice bloke too."

Effie shook her head. "I've been at my wit's end."

"You're in for a hell of a time. You're going to need help. You need to get a diagnosis," said Gary. "And the sooner the better. It'll take longer than you think."

"I... I don't know..."

Gary patted the car on the bonnet. "I've got the roof and the boot closed," he said. "But the mechanism is broken. It needs replacing. You'll have to go back to the manufacturer's garage for that. It won't be cheap." He grinned. "That's the trouble with these gimmicky cars. Things do tend to go wrong." His brow puckered. "Where did you buy it?"

Effie frowned. "Er... Greenwoods... in Farnden..." she said.

"Yeah. That's the place... take it back there." He handed her back the keys.

"The bill?"

He shook his head. "Not just for that," he said. "And remember, whatever people say about your hubby... he's a great bloke... he can't help what's happening to him."

It took two days for Greenwood Motors to get the spare part for the car and another morning to fit it. It took two whole weeks to get an appointment with Dr Andrews. As she drove into the car park of the Park Health Centre she remembered the first time she'd made an appointment to talk to Dr Andrews about Lionel.

It must have been over two years ago, and Lionel had just come home from an annual medical check-up. "How did you get on?" she'd asked him.

"Fine," he had said, as he always did. Fine, given that he kept taking the tablets, presumably. Effie didn't think Lionel was fine. Lionel was a wreck. It couldn't go on like this.

So she had made an appointment, walked into Dr Andrews' surgery, sat down, and burst into tears.

"I'm sorry..." she stuttered. "It's about my husband."

"Yes?" Dr Andrews pushed a box of tissues across his desk towards her. She'd taken one and blown her nose.

"He comes in here for his check-ups," she'd sobbed, the tissue scrunched in her left hand. She'd taken a deep breath. "Then he comes home and tells me he's fine. He isn't fine. I know he isn't."

The doctor pulled up Lionel's records on his computer screen then turned to her. "We have never said he's fine," he said. "He has COPD."

"COPD?"

"Chronic Obstructive Pulmonary Disease, caused by smoking." He waited for Effie to assimilate the information.

"How much does he drink?" he asked.

Effie sniffed and wiped the tears that were spilling down her face. "About... a bottle of spirits a day," she'd said. "Vodka at lunchtime, whisky in the evening."

Dr Andrews had expressed no surprise. "It's a lifestyle choice. He's going downhill and there's nothing we, or anyone else, can do about it. It's too late. He won't listen to us. He won't help himself. He thinks he's immortal and that our job is to repair any damage he's done."

The impression Dr Andrews had given Effie at that time, was that this particular patient had driven him to the limits of his patience and was nothing but a waste of space.

He'd leant forward. "Now the person I'm worried about is you. You're a healthy woman and you have years ahead of you. How do you cope?" He pushed the box of tissues a little nearer.

Effie took one, blew her nose again and took a deep breath.

"I mean it, how are you coping?"

"I suppose... I lead the life of a widow really. Lionel won't go anywhere with me. We don't go to pubs, cinemas... anywhere. He won't go on aeroplanes – partly because of the smoking restrictions I suppose, but mainly, I think... he just doesn't want to. So we have no holidays. He's so rude that all our friends have dropped us. His behaviour has destroyed our social life."

She'd taken another tissue and wiped her eyes. The sobbing had subsided.

"The only thing he does now is play bridge, but not with me. He's too impatient."

"And your marriage?"

Effie took a few deep breaths. "He doesn't sleep with me. He moved into the spare room four years ago. We weren't sleeping well but I was... surprised when he actually shifted his things. I thought he might come back sometimes for a... well... but he never did. And now..." Her voice faded. The last thing she'd want now was that unwashed snoring wreck of humanity back in her bed.

"And how does that make you feel?"

Effie had paused. "Lonely."

Should she tell him about Matt? "I have my own friends now. My own social life," she said. "I have things to do... tennis... music... other things."

Dr Andrews listened attentively.

She continued. "I go on holidays, sometimes on my own, sometimes with... other people." She decided to tell him about Matt. "I have a... a gentleman friend..." There, she had said it. "But he lives in California, so I don't see him very often. We meet up when and where we can."

She had first met Matt years ago, when both their marriages had been viable, if not perfect. There had been a spark, and they'd kept in touch. Christmas cards at first. Emails later. And then, a couple of months ago, she'd taken a solo touring holiday to his part of the world. And she'd looked him up, not knowing what to expect. The spark was still there, and with each of them now living in the shadow of a dysfunctional marriage, they virtually fell into each other's arms. Effie had delayed her flight home and they had embarked on a crazy, romantic, long-distance affair. Effie had been shocked at the physicality of her response to him. And the joy in the pleasure they shared. In the light of Lionel's changed behaviour, his altered personality, she had felt no guilt.

Lionel was an alcoholic. Matt was an escape.

Dr Andrews nodded. "That's good. You can't do anything about Lionel. It's important that you look after yourself. You go ahead – enjoy some holidays with your lover. You deserve all the joy you can get." He had leaned forward and said earnestly, "There is no future for you with Lionel. Have you thought about seeing a solicitor?"

"Er... no. I've thought about how I can go on like this, but..."

"Well, do so. You've been doing wonderful job with a very difficult man. You don't have to do it forever. And don't feel guilty."

She had stopped crying, but she had left the surgery thinking that nothing, absolutely nothing, had been resolved.

And three days later Lionel had collapsed on the steps to the front door.

He had spent two weeks in intensive care and five weeks in hospital. There were three days when the doctors thought he might die. At least, they said he was *very poorly*, which Effie knew was a euphemism for *might die*. When pressed, they agreed that he *might not survive* which was a slightly weaker euphemism for *might die*. One of the junior doctors had been more honest. He'd said to Effie, 'We might be able to save his life, but we won't be able to make him better."

Back then she didn't understand the full significance of the statement. What was worrying her at the time was: how would she organise a funeral? Who would come? Who could she ask to give a eulogy? Lionel had fallen out with his family and lost all his friends. There was only immediate family left. And they were all sick of him.

Each night she'd emailed Matt in California. He'd been her rock, the person who'd let her pour out her anxieties across cyberspace. And oh, did she long to see him in the flesh again! Of course, being a rock is quite easy. You don't actually have to do anything.

But Lionel hadn't died, and there'd been no funeral. The problem was on hold.

And it was still, all this time later, on hold.

She parked the car in the Parkside Health Centre car park and closed the roof. This time the mechanism worked perfectly. So it should. The repair had cost enough. She clicked the roof clips down and got out. Here we go again, she thought as she entered the reception area.

"It's about Lionel," she said to Dr Andrews.

"Yes," he said flatly.

"I think he might have dementia."

Dr Andrews sat back in his chair and took a deep breath. "Now, Mrs Butler, what gives you that idea?"

"Well... it was Gary Barton... you know... he runs Barton's Garage. He fixes our cars. He's known us for years. He said so."

Dr Andrews smiled slowly. "So you have a garage mechanic's diagnosis of your husband's mental health?" he said. Then he laughed. "Would you trust me to service your car?"

Effie gave a nervous laugh. She saw his point. "Well... he said he recognised the symptoms. His father-in-law had it."

Dr Andrews nodded. "Okay." He paused. "Has Lionel ever got lost going somewhere he knows very well? That tends to be an early sign."

Effie slowly shook her head. "Not as far as I know."

"Look," said Dr Andrews. "Isn't Lionel a bridge player?" He was looking at his computer screen.

Effie nodded. "He's very good."

"Dementia affects short-term memory. He wouldn't be able to play bridge if he had dementia."

"Oh," said Effie. "It's just that his behaviour..."

"I know about his behaviour. He is rude, aggressive, and objectionable. There are staff in this surgery who have refused to work with him."

Effie frowned. "What? Who?"

"Practice nurses, secretaries, receptionists. None of them can understand why you're still married to him. Neither can I."

Effie frowned. "What does he do?" It was a silly question. She knew what he did. The swearing. The angry impatience if they were running a little late. It was endless.

"He has what we call an *extreme personality*. As people age, their personality traits tend to be exaggerated."

"It's very difficult," she said. "He did give up drinking after that spell in hospital."

"Yes, that amazed me," said the doctor. He smiled. "I read him the riot act, but I didn't think it would have any effect. At least his liver recovered."

"But it didn't make much difference to his behaviour," said Effie. "He still has what I believe is called the alcoholic personality."

"That's inevitable. Once an alcoholic..." Then, "How are you?" he asked.

She shrugged.

"You've stuck with him," he pointed out.

She nodded. "Just about," she said.

"Still getting away from time to time?"

She nodded again. In the last couple of years, she and Matt had met up all over the world. Matt was a travel writer who went to all sorts of locations and was often able to take her with him. It was a whirlwind romance, at a time of life when things like whirlwind romances didn't happen. She smiled at the recollection of getting off aeroplanes in Florida or Venice or Chile, the queuing forever to get through immigration. Scanning the sea of faces in the arrivals lounge. And that moment of magic when she and Matt made eye contact.

Lionel had asked no questions. That in itself was weird. He hadn't wanted to take holidays abroad. She had. So be it. So long as he didn't have to travel with her, he didn't appear to care who did. If it hadn't been for Matt lifting her out of the dreariness of her home life, maybe she would have left Lionel by now. Maybe she still should.

Then Dr Andrews changed the subject. "Did you know I'm leaving in a couple of months' time?" he said.

"Er... yes... someone mentioned it. Good luck with the move, and your new job."

"Thank you. Lionel will go on Dr Dauncey's list. He does already know him quite well."

Effie nodded.

Dr Andrews keyed something into his computer, then looked at her. He tapped his pen on the desk, then said slowly, "Believe me, Mrs Butler, it isn't dementia."

CHAPTER 3

Lionel and the Bridge Club

Lionel swings the green Jaguar into the car park and pulls into the space next to the chairman's BMW. He puts out his cigarette in the ash tray, gets out and pushes the car door closed.

He pauses in the doorway. There are nine bridge tables, each laid with green cloths, and four bidding boxes. His partner, Alan, is already there and is seated West on table three. Lionel goes in and pushes the chair back to sit opposite in position East.

"Why are we sitting East-West?" he demands.

"I need to keep moving. Since my knee replacement, I tend to seize up if I sit still too long."

Lionel grunts irritably as he sits down in position East. He likes sitting North. He likes to be in control of the scoring.

"Good evening, Lionel," says Alan pointedly.

"Good evening, Alan," recites Lionel in response. There are bridge etiquette rules about greeting each other courteously. Lionel has frequently been told off for not observing the correct protocol.

"How are you?" says Alan.

"Average."

Lionel does not return the question, partly because he doesn't want a description of the state of Alan's knee and partly because he can't be bothered. Alan asks, "What system are we playing tonight?"

Alan is Lionel's partner every second Thursday of every month. They each have other partners for other nights. Lionel likes to play two or three times a week, but just recently it's been more difficult arranging things. He's had many partners over the years and at one time the phone didn't stop ringing with people wanting to fix bridge dates with him.

He remembers one of his early partners, a flirtatious old biddy called Babs. She used to joke that he was her favourite toy boy as well as her favourite partner. And he used to say that she was his favourite tart and she'd shriek with vulgar laughter. She was pushing seventy when they started playing together. With her white stiletto heels, her wrinkly cleavage and her leopard print trousers, she'd been a breath of fresh air in an otherwise staid environment.

And so had he, she told him. "We need more members like you," she'd said. "People who can crack a joke." She was a brilliant player but it didn't stop her dying of drink.

Lionel likes to crack a joke or two. You need someone to lighten things up in a place like this. But they're a gloomy bunch. Some of them laugh at his jokes but some of them just glare at him.

Lionel has been a member of the Dalton Heath Bridge Club for over thirty years. He played with Effie in the early days. They had to get babysitters back then. But Effie's useless at cards and she never got any better. But they made good friends through the bridge club and it was the basis of much of their social life at one time.

Lionel and Alan discuss their bidding system and agree on five-card majors with a strong no trump. "What discards?" asks Alan.

"Good evening, gentlemen, may we join you?" comes the instantly recognisable tone of Flora Mackenzie. Her shrill Scottish lilt is unmistakable. She sits South while her husband takes the North position.

"Of course ye may," squeaks Lionel in an exaggerated Scottish accent. He's good at accents and he likes to imitate people. He laughs.

Flora presses her lips tightly together. Her husband makes an odd noise in his throat which isn't exactly a laugh.

"That was a joke," says Lionel.

Alan fixes him. "Lionel," he says quietly. "It isn't new and it isn't funny."

Lionel shrugs. He is about to make a remark about some people being too sensitive, and others being too humourless, but the director is issuing instructions to start play.

The first hand is a bit of a gamble but Lionel makes his four-spade contract. Flora pauses forever on that last but one trick, dithering whether to lead out her ten of hearts or seven of clubs. "Just play a card," says Lionel. He rocks his chair impatiently. He stares fixedly at her.

"I'm thinking," she says.

"It doesn't matter," he says. He knows exactly which two cards are in her hand.

She finally lays one down.

"There," he says triumphantly, as he takes the trick with the last trump. "I told you it didn't matter."

"Well played," says Alan.

"They let me off the hook. Flora shouldn't have put up her queen of hearts." He looks at her. "You'd have got me down if you hadn't done that."

Flora looks down. Her face is pale and her hands are shaking.

"It's only a game," says her husband.

"Will you move, please?" calls the director when the first three hands have been completed. "Players up one, cards down one," he adds.

There's not much space between the tables and there's a bit of a kerfuffle when Minnie Armitage, who never looks where she's going, bumps into Lionel. "Careful," he shouts. "Look where you're effing going." He knows he mustn't swear here. The chairman told him so in a letter. Didn't have the balls to speak to him face to face. So he has to say things like 'Eff' or 'Effing'. Or maybe 'Sugar' sometimes.

He takes his seat at the next table. But as soon as he settles, he realises that the chair he's taken is one of the old soggy ones that ought to be replaced. He stands up and drags it to the edge of the room and fetches another from an unoccupied table, and sits down for the second time.

"Good evening," says the new North player.

Lionel wriggles in the chair to get himself comfortable. "That's better," he says when he's finally seated.

"Are you ready?" asks North.

"Of course I'm ready," snaps Lionel. "Let's get on with it." He's ready for a cigarette and he's hoping he'll be dummy.

By the time he is dummy they've played two more hands and his partner is playing a six-heart contract. "Good luck," says Lionel as the opening lead is played. He lays his cards down and hurries outside, taking a quick look at South's cards as he walks past. He sees instantly that the contract is makeable.

It takes just about as long to smoke a cigarette as it does to play a hand of bridge. Sometimes a bit longer.

"How did you do?" he asks as he hurries back.

"One down, I'm afraid," says Alan.

"You didn't finesse the queen of diamonds?"

Alan shakes his head. "No. Went for the drop. Sorry."

Lionel exhales impatiently. "Fucking idiot!" he mutters to himself.

Jacintha Maloney sits North, partnered by Jeff Bowling. Lionel stares at Jacintha. She is huge. Her backside hangs over the sides of the chair. Not the sort of person you'd want to sit beside on an aeroplane.

Jeff wins the contract and Alan leads a card through Jacintha's dummy. She lays down her cards and stands. "I won't be a minute," she says as she turns towards the toilets.

"Can't imagine the loo's strong enough to hold her fat arse," remarks Lionel in a loud whisper.

"Shhhh," says Alan. "It's you to play."

Jacintha returns in time for the last trick of the contract.

Lionel looks up at her and beams. "Everything come out all right?" he asks lightly.

She purses her lips and pushes forward the final card.

"There – your partner's made an extra trick. You did well to set up the diamonds," Lionel compliments North.

The evening is over and the bridge players have played twenty-seven hands of duplicate bridge. Some are exhausted with the concentration required. Others are stimulated by the mental challenge.

Lionel and Alan have come second with over sixty percent. If it hadn't been for Alan's mistake they'd have come top. Lionel doesn't need to point that out to his partner, but he does. After all, if you don't tell people what they've done wrong, they'll never learn. He's only being helpful.

"Bye, Lionel. Thanks for the game," says Alan as they head for the door.

"Thank you. See you in a fortnight."

"Actually," begins Alan, "I'm not sure I'm free... I'll email you."

"Excuse me, Lionel?" interrupts the club chairman who has

hurried after them.

"Yes," says Lionel, turning.

"Could I have a private word with you?"

Lionel bristles. "Okay, Charles. If you must. What is it?"

They wait for the stragglers to leave the bridge room and allow them some privacy. "It's just that..." The chairman hesitates. "There's been another official complaint about you."

"What? Why?"

"I just wanted to warn you. You'll be getting a letter from the chairman of the Conduct Committee."

"Conduct Committee? What the fuck is that?"

The chairman takes a deep, drawn-out breath. "It's a subcommittee. Its duties are summarised on the website. The letter will explain it all. This can't go on, you know. We can't discuss it here, but you don't seem to have any understanding of a normal, acceptable way to behave in company. Goodnight, Lionel."

"Just a minute," Lionel calls back the chairman.

"Yes?"

"This letter? It'll be addressed to me? Not Effie?"

"Of course, Lionel. This situation has nothing to do with Effie."

Lionel nods happily. "That's okay then."

As Lionel heads for the door he notices Jean Williams stretching to reach to her coat from the row of hooks by the door. She used to be one of his partners. He lifts down the coat and holds it for her. She is getting increasingly disabled with her crooked shoulders and her wasted body. "Keep your shoulders back!" he says lightly as he helps her on with the coat. "Want a lift home?" he asks as an afterthought.

She shakes her head. "I ordered a taxi," she says. "It'll be here in minute."

"Please yourself," he says.

As Lionel gets into his green Jag, he lights a cigarette and opens the window.

CHAPTER 4

An Invitation to a Party

"I think I'll go for the prawn salad," Effie decided. She passed the card across and took a sip of her Pinot Grigio.

Sandra considered the menu. "Bacon and Brie baguette for me," she said. "I'll go and order."

Effie and Sandra met for lunch every few months. They were, Effie supposed, 'ladies who lunch', though the term seemed patronising. This time they were in the King's Arms. They had supported each other through a lot of changes and liked to keep in touch.

"How's Lionel?" asked Sandra when she returned from the bar.

Effie grimaced. "Difficult," she said. She didn't want to talk about Lionel. "How's Keith?" she asked.

"Fine. Still keeping fit. Still into health food and yoga."

"Can't be bad," said Effie.

Sandra leaned forward and rested her elbows on the table, her chin on her interlocked fingers. "It's our tenth wedding anniversary this year," she said.

"Ten years!" Effie reacted. "Surely not!"

Sandra smiled. "The years go by."

"They've been good ones for you two, haven't they?"

Sandra nodded in agreement.

"Makes up for the rotten time you had before," said Effie thoughtfully.

"I was lucky to find him."

"He was lucky to find you," Effie said.

Sandra lowered her arms. "Maybe we all make our own luck. At least, you have to be out there to recognise it."

It was a second marriage for both Sandra and Keith. Sandra's first husband had been killed in a car crash. A country road. A car on the wrong side. No way could anyone have made that sort of luck. Effie and Lionel had been close to the couple for years, and it had seemed as though Sandra would never get over his loss. But she did, and five years later she met a personable divorcee on a tennis holiday in Portugal. His name was Keith and she'd married him.

"We're planning a wedding anniversary party," she said. "We're booking the Castle Restaurant."

"Very nice," remarked Effie. The Castle Restaurant was one of the best in the area and the setting was glorious.

"The thing is..." Sandra hesitated.

"Yes?"

Sandra took a deep breath. It was as though she'd been rehearsing what she was going to say. "I'd like you to be there, but I don't want to ask Lionel. Is it possible for me to invite you on your own?"

The waitress arrived at the table. "Prawn salad?" she said. "Baguette? Would you like mayonnaise?" She put down the plates. "Enjoy your meal," she said as she left.

Sandra was still looking askance at Effie.

Effie unfolded her paper napkin and spread it on her lap. She was thinking. Then she replied with a question. "When is it to be?" she asked, mainly to delay her response.

Sandra cut her baguette in half. Then she continued without

reference to the question. "The thing is, I don't want Lionel upsetting our guests. I don't know what's happened to him, but he's not capable of socialising without being rude. I think he'd ruin the whole occasion. Keith agrees with me, but we'd both like you to come."

Effie's mind went into overdrive. This was the first occasion of this type to which she had been invited for ages. She and Lionel had long been dropped from the social circle they'd once enjoyed. It had happened gradually, but the married couples they knew had faded from their lives. Even Lionel's own brother was avoiding contact. The first clue that this was happening had been given by the couple who used to invite them on New Year's Eve.

"Did you know that Christabel and Charles Jones are having their usual New Year thrash?" she had commented to Lionel. This had been some years ago.

He'd shrugged in that way of his.

"Funny they haven't asked us," Effie had continued.

And Lionel had said something odd. "Charles doesn't like my jokes," he'd said. "He's got no sense of humour."

Effie had frowned. "He's rather serious," she agreed, "but he's a nice man." And there were others who didn't like Lionel's jokes. "How did you upset him?" she'd asked.

But Lionel hadn't replied. Just that shrug again.

Later they had been dropped by the group who organised social bridge evenings. And the one that planned the theatre trips. The dinner parties, the summer barbecues and the Christmas drinks invitations all dried up. When Effie had organised a summer party on the lawn, a surprising number of invitations were turned down. Charles and Christabel's refusal had been by the curtest email you could have imagined. She'd found out later the reason for this through a gossipy acquaintance. Apparently Christabel had offered

Lionel a glass of wine at that last party. He'd snapped at her and said, "No, you silly bitch. Don't you know I drink whisky?" And Charles had decided that no way would a man who called his wife a bitch ever enter his home again.

Effie looked at Sandra and smiled. "I'd be delighted to come," she said. She was grateful to be asked in her own right. It was a recognition that she wasn't just one half of Lionel-and-Effie.

"Great!" said Sandra, and fished in her handbag for the invitation. "I've already written it, but if you'd said you couldn't come on your own I would have ripped it up."

"Thank you." She took another sip of her wine. "Cheers!" she said, raising her glass. "Congratulations!"

"No presents," added Sandra. She laughed. "After all, if we haven't got what we want by now, no one can buy it for us."

Effie speared a prawn and put it in her mouth. "Sandra?" she asked. "Yes."

"Ten years ago, Lionel gave the speech at your and Keith's wedding."

Sandra nodded slowly. "I know."

"You must have liked him, valued him, back then."

"Of course I did. He was so supportive when Robert died. If it hadn't been for you two... I was cracking up at one point."

Effie thought. "I know how you feel about him now. I understand completely. But can you remember how and when he changed?"

Sandra took a bite of her baguette and shook her head as she finished the mouthful. "It was gradual. He used to call me his 'favourite tart'. It was a joke, I know it was, but it got that it was no longer funny. The humour got lost in the repetition. Keith found it offensive."

There was a pause, then Sandra looked up from her food to say,

"Remember, I partnered Lionel at the bridge club for a while? He'd come up with snide remarks about my play. And the things he'd say to the opposition! It was uncomfortable. He used to tease the Kelly sisters for being overweight. He was drinking too much, of course."

"And I was the last to realise it," Effie said sadly. "I kept making excuses for him. You do that when someone you love is behaving badly. Though he did come off the booze after that scare in hospital."

"Mmmm," said Sandra. "I think the damage was already done. Once an alcoholic... I think they call it 'wet brain'."

Effie frowned. 'Wet brain'? She hadn't heard of that. She sipped her wine.

Sandra changed the subject. "How's the house in Spain?"

Effie shrugged. "Okay. The lettings are just about paying for its keep till I decide what to do with it."

Sandra nodded. "Have you been away?"

"I'm still going to Spain once or twice a year. Mainly to keep an eye on the house. And I visit Nigel and the family in Berlin. On my own, of course."

"I see you're still travelling elsewhere?" Sandra said.

Effie looked down. "You've been looking at Facebook?"

Sandra looked at her. "You don't give much away, do you? But a glacier, a volcano and a desert has to mean something. How's your... er... 'travelling companion'?"

"Matt, you mean?" said Effie archly. Sandra was one of the few people who knew about Matt. "Very well, thank you. We've a couple more things planned."

"And what does Lionel think about the... er... affair?"

"I don't know. I don't know what he thinks, or if he thinks, about anything. Sandra, I've tried to talk about so much... his health... our marriage... but he just clams up."

"And Matt's wife? What about her?"

"She doesn't know."

"Mmmm." Sandra's lips were pressed tightly together.

"Do you disapprove?"

"Heavens, no! You have to take your happiness where you can." She raised her glass. "Good luck to you both."

"I'm flying to Manaus after Christmas."

"Manaus? Wherever's that?"

Effie laughed. "I had to look it up. It's in the middle of Brazil. We're going down the Amazon."

"Wow!"

When she got home, Effie Googled 'wet brain'. And up came the name 'Korsakoff's Syndrome'. And something about thiamine supplements. Hadn't Lionel been on thiamine at one point? Why had that been stopped?

Effie stood before the mirror and considered herself. She was wearing the dress she had bought for that first trip with Matt. The memories were still sharply focussed.

It had been wonderful to have a reason to buy new clothes, and to have someone who would appreciate them. The dress was a bright red shift with a scooped neckline and a black trim. She'd bought a matching red bra and pants to wear under it. The first time she'd worn it to dinner, the neck had gaped a little and must have showed the top of her bra, because Matt had whispered in her ear as the waiter poured the wine, "Are you wearing red knickers?"

And she'd lowered her lashes and said, "That's for me to know and you to find out!"

He had put his hand on her knee and said he couldn't wait.

Then she'd felt troubled because the line, 'That's for me to know and you to find out,' was a favourite quote of Lionel's. Why had that come into her head just then? Why couldn't she get Lionel out of her brain, even when she was on the other side of the world with this gorgeous romantic man?

Everyone here in Dalton Heath would be seeing the dress for the first time. The high-heeled strappy sandals had been around for years and had served her well. Bare legs that were nicely tanned. Red varnish on her toenails matched her dress. She swivelled around to view herself from the back. All okay. It hung smoothly. She picked up the invitation to check the time. Seven-thirty for eight, it said. But the significant thing about it was that it was addressed to her and her alone.

Effie put the invitation back in her handbag and went downstairs, a little cautiously on the high-heeled sandals. "How do I look?" she said to Lionel, parading before him.

"Okay," he said.

"Do you like the dress?"

"Yeah," he said. "It's okay."

"Lionel, I am going to a party. I've had my hair done, I've had my nails done, and I'm wearing my prettiest dress. I'm sorry you haven't been invited, but it would be really good, if just once, you could say something nice to me."

He gave her a look that indicated she might have been speaking in a foreign language. And from the gutter at that.

The taxi would be here in a moment. She wanted to be free to have a drink or two at the party and she could hardly ask Lionel to give her a lift. She had told him the reason he'd not been invited. She'd thought he'd be gutted, but he'd shrugged his shoulders and muttered something about not wanting to be lumbered with Sandra and Keith's boring friends.

She felt awkward arriving on her own, but as she stood uncertainly in the doorway of the restaurant, wondering how many of these people she knew, Keith spotted her and came across.

"Wow!" he said, giving her a hug and a kiss. "You look gorgeous." And he put a glass of champagne in her hand and ushered her towards a group of old friends whom she hadn't seen for a while. No one asked about Lionel. She suspected that they'd been briefed why he wasn't here.

There was a table plan and Effie found herself sitting next to a sun-weathered man with heavy framed glasses and longish greying hair pulled back into a pony tail. He wore a black shirt and a cream, rather creased, linen jacket. He was attractive in a dissolute sort of way.

"Hi, Effie," he said, as he shook hands with her.

"Hello…" Her eyes flicked to the name label on the table in front of him, "Jacob," she said.

"Jake," he corrected with a smile that revealed white, but crooked teeth.

A waitress approached the table. "Red or white wine?" she asked.

Did Effie recognise him? "Have we met before?" she asked as she took a sip of white wine.

"Yes. At Robert's funeral, and again at Sandra and Keith's wedding. I remember you because your husband gave that brilliant speech… at least…" He corrected himself. "No, I remember you because you're charming and attractive, and you were wearing red, like you are now. A lady in red. Only last time you had a hat." He raised his glass, and swirled the wine around. "Cheers," he said.

Effie remembered. She'd worn an enormous flowery hat that kept falling off. She couldn't keep it on through the meal and she'd tried to hang it on the back of her chair. Then Jake had picked it up and plonked it on top of one of the floral table decorations. "What's another dozen roses between guests?" he'd remarked lightly.

"But I remember your husband because of the wedding speech. It was brilliant. He made us all laugh. But it had a touch of poignancy about it too. And I also remember him because I talked to him about amateur dramatics afterwards. Lionel Butler... that's right, isn't it? I was trying to set up a fringe theatre at the time and we had a lot in common. I wanted him for a play I was hoping to put on, but it didn't happen. Then the theatre folded."

"That's a pity," she said.

"It needed an accountant." He paused. "I'm Sandra's cousin by the way, the only one of the family who isn't an accountant or a lawyer or the like."

"So what are you?" she asked.

"I think the technical term is 'resting'."

"You're an actor?"

"Sometimes. Sometimes I'm a writer. Sometimes I'm a gardener. But mostly, I'm a bit of a layabout."

"That sounds more fun than accountancy," Effie remarked.

Another waitress had arrived. "Crab cocktail or melon with Parma ham?" she was asking before putting a plate before each guest.

"Thank you," said Effie. "This looks nice." She unfolded her napkin and spread it on her lap.

He was also something of charmer, she was thinking. At the wedding... she forced her mind back... there had been a wife... a pretty woman with thick dark curls... like a gypsy...

"I think I remember your wife," she said.

"Do you?" He pressed his lips tightly together. "She wouldn't remember you," he said. "Not now."

There was a silence. What did that mean? Effie wondered. A lot can happen in ten years.

"So where's Lionel?" he asked. He glanced at her left hand, evidently noting her rings.

"Oh..." If he didn't know why Lionel wasn't here, she wasn't going to tell him. The explanation would be tortuous. "He's not very well at the moment," she said.

"That's a shame."

"Yes."

"For him, I mean." Very lightly, he touched her right wrist and trailed his fingertips over the back of her hand.

Then he said, "For me, it's a bit of luck."

CHAPTER 5

A Visit to the Library

Lionel puts on his coat, checks he has his cigarettes, his lighter and his puffer. His credit cards are in his top shirt pocket with his blue rollerball pen, and today he has his library card with them. This morning he is going to the library. He has found that numbers of retired people go to the library each morning. It is somewhere to go. Sometimes he sees someone he knows and he likes that.

At home he gets the *Daily Telegraph* during the week, the *Sunday Times* on Sundays and the *Dalton Heath Advertiser* on Thursdays. They used to be delivered by a boy on a bike. But now a car pulls up outside the house and somebody runs up the drive with the paper or papers for that day. The *Daily Telegraph* has always been the best paper for sport, and he used to do the crossword on the train on the way to work. Then, after he retired, he would do it at home, and sometimes Effie would help him if he got stuck. She wasn't very good at crosswords, but it was nice to have something to discuss with her. But it's not the same as it used to be. The clues have got more difficult. Some of those long anagrams are impossible, and things have all got so obscure.

In the library they have newspapers and you can sit at a table and read them all morning if you like. Some people do. The library has all the national dailies and Sundays, and quite a few local papers. Magazines too. He likes to look at the papers like he did when he was at work.

He parks his green Jaguar right outside the library. He goes up to the glass door which opens automatically, and a woman with a pushchair is coming out. He stands there. She is in his way. Hasn't she noticed him? He stamps his feet to get her attention. "You're in my effing way!" he says. She frowns and adjusts the pushchair to give him space to get past her. "Thank you!" he sneers. Why don't people look where they're going?

It isn't like libraries used to be. It's not just books, though there are rows and rows of books. He pulls the odd one from a shelf and puts it back. Too much choice. There are computers too. And rows of DVDs. He looks at some of those. Some of them he knows. *The Sound of Music. Mary Poppins.* Some of them they've got at home anyway, he thinks.

There's a children's section where sometimes they have story afternoons. Mothers bring their children and somebody reads a story to them. It's nice to listen to stories. And it's nice to watch the little faces all wide-eyed and attentive. Some of them anyway.

One of the librarians is following him around. He swings round and glares at her.

"Can I help you, sir?" she asks.

He frowns. He doesn't know what he wants or what he's looking for. "I'm just looking," he says. Then, irritated at her interference, "Isn't that allowed?"

"Er... yes, of course, sir."

He is aware of her watching him and he doesn't like that.

He heads for the big table where people are reading the daily papers. There is one spare chair so he sits down. The paper nearest him is the *Daily Telegraph*, but he can look at that at home. His fellow readers look a bit gloomy so he decides he will cheer them up with a joke.

He looks at a man who is reading the *Daily Mirror*. "Hey, you. Do you know who the readers of that paper are?" he asks.

The man looks at him, puzzled. "Do I need to?" he asks.

Lionel begins his joke. "The *Daily Mirror* is read by people who think they run the country." A couple of people look up from their papers. "The *Guardian* is read by people who think they ought to run the country." Everybody has stopped reading. He grins. He is enjoying this. "The *Times* is read by people who actually do run the country. The *Daily Mail* is read by the wives of the people who run the country. The *Financial Times* is read by people who own the country."

They are all looking at him now, enjoying his performance. And the librarian is coming across. He scowls and gives her the V-sign.

He continues happily. "The *Morning Star* is read by people who think the country ought to be run by another country, and the *Daily Telegraph* is read by people who think it is!" He laughs raucously and begins the punch line. "And the *Sun* readers couldn't care less who runs the country so long as she's got big tits!"

One man laughs aloud. Two women titter a bit and someone whispers, "That's from *Yes Minister*."

Lionel shakes his head. "Oh yeah? I was in advertising. I was a media man. *Yes Minister* got it from us!" He laughs again.

The librarian is standing there, arms folded. "Excuse me, Mr Butler, but this is an area for quiet reading. Please could you read in silence?"

He shrugs and looks down at the *Daily Telegraph*. He wants to look at the *Argus*. "Have you got the *Argus*?" he asks her.

"I've got it," says the woman opposite, but I'm going now." She pushes the *Argus* towards him. As she gets up she looks at the librarian, puts her forefinger to her temple and pretends to screw it round in a 'he's bonkers' gesture.

They're all bonkers, thinks Lionel.

Anyway, Lionel has got his *Argus*. He spreads it out on the table before him, and flicks through it, noting some of the headlines. Some of the sports results. Then he turns to the cryptic crossword. He runs through the clues. Yes, here's one he can do. He takes his blue rollerball pen ready. This one is an anagram. He writes the letters in a circle and thinks about it. He leans back. He'd prefer to do this at home. And he's ready for a cigarette. If he does the crossword at home and he gets stuck, Effie might be able to get him going again. None of this lot look as though they'd help him out. He folds the page of paper, carefully tears out the crossword section, folds it smaller and puts it in his pocket. He'll finish it later, like he did yesterday and the day before and the day before that.

"You can't do that!" reacts the woman sitting opposite him.

He frowns. "What?"

"You can't tear bits out of the paper."

"Yes, I can. I just have."

Another woman hisses at her. "Just ignore him. He's a bit of a nutter but he's quite harmless."

"That's not the point," whispers the first woman. Then to him, "It's not your paper. You can't rip it up! You can't take bits of it away... It's... stealing."

He takes the crossword from his pocket. "What difference does it make?" he says. "I'm allowed to do the crossword sitting here, which means no one else can do it. And look..." He turns the crossword over. "There's only an advert on the back. So all I'm doing is depriving some idiot of reading a fucking stupid advert. You can't call that stealing!" And he refolds the crossword and puts it back in his pocket. "Logic," he says. "Logic." He stands up and turns to leave.

"Mr Butler," calls the librarian as he heads for the exit.

He stops.

"Please could you have a private word with our chief librarian? Would you come this way to the office?"

They are all mentally ill, thinks Lionel. You can have kids yelling their heads off and no one cares a fuck, but if he cracks a joke or two to lighten the atmosphere, they call it 'inappropriate behaviour' or 'verbal aggression'. Last time this happened he was banned from entering the library for three months. This time it is permanent. The chief librarian reads the letter to him, puts it in an envelope and hands it to him. She is a tall, thin woman. Hard angles to her body. Hard angles to her face. What a bitch!

"Would you like to hand me your library card?" she says.

"I'd like to stick it right up your..." Something, some vestige of what he used to understand about good manners makes him stop. He gives her the card.

She has flat shoes, a flat chest, a dowdy skirt and heavily framed glasses. The archetypal old maid. A dried up old virgin. He folds the envelope and puts it in the inside pocket of his jacket.

"If you enter the premises it will be regarded as trespassing and we will inform the police," she says.

He turns on his heel.

"Goodbye, Mr Butler," she calls after him.

He doesn't reply.

He gets into his car and pulls away. He is angry and he puts his foot down. Suddenly a car pulls out from a parking place the other side of the road. He yanks the brakes on and stops just in time. He opens the window and waves two fingers at the driver. "Wanker!" he shouts. He takes a deep breath. That was a near miss. He must be more careful.

He drives down to Grove Road where the paper shop is. It's time he paid the bill anyway.

"Hello, Mr Butler, sir," says Mr Patel cheerfully. "Nice day."

"Velly nice day," says Lionel, putting on an Asian accent.

Mr Patel laughs.

Lionel likes Mr Patel. He always laughs at his jokes. "I need to pay our bill." He hands his debit card across and Mr Patel puts it in the machine.

"How are you today, Mr Butler?" says Mr Patel.

Lionel shrugs. "Average."

Mr Patel laughs again. "You are always average, Mr Butler," he says as he processes the card. He hands the machine across. Just for a fraction of a second Lionel can't think of his pin number. Then it comes to him and he keys it in.

"Average is not bad," continues Mr Patel. "That is something to be grateful for."

Lionel laughs. "That's true." Then he asks, "Could you add the *Argus* to our regular order?"

"Yes, indeed I can. A good paper, the *Argus*."

"Yes," says Lionel. "I like the crossword. It's easier than the *Telegraph*."

Mr Patel gets out his book. "Starting tomorrow?" he checks. He is writing in his book.

Lionel nods. "Yes, please."

"How's the car?" asks Mr Patel.

"Oh, very nice. Comfortable. Very smooth. I'd recommend an X-Type any day. You should get one."

"Yes, indeed, Mr Butler. Maybe next year if business is good, I'll follow your very excellent advice and buy one."

Lionel is pleased. "You could pick up a second-hand one at a very good price," he suggests. "Though they do drink gallons of petrol."

"I'll look out for one," says Mr Patel. "Enjoy the *Argus*."

"Yes," says, Lionel, "I will." Then, "Goodbye. See you next time."

"Goodbye Mr Butler. Take care."

Why do they all say, 'take care'? Lionel wonders. Still, it's not as stupid as 'have a nice day'. What's wrong with an old-fashioned 'goodbye'? Still, he likes Mr Patel.

As he gets back into his car and pulls away he thinks, Why can't everyone be like that nice Mr Patel?

CHAPTER 6

A Routine Health Check

"Goodnight," said Effie.

Lionel was seated at his table in his usual chair. He was working on a Sudoku puzzle. He looked at his watch and remarked, "It's early for you, isn't it?" He always commented on her timing. She might be early or she might be late, or just sometimes he would say, "Yes, it's your bedtime, isn't it?" She didn't think she had a bedtime but Lionel evidently had the precise hour and minutes inscribed somewhere in his brain. He tilted his head, ready for her goodnight kiss.

"What day is it tomorrow?" was his next question. Then he answered it himself. "Friday. Got anything on?" The predictability of his dialogue drove her to distraction.

"I've a doctor's appointment," she said.

"What time?" he asked. He didn't ask what the appointment was for. That wouldn't have concerned him. Though it should set up an alert in his mind. What would happen to him if she were ill?

"Ten to nine," she said. "I'll be gone before you're up. In fact, I'll probably be back before you're up."

He reached for his diary, found the page and wrote: *Effie. Doctor. 8.50am*. Beside him was a glass of cola, probably mixed with ginger ale. He'd given up drinking alcohol when he came out of hospital, but he'd retained the ritual. He'd substituted cola with ginger ale for whisky and ginger ale in the evening, and tonic with lime juice, for vodka and tonic at lunchtime. The glasses – the heavy, squat whisky glasses and the tall, elegant gin and tonic glasses – were the remains of the crystal sets they had when they were first married. They were all kept in the drinks cabinet in the living room, just as they had always been, but now alongside bottles of low-calorie fizzy drinks. Effie suspected that Lionel was now addicted to aspartame, but that had to be a whole lot better than alcohol.

"Have you taken your pills?" she asked.

"I'm just about to."

The appointment at the surgery was for a routine health check. When you reached that magic age, you got a letter in the post inviting you to make an appointment. Effie was to see a practice nurse. She'd be fine – she knew that. She didn't smoke, she wasn't overweight, and she ate and drank sensibly. What could possibly be wrong?

She had given up drinking alcohol completely the year Lionel nearly died of drink. She'd given away all the unopened bottles of spirits and wine in the house, and poured the opened ones down the drain. She'd felt an irrational hatred of alcohol which she blamed for ruining Lionel's life, her life, and to some extent the lives of their children. Later, she'd gone back to enjoying a glass of wine from time to time, but she was careful not to let it become a habit.

She liked and enjoyed the activities that kept her fit – walking, tennis, exercise classes. The only thing wrong with her was the stress of living with Lionel. And stress wasn't an illness.

Or was it?

"Good morning, Mrs Butler," said the practice nurse cheerfully. According to her badge her name was Doreen and according to her size she was in grave danger of developing diabetes, heart disease and all the other things that are reputed to be caused by obesity.

"Do sit down," said Doreen.

Effie wondered if Doreen realised she was Lionel's wife. Probably. Everyone in the surgery knew Lionel Butler. Most of them had been insulted by him.

Doreen weighed her, measured her and calculated a body mass index that was considered healthy. Her blood pressure was higher than she expected.

"Why's that?" asked Effie.

Doreen didn't have an answer. "It's nothing to worry about," she said. She questioned her on her exercise routines and finally took a blood test to measure her cholesterol level. Just a finger prick.

"Now that is rather high," said Doreen thoughtfully.

Effie frowned. "But... but it can't be. I eat all the right things."

Doreen gave her some advice about good cholesterol and bad cholesterol and how to adjust your diet to deal with the problem. And then gave her a leaflet that said it all again in more detail.

"If that doesn't work, Doctor Dauncey might consider prescribing a statin, to reduce the risk of heart disease."

Effie felt a sensation of disbelief. No! No! she screamed inside her head. She couldn't be in danger of heart disease! A feeling of panic arose within her. She started to shake as her breathing speeded up. She couldn't be ill, she told herself. She couldn't cope with Lionel if she fell ill. She wasn't coping now and if anything else went wrong she'd fall apart. A lump rose in her throat, and tears brimmed her eyes. It was though she had been switched from her calm controlled outer mode to her out-of-control panic inner mode.

"It's nothing to worry about," said Doreen, putting a hand on her forearm. "It's just a precaution."

Effie shook. "I'm sorry... it's not this... it's other things," she began. "I can't cope," she sobbed. "It's my husband... He's so difficult and I can't cope anymore... I don't know what to do. It just goes on and on and on. Year after year after year. Nobody understands. I can't deal with it..."

And then her whole body was wracked with huge sobs and her nose was running and tears were pouring down her face and she was rocking helplessly back and forth on her chair... "He's mentally ill. I don't know what it's called but he's mad as a hatter. I know he is... and no one believes me. A hundred years ago you lot would have put him in a strait jacket and locked him up. I can't reason with him. People think it's my fault... and I'm so tired. I can't sleep. I pace round the house at night, churning it all over." She leaned forward in her chair with her head in her hands, almost resting on her knees. "It all grows to fill my head and I think my brain is going to burst. If only..." She was spluttering in her distress. She sat up and froze, her face wet with tears. Then she said quietly, "If only he could say something nice to me... just once..." And then she groaned and shuddered as the weeping enveloped her all over again.

Doreen handed her some tissues, lifted the phone, and pressed a button. "Could I have some help?" she asked into the mouthpiece.

And then there was another practice nurse in the room. "It's all right, Effie," came the words. Someone was stroking her hair, but that only made her cry more. "We do understand," she said. "We do know him. We only see him at the odd appointment and he's difficult then. We don't know how you can live with him day after day after day. You're doing marvellously."

Effie shook her head wildly from side to side. "No, I'm not. You don't understand," she spluttered through her tears. "You couldn't possibly."

And the next thing Doctor Dauncey was standing there.

"Okay," he said. "Enough is enough. Something has to be done."

Her tears had subsided, at least for the time being. And she sat, her composure on a knife-edge, breathing evenly and with a tissue clutched in her left hand, just in case. They had given her a cup of tea, that British panacea for all ills, and she was now in Dr Dauncey's office. The morning surgery was over.

"I'm so sorry. Thank you for fitting me in," she said. "I'm all right. Really, I'm all right. I just get upset sometimes. Mostly I'm fine. It's just that Lionel..."

"Lionel needs to be diagnosed. This has gone on long enough," he said thoughtfully. "I'll refer him to the mental health team. There's certainly something wrong. He needs to be tested."

Effie sighed with relief. Someone was at last listening to her. Someone was going to do something. "Do you think it might be a condition called Korsakoff's Syndrome?" she asked. "Do you know about it?"

He frowned. He evidently didn't.

"It's a type of dementia caused by lack of vitamin B," she said. "Usually as a result of alcohol abuse."

He smiled. "You've been doing your homework?" he remarked.

"A friend knew something about it, except she called it 'wet brain'. Then I looked it up online."

Dr Dauncey nodded. "There are certainly a number of alcohol-related dementias. And it seems likely one of them might account for Lionel's behaviour."

"He did stop drinking," said Effie, "after he came out of hospital. But that doesn't mean the damage isn't done, does it?" she asked, looking up at him.

"No indeed. We'll refer him. And I'll refer you to the mental health team too. You need help with your anxiety. And meanwhile, I recommend you join Al-Anon. It's a self-help group linked to AA, and it's there to help families of alcoholics and recovered alcoholics. Not that alcoholics ever recover. There's branch in Dalton Heath."

Effie nodded. "I know about Al-Anon. I went to some meetings about ten years ago when I realised just how much Lionel was drinking. I went to the group in Brighton." She laughed. "It was a long drive, but I was afraid that if I went locally I might bump into someone I know."

"And did it help?"

She shook her head. "I thought I'd learn how to stop him drinking, but it wasn't about that."

"No. It's to help you. Give it another try."

"I will," said Effie. "I've got nothing to lose." She looked up at him. "And I'll go to the local one this time." She laughed weakly. "I'm past caring who knows now."

Dr Dauncey smiled benignly. He was a kind man.

"You know, a couple of months after he came out of hospital I had to take him back there for an angiogram. We were kept waiting for hours. His notes were lying on a hospital bed in a big fat file marked 'confidential'. I passed the time reading them. Do you realise that the first time alcohol abuse was mentioned in those notes was nearly twenty years ago!"

Dr Dauncey gave a nod and a 'Hmmm' that indicated he wasn't in the least surprised.

"Well, I couldn't believe it." She chewed her lower lip and shook her head. "Why didn't I know? Why didn't I see it? It took me another ten years to even suspect there was a problem! I've been so stupid. Maybe if I'd realised..."

Dr Dauncey interrupted sharply, "No, Mrs Butler. Even if you'd realised your husband was an alcoholic, there wouldn't have been a thing you could do." He leaned forward and said slowly, "You must understand. It isn't your fault."

CHAPTER 7

P is for Psycho

The doorbell rings.

Lionel feels a flash of irritation at the interruption of his routine. He looks up from his table where he has been settled since he got up. His table is at the end of the living room which is really a sun lounge extension. He likes to sit there. He has a general view of the garden but he can still keep an eye on the living room. The *Radio Times* is open on the table and he has nearly finished marking the programmes he intends to watch tonight. He is using his blue rollerball pen. Usually the daily paper is open too on the crossword page, together with his Sudoku book, his diary and his address book. Sometimes any mail that arrives in the post is there too. But Effie has been tidying up so things have been put away. Things aren't quite the way he likes them. He never likes it when she tidies up.

He hears Effie open the front door. "Hello, pleased to meet you..." he hears. "Did you find the house all right...?"

Well of course they did. They wouldn't be here otherwise. Effie has told him that someone from the Larwood Mental Health team is coming to see him and he has written in his diary. *Memory Assessment, 11.15am.* Effie's got a fucking nerve thinking his memory needs to be assessed. He can remember every hand he played at the bridge club last night. He and Derek were top again with seventy-two percent. You can't do that if you can't remember the cards. Effie's so scatty that when she plays she can't even remember how many trumps are out. Not that she's played with him for ages. She's says it's stressful for married couples to play bridge together.

He's not playing as much as he'd like either, Lionel reflects. His partners keep making excuses. And even Derek said he might be too busy next week. Lionel frowns. Derek seemed upset when he joked about that stupid opening lead he made. It was only a joke.

The door to the living room opens and Effie ushers in the visitor.

"This is my husband, Lionel," she says. "Lionel, this is Sandy Thomas who's a psychiatric nurse. She's come to give you some of those tests I mentioned."

Is that what psychiatric nurses do? he wonders, but he shakes hands with her. "My wife wants to have me locked up," he says. Then he laughs and the psychiatric nurse giggles a bit. It's a silly sort of squeaky giggle so he imitates it.

Effie glares at him.

"That was a joke," he says.

"Do sit down," says Effie to the psychiatric nurse, indicating the sofa. "Would you like a coffee?"

"I'd love one," she says brightly. "Milk, no sugar. But I'll sit at the table with Lionel, if I may. Is that all right Lionel?"

"Sit where you like. I don't care," he says.

"Thank you," she says and she pulls up a chair and sits next to him. Actually he does care, and he finds she's a bit too close for comfort. He'd be much happier if she were across the room on the sofa.

She gets out an A4 file and puts it in front of her on the table. "Lovely garden," she says, looking out of the window. "Do you do it?"

"No," he says.

She has heavy, dark-framed, square glasses and long brown hair that's very straight and smooth. One side of her hair is tucked behind one ear, but the other hangs loosely forward. He leans towards her and pushes the loose side behind her other ear. That's better, he thinks. Now she's symmetrical.

She doesn't react at first. It's as though she's frozen. Then she smiles. "Thank you," she says.

"That's all right," he says. "No problem."

Effie comes in with the coffee and a plate of biscuits. There are biscuits of different shapes and colours but there are no fig rolls.

"Thank you," says the psychiatric nurse as Effie puts the coffee down.

"Would you like a fig roll?" asks Lionel. And he takes an open box of fig rolls from the book shelf where Effie put it when she was tidying up.

"No, thank you," she says. "I'll have a bourbon." She takes a dark brown biscuit that is a rectangle. "Do you like fig rolls?" she asks.

He nods as he takes one.

"He eats two or three packets a day," says Effie.

"No, I don't," he says.

Effie puckers her lips tightly in a way that means she disagrees but she's not going to argue.

The psychiatric nurse dips her bourbon biscuit in her coffee. "Do you mind if I dunk it?" she asks. "I love them soggy."

"Do what you like. I don't care," says Lionel.

"Nice pictures," she says, looking at the walls. "Are they your grandchildren?"

"Yes," he says.

"Aren't you lucky? You must be very proud. How many have you got?"

"Four," he says. "Look. One, two, three, four." He gives her a triumphant look. "See, I can count. Can't you? Nothing wrong with my brain!"

"What are their names?"

"Mariella... Cameron... Alicia..." he says, pointing at each in turn. Then he falters. "Baby," he says finally.

"They're lovely," says the psychiatric nurse. "Do they live locally?"

Lionel frowns. "Those two do, but those live in Berlin. Our son married a German girl."

"How interesting! Berlin's such an exciting city, don't you think?"

"Don't know. Don't care!" says Lionel. He looks at his watch. "Isn't it time you went?" he asks.

"I won't be long, but I'm hoping you'll be able to answer some questions. We know you haven't been very well and we might be able to find out what's wrong."

"I'm fine. There's nothing wrong with me."

She has opened her file and is looking at some papers. She has a pen at the ready. It's black with a gold top.

"It won't take very long. I expect you'll find it very easy."

He shrugs.

"Okay?" she prompts.

When he says nothing, she continues. "Can you tell me what day it is?"

"Friday," he says.

"And the date?"

"Friday the fifteenth of August." He looks at his watch. "And it's eleven forty-five in the morning which is the same thing as a quarter to twelve, and this is so-o boring."

"Can you tell me the name of our queen?"

"Elizabeth!" he snarls.

"And her eldest son?"

"Prince Charles, for Chrissake. What is all this about?"

"Can you count downwards from twenty? In ones."

Lionel rolled his eyes. "Twenty, nineteen, eighteen, seventeen..."

"Well done. I'm going to tell you three words now. See if you can remember them: plate, apple, car.

"Plate, apple, car," he repeats.

"That's right. Try to remember them because I'll come back to them later."

She puts five cards in front of him. "Can you read these words?" she says. Each card has a word printed on it. "'Course I can!" he reacts impatiently.

"Read them aloud, please." She points at each in turn.

They are rhyming words. "Hoot... loot... soot... boot... foot... coot," he says as she points.

He frowns. Something wasn't right, he thinks.

Then she points back to a couple of them.

"Soot, foot," he says.

"Well done. Just checking," she says. Then she gives him a piece of paper with a drawing on it. It's just a square with a circle inside it and a diagonal joining opposite corners of the square. "Can you copy the drawing?" she asks.

"Yeah... if have to. But I'll use my pen, if you don't mind." He draws.

"Can you remember the three words I told you earlier?"

He thought. "Apple," he says. Then he frowns. "Car...? Cup? Look, this is getting really boring. Isn't it time you left?"

"It won't take much longer."

"Well, I'm sick of it. This is my house and I want you to get the hell out of here."

"You want me to go?"

"Yes."

She shrugs. "Very well then..."

Effie has been sitting on the sofa. She stands up and crosses to the table and puts her hand on his shoulder. "Look, Lionel. Sandy's come all the way from Brighton. You might as well let her finish properly. Otherwise it'll be a wasted journey for her. Please."

He shrugs.

"It won't take long now," says the psychiatric nurse.

"Okay," he says sulkily. "But get on with it."

The woman hands him a piece of plain A4 paper. "Could you fold it in half and drop it on the floor?"

He stares at her in astonishment. "You mean like this?" he says as he folds it. "And like this?" as he drops it.

"And Lionel, could you tell me some words beginning with P?"

He smiles. "*Possibly*," he says.

"Go on then," she prompts.

"I just did, *probably*." He grins. "You're not too bright, are you? "How about, *Psychology, Pterodactyl, Photography, Pneumonia, Phlegmatic?*" He laughs. "Bet you can't spell that little lot, can you? If you ask me your little test's a bit of a *Pig-in-a-Poke*."

"Thank you, Lionel. I'm impressed."

She writes in her notebook, then says, "And can you say a sentence? Any sentence."

He glares her. "Why don't you fuck off!" he says. "Will that do?"

"That's fine," she says, suppressing a smile. "Do think you could write it down?" She gives him a piece of paper and he writes with his blue rollerball pen. He'd better not write *fuck*, he thinks. People are so sensitive. So he writes '*Why don't you eff off.*' Then he looks at it and changes his full stop into a question mark.

"Very well done. Can you count down from a hundred in threes?"

"Threes? Isn't that a bit easy? How about sevens?"

"If you like."

He starts. "One hundred, ninety-three, eight-six, seventy-nine, seventy-two..."

"That's great," she says. "No need to go on."

"I've started so I'll finish," he snarls angrily. "Sixty-five, fifty-eight, fifty-one, forty-four, thirty-seven, thirty, twenty-three, sixteen, nine, two, minus five, minus twelve, minus nineteen..."

She puts up a hand. "That's enough!" she grins. "I thought you wanted to get rid of me! But very well done," she says.

"Yeah. Bet *she* couldn't do that," he sneers. "Could you, Effie?"

The psychiatric nurse gives him another piece of paper. "And can you draw the drawing you did before?"

He stares at her. "What drawing?" he asks.

CHAPTER 8

A Visit from the Police

As Effie opened the front door she felt a sinking sensation in her stomach.

Not again! she thought.

The uniforms of the two figures on the steps told her instantly that Lionel was in trouble. And not for the first time. The white shirts, the navy jerkins with buttoned pockets, and the tailored trousers were in themselves non-committal. It was the hat with the blue and white checked band that was the identifying feature. And the badge on it that announced that the wearer was a PCSO. A Police Community Support Officer.

"Good afternoon, Mrs Butler," were the opening words from the one she had met last time. "Mo Gorridge, Community Support Police," the woman officer said by way of a reminder. She smiled. "We met before."

Effie nodded and shook hands with her.

"And this is my colleague, David Armitage. I was with another colleague, last time, if you remember."

Effie was hardly likely to forget. It wasn't every day you had the police turning up on your doorstep. "Yes – after the fracas in the Leisure Centre." Effie gave a wry smile. "I won't say it's nice to see you, Officer, because I have a feeling you have bad news for me." Last time they had delivered the letter banning Lionel from ever entering the Leisure Centre premises again. "Has he been there again? Has he been making a nuisance of himself?"

"Not at the Leisure Centre," said Mo Gorringe.

"You'd better come in," said Effie. "You can tell him yourself what this is all about."

She showed them into the living room. Lionel was seated at his table, an open packet of fig roll biscuits next to his Sudoku book before him.

"Lionel, do you remember Mo Gorringe?" she said.

He looked up blankly.

"She came to talk to us about that problem at the Leisure Centre."

He shrugged and grunted but he wasn't revealing whether or not he remembered the situation. She suspected he didn't.

"Good afternoon, Mr Butler," said Mo brightly. "This is my colleague, David Armitage."

"Do sit down." suggested Effie. "Would you like a cup of something? Tea? Coffee?"

They sat side by side on the sofa, but declined the offer of drinks.

Mo turned to address Lionel. "Mr Butler, did you tell your wife about what happened at Dunfords Supermarket this morning?"

Lionel was concentrating on his Sudoku. He grunted a noise that evidently meant no.

"I know he got home without doing the shopping he wanted. But I assumed he'd forgotten what he went for. What happened, Lionel?" asked Effie.

He didn't look up. "Don't know. Don't care. Lot of fuss about nothing," he mumbled.

Effie looked questioningly at Mo.

"Are you aware, Mrs Butler, that your husband was banned from entering Dunfords Supermarket nearly two years ago?"

"Two years!" Effie reacted. She had that sick sensation in her stomach again. "I'd no idea. Whatever for?"

"We haven't seen the written report from the incident, but this morning one of the members of staff recognised him and reported the fact to the security officer on duty. He approached Mr Butler to ask him to leave, but he wouldn't. He said he wasn't going till he'd done his shopping, and stamped off, swearing and cursing. He bumped his trolley into someone else's trolley and swore at them."

Effie felt sick.

"The security officer called two of our team who happened to be on duty around the entrance and they asked him to leave. Which he did eventually, but not before another round of abuse."

"Lionel, why didn't you tell me?"

Lionel looked at his watch. "It's time for my afternoon nap," he said. "I'm going up now." He stood up from the table, and walked past the two officers. "See you later," he said to Effie as he left the room.

"I'm sorry," said Effie. She shook her head. The embarrassment, the humiliation. It was just one thing after another. "The thing is," said Effie, "he is now under the Larwood Mental Health team. He's in the process of diagnosis. We're waiting for a brain scan. But meanwhile they've put him on medication that is supposed to settle him. He's not as aggressive as he was before. He's calmer. Everyone says so."

"My officers said he was highly abusive."

"Yes, but that must have been because he was approached by the security staff. That would have confused him. If it hadn't been for that, he'd have got round the store, paid his bill, and been no trouble to anyone."

Mo shrugged. "Maybe."

"A bit of shopping is all he can do now," Effie explained. "It gets him out of the house. It's good for him to go shopping. If he can't do that his life will be totally empty. I mean, there's all this stuff in the press saying we're supposed to be a dementia-friendly society. Do you think I should go and talk to the manager? Explain about the medication? Do you think he might give him a second chance?"

No way was the manager of Dunfords prepared to give Lionel a second chance.

Effie spoke first to the girl in customer services. "Could I have a word with the manager?" she asked.

"What's it about?" asked the girl.

"It's about my husband, Lionel Butler. The community police have told me he's been banned from using the store. I wanted to find out what's happened."

The girl phoned for the manager and five minutes later he appeared. He was wearing a red polo shirt and a jumper with a badge saying *Tom Mackenzie. Store Manager*. She'd been expecting a man in a suit, but presumably that was her old-fashioned attitude to business.

"Good afternoon, Mrs Butler," he said. "What can I do for you?"

"Er... do you think I could speak to you in private?" she asked.

"Er... yes... I suppose so," he said.

She expected to be taken to his office. Presumably store managers at Dunfords do have offices. But no, he showed her towards a door that led into what appeared to be a stock room. There was nowhere to sit. It was private but not in any way comfortable.

"I've learned that my husband was banned from using this store two years ago. I wonder if you can tell me why?"

"He was a danger to the well-being of our staff and customers."

"A danger? Was he violent?"

"No, but his aggressive language and inappropriate behaviour was offensive."

Effie took a deep breath. "He has a form of dementia, and is in the process of being diagnosed by the Larwood Mental Health team. I'm sure an organisation the size of Dunfords must have a dementia-friendly policy."

"We also have a zero-tolerance policy when it comes to threatening behaviour."

"Threatening?"

"Mrs Butler, we are happy for him to shop here with you, but he is banned from coming here on his own."

"So you're discriminating against him on the grounds of ill health? That must be illegal."

"Hardly. Dunfords Supermarket is a private organisation which invites members of the public to shop here. We don't have to invite anyone, any more than you have to invite anyone into your own home."

"He's ill. He can't help it. If he can't go shopping on his own..." Effie's voice was getting agitated. She mustn't cry. She took a deep breath. "He's being treated. He's on a medication that calms him down. Can't you give him a second chance?" she appealed. She was becoming tearful again.

The manager was cool and unmoved. Of course, that was why he was a manager.

"It didn't calm him down this morning. I'm sorry, Mrs Butler. We will allow him here if you supervise him. I have a duty to my staff and customers. That's all I can offer, I'm afraid."

And that was that. He showed her out of the stock room, and she left in tears, feeling an absolute idiot. She also felt angry.

Okay, she decided. She'd go shopping with Lionel and find out for herself just what his behaviour was like. Maybe if they shopped there a few times with no problems, then Mr Tom Zero Tolerance Mackenzie might relent.

She left it a week and then wrote a letter.

Dear Tom Mackenzie

Lionel Butler : Exclusion from Store

Many thanks for talking to me last week. I apologise for allowing myself to become so distressed. My husband's illness is difficult and I do not always cope as well as I should.

I am hoping it will still be acceptable, as we discussed, for me to shop with my husband in the store. If so, I should like to do so on Monday (tomorrow) morning at about 11.00am. I hope there will be no problems, but if he upsets anyone, then I assure you I will make it the last and only time.

Thank you for your tolerance.

Kind regards

Frances Butler (Mrs)

She signed the letter, put it in an envelope, addressed it and sealed it. Tolerance! That man was a monster.

She drove to Dunfords, parked her car in the car park, then took the letter to customer services and asked if it could be delivered promptly to the store manager.

So far so good. Three letters, three shopping expeditions, no crises. And no replies to her letters. Not that escorting Lionel round the shopping aisles of a supermarket was Effie's idea of a fun outing. Especially when she was being followed at a discreet distance by a security officer. Time to go one stage further: -

Dear Tom Mackenzie

Lionel Butler: Exclusion from Store

I should like to visit Dunfords Supermarket store with my husband on Tuesday morning at about 11.00am. There have been no problems on the last three occasions, so please may I sit in the cafeteria and allow Lionel the freedom to shop on his own? His psychiatrist encourages the maintenance of independence for such patients for as long as is possible. I imagine you will need to inform your security officer on duty. I am hoping that there will be no problems, but if he offends anyone then I shall accept that we will not use the store in future.

I assure you that, although Lionel's illness has made him very unpleasant, he is harmless. Under his present medication he is calmer and quieter than when the ban was imposed.

Let me know if you are not happy with this. Meanwhile, thank you for your support in this difficult matter.

Kind regards

Frances Butler (Mrs)

Effie enjoyed sitting in the cafeteria in Dunfords more than she expected. The coffee wasn't too bad and carrot cake was excellent. She'd brought a book with her and nobody bothered her. It wasn't a bad way of passing half an hour or so. Undoubtedly Lionel was being closely tailed by whichever security officer happened to be on duty.

A couple of days later she learned something new.

And she wrote her final letter to the manager.

Dear Tom Mackenzie

Lionel Butler : Exclusion from Store

As you know I have visited the store with Lionel a few times now, initially shopping with him, and then waiting in the cafeteria while he shopped alone. Thank you for your support in this. As far I know there have been no problems and I have reached the stage where I should like to ask you if you would consider lifting the ban on his using the store unsupervised?

Unfortunately something has occurred which renders my request somewhat academic. I have discovered that in the last week or so Lionel has been to your store unescorted on at least two occasions. (Friends of mine observed him and informed me.) As you know Lionel is mentally ill and has probably either forgotten or does not understand that he is not supposed to go to Dunfords Supermarket alone. I cannot supervise him at all times.

I do hope you will not have further problems with him. If you do it would be best to call Mo Gorringe, Community Police Support Officer. She knows us well and understands the situation.

I do not feel able to do any more. Thank you for your support.

Kind regards

Effie Butler

(Copy to Mo Gorringe, Community Police Support)

Effie smiled as she signed the letter, and this time she put a stamp on the envelope. This was her fifth letter to Tom Mackenzie. He hadn't replied to any of the others so she wasn't expecting a reply to this one. But she had done everything she could, and she had, as they say, put the ball in his court.

If Tom Mackenzie wanted to have Lionel Butler arrested, well let him!

CHAPTER 9

A Smashing Time

Lionel pours olive oil over his dinner. He is sitting at the kitchen table across from Effie. It is seven thirty and time for dinner. There is a piece of chicken from the casserole that Effie has cooked, and some broccoli. He likes chicken the way she does it, nice and soft with whole chunks of garlic and tasty gravy. There is never enough gravy and that's why he pours olive oil over it. He likes olive oil. He always pours it on his dinner. He puts salt on it. He sees Effie wince. He knows she thinks he eats far too much salt.

"I'll take it next door," he says. He likes to eat in front of the TV. If he eats with Effie in the kitchen she always asks him questions. She's always going on about things. On and on and on. And she watches him eat his food. Stares at him and tells him off if he spills anything.

"Okay," she says tightly. "If you don't want to talk to me."

He pushes back his chair ready to stand up. "I want to watch *Coast*." He likes *Coast*, though he thinks that the Scottish presenter should get his hair cut. Who does the man think he is? Effie likes his long hair and says he makes her think of Heathcliff. He can't remember who Heathcliff is, but he thinks Laurence Olivier played him in a film. He remembers Laurence Olivier.

"Not much point in us living together, is there?" she says.

He frowns. She is in one of her moods. He picks up the *Radio Times* from the kitchen table in his left hand. He needs to check what programmes he has marked for tonight. He mustn't miss anything.

"Is there?" she repeats loudly.

He picks up his plate with its chicken and its broccoli and its olive oil and he turns towards the kitchen door.

"Hold it straight!" she shouts. She stands up and grabs his plate from him.

He stares at her. What's the matter with her? She's losing it. She really is.

"Look!" she shouts. "You've spilt olive oil on the floor. And now you're going to tread in it. Like you always do."

He takes a piece of kitchen roll and bends to mop up the dribble of oil. But he's stiff and he can't bend.

"That's no good," she shouts. "I'll have to wash the whole thing properly with the bucket and the mop and floor cleaner. Like I did yesterday, and the day before and the day before that. All because of your stupid olive oil."

He picks up his plate and turns away.

"I've had enough," she shouts. "I've had just about as much as I can take. More than I can take."

"What's the matter?" asks Lionel.

She takes a deep breath. "I want us to split up," she says. "I want us to put the house on the market and buy two smaller places."

He frowns. All because of the olive oil? She's bonkers. "That would be a pity," he says. "We're happily married."

"You might be, but I'm not," she says. "What's the point of us being together? We don't talk, we don't go anywhere, we don't have any friends. And as for sex..." She splutters. "Everything is all over.

71

All I ever do is clear up after you!"

Suddenly she picks up her own plate, lifts it high, and smashes it as hard as she can on the floor. The chicken goes one way, the broccoli goes another, and pieces of china scatter in all directions. Splatters of gravy are everywhere. Now the floor really will need mopping.

"What did you do that for?" he asks.

But Effie is slumped on the floor, sitting in some gravy, rocking back and fore and weeping copiously with her face in her hands. What is it with her?

"Are you mentally ill?" he demands.

She sobs. "I... expect so," she manages, through the tears and heaving sobs. "Anyone in my situation would be."

He can't stand it when she cries.

He carries his plate and his *Radio Times* into the dining room and switches on the TV. That presenter with the long hair has a nice Scottish accent. There are a lot of cliffs and a lot of birds to look at. Scenery too. The chicken is tasty.

Later Effie puts her head around the door. She has stopped crying. She always does in the end.

"I'm going to an Al-Anon meeting," she says.

"What's that?" he asks.

"I've told you before. It's a support group for families and friends of alcoholics. It's for people like me whose lives have been ruined by alcohol."

That's stupid, he thinks. "I'm not an alcoholic," he says. "I don't drink anymore."

She takes a deep breath. "Well you used to. It ruined your health and it ruined your brain. You're a wreck and it's all your fault."

"Well, I'm getting older. What do you expect?"

"And it ruined our marriage," she says. "That's a wreck too. I can't go on like this." She closes her eyes and grits her teeth. "I want us to split up."

He shrugs. She'll calm down in a day or two, he thinks. "All right," he says, "if that's what you want we can get a divorce." He looks at his watch. "What time will you be back?"

"I don't know," she hisses impatiently.

Why does she have to be so vague? His watch says it's twenty-five to eight now. He will finish his dinner and at eight o'clock, when *Coast* is over, he will go up to his room and have a cigarette. "Approximately?" he asks.

CHAPTER 10

Three C-Words

Effie had been meaning to go to Al-Anon ever since her discussion with Dr Dauncey. She'd been on the edge of taking the plunge a couple of times. But something had held her back. But her outburst over Lionel's spilt olive oil showed that she needed help. Now was as good a time as any. Would she, she wondered, know anyone there?

She arrived a few minutes early and a man was arranging two folding tables side by side in the centre of the room.

"Good evening," he said with a welcoming smile.

"Al-Anon?" she checked.

"Welcome. Do come in." He offered his hand. "I'm Andy."

"Hello, Andy. I'm Effie," she said.

He offered her a chair pulled from a stack and put others in place around the table.

"How many do you expect?" she asked.

"Oh... it varies. Six or seven... just depends... I'll put the kettle on," he said. "Tea or coffee?" He got some mugs down from a cupboard.

A couple of others arrived and sat down, while Andy was sticking notices on the walls with Blu Tack, each one giving words of advice.

One day at a time.

Let go, let God.

It begins with me.

Then he put some leaflets on the table. "Are you new to Al-Anon?" he asked.

"I went to the branch in Brighton some years ago. But there were so many people there, I found it rather daunting. I didn't stick with it, but the problem hasn't gone away."

"Al-Anon problems don't," he said. "But we're a small and friendly group. People come and go as they feel the need."

And two more arrived. Teas and coffees were distributed and Andy sat down. He opened the meeting with, "I welcome you to this Al-Anon family group..."

Some of the members had books, but Andy passed her a card so that she could take her turn to read from a list of what were called the twelve steps to recovery. She remembered that the pre-determined ritual was what had made her feel so uncomfortable last time. Of course, last time she had thought that Al-Anon would be showing her how to stop Lionel drinking. This time she realised that the whole philosophy of Al-Anon was that alcoholism was a family illness, and that while the alcoholics themselves were not treatable, their families were.

The first step on her road to recovery would be to admit that she was *powerless over alcohol* and that her life *had become unmanageable*.

That was ok. She'd accepted that some time ago. And she'd even accepted that Lionel's giving up drinking after he came out of hospital had not enabled him to revert to some long-forgotten non-alcoholic personality.

What was not okay, was the references to God, or to some other indeterminate Higher Power. Nor was the requirement for her to make amends for her *wrongdoings, her shortcomings, and her defects of character*. Was she to blame for all this? And as for asking God, if he or she existed, for forgiveness? She just didn't get it.

But she was here and she might as well listen.

After the twelve steps were read aloud the twelve traditions of Al-Anon followed. And then it was time for each member to speak of their problems.

"Would you like to start, Zoe?" said Andy to the woman on his right.

"My name's Zoe, and my alcoholic is my ex-husband."

Well done, you've got rid of him, thought Effie. Why is an ex-husband still a problem?

"He took his share of the money and went off to Thailand for a holiday. Well, we heard he married a Thai girl and is not planning to come home ever. The children are gutted and I feel awful for them. Not that I ever want to see him again."

Not surprised, thought Effie.

"Thank you, Zoe," said Andy.

The next one was Eileen. "My name is Eileen and my alcoholic is my husband."

Effie noted the use of the term 'my alcoholic'. A bit like 'my cat' or 'my dog'. No way was an alcoholic a family pet. If he were, Effie thought wryly, you could have him put down.

Eileen's husband was driving her to distraction. So many parallels with Effie's own experiences. The obsessions, the compulsions, the embarrassing behaviour, the rudeness. And on top of that he hadn't worked in years, so poor Eileen was struggling to maintain the household finances.

You have to count your blessings, thought Effie. At least Lionel's behavioural problems hadn't started until he was approaching retirement. Although, looking back, maybe the loss of those last clients had something to do with his drinking.

It was Effie's turn. "I'm Effie and my alcoholic is my husband." She smiled at Eileen. She felt there was a bond there. "He gave up drinking three years ago after nearly dying of heart failure, but the damage was done. He's verbally aggressive. He has obsessions – food obsessions, time obsessions, verbal obsessions. His behaviour is bizarre. He is under the mental health team at Larwood, and we're waiting for a scan, but I think he's probably got Korsakoff's Syndrome, which is an alcohol-induced dementia."

Eileen nodded. "I've read about that," she said. "I'd like to get Roland tested."

Effie continued. "When I went to Al-Anon some years ago, I was hoping I'd learn how to stop him drinking. I didn't know then that it couldn't be done. Now I'm here to learn how to live with a recovered alcoholic. Thank you."

"Thank you for sharing that with us," said Andy. "Though we do all know that there is no such thing as a 'recovered alcoholic'."

Andy's alcoholic was his son, and his aim was to distance himself from the problem. He had helped his son out too many times, bailed him out from jail, given him money, and let him come back to live at home. But always the boy – who was no longer a boy – went back to his old ways. There was nothing Andy could do for him. Andy was coming to Al-Anon to learn to let go. But it was obvious that he never would.

The session closed with the group saying the Serenity Prayer together.

God, grant me the serenity to accept the things I cannot change,
The courage to change the things I can,
And the wisdom to know the difference.

Serenity. That was the aim. There were no solutions.

During the course of the evening Effie learned about the three Cs of alcoholism: You cannot *Cause* it, you cannot *Cure* it and you cannot *Control* it.

Effie thought about that as she walked home in the dark. Was it true? Was it a cop-out, an abdication of responsibility? Was there not some point in Effie's past life with Lionel, when she should have recognised the seriousness of his drinking, and when she might have been able to do something about it?

Who knew?

Later, Effie would realise that the maxim of the three Cs could also be applied to another disease. But that night Effie had yet to hear of FTD.

"Hello," called Lionel as Effie pushed open the front door.

She walked into the living room. Lionel was seated in his usual place at the usual table. "Where've you been?" he asked.

"Al-Anon," she said.

"What the fuck's Al-Anon?" he asked.

Next morning, Effie picked up the local paper. The house was peaceful and this was a good time to sit quietly and read the headlines. Lionel was still in bed. Asleep presumably. Unless, of course, he were dead. He might have died in the night. There'd been a time when he'd first come out of hospital, when she'd creep up to his room to check that he was still alive. A bit like you do with a new-born baby. That was three years ago when she still had hope. But now she didn't bother. If he were in the process of dying, she wouldn't want to interrupt.

The lead story in the paper was about a car crash. Three young people, a car, and lamp post were involved. And two of those young people were dead. It had taken place in the early hours of the morning and the crash victims had been partying. Drinking. She thought of the parents, the families, the friends. So much damage to so many lives. Alcohol was to blame. How would they all cope?

What was it about Al-Anon? The philosophy of handing your life over to a Higher Power made no sense to her. Any strength had to come from within. Surely? Of course, if you believed, really believed, that there was something out there watching over you, then you were very lucky. Maybe that belief helped you find the strength within. But mostly you had to get your act together and get on with it.

And some of those people who'd poured out their problems last night shouldn't be getting on with it. They should be getting out of it. The young woman whose partner was drinking her into penury. She had everything going for her. Young, attractive, intelligent. Why was she allowing that useless man to drag her down? All she had to do was get out. It seemed so simple.

Is that what I should have done? Effie wondered. Is that what I should still do?

She turned the pages. What was the house worth? Unless you were actually house hunting you lost track of what was happening to the housing market. She reached the property section and looked to see what was for sale. There was one she recognised. A bit bigger than theirs, she noted, but not such a nice road. A sum of money like that would have been a fortune when she was a girl. Was it enough to buy two smaller properties? One for him and one for her? She'd like to talk to him about it, but she knew he wouldn't listen. He'd grunt and look down at his Sudoku puzzle. Or he'd grunt and walk out of the room.

She turned the page and looked at some flats for sale. Perhaps they could buy a flat each. A one-bedroom flat would be fine for Lionel, but she'd need a bit more space for when the grandchildren stayed. She looked at some possibilities. But it was practicalities that would be the problem. No way could they tie in the sale of one home and the purchase of two others simultaneously. The property market wasn't like that. What they'd need to do, was find something for Lionel, sell the house, then she could rent something while she decided what to do. Sheltered housing would be best for Lionel. After all, he could barely change a light bulb, these days. But to even embark upon such a plan she would have to put the house on the market. And she couldn't do that without him agreeing. And how could she get him to agree when he wouldn't even talk about it? She was trapped.

She turned to the next page. These were properties to let. As she ran her eye down the page, one caught her attention. It was a six-month let. And it was furnished. It was in Farnford, the village where Effie played tennis. In fact, the tennis club there was a lifeline to her sanity. She read the advert carefully. Fully furnished and equipped. Did that mean you could just move in? she wondered. Like tomorrow? She reached for the phone and made an appointment to view it.

"It's just round the corner," said the estate agent when she arrived.

It was an end-of-terrace cottage down the lane between the pub and the church. You had to turn into a narrow alley between the house and the garage to get to the front door which was really a side door. The owners had gone to Australia for six months, the estate agent explained. What they wanted, apart from six months' rent, was someone quiet and reliable to occupy it. What they didn't want was a group of youngsters throwing parties.

She would be an eminently suitable tenant, thought Effie. Peace and quiet was what she was seeking.

There was a kitchen with dishwasher, washing machine and cupboards stocked with crockery, glassware, saucepans and cutlery. There was a kettle, an iron and a microwave. The living room had a sofa, two chairs, a TV, a well-stocked bookcase and a coffee table. And it had French windows out into a secluded garden with a modest patio, a small lawn and shrubbed borders. Upstairs was a bedroom and a bathroom, along with a second bedroom that was, explained the agent, kept locked. That was where the owners had put their private belongings while they were abroad.

The only windows that overlooked the lane were those of the locked bedroom whose curtains were closed, and that of the bathroom window, which was frosted. No one would need to know she was there, thought Effie. She could hide from Lionel. She could hide from the world. She could have six months here to restore her sanity and decide what she was going to do with her life.

"How quickly could I move in?" she asked the estate agent.

He considered. "It's just a matter of sorting out the electricity, gas, and rates," he said. "That can all be done with a couple of phone calls. You could move in tomorrow if you can pay a month's rent and sign the contract."

She did some rough calculations. The rent plus the maintenance of a second home for six months. She'd have to cash in some savings. It was a lot of money. But who can put a price on sanity? It would give her some space. Some time to think things through. One part of her mind told her that this was a wild fantasy. The other part told her that it must have been meant. A cottage like this coming up just as she felt she could cope no longer.

"And how long have I got to make up my mind?" she asked.

He shrugged. "We've had a couple of enquiries, but nothing definite. Who knows?"

And then she remembered her car.

"And the garage?" she asked. "Can I see the garage?"

"The owners weren't planning to let that. They've left a car there. You can park in the village. It's no problem."

Effie frowned. It is for me, she thought. Her bright green ostentatious car was parked right now in the main street, outside the estate agent's office where everyone could see it. And most people she knew could recognise it.

"Can I see the garage?" she asked.

The garage door was unlocked and falling off its hinges. And inside was an old sports car with a broken canvas roof. Effie smiled. It was an MGB. Red, or at least it was where the rust hadn't come through. The very sight of it took her back in time.

It was the first holiday she and Lionel had taken after getting married. Their honeymoon. She hadn't thought of it as a honeymoon as they'd been living together before they were married. Everyone does that now, but it was unusual back then. And they'd been to Tenerife, which for her, in those days, was an adventure. They'd stayed on the wild side of the island on a bay overlooked by magnificent black cliffs that towered a couple of thousand feet above a deep blue sea. Each morning Lionel ordered morning tea to be brought to the room and usually they took it out on the balcony to enjoy the view. In the evening, they had drinks in the room as the sun went down. Lionel had bought bottles of duty-free whisky and gin at the airport and he'd bring Effie a gin and tonic in the bath before they went down for dinner. Sometimes he would get in the bath with her and sometimes they were late for dinner. She closed her eyes as she remembered the lovemaking. They had a bottle of wine, sometimes two, at dinner, and then maybe dancing, a walk on moonlit beach and more lovemaking. It was magic, but she could see now that both of them had been drinking far too much.

What she also remembered was the red MGB they hired. It had taken a few days to see the island. Such fun with the roof open. But the highlight was that drive up to the ancient volcano. The ascent via those lethal hairpin bends as the road climbed through the pine trees to a desert of ancient lava formations that changed from red to gold to black in swirls of contrasting colour that took Effie's breath away. Sometimes it was fear of the steepness of the bends, sometimes the sheer awesome beauty of the landscape that thrilled her. They drove through patches of white cloud, and it was cold, very cold, by the time they reached the top.

"One degree for every three hundred feet," Lionel had said.

And then the further ascent by cable car to the summit where they climbed to look into the caldera. The air was thick with the smell of sulphur and the rough pumice was edged with bright yellow crystals.

And down at the bottom of the cable car was parked the red MGB, looking like a toy so far below. It was new and shiny, unlike this one which could only be fit for scrap.

Effie ran her hands over the damaged paintwork. A spider had spun a web across the steering wheel.

"I'd have to have the garage," Effie said to the agent. "I couldn't take it otherwise."

"Well..." There was a hesitation. "I suppose the owner might consider storing the car elsewhere," pondered the agent.

Or getting rid of it, thought Effie. Surely he couldn't be planning to restore this lump of rusty metal to its former glory?

"The house," said Effie, "is exactly what I need, but I have to be able to park."

"I'll ask him," said the agent.

Effie went home fantasising about the future. She hadn't caused Lionel's symptoms. She couldn't cure them, or control them. Maybe, just maybe, she could escape from them.

CHAPTER 11

A First Brain Scan

"You mean down here?" says Lionel, turning into the road that leads past A&E. He's been to this hospital before. He must have done. He doesn't remember what he came for, but he knows he did. He thinks something has changed.

Effie is reading the instructions. "It says go right to the end of the building and turn right into the courtyard behind A&E. The MRI Centre is opposite."

"Here?" says Lionel. What's an MRI Centre? he is wondering. And why do they have to go there?

"Yes, but you'd better go on. We can't park here. We might have to go back to the main car park."

Lionel frowns. Effie always finds problems when there aren't any. "Yes, we can. Look there's a space."

"It's a disabled space. You're not disabled."

Why does she fuss so? he thinks. Parking a car is no big deal. "Yeah. Well you seem to think I am. We wouldn't be here if you didn't." He pulls up, puts the green Jaguar into reverse and neatly parks it. "There!" he says triumphantly. "What's wrong with that?

Effie frowns. "We should really go to the main car park."

Lionel exhales impatiently. She is such a stickler for stupid rules.

"Well, we're here now." He opens the driver's door, swings his legs sideways and stands up. For a moment he feels a little dizzy. He must have stood up too quickly. He takes his cigarettes out of his coat pocket and feels for his lighter. He'll feel better in a minute, he thinks, as he lights up and inhales deeply.

"Where do we go?" he asks.

Effie is out of the car now and points to the double swing doors with the sign saying *MRI Centre* over the top.

"Must be in there."

He takes a couple more puffs, puts out his cigarette, replaces the unsmoked half in the box, and follows Effie in. They report to reception and are invited to take a seat alongside other patients. Lionel glances at his watch. His appointment is in ten minutes. Why did Effie insist on setting out so early?

"I'm just going outside," he says.

He relights his cigarette and paces up and down. He checks his watch, puts out his cigarette and goes back inside.

"Is the doctor ready for me?" he asks the receptionist.

"You're not seeing a doctor, Mr Butler. You're here for an MRI scan. You'll be seeing a radiologist."

He frowns. He doesn't know what an MRI scan is. Nor does he want to know. Why is he here?

He points to his watch. "Are you running on time?" he asks.

The receptionist nods. "More or less," she says. "Do sit down."

"Come and sit down," prompts Effie and pats the seat of the chair beside her.

He sits. "What time's your appointment?" he asks the man sitting next to him.

The man looks at the clock on the wall and sighs. "Fifteen minutes ago," he says in a resigned tone.

"What time?" repeats Lionel.

"Eleven fifteen," replies the man.

"Christ! That's before me!" He stands up and goes back to the reception desk. "How many people before me?" he asks.

"Only one," says the receptionist. She smiles tightly. "We're trying to catch up."

What is it with the appointment system? Why can't they be more accurate? He looks at Effie. "I'm going outside for a bit," he says. He needs to have another puff just before he goes in, because God knows when he'll be able to get out.

Effie shrugs and gives him that anxious smile of hers. "Check the car's okay," she says.

He shakes his head. Of course the car's okay, he thinks. He wanders across the courtyard. Why do they need so many disabled spaces? he wonders. Didn't look like anyone in that waiting room was disabled.

He sits on a wall. What a stupid way to spend an afternoon, he thinks. Then Effie comes hurrying out. "They're ready for you," she calls.

"Good morning Mr Butler," says a man. "I'm Abdul Ahmed, your radiographer," he says as they shake hands. "I'm going to be taking some pictures of your brain."

Are you indeed? thinks Lionel. "If I have one!" he remarks. "*She* doesn't think I have," he adds, grinning at Effie.

The radiographer's face remains impassive. That's the trouble with these foreigners, thinks Lionel. They don't understand the British sense of humour. Come to think of it, Effie doesn't seem to understand his jokes any more.

"You'll need to... your... your watch..."

Lionel frowns. He can't follow what this foreigner is saying.

Babble-abble-abble. It's his accent. Why don't they teach these idiots to speak properly?

"Speak English!" he shouts at the man.

Effie interrupts. "My husband can't hear very well," she says in that ameliorating tone she sometimes has.

"Yes, I can!" he shouts. "I just can't follow his gobbledegook foreign accent."

The man speaks more slowly. "You need to remove your belt and your watch. Any money. Anything made of metal," he says. "You can use one of these lockers."

As Lionel puts his belongings in the locker, the radiographer addresses Effie. "Mrs Butler?" he asks.

"Yes?"

"He doesn't like my colour?" he says quietly to her, though this time Lionel can hear every word.

Effie sighs. "It's not that. He'd be just as rude if you were Scottish. I'm sorry, but it's because of his behaviour we're here."

"Will you be staying with him during the scan?" he asks.

She nods again. "Yes, please."

"Good. Perhaps you'd remove your watch and any jewellery too."

They are shown into a room which is empty except for two chairs and what they are soon to discover is the MRI scanning machine.

"You can sit on this chair," says the radiographer, to Effie. You may like to use these earplugs. It will be noisy.

Effie sits.

He gives Lionel a set of earphones. "And Mr Butler, will you lie down here and make yourself comfortable."

Lionel sits on a flat bed thing and swivels sideways to lie down. Comfortable? Some chance!

"When I start the machine you'll be slowly moved into it to have the pictures taken. You will find it noisy, which is why you need the headphones. Don't worry about anything. Just relax and lie as still as you possibly can. I'll be in the next room behind that window."

Relax. How do they expect him to relax? The whole place looks like something out of Star Wars.

Effie stretches an arm forwards and caresses his shoulder. She says something, but now that he's got the headphones on he doesn't know what it is. What a nightmare!

And it is. The headphones don't block out the noise. The banging, the grinding. How long is it this going on? He wants to get out. He bangs on the roof. "Haven't we finished yet?" he shouts.

And then it stops.

"I'm sorry, Mr Butler," comes a voice from somewhere. "I'm, afraid you're not lying sufficiently still for clear images. Could we try again, please?"

"No, we couldn't," reacts Lionel, sitting up on the flat bed. "I'm not going through all that again."

The radiographer comes back in the room. "We've time to make one more attempt. And if you could concentrate on lying very still."

"Please, Lionel," says Effie, "we're here now. You might as well get the tests done."

He glares at her and sighs. He'd better do what she wants. She's been threatening to move out and live somewhere else just recently. She doesn't mean it, of course. But he needs to humour her. "Okay. I'll try."

The radiographer nods. "That's splendid, Mr Butler."

"Lie there and count to a thousand," says Effie.

And it starts all over again.

He decides to count in seventeens. Seventeen, thirty-four, fifty-one, sixty-eight... he begins inside his head. The noise is horrendous...

a hundred and seventy, a hundred and eighty-seven... he continues. And then the numbers are merging together and he has lost his place because the noise is so awful, but it doesn't matter anymore because he is too tired to worry about it.

"Well done!" says the radiographer when all has gone quiet. "I've got some clear images," he adds.

"What do they show?" asks Effie.

The radiographer smiles. "It's not my job to interpret them. I'll be sending the results to Dr Hazan.

"But do they show I've got a brain?" asks Lionel, tapping his head.

The radiographer laughs. "Oh yes. There's a brain in there all right. A very active one."

Lionel sniggers. "Ha-ha," he says to Effie. "You thought my head was stuffed with cotton wool!"

CHAPTER 12

Effie and the Bridge Club

"Ah well," said Barbara. "Another disastrous evening."

Barbara was Effie's bridge partner. They got on well, but they didn't play bridge well. They'd been to lessons and learned the rules of the game, but Effie had accepted that neither of them had a flair for cards, and neither of them had the powers of concentration or memory that were needed to be a good player. Especially Effie. Perhaps she just didn't care enough.

Unlike Lionel.

Lionel was a card sharp. He had a memory for the cards and an intuitive understanding of chance. In the early days he'd played poker, and mostly he'd won. Then one day shortly after they'd moved in together and they were planning to buy a home, he got back at four in the morning having lost a lot more than was sensible. Effie was upset and Lionel had the intelligence to give up. Later, after they'd settled down and started a family, they both learned to play bridge, and for a while had partnered each other. Much of their social life was centred on bridge. They played socially with friends – bridge fours, or eights, or twelves in each other's homes. Sometimes these occasions were accompanied by dinner, always by drinks. Lionel drank whisky in those days, but he knew when to stop. Later, things were different.

It was their membership of the Dalton Health Bridge Club that enabled them to develop their skills further.

Lionel in particular.

There had come a time when Effie felt inadequate as his partner. The thing was, she knew him too well. That movement of his right eyebrow when she played the wrong card. That slight, *ahem,* when she made a mistake. That little laugh that was almost a snigger undermined her confidence. And the analysis of the card play when it was all over had been tortuous. After all, it was only a game. Wasn't it?

As Effie had played less, Lionel had played more. And with better and better partners. For some years the phone had rung almost daily, either with calls from people who wanted to partner him, or from people who had partnered him and wanted to discuss the intricacies of the card play. He'd been a popular man in those days and he'd been in demand.

Unlike now.

These days Effie played more, and Lionel played less.

The results were analysed by computer, and even before leaving the room, Effie and Barbara knew that they had achieved only forty-one percent of a possible score and had come second to bottom in the ranking. Lionel would have discovered this online by the time Effie got home and printed off the results table. She knew he'd make scathing remarks about the hopelessness of her bridge-playing skills.

"Wasn't so bad," said Effie to Barbara. "You played that slam well, and if I hadn't revoked against Derek and Sam we'd have done a bit better."

Barbara grinned. "Okay for next week?" she said as she put on her coat.

Effie nodded. "See you then, and I'll try..."

"How about other things?" asked Barbara. "Did you decide about moving out?"

"Renting the cottage?" Effie had confided in Barbara about her discussions with the estate agent. She should have kept it to herself really, but sometimes she needed someone to talk to. "There isn't a garage. I wouldn't be able to park."

Barbara looked sceptical. "That's just an excuse," she said. "The least of your problems."

Yes. There were other reasons. She couldn't bring herself to do it. Not now she knew Lionel was ill. "I should have done it before."

"Before what?"

"Before I knew that Lionel couldn't cope on his own." But if she had...

"Effie!" came a voice.

Effie turned. It was Derek calling from across the room. "Could I have a word?"

"Bye," she said to Barbara. "Talk to you next time." She joined Derek.

Derek had been one of Lionel's most regular and most loyal bridge partners for many years. "A couple of things," he said, his voice lowered. He evidently didn't want to be overheard.

"Yes?"

"I thought I should tell you that I've told Lionel I'm not going to partner him anymore."

Effie closed her eyes, her heart sinking. She nodded. "Thanks for letting me know."

"I feel awful about it, but it's all got so difficult. The things he comes up with. You can't imagine..."

"Yes, I can. I know what he's like," responded Effie. Nevertheless, she felt awful. If Derek was giving up on Lionel, who would be left?

"I'm so sorry. I mean, I used to enjoy playing with him so much. But..."

"I quite understand. Thank you for sticking it out so long."

"I think all his old friends now realise he's ill, but the youngsters here..." He glanced around to check no one was listening. "They just think he's one grade worse than the archetypal grumpy old man. Did you know there's been another formal complaint about him?"

"Another?" Effie reacted. How many had there been? "No. I don't know anything."

"He's going to get another letter. I got here early tonight and happened to overhear Charles and Helen discussing him in the office. Charles said, 'Something's got to be done.'"

"You mean they're going to throw him out of the club?" asked Effie. Why can't they talk to me about it? she asked herself. She was a member. She was Lionel's wife. Why was she always the last to know what was going on?

"Not just like that. There are procedures that have to be followed, but I think they're starting them."

Effie shook her head despairingly. "I don't know what to do," she cried. She felt a tremor in her voice. "I don't know how to cope with all this."

Derek shook his head. "I'm sorry. I didn't mean to upset you. I shouldn't have told you."

The bridge room was empty now and the director was waiting to lock up.

"I'm glad you did. Thank you."

It was late morning the following day and Effie could hear Lionel on the phone. "Any chance of a game next week?" he was saying.

Effie paused in the doorway. He didn't realise she was back home.

"Well what about the week after?" she heard him ask.

Effie cringed. One of his partners was making excuses. Whoever it was didn't want to play with him and didn't have the balls to say so.

"Oh well, see how you're fixed. Maybe next month," he said finally, his tone heavy with disappointment. He paused, perhaps waiting for a positive response. "Bye then," he said sadly and put the phone down.

She peered around the edge of the door. He was flicking though his address book. He dialled another number and began the same process all over again. He got much the same response. When the phone clicked off she breezed into the room.

"Okay?" she asked.

He shrugged. "Can't get a game next week," he said.

"What about Nick?" she suggested.

"Could do," he said uncertainly. "He sent an email."

"Saying?" said Effie.

Lionel frowned and took a deep breath. "He said he'd been forced to rearrange his bridge commitments. The third Monday of the month is no longer available."

Effie gritted her teeth.

"I could phone him and see if he's got another day," said Lionel a little more brightly.

The bastard! Why couldn't Nick be honest about it? Was Derek the only decent person in the club?

"I wouldn't do that," she said evenly. She took a deep breath. "He'd have said if he had. Lionel, you must realise that your behaviour at the bridge club makes it very difficult for people to play with you. It's your fault."

"Oh, for Chrissake! You're always getting at me!"

She forced herself to speak slowly. "I don't know for sure, but I suspect they don't like the swearing, the jokey put-downs, the walking about when you're dummy."

"I don't swear," he reacted.

"You say, 'Eff, eff, eff.' They know what it means."

Lionel glared at her. "Eff is for 'friendly'," he snarled. Then he grinned. "Eff is for Effie!" he said triumphantly. And he laughed as though he'd said something clever. "Effie, effing Effie, the love of my life."

She smiled. He just didn't get it. "Would you like to play with me next week?" she offered.

He gave her a bitter look. "I'm not that desperate," he sneered.

She felt she'd been slapped in the face with a wet cloth. "Please yourself," she said, "but you may find that when everyone else has ditched you, you won't have any choice." She turned on her heel. "I've got to unload the shopping."

At three o'clock Lionel went off for his afternoon nap. Effie knew he would sleep at least until five, so she had plenty of time to get on with things. The phone list of the bridge club members was pinned to the notice board. She got it down and scanned the names of the committee. Helen first. She was the secretary. She was a retired nurse and must have dealt with some difficult patients in her time. Maybe she'd been a bit more understanding than those ex-lawyers and accountants who were trying to run the club like a multinational company.

"Hello. Is that Helen? It's Effie Butler."

"Hello, Effie." The tone was flat and not particularly welcoming.

"It's about Lionel," she said.

"Yes?"

"I heard some gossip that there's been a complaint about him?" she said. "I wondered if it were true?"

Helen wasn't giving anything away. Tight-lipped bitch. "I think it would best if you phoned Toby Mulligan. He's the chairman of the Conduct Committee. He's the one who's dealing with the situation."

Situation? What was that supposed to mean?

"Very well. Thank you. Goodbye."

She dialled Toby's number and asked him the same question.

He was more forthcoming. "There've been two complaints. I'm going to deliver a letter about the second one later today. I'll put it through your letter box. That way I'll be sure he'll get it."

Will you be sure he'll read it? Effie asked silently inside her head. Let alone understand what it's all about. "Can you tell me what he's done?" she asked.

Toby sighed. "It's difficult. He makes inappropriate jokes. He uses unacceptable language. He makes unsuitable remarks."

Inappropriate. Unacceptable. Unsuitable. What do all these platitudes mean?

"Such as?" she said.

Toby elaborated a little. "He comments on people's appearance. He imitates accents, mannerisms. Stares at them in a way that makes them nervous."

"He isn't vindictive," said Effie. "You do realise he has some sort of mental illness. We're waiting for a diagnosis," she added.

"What difference will that make?" said Toby.

Effie frowned. How he could be so flippant? A diagnosis would make all the difference. It would mean they could understand what was making Lionel behave the way he did. People would sympathise with him rather than criticise him. Wouldn't they?

What she said was, "You never know – it might be treatable."

"Possibly," said Toby, "but unlikely. And not in time for us to deal with this particular situation."

There it was again – *situation.*

He continued, "There are members who have left the club because Lionel makes them feel uncomfortable. When they see him arrive they're intimidated. They're waiting for him to reach their table and say something or do something unacceptable."

"You mean something rude," said Effie.

"Yes."

Then why didn't he say so? And Lionel wasn't the only member of that club who made people feel uncomfortable. She could think of at least three – all patronising county players – who treated occasional players like herself as though they were something the cat sicked up.

"So are you going to chuck him out?" she asked.

"It's not that simple. After three letters from the Conduct Committee the matter will be passed to the Disciplinary Committee, which is nothing to do with me. It'll be someone else's problem."

"He's ill, Toby. Bridge is the only thing he can still do. He'll have nothing left in his life if you stop him playing bridge."

"We realise that. That's why we've been bending over backwards to be tolerant."

Have you really? she wondered. "It would have been nice," she said, "if someone had told me what was going on. Hearing it on the grapevine was a nasty shock."

"It's between him and the bridge club. We have no official right to approach you, just because..."

"...Just because I'm his wife," she completed for him. "Only his wife. No one important."

The letter fell on the doormat an hour later. It was addressed to Lionel and marked *by hand.* Effie picked it up, turned it over, and wondered about opening it. But she carried it into the lounge and placed it on Lionel's table next to his Sudoku book.

Later, he came down from his afternoon nap and settled at his table.

She watched him open the envelope, skim through the letter inside, then fold it small and put it in his back pocket.

"What's that?" she asked.

"Nothing," he growled.

CHAPTER 13

D-Day!

D is for Diagnosis. Another month, another appointment. Lionel is sick of appointments. This one is at the Larwood Mental Health Centre and he is to see Dr Hazan. Effie says Dr Hazan is a psychiatrist. A shrink. What do shrinks do? In films they put you on a couch and ask you questions about your sex life. Funny how he lost interest in sex. Good thing too, given that there's no way he could get it up these days. Still, what do you expect after all those years of marriage?

For this appointment he parks in a parking space that is marked *deliveries only* and this time Effie doesn't say a word. She has already snapped at him for overtaking that idiot lorry driver and she's gone into one of her silent moods.

They have to press a doorbell and somebody inside takes a peek at you, clicks the door open and lets you in. Security. They have to have security because they're dealing with a load of nutters. There is a waiting room where you have to sign in a book and write the time down.

"Dr Hazan won't be long," says the receptionist. "Do take a seat."

He sits one side of the room and Effie sits the other. She's avoiding eye contact with him. She picks up a magazine.

He looks at his watch and stands up again to go back to the desk.

"How long will it be?" he asks.

"Not long. There's a patient with Doctor Hazan now."

Lionel takes a quick glance at Effie who has her nose in her magazine. He can see she's concentrating on ignoring him. He pushes open the door, goes outside and lights up a cigarette.

He only has time for a couple of puffs before the door opens and Effie says: "Hurry up, Lionel. They're ready for us."

He inhales deeply, then puts out the cigarette and puts what's left of it back in the box. He seems to be living life at half a cigarette at a time.

"Good afternoon, Mr Butler," says a young man who extends his hand. "I'm David Anderson, I'm..."

"I thought we were seeing Dr Hazan," reacts Lionel.

"You are. I'm a psychiatric nurse and I'm going to take down some information first. Would you come this way please?"

He leads them through fire doors, along corridors, up stairs and around corners to a room where there is a circle of armchairs with fake leather upholstery and wooden arms. "Do take a seat," he says.

"Where?" asks Lionel, considering the options.

"Wherever you like."

"I don't like. I don't want to be here."

Effie is already seated. She grits her teeth in that way she has. "Just sit down, Lionel," she hisses.

He does.

"So, how are you?" asks the psychiatric nurse.

"Same as yesterday," says Lionel flatly. Why do people always ask you how you are? They don't mean it. It's just something they say.

"And how were you yesterday?" continues the nurse.

"Average," says Lionel.

"Which is?"

"I'm a wreck. An old git. What do you expect at my age?"

The psychiatric nurse is making notes. "Do you know what day of the week it is?" he asks.

"Friday," says Lionel. Here we go again, he thinks. More stupid questions. He knows the day, the date, the year, and the name of the prime minister. Has he done all this before? Or did he imagine it? He's forgotten the name of the psychiatric nurse though. But that might be because it doesn't interest him. "This is so-o boring," he says.

"What floor are we on?" is another question.

Good grief! All those stairs and corridors. Is he supposed to remember? He glances out of the window. There is a group of nursing staff down there smoking cigarettes. "Upstairs," he says. He thinks. "First floor."

"Very good. Mr Butler, do you understand why you're here?"

No, he doesn't understand that. He doesn't understand what any of this fuss is about. It's been going on and on and on and on. They're all bonkers. The bridge club nutters, the supermarket staff, the people at the leisure centre. They just don't get it. And *she* is the worst of the lot. He raises his finger and points it accusingly at Effie. "Because *she* said so," he snarls.

David Anderson thanks him. "I'll just go and fetch Dr Hazan," he says.

Dr Hazan is all smiles and teeth set against coffee-coloured skin, and much to Lionel's surprise, he speaks with an English accent. A proper upmarket English accent. Lionel likes that.

"Good afternoon," he says. "Pleased to meet you, Mr Butler. I'm Dr Hazan." He shakes hands with him. And then with Effie. "Good afternoon, Mrs Butler."

Dr Hazan sits down, a file in his hands. "So, Mr Butler," he says. "How are you?"

Here we go again. "That other bloke asked me that," he says.

"Yes, but I need to you to tell me."

"Average," says Lionel.

Dr Hazan smiles. "And what do you mean by *average?*" he asks.

"What?" says Lionel.

"Well. I understand you used to be a bit of a statistician? Now, the *average* price of a loaf of bread in the supermarket is the total price of all the loaves of bread in the supermarket divided by the number of loaves. Or that's what I was taught in maths at school. I wonder how that relates to your feeling *average?*"

Lionel smiles to himself. "I was speaking metaphorically, not statistically," he says. He laughs.

"Indeed?" says the psychiatrist. "I can see there's nothing wrong with your semantic skills."

"That's good," says Lionel. "Clever dick, Dr..." He realises he's forgotten the wretched man's name. Not that he knows what 'semantic skills' are anyway.

The psychiatrist makes some notes, then looks up at him. "Do you understand why you're here?"

"No, I don't. And I'm getting pretty pissed off. You tell me!"

"Yes, Mr Butler, that's exactly what I intend to do. We've had the results of your brain scan from the hospital. The images of your brain."

"Oh yeah?" Lionel senses Effie sitting up to attention.

"You have a neurological disease which is called frontotemporal dementia."

Lionel frowns. Neuro...? Fronto-what? his mind echoes.

Dr Hazan is still talking. "FTD is what we usually call it. It used to be called Pick's Disease. It's a complex degenerative condition caused by a deterioration of specific parts of the brain that are called the frontotemporal lobes."

Lionel frowns.

"That's this part here," says Dr Hazan, pointing to his own forehead. "In the front. It deals with communication, sympathy, empathy and language. It's what enables us to socialise." He looks at Lionel. "Did you follow that?"

"What?"

"Do you understand what I said?"

Lionel frowns. "Well, yes..."

"Can you explain it back to me then?"

"Explain what?"

"What I just told you."

"Yes...no... sort of... fucking hell! Whatever for?" Lionel frowns and shakes his head crossly.

The psychiatrist continues, but is addressing Effie now. "The atrophy is quite marked, fairly advanced. It's the reason some people have found his behaviour..." he hesitates... "inappropriate."

Effie sighs. She looks relieved for some reason. "This... FTD... is it caused by alcohol?" asks Effie.

Dr Hazan shakes his head. "Well, it wouldn't help, but no. There is no cause as far we know."

"And no cure?" asks Effie.

"Not at present," says Dr Hazan. "I'm sorry."

"And no control," says Effie softly, more to herself than anyone else. "The three Cs..."

"I beg your pardon?" says the psychiatrist.

She smiles. "The three C's of alcoholism... you can't *cause* it, you can't *cure* it and you can't *control* it. That's what Al-Anon taught me. Is it the same with FTD?"

Dr Hazan shrugs, and then nods slowly. "Pretty well. We may be able help to *control* some of the symptoms," he says, "but there is, as yet, no cure."

"And it's not caused by Lionel's past lifestyle?" she checks. "He was an alcoholic."

"No, I wasn't!" interrupts Lionel. Effie and this idiot are talking about him as though he wasn't there. Is that rude or what?

Effie looks down.

Dr Hazan looks at his notes. "There is a history of alcohol abuse," he says, "but that's not the cause." He frowns. "It is just possible that the disease caused the obsessive drinking." He smiles at Effie. "He would have developed this disease even if he'd been a teetotaller all his life. We know of no cause and no cure."

"Right," says Lionel, standing up. "If there's no cure for this fucking fronto-whatever-it-is you say I've got, I might as well piss off. I'm going for a fag."

He stands up and heads out of the door and into the corridor, just as the psychiatric nurse reappears.

"David, would you show Mr Butler to the waiting room?" asks the psychiatrist. "I'd like a few words with Mrs Butler. She'll join him in a minute or two."

"This way," says the psychiatric nurse. "...No, not that door... Yes, it is a bit of a rabbit warren... it takes a bit of getting used to. Perhaps you'd like to wait here? I'm sure your wife won't be long." He extends his hand to Lionel. "Nice to meet you, Mr Butler. See you next time."

Stuff the waiting room! thinks Lionel. He's not going to sit around here with all these nutters. You can tell they've lost it, just by looking at them.

"Could you sign, out, please, sir?" says the receptionist as he leaves.

"I could, but I'm fucking not going to," he says irritably.

Then, What a bloody waste of time, thinks Lionel as he takes his car keys from his pocket and clicks open the driver's door. He gets into the car and lights a cigarette. A new one this time. He turns on the ignition, and starts up. It isn't until he's parked the green Jaguar on the front drive of his home that he realises that something is missing. He opens the front door of the house and calls. "Effie?" He walks into the living room. Where the hell has she gone?

CHAPTER 14

A Steep Learning Curve

"It's a lot for you to take in," said Dr Hazan.

Effie shook her head, bemused, confused, shaken. "I can't believe it. I was so sure the diagnosis would be Korsakoff's Syndrome," she said, "because he used to be... such a heavy drinker."

"I thought that too," said the psychiatrist.

"I thought it was all his fault," she added. She gnawed her lower lip, and her brow furrowed with anxiety. Guilt, even. "I've been so angry with him. Ruining our lives with his stupid attitudes and dreadful behaviour. I'd thought about leaving him... Now..." Effie's mind was buzzing. This illness that Lionel had... this disease... Was it really just bad luck? Nothing to do with his lifestyle? Whatever the reason, she was his wife. She had a duty to support him. *In sickness and in health*... That's what she had promised. "What's the prognosis?" she asked.

The doctor shrugged. "It's a degenerative illness," he said. "He will need full-time care at the end."

"How long?" asked Effie.

"It's hard to say. Every case is different. Could be two years. Could be ten. Even twenty."

"And no treatment?"

Dr Hazan shook his head. "No. But we may be able to help with the behavioural symptoms. I'm prescribing a medication which should calm him down. We'll start him off on a low dose for the first month and we'll see how it goes." He handed her a prescription. "It may make him sleepy, so best for him to take it in the evening."

"And in the shorter term?"

"In the shorter term, you're the one who'll need help." He handed her a stack of leaflets and a booklet.

Effie flicked through. This was a new world. The world of dementia. The world of FTD.

"You'll need to inform the DVLA," Dr Hazan said.

Effie frowned. "Will he have to give up driving?" she asked.

"Not necessarily straight away. They might ask him to take a test. But his insurance company will have to be told." He paused. Then he said, "He shouldn't be left on his own for too long."

"What!" reacted Effie. "That's ridiculous! I go out all the time. He doesn't mind. I even go on holiday on my own. I'd go mad if I didn't. I need to get away."

"Well... you must judge for yourself. It's a risk, and it will be an increasing risk as the disease progresses. You'll need to find out about available help. Those leaflets will give you some ideas."

"If I go away you mean, on holiday for example?" She was going away in January. She was going to have the holiday of a lifetime with her lover. But she wasn't going to tell Dr Hazan about Matt.

"You need to explore the different possibilities. Carers can visit, or you can book residential respite care. You should try and get things in place ready for when you need them." He paused. "And you will need them."

That's right – shift the responsibility onto me, thought Effie. "Very well," she said.

108

Then, "Any more questions?" he asked.

"Not at the moment," said Effie. There were dozens of questions, all jostling for position in her mind. What would Lionel be like? How long would it take? How would she be able to cope? But she needed to settle down and go through all this information first. She stood up. "He'll be getting impatient," she said. "I'd better go."

"Make an appointment with David Anderson in a month," he said, "to monitor the medication."

As Dr Hazan showed her back along corridors, through doorways and down staircases towards the exit of this rambling old building, she wondered if she'd have remembered the way on her own. She wondered what was going on in her own brain.

There was no sign of Lionel when Dr Hazan delivered her back to the waiting room. "Don't worry," she said. "He'll have gone out for a cigarette. Thank you for your help." They shook hands and he held the heavy glass door for her to leave the building. Her eyes scanned the car park. Good, there was the green X-Type Jag. This time parked properly in a marked parking space. She hurried across, opened the front passenger door and let herself in. "Well done. You moved the car?" she said to Lionel.

"No, I didn't," he said.

"Yes, you did. It was parked there, in that disabled space." She pointed at a red Mini. Without a disabled badge, she noticed – Lionel was evidently not the only person who didn't worry about parking regulations.

"No, it wasn't. I've waiting been here for fucking hours."

Effie pressed her lips tightly together. "Shall we go home?" she said brightly.

Five minutes later, Lionel parked the Jaguar in its usual place on the drive, and Effie got out of the car and headed for the front door.

That was odd, she thought. She was about to put her key in the lock when she realised that she didn't need to. It was already open. She must have left the door on the latch. That was a worry. Anyone could have come in.

While Lionel was having his afternoon nap, Effie sat on the sofa working her way through the documentation that Dr Hazan had given her.

First, she studied a leaflet about FTD. Reading it was almost like coming home. This was Lionel. The symptoms described fitted almost everything that had become familiar to her these past few years.

The repetition of phrases. "Nice to see you... to see you nice," was a favourite of Lionel's, every time he said goodbye to someone. *Every* time. He could do a very good imitation of Bruce Forsyth's delivery, but oh did it irritate her!

The obsessions with food. Three packets of fig roll biscuits *every day* was beyond belief. The curious lunch of one sardine from a tin and a spoonful of cold baked beans all smothered with olive oil. *Every* day at *exactly* one o'clock.

The inappropriate remarks, the swearing and the embarrassing behaviour were what had alienated their friends. The loss of interest in other people and the lack of sympathy and empathy were all symptoms of FTD. There it was in black and white.

This was what Lionel had become. This was his restricted world, and now it was hers too.

And the information that, unlike in the case of Alzheimer's Disease, memory tends not to be a problem in the early stages of FTD, also rang true. The fact that Lionel could still play bridge, still remember the cards, fitted in with that.

On the back of the leaflet was a heading, *Other useful organisations.* The contact details of the *Frontotemporal Support Group (Formerly Pick's Disease Support Group).* That sounded useful, Effie thought. She'd give them a ring later. She didn't then know just how important to her that group was to become.

There were other leaflets about local care companies. Effie looked at each in turn.

Primacare was a possibility. They were based in Dalton Heath and provided carers at any time of the day from anything from fifteen minutes up to all day. Fifteen minutes wasn't long, Effie thought, but it was long enough to check that a patient was okay, that he hadn't fallen down stairs or had a heart attack. *Free assessment* the leaflet said. There was a phone number and an email address and a website. Effie would take a look later and give them a ring. It would be a good move to have Lionel assessed so that all was in place when she needed help.

Effie felt shaky. Spaced out. The diagnosis was a shock. But it was also a relief. Now there was a reason for the way Lionel behaved. It wasn't his fault. She must stop blaming him. The anger and resentment she had been feeling were no longer justified. She could tell people he was a sick man and there was a name for his disease. Now they would understand and sympathise.

The first person Effie phoned was Suzie. She hadn't heard of FTD which, given that she was a nurse, was surprising.

"It's a relief to have a diagnosis," Effie said.

"Oh, Mum, what difference does it make?" Suzie asked. "Dad's rude and objectionable. Why do they need to give it a name?"

"Well... they're putting him on something that should calm him down." Effie felt suddenly tearful. She swallowed hard. It made a huge difference. Couldn't Suzie see that?

"Well, let's hope it works," said Suzie.

"Yes... I hope so." She knew Suzie couldn't stand it when she cried. "I must go. We'll see you Christmas Day," she said.

Suzie, Effie knew, was still experiencing a certain amount of juvenile angst against Lionel. They had argued heatedly through her teens, and the outbursts had continued with reduced frequency but increased intensity ever since.

Then Effie phoned Nigel in Berlin to give him the facts. "I'll look it up," he said, "but make sure you look after yourself."

She knew she had to tell Lionel's brother and sister-in-law but she was nervous about calling them. It was months since they'd seen Michael and Joanna. Effie used to be good friends with Joanna. They'd get together when their children were young, and at Christmas and bank holidays they'd meet up for family parties and outings. But in recent years the meetings and the phone calls had become fewer and further between. The last time they'd spoken on the phone she'd had to endure Joanna's diatribe about how badly Lionel had behaved at their daughter's wedding reception. Did Joanna think Effie didn't know all this? Eventually Effie had said, "I'm sorry, I've got to go — someone's at the door." And she'd hung up.

But she should tell them about the diagnosis. Maybe they'd be more sympathetic once they understood.

She checked the phone book and started keying in the number. Which of the two of them would pick it up? Michael or Joanna? How would she explain it all? Would she cry? She felt that lump in her throat rising. She was finding it increasingly difficult to talk to people without crying. The tears would just spring from nowhere. And what would she say if they were out and the answerphone clicked in? It was all so difficult.

Perhaps she should send an email? But emails were forever.

Emails could be copied, forwarded, altered. Perhaps this was something that should be written in a letter. She put down the phone.

She tried to make the letter friendly and factual. Unemotional. She used a proper fountain pen with real ink and it took her three attempts to write it without any crossings out. She explained about the brain scan showing the loss of brain cells. She explained how the illness accounted for the offensive behaviour that had been so distressing in recent years. And she explained that the disease was degenerative and would eventually lead to total incapacity and death.

She paused for a long time thinking about how to end the letter, but finally wrote, *love Effie xx.* She didn't write, *see you soon,* as it might have sounded presumptuous, but she hoped that she would see them soon. Perhaps now Michael would feel more warmly towards his poor sick brother.

She addressed the envelope, put a first-class stamp on it, and walked down the road to post it.

Lionel was still asleep when she got back.

Then she turned to the *Dementia Guide,* a thick booklet, largely addressed to recently diagnosed dementia patients and advising them on *living well after diagnosis.* On page sixty-five was a section on driving. How many dementia patients would manage to read as far as page sixty-five? wondered Effie. It said *you must inform the DVLA about your diagnosis of dementia. You must also tell your car insurance company.*

Lionel would never do that, Effie realised. And she could just imagine his reaction if she were to suggest it to him. She had better do it herself. What would happen if she didn't? Nothing probably, but if he had an accident his insurance might be turn out to be invalid. She went upstairs to the spare bedroom she used as a study. She sat before the computer to write two letters, one to the DVLA and one to the insurance company.

Dear Sirs,

This is to inform you that my husband, Lionel Butler, of the above address, has recently been diagnosed with FTD (frontotemporal dementia). His driving skills remain unaffected by the condition, but I understand that you should be informed.

Yours sincerely

Frances Butler (Mrs)

She printed off the letters, then signed, folded and stuck them in envelopes. She felt like a traitor as she hurried down the road to post them. Lionel loved his car, and it would break his heart to have to give up driving. She asked herself, how could she do this to him? Then, how could she not? She'd only been back five minutes when there was a ring on the doorbell.

"Good afternoon Mrs Butler," came a voice as she opened the door. Two uniformed police officers stood there.

She sighed. "Good afternoon, Officers," she replied.

"Is Mr Butler in?" was the response.

Effie recognised one of them and peered at the badge. "It's Mo Gorringe?" she checked.

"Yes, Mrs Butler, and this is my colleague, Constable Darren Arkwright of the traffic police."

"Lionel's having his afternoon nap," she said flatly. "Come in." She showed the two officers into the living room and they sat side by side on the sofa.

"Who's he upset this time?" she asked.

"It's a traffic matter," said Darren Arkwright.

"That makes a change," said Effie. "I'll go and get him up. Would you like a cup of tea while you're waiting?"

"No, thank you. We're fine."

She headed up the stairs and pushed open Lionel's bedroom door. She touched him on the shoulder and he reacted like he'd been hit. "Wassamatter?" he snarled.

"You have to get up. The police are here." She gritted her teeth. "Again!"

When Lionel appeared and had settled down in his usual chair, the traffic officer read an account of the incident. Lionel's Jaguar, he explained, had been parked outside Boots on a double yellow line. He came out of Boots and got into the car, not noticing the parking ticket under his windscreen wiper.

"Yes, I did!" said Lionel.

Lionel was no stranger to parking tickets. He never told Effie about them, but she noticed the entries on the bank statement. An unexplained seventy pounds usually turned out to be a parking ticket.

The officer continued. Lionel had started the car and pulled away without indicating, almost knocking down a pedestrian who was crossing the road while pushing a pram with one arm and holding the hand of a small child with the other.

"She should have used the pedestrian crossing!" Lionel reacted crossly.

The police officer continued. Lionel had opened the driver's window, sworn at the woman, telling her she was lucky to have kids and she should take more care of them. And then he had accelerated, entering the pedestrian crossing as the lights turned red, and just touching another pedestrian with his wing mirror.

"I waved him down," said the officer. "But he ignored me, and continued down the High Street."

"I fucking didn't!" reacted Lionel. He stood up.

Effie sighed. She could just imagine the situation. The week before Christmas. Too many cars. Too many people under stress.

Harassed. Loaded with shopping they couldn't afford, and presents that nobody needed. That was what Christmas was all about. No wonder people crossed roads without looking properly. Why couldn't Lionel just have apologised to the woman, instead of hurling insults at her?

"Mr Butler," said Darren Arkwright. "I have informed you of the circumstances and I should now like to invite you to hand in your driving licence."

"What?!" reacted, Lionel, taking a step nearer.

"I should like to invite you to hand in your driving licence."

"You mean to you? Now? So I couldn't drive?"

"Yes."

"No. No. Not bloody likely. No way! And you can get the fuck out of here!"

"Lionel. Calm down. They have a job to do. Swearing won't help."

"Are you declining my invitation, sir?"

"Yeah. 'Course I am."

"In that case, sir, if you are declining my invitation to hand in your driving licence, I do have to fill in a form, a copy of which will be passed to the DVLA. You may be required to take a driving test."

"Since I saw you last," Effie explained to Mo Gorringe, "Lionel has been diagnosed with the disease, frontotemporal dementia. It's a form of dementia that affects behaviour, social skills, communication. Have you heard of it?"

She nodded. "Yes, I have."

"Then you'll know he can't help his aggressive responses to difficult situations."

"Which some might describe as road rage," remarked the officer.

Effie continued, "Which wouldn't be his fault," she explained. "He has been prescribed medication which should calm him down.

So when it's had a chance to take effect I'm hoping these situations won't arise anymore." Effie paused. "I have posted letters to the DVLA and to Lionel's insurance company to inform them of the diagnosis," said Effie. "So the matter is in hand."

Mo Gorringe nodded thoughtfully. "In that case this report may not make any difference. You may hear from the DVLA before it's processed."

"How long do you think that'll be?" asked Effie.

The following day Effie received a text message on her mobile phone.

Letter received. Content noted. Love J&M xx.

Effie stared in astonishment at the words from her brother- and sister-in-law. Was that it? No message of sympathy? No good wishes for the appalling future that this disease would bring. Nothing. How could they be so utterly heartless? Was it her they were trying to punish? What had she done wrong?

She cried and she cried and she cried.

That night, in the grips of insomnia, she got out of bed, slipped on her dressing gown and went to the study to switch on the computer. She opened her Facebook account. There was a photo of one of Lionel's nephews, Joanna and Michael's eldest, catching a big fish. There was a piece about a niece bumping into a celebrity on the train. Someone else had done a parachute jump for charity. And someone was feeling fed up and couldn't decide what to have for supper. With photographs, of course. What trivia!

Facebook friends! What did that mean? Joanna was a 'Facebook friend' and so were her offspring, Lionel's nieces and nephews. Effie clicked over to Joanna's page. There was an effusive thank you to her children for organising a birthday party for her. Lots of love and kisses for the whole world to see. What Effie noted was that she and Lionel had not been invited to the party. Effie and Lionel, after all these years of family contact, were off Michael and Joanna's invitation list.

Effie sighed. She and Lionel were off all invitation lists. Lionel's illness had frightened away all those people she'd once believed were friends. The isolation this illness caused was absolute.

She looked again at her mobile phone and reread the text message. *Letter received. Content noted, love J&M xx.*

What coldness! No, she could never forgive that.

Tears trickled down her face. Silent tears. She looked down her Facebook list of so-called friends. Was there one single person on that list that she felt she could phone, here and now in the middle of night, to say she felt desperate?

She clicked on a menu, and then another. Could you ever close down a Facebook account? Would her details, her silly snapshots and her trite remarks be saved forever in that great computer in the sky? And then there was another menu, and another one asking if she was sure. Yes, of course she was sure. This whole scenario was lot of silly nonsense. She clicked on 'yes' and sat back.

She was tired, very tired. Her isolation was complete. She'd learned a lot of things in the last couple of days, the most important of which was the fact that she was utterly on her own. She had a new role. Not only was she a wife, mother and grandmother. She was also a carer. An FTD carer. What that was going to entail?

She was scared.

CHAPTER 15

A Joke Too Far

Tonight, Lionel is going to play bridge with Effie. Lionel has written it in his diary. He always keeps his diary up to date. *Bridge – Effie,* he has written with his blue rollerball pen. He isn't keen on playing with Effie. She can't concentrate. Can't remember what cards are gone. And she's always a trick light in three no trumps. But she is better than no partner at all.

Lionel has spent the morning at his table in the living room. He has read the newspaper and done two and a half Sudokus. Now it is one o'clock so it is lunchtime. He goes into the kitchen and puts a sardine, a hunk of Camembert cheese and a spoonful of baked beans on a plate. Then he adds olive oil. He carries it into the dining room to eat. There is another TV in the dining room. He switches it on to watch the BBC one o'clock news while he is eating. There is a laptop computer on the dining room table and when he has finished eating he clicks the mouse to open his bridge-playing game. He will play bridge against the computer until three o'clock, when it will be time for his afternoon nap.

Effie comes in carrying a piece of paper. "Now look, Lionel," she says. "If you're going to play bridge with me tonight, you must try and behave."

He is looking at the computer screen. "I do behave," he says. He looks at the images of the cards the computer has just dealt. "Four spades is the right bid."

"A lot of people say you don't. And we want to prove them wrong, don't we Lionel?"

"Give it a break, Effie!" he snaps. "I'm not a child."

"Sometimes you behave like one."

He is about to protest further, but she hands him the piece of paper.

"What's this?" he says.

"I've written you a letter, Lionel. I know you won't listen to what I have to say, not without us having a row, so I've written it all down. Now I'm going out. Please read what I've written and think about it. It's important."

Lionel looks at the screen. He covers East's jack of hearts with the queen.

"Look, Lionel. There are people at the Dalton Heath Bridge Club who want to get rid of you. Don't give them any excuses. I'm going out now."

"Where're you going?"

"Shopping."

"When'll you be back?"

"I don't know," she says. "Goodbye."

He listens to the front door slam. She'll be getting into her car now, starting it up, and reversing into the road. Why doesn't she ever go out frontwards? he wonders. He plays the hand, makes the contract then looks at the paper she had given him. He begins to read.

Dear Lionel

As it's impossible for us to have a conversation without you getting cross, and me getting upset, I've decided to write to you.

Your behaviour at the bridge club upsets people. The committee want to throw you out. When you are there, people are on edge. If you don't wasn't to upset people, here is my advice.

1. *Be quiet and unobtrusive.*

2. *Say, 'good evening', and 'thank you for the game', but as little else as possible.*

3. *Do not make a stupid remark and then tell people it was a joke. It wasn't.*

4. *Do not swear in any way. 'F. F. F.' is swearing.*

5. *Avoid fidgeting. Do not scratch. If you itch put up with it.*

6. *Do not swap chairs over. If some of the chairs are uncomfortable put up with it.*

7. *Do not leave your partner to play your dummy hand more than absolutely necessary. One cigarette break and one loo break is more than enough.*

8. *Do not wander around the room.*

9. *Do not stare at people across the room.*

10. *Do not put people down. e.g. Do not look at people who have been a bit slow, and say, "That wasn't very difficult!" It's a put-down.*

11. *If someone has not heard you, don't put your hands around your mouth and shout.*

12. *If you have not heard what someone has said, don't put your hand to your ears and shout 'What?'*

I am only trying to help. If you can't change, you will have to give up bridge and that would be a great shame.

I do care.

Love Effie xxx

Why are they all so fucking sensitive? Lionel asks himself. The place needs livening up. It needs someone with a sense of humour.

Lionel stands outside the Dalton Heath Bridge Club. He wants one last cigarette.

"You grab a table," he says to Effie. "I'll join you in minute."

Through the double glass doors, he watches her step into the room, take off her coat, and hang it up. Then he sees her pause and look uncertainly around the room wondering where to sit. Someone waves to her and he sees her join a table occupied by Katy and Theo Crossland. Lionel smiles. He likes those two. He finishes his cigarette and crosses the room to sit opposite Effie.

"Good evening," says Lionel to their opponents. "Have you met my daughter, Effie?" he adds. And then he laughs at his joke.

"Stop it, Lionel!" Effie hisses.

Why doesn't she like that joke? he wonders. It's meant to be a compliment.

Theo plays along with it. "We have indeed. She's delightful. And this is my niece, Katy," he says.

Lionel laughs, pleased that someone enjoys his humour.

Effie speaks to Katy in a low voice. "He said that to a doctor when he was in hospital," she says. "And the doctor thought he was confused and meant it."

Lionel stands up again. "I hate these new chairs," he says, and drags it across the room to replace it with an old style one. "That's better," he says, and beams at them all.

Effie glares at him.

The cards are in place and it is time for Katy to open the bidding. She is slow and indecisive and Lionel hums a bit and taps his feet while they wait. Finally, Effie wins the bidding, Katy leads a low heart and Lionel lays down his dummy. "There you are," he says. "All depends on you playing one card right."

Effie frowns.

He stands up. "I'm just going outside a minute. Is that all right?"

Effie grits her teeth. "I'd prefer you to play dummy's cards for me," she says.

"That's okay," interjects Theo. "I'll do it."

Lionel watches from the doorway. He smokes half a cigarette, puts it out, and then rejoins the table.

Effie has gone one down.

"Didn't you take the spade finesse?" asks Lionel.

"I didn't think I needed to," she says.

"It was your only chance," he says.

While they are playing the next hand, one of the players from another table eases past them to go to the cloakroom. It's Janey Caldecott, a very nice lady who is grossly obese. Lionel looks up from his cards and watches her bottom wobble as she struggles to get between the lines of tables. "Wibble wobble, jelly on a plate," he remarks. And he looks round the room to see who had overheard his joke. Then he laughs.

"Lionel!" hisses Effie.

It is time to move to the next table, where they will meet new opponents and play two new hands of cards. Lionel hopes it'll be someone amusing.

"Thank you for the game," Effie says to Katy and Theo.

"Thank you for the game," imitates Lionel. "Have a nice evening." He looks at Effie triumphantly. "See, I can be polite," he whispers.

"Good evening," says Effie as they join the next table.

Their opponents this time are Sophie White and Craig Grant, both rather younger than the majority of club members. Sophie is slender with long blonde hair and a golden suntan. Craig is a rugged sort of bloke with a thick dark beard. Not the kind of man you'd want to bump into on a dark night.

They settle down and pick up their cards. It is Sophie's opening bid.

Lionel sorts his cards quickly then watches Sophie consider hers. He can see her counting under her breath. She has a sensuous mouth. And that shiny red lipstick is deliberately provocative. Not to mention the cleavage not quite concealed by that lacy top. He looks at Craig. He knows Craig has a dreary plain wife he used to partner a while ago. He must fancy Sophie. How could he not? Sitting opposite her all evening and watching that moist pink tongue lick the corner of her mouth. She is fucking gorgeous. She must turn him on.

Lionel turns towards Craig and says cheerily, "Have you got an erection?"

There is a silence.

"Lionel!" hisses Effie. "You can't say things like that."

Lionel shrugs. Just one of his jokey remarks. Why do they all look so shocked?

Craig gives a weak laugh and mutters something about the bridge hands being somewhat unstimulating tonight.

And Sophie's eyes are fixed on her cards. She grits her teeth and lays down her bidding card.

There are twenty more hands to play and not once does Effie look at Lionel. For some reason she's gone into one of her big sulks. And she really glares at him when he goes off to the loo.

"Sorry to keep you waiting," he says when he gets back. He smiles at Effie. "Or would you prefer me to piss on the floor?"

The evening is over.

"Was that all right?" he says brightly when they get back in the car. "Did I behave all right?"

"No, you didn't!" Effie explodes. "Lionel, you can't say things like that to people!"

"Things like what?" He puts the car into drive and it moves forward.

Effie raises her hands. "You can't ask a man in public if he's got an erection. It's just... just... not done."

"It was a joke," Lionel protests.

"It was a joke too far!"

Lionel turns right on to the main road. "Craig didn't mind. He's a good bloke."

"Well, Sophie did," Effie says. "She'll put in a complaint. I know she will." Then Effie giggles.

Lionel likes that. It's nice to hear Effie giggle. She used to giggle a lot.

"If he did have an erection," she says, "it wasn't very big."

CHAPTER 16

C is for Christmas

C is for Christmas. Don't mention Christmas.

Christmas went wrong.

Well, it always does, thought Effie, but never in quite the way you expect.

To start with, it was shadowed by the next letter from the Dalton Heath Bridge Club. This dropped through the letter box along with the last two Christmas cards of the season.

Effie picked it up, saw that it was addressed to Lionel and marked *by hand*. She knew instantly that this was the letter from the bridge club. How come it had taken so long? Presumably they'd had to fix a committee meeting to discuss poor demented Lionel. This one Effie decided to read. She opened the envelope and pulled out two pages of close typing from the *Chairman and Secretary of the Conduct Committee (CC)*, Toby Mulligan. These people who ran the bridge club liked committees. They liked rules and regulations and hiding behind rhetoric. Somewhere in the middle of the letter were a few lines describing Lionel's stupid remark about Craig's possible erection. The rest of it referred to things like *Our Constitution under clause 17*, and *Law 74 of the Laws of Duplicate Bridge*. The phrases, *you will be aware that*, and, *you will recollect that*, were used to begin three different paragraphs.

No! protested Effie inside her head. Lionel will not recollect what happened. And he will not be aware that *his behaviour does not conform to the standards of play, courtesy and personal deportment prescribed by the byelaws and regulations of the English Bridge Union.*

Dear God, were the previous letters written in this language? No way would Lionel have understood them. Don't these idiots know he's ill?

In view of the above, said the letter, *the CC has determined that further action is warranted.*

Ah ha! So they are going to chuck him out, thought Effie. Well, what did it matter? All his partners had ditched him, and after last time she'd never dare partner him again. But no. Lionel was invited to *make a written response.* They were planning to drag it on longer. More meetings. More rhetoric. What did they think he was going to write?

She went upstairs and took a new envelope from her desk. She typed Lionel's name, his address and the words, *by hand,* on the envelope, refolded the letter and put it inside. She sealed the envelope, carried the letter downstairs and placed it on the door mat exactly where she had found it. Sooner or later Lionel would pick it up. He would open it and look at it. Whether he would understand what it was about was anyone's guess. Then she tore the envelope in which the letter had arrived into tiny pieces.

What she had to do now, was finish wrapping the Christmas presents.

They were invited to Suzie and Dudley's for Christmas Day, and credit where it's due, their daughter and son-in-law were now making an effort to accommodate Lionel and his bizarre habits. Since the diagnosis they had realised that his obsessions with routine, which had driven everyone mad for years, were all part of the illness. They were trying to be sympathetic.

So lunch was planned to be at one o'clock, Lionel's routine lunchtime. This was earlier than Suzie and Dudley would have chosen, but that's how you accommodate people with FTD. The plan was for Lionel to arrive at twelve-thirty in time for lunch, and then leave at two-fifteen in order to get back home in time for his afternoon nap at precisely three o'clock. Suzie had suggested that he might have his afternoon nap in their spare bedroom, but that idea went down like a lead balloon.

So that Effie wouldn't be constrained by Lionel's timetable, they decided to go in two cars. Lionel in his and she in hers. That way she could arrive earlier, give Suzie a hand with the lunch preparations, and participate in the 'present-opening' ceremony. Later she could come home whenever she liked. Which would most probably be after afternoon tea with Christmas cake and maybe a game of Trivial Pursuit or Monopoly.

"You remember the way?" she said to Lionel before she left, her car loaded with presents. He was up, but not yet dressed.

"Of course I do!" reacted Lionel. "I've been there often enough."

Lionel liked going to Suzie's, provided it wasn't for too long. Obviously he liked seeing the grandchildren, but Effie thought it was also partly because Suzie kept chickens. Something that reminded him of his childhood.

"You will have a shower and shave before you come, won't you?"

He grunted.

"And put on clean clothes? I've put them out for you."

"Of course I will."

"Well, I'll be off now. See you later."

Effie parked in Suzie's and Dudley's drive, unloaded the presents and rang the doorbell.

"Happy Christmas!"

The children ran up to her excitedly. Big hugs all round. Kisses for everyone.

"Where's Grampa?" asked the eldest.

"He's coming later. He'll be here in time for lunch."

It was time to open the presents. There was sparkling wine for the adults while the children ripped off the paper and shrieked with excitement at their new acquisitions. Within minutes a tidy living room disintegrated into a chaotic spread of Christmas packaging and crushed crisps. Effie held back on the bubbly. She knew there'd be wine with the Christmas lunch, and sooner or later – hopefully later – she would have to drive home.

It was just gone one o'clock. The turkey, traditionally garnished with bacon rolls and watercress, was on the table waiting to be carved. A stack of oven-warmed plates stood in readiness. Effie carried in dishes of vegetables, and checked that the cranberry sauce, the bread sauce and the condiments were all in place, along with wine glasses, napkins, and Christmas crackers.

"It's so pretty," said Effie as she lit the candles.

Dudley was sharpening the carving knife. He looked as though he wouldn't mind sticking it into to someone.

Everyone was ready.

Except Lionel.

Effie called the home number on her mobile. It rang until the answerphone clicked in, so she knew he must have left.

"Where's Dad?" snarled Suzie.

Effie shrugged her shoulders. "He must be nearly here."

"We've bust a gut getting lunch ready this early, just to please him, and he can't even be bothered to get here on time."

Effie gnawed her lower lip. "Well, let's get started. It always takes a while to dish up. I expect he'll turn up by the time we start eating."

He didn't.

Everyone tucked in. "Lovely roast potatoes," said Effie.

"Cheers!" said Dudley, raising his glass.

"Happy Christmas!" said Effie, raising hers.

Suzie remained grimly silent.

"Let's pull the crackers?" cried one of the children.

And after a short interlude of paper hats and jokes, the only sound was that of jaws chomping on turkey, knives scraping on plates and glasses clunking on the table.

But the celebration was shadowed by anxiety.

"D'you think Grampa's had a crash?" piped up little Cameron.

Out of the mouths of babes, thought Effie.

"He could have forgotten to buy petrol," suggested his sister. "Grampa's always forgetting things."

"Shall I go and look for him?" said Dudley. "He can't be far."

Effie felt a flash of irritation. Why couldn't Lionel have learned to use a mobile phone? She'd bought one for him a couple of years ago, and insisted he take it in the car with him. But he'd never got the hang of it, and even if he had, she doubted whether it would cross his mind to use it. Not even in a crisis.

Effie hesitated. "If you don't mind, Dudley."

Dudley was back in twenty minutes. "He's not between here and the motorway. I wonder if he's changed his mind and gone home. I didn't want to go all the way."

Effie called their home number, and this time she left a message on the answerphone. "Lionel. We're worried. Please call us the minute you get this."

"Anyone ready for seconds?" asked Suzie.

"There could have been an accident or a breakdown," said Effie. "He wouldn't be able to ask for help. He wouldn't think of contacting us."

"I'll call the police," said Dudley. "See if they've had any accident reports in the area."

Dudley went to check the number of the local police force and make the call.

"They haven't," he told them when he came back. "But I gave them details about the car. They'll radio all their patrol cars with the information and they'll call us if they find him."

"Thanks Dudley. That's great."

"Funny thing was..." His brow furrowed.

"Yes?"

"The instant I mentioned the car, and gave them his name... they knew about him. They know who he is, you know."

Effie shrugged. "That doesn't surprise me one bit."

"Who's ready for Christmas pud?" said Suzie. She was carrying a platter containing a Christmas pudding topped with a sprig of holly. Blue flames licked around the edge.

The phone rang. "That must be him!" said Effie.

Dudley hurried to get it. He carried the handset back into the dining room.

He held his hand over the mouthpiece and whispered, "It's the police. They've found him. He continued to listen. "Yes, thank you very much, Officer," he said. "That is a relief." He put the phone down. "He was driving north from the Dalton Heath bypass. Quite the wrong direction. He seems to have taken a wrong turning and got totally confused."

Effie put her elbows on the table and rested her face on her hands.

"Oh, no!" she groaned. It wasn't the fact he'd got lost that troubled her. It was the fact that it represented another stage in his illness.

"Where on earth did he think he was going?" asked Suzie.

Dudley continued with his account. "They're escorting him back to your house now and he should be there shortly. Apparently he was somewhat abusive when they stopped him."

"I bet he was!" said Effie.

"But now he's being quite cooperative."

She stood up. "I'd better go back home. See how he is. The police might want to talk to me." She headed for the hall and put on her coat. "Sorry to break up the party."

Suzie pressed her lips tightly together. "Some party!" she said bitterly.

CHAPTER 17

A Police Escort

A siren is sounding. It's a horrible noise and Lionel would like to put his hands over his ears. But you can't when you're driving. Where is it coming from? Lionel sees a light flashing in his wing mirror. The police car must be chasing someone. He slows and pulls closer to the side of the road. The police car overtakes Lionel, but instead of accelerating, it slows down, an arm waving out of the driver's window. Lionel slows down too. What the fuck is all this about? Christmas Day. Maybe they're doing random breathalyser tests. Ah ha! He doesn't drink anymore. Can't catch me! he thinks. And puts two fingers up at them.

Two policemen get out and walk back to speak to Lionel. He opens the driver's window. "What the fuck's going on?" he snarls.

"Good afternoon, Mr Butler?" says one of them. "I'm PC Chambers and this is PC Smithson."

Lionel glares at them. "How the hell d'you know who I am?"

"Your family called. They were anxious that you might have got lost. Are you all right, sir?" says the police officer.

"Of course I'm all right!" reacts Lionel.

Why shouldn't he be? Everybody gets lost sometimes. He frowns. It's not like him to get lost like that though. He can't remember how it happened. He must have taken a wrong turning somewhere.

"Your family were worried. They were expecting you for Christmas lunch."

"Yeah. Well. I don't like Christmas lunch. Too much food, too much noise, too much fuss," he says.

"I entirely agree with you, Mr Butler," says PC Chambers. "That's why we like being out on duty on Christmas Day." He grins. "Don't we, PC Smithson?"

There is a moment's pause. Then PC Smithson says, "So where are you off to now, Mr Butler."

"Home. Dalton Heath. For a bit of peace and quiet."

"Well, you might have taken a wrong turning somewhere. This isn't the way to Dalton Heath."

Lionel frowns. Not like him to get lost. How did he do that?

"Tell you what. We've got to go there now. Would you like to follow us? We'll lead you back home."

Lionel thinks. Where did he go wrong? He smiles. "Thank you very much, Officer," he says.

Lionel puts his key in the lock and opens the front door. It has been a new experience following a police car home, and the two young guys were pleasant enough.

He is aware of the police car still parked at the bottom of the drive. He turns and looks. "You don't need to hang around," he says to the policeman who's got out of the passenger door of the police car and looks like he might follow him in. He doesn't want them in the house with him. "Haven't you got any burglars to catch?"

"We'll just wait in the car till your wife gets home. She's on her way."

"Oh. Right." He hesitates. "Do you want some coffee?" he asks.

He could make some, and bring two mugs outside, like he does for the window cleaner and the gardener.

The guy smiles. "Thank you, sir, but we're fine."

He shrugs, pauses for a moment, then goes inside and slams the front door. He exhales with relief. It is so very good to be home. He is so tired. He puts his keys on the right-hand hook by the front door, takes off his coat and hangs it on the banister post. Then he goes straight into the kitchen and switches on the kettle ready to make a mug of coffee. He needs a coffee. Then he looks at his watch. Christ! It's long past coffee time. It's even past lunchtime! He's been on the road for hours. And he's hungry. What should he do next? Eat. Sleep. Eat. Everything's out of sync and he doesn't know what to do first.

He pours himself a tonic with lime juice and he makes his lunch. A sardine. A spoonful of baked beans and some olive oil, and he takes it into the dining room. He's glad he hasn't got to sit down with a noisy family and a Christmas turkey. He hates noise. Children shrieking, adults telling jokes. Noise hurts his ears.

What else would they have? Crackers? Candles? He can do without all that too. His laptop is there on the dining room table. Already switched on but with that picture of somewhere he and Effie went on holiday. He knows that if he jiggles the mouse the picture will go away and he'll be able to find his bridge game. He doesn't know how it happens, but as he picks up the TV remote control, his elbow catches his tonic bottle which falls sideways and rolls across the table toward the laptop. The keyboard, screen and mouse, all fall with a resounding crash to the floor. The tonic bottle follows.

"Fuck, fuck, fuck!" he says aloud as his sardine slides off the plate onto the table. There's a puddle of olive oil soaking into the tablecloth. Effie won't like that. He puts the sardine back on his plate and switches on the TV. He wants to watch the BBC lunchtime news, but it's not lunchtime any more, and anyway it's Christmas Day and the TV programmes are out of sync too. What he gets is the Queen reading her Christmas message. Oh well, that'll do. Something to watch. She's nice, the Queen. Looks nice. Sounds nice. He sips his glass of tonic and lime and eats his sardine and his beans. It's time for his afternoon nap. He looks at the laptop on the floor. The screen has almost broken away from the keyboard now. He'll pick it up later, he thinks.

As he carries his plate back to the kitchen, he can see through the hall window that the police car is still there in the road, but that Effie's car is now in the drive behind his. She has got out and is talking to the policemen.

He goes back to the dining room to pick up the laptop and puts it back on the table in its usual place. The screen is all wobbly now as its hinges are broken. So he props it up against a cola bottle. He jiggles the mouse and the usual screen comes up. He clicks on the bridge programme picture and it opens as usual. Thank goodness for that. He doesn't want Effie to go on at him about dropping it and breaking it. She's going to be mad enough about him not finding his way to Suzie's, and missing Christmas Day with the grandchildren. He watches through the window as she speaks with the policemen.

Lionel opens the front door.

"Thank you so much," Lionel hears Effie say to them.

He watches her wave as the police car pulls away. Then she runs up the steps to greet him. She is going to be so cross with him.

She throws her arms around him and gives him a big hug. "Oh, my poor Lionel!" she says. "I've been so worried. Are you all right?"

And she kisses him too. Kisses his face, his mouth, his forehead, like she really cares. "My lovey," she says.

"I'm fine. I'm sorry I got lost. Was Suzie cross? I'm sorry I missed..."

"That doesn't matter. Just so long as you're all right. We were so worried."

And she leads him into the living room and gives him another hug.

"It's time for my afternoon nap," he says.

"Yes, of course it is," she says. "You must be exhausted, driving all that way!"

And she hugs him again.

Yes, he is very, very tired. But it feels good to have her arms around him. It's like the two of them belong together like this. Like they always did. Like they always will. Always.

"My Effie!" he murmurs into her hair.

Later, after he gets up from his nap, she says to him, "What happened to the laptop?"

"Nothing," he says. "It's fine."

CHAPTER 18

Two-Timing

Short haul takes the best part of a day. Long haul is nearer two days.

This time tomorrow, Effie thought, she would be in another climate on another continent with another man. Only she didn't know what 'this time tomorrow' really meant. Dealing with time changes always confused her.

She'd taken to wearing two watches on her wrist when she travelled. Watch number one was set to UK time, and watch number two to whatever country she was in. That way she could look at her UK watch and know instantly what Lionel was doing. It helped her work out when to phone him, which wasn't easy. Mostly he would get up at about ten, go somewhere in his car at eleven, then get home for lunch at exactly one o'clock. Then he would eat in front of the TV in the dining room while playing bridge on his laptop and watching the BBC News. This was followed by what he called an afternoon kip but was actually a proper sleep. He would go upstairs to bed at three o'clock for two and half hours precisely. Since Effie's previous trip, his bridge club attendance had come to an end so at least she knew he'd be at home in the evenings.

On one of their early trips Matt had laughed at Effie's two watches and told her she was two-timing. Yes, she was. In both senses. But in the beginning she'd been so angry at the state of her marriage she'd felt no guilt. She'd had to tell Lionel where she was going, of course, and with whom. A woman can't go halfway round the world with no explanation. On one occasion, Lionel had said to her, "This travel companion of yours – Matt – are you having an affair with him?"

"Matt?" she had reacted. "He's... just... someone to travel with," she'd said. "You know how I always liked seeing new places. And when you lost interest..."

And Lionel had stood up to leave the room. He must have known she was lying.

"Would you mind," she had asked, "if he were anything more?"

"Yes, in principle," he'd said without stopping.

What was that supposed to mean? Did he mean that in practice he wouldn't mind?

After a few minutes he had returned, grim-faced, and sat in his usual chair.

"Can we talk about it?" she'd asked.

"No."

"I mean, can we talk about us?" She had looked at him, hoping for some sort of response.

"Stop staring at me," he had said.

In any normal marriage there'd have been a huge row. But it wasn't a normal marriage.

This time Effie knew that Lionel's behaviour was not his fault, so it was different. "I'm going to bed," she said. "It's an early start."

She woke Lionel to say goodbye to him. He was in his bed wearing yesterday's shirt, the duvet pushed away, the room smelling stale. He wasn't a pretty sight, and she couldn't help comparing his wasted flesh and his blemished skin with her memories of the smooth tan and taut muscles of the young man she'd fallen in love with so long before.

"The taxi's here," she said.

The driver was putting her suitcase in the taxi. She heard the boot close.

Lionel sat up a bit and Effie put her arms around his thin and bony shoulders. She kissed the top of his head.

"Phone me," he said.

"I will, when I can."

He hugged her. "My Effie," he said with what seemed like real affection. And she felt her emotions stir. With what? Love? Guilt? Who knows? And what was Lionel feeling? If anything.

When she got to Paris, which was in quite the wrong direction for her destination, she moved watch number two on one hour. She had five thousand miles to travel as the crow flies. But she was flying on an aeroplane, not on a crow.

The next flight change was Sao Paulo, which was the best part of two thousand miles south of her destination. Brazil is a big place. And finally, she looked out of her window and beneath the hazy blue sky and she could see thick green vegetation divided by a river of brown water winding its way through the dark jungle. This was Amazonia. She put the hands of watch number two back five hours.

She stood at the baggage reclaim waiting for her suitcase. Each time someone was ready with their belongings, automatic doors slid open to allow them through into the arrivals hall so she had repeated glimpses of those waiting to meet the new arrivals. Mostly locals. She also felt repeated draughts of tropical warmth competing with the cool of the air conditioning. On the third time, Effie spotted Matt waiting for her. She jumped and waved to him and he grinned and waved back. He blew a kiss and the doors closed again. Next time she noted that he was dressed in shorts, T-shirt and an Indiana Jones-style sunhat. She was brimming with joy. Then her suitcase appeared on the carousel. At last it was her turn to hurry through. And she was in Matt's arms and he was smiling and laughing and hugging and kissing and telling her how much he had missed her. She felt almost faint with excitement but maybe it was the heat and the humidity of the Amazonian climate or the tiredness of the long journey that was affecting her.

"This way," he said, taking her suitcase. Its wheels rattled on the paving.

He led her to a local bus that took them through the busy streets to the port. And there was the ship, white and gleaming against the murky river. The *Delfine Princessa* towered over the local river boats, their open decks packed with passengers, some chatting in family groups, others sitting, even sleeping, in brightly coloured cloth hammocks that swung from hooks above. On one deck, a wizened man in underpants stood at a single washbasin cleaning his teeth. Matt lifted his camera and took a photograph. Photography was part of Matt's business, and quirky shots were his speciality.

"Fancy going upstream in one of those?" said Matt. "Bring your own hammock. One washbasin on the lower deck. One loo in the stern. That's what I did last year. What do you reckon?"

She smiled weakly. "I think this is a big enough adventure for me," she said.

They made their way along a wooden walkway. The water lapped on a sandy beach that was littered with detritus washed ashore by the mighty river. Branches of trees and clumps of vegetation were polluted with plastic bottles, shredded polythene sheeting, and tangled rope. All mixed with rotting sludge and dead fish. Whereas in Brighton, seagulls would search such rubbish for tasty delicacies, here sinister black Amazon vultures did the same task. One pecked at what might have been a dead dog. Others wheeled overhead, waiting and watching.

"Look over there," said Matt. He pointed to what was effectively an island of floating vegetation, decaying rubbish and the inevitable plastic.

"What?" she said.

"See the alligators?"

She looked more carefully. There were two. One must have been three metres long. They waited and they watched.

"The ships chuck out so much waste. It's easier for them than hunting," said Matt.

It was time to go aboard. There was paperwork to be checked and a security procedure to be followed. And then she was in the air-conditioned cool and Matt was leading her to his cabin. Except it was called a stateroom, though that seemed somewhat pretentious.

"I need a shower," she said when Matt put his arms around her. It felt so good. Strong arms holding her close.

He smiled. "You have your shower," he said. "I'll open the champagne."

She checked her UK watch as she removed it. Lionel would be having his afternoon kip. She would call him later.

There was so much catching up to do with Matt. Some of it was physical. There was a mutual shyness as they tentatively relearned each other's bodies.

"How's Pandora?" she asked over dinner. The dining room in the *Delfine Princessa* was like fairyland. The lights that hung from the ceiling were exquisite, as were the exotic wall hangings and the decorative pillars. Effie had never understood Pandora's attitude to her husband. Why didn't she ever travel with him?

He shrugged. "She's okay."

Other people's marriages are beyond understanding. "What would she do if she knew I were here with you?"

"She'd go berserk. She'd divorce me."

"Would you mind?"

"It would be... inconvenient."

Is convenience the glue that holds most marriages together? Effie wondered.

He took her hand across the table. "We're here together, and I love you," he said. "That's what matters."

She remembered that she hadn't told Lionel she'd arrived safely. She looked at her UK watch. He'd have woken from his afternoon nap and would be wondering why he hadn't heard from her.

"Will my mobile work from here?" she asked.

"Should do, while we're in port."

"I'd better call home," she said.

"How is he?" asked Matt, when she'd made the call.

And she told him about Lionel's diagnosis and its implications. She went into far too much detail and at one point Matt's eyes seemed to glaze over. She needed to change the subject. It wasn't as if she hadn't already told him. They'd been emailing each other every day and Skyping at least once a week. So it wasn't news to him.

Next day was New Year's Eve and they were due to sail at sunset, so they had to fit in what they could. In the morning they took a tourist boat trip across the river and into the jungle. They walked to a lake where giant lily pads, like the ones you see at Kew Gardens, floated between pink waxy flower heads. Matt photographed long-legged jacanas walking from leaf to leaf, while a caiman lay in wait beneath. When they got back to the jetty a mother with a little girl sat with a sloth wrapped around her neck.

"He's lovely," Effie said, taking the furry creature in her arms.

Matt grinned, took a photo, and gave the mother some coins.

In the afternoon they walked into the town. The heat, the colour and the music was magic. Bars with live bands. That South American beat that makes you want to dance. Food stalls selling spicy delicacies under bright canopies. Street markets alive with bustle and song. Effie was walking hand in hand with Matt when she felt something scratch the back of her neck. For an instant she thought of the claws of those black vultures that populated the port area. But as she put her hand up to feel, she saw a wiry young man disappear between two market stalls.

"My necklace!" she cried. She should have shouted, "Stop. Thief!" That's what they do in films. But she didn't. And the man was gone. She said to Matt, "My gold chain with my cartouche!"

She touched her neck where she'd felt the hand grab at her. It was bare and she felt weird. As though she were dirty. She'd have liked to scrub it off.

She felt as though a bubble of joy had burst. Lionel had bought her that cartouche in Cairo. She wore it constantly, which was why she hadn't thought of taking it off. How stupid! Every traveller knew that you shouldn't wear gold jewellery in a South American street market. As they walked back to the ship she was thinking of Lionel and the good times they'd had together and how they had all slipped away. Like the cartouche.

The sun was setting as the ship set sail. A band played for the sail-away party and Effie and Matt leaned over the barrier sipping their sail-away cocktails as the city lights faded into the distance. The ship glided between the lush green banks of the Amazon. Darkness fell.

"We'd better get changed," said Matt. "Formal dinner tonight." He smiled. "And dancing."

Effie's evening dress was about twenty-five years old. She'd bought it for a business function of Lionel's. It had a glittery blue bodice and black taffeta tiered skirt. She'd had to let it out a bit but she still felt good in it.

"You look gorgeous," said Matt when she was ready. And he got his camera out to take a few shots of her. "I feel so proud of you," he murmured later as they entered the dining room.

There was a succession of bands through the evening, and they saw the New Year in on the pool deck. Then they went up to the top deck to get away from the revellers. They leaned over the barrier to look at the water.

The jungle on the banks of the river was deep and dark, and the inky black sky studded with more stars than you ever saw at home.

Effie looked at her UK watch. "It's already next year at home," she said. She thought of poor Lionel, all on his own on New Year's Eve. She remembered New Year's Eve celebrations they had shared in the past. Walking home in the cold because they'd drunk too much to drive and there were no taxis available. "I wonder if he's asleep," she said. She felt a lump rising in her throat. Tears pricked her eyes.

"What does it matter?" snapped Matt.

She looked up in response to his tone. "What's wrong, Matt?"

He held both her shoulders and looked into her face. "Effie, we are on a beautiful ship sailing down the Amazon. It is warm and it is clear and we are thousands of miles from our homes. This is the most romantic setting I could possibly imagine. You have been talking about Lionel most of the evening and I know you haven't stopped thinking about him for one moment. Effie, I am married too, but I'm in love with you. And when I'm with you I forget about Pandora. I forget about my other life. What has changed?"

Tears brimmed in Effie's eyes and trickled down her cheeks. She rested her face against the lapel of Matt's tuxedo so that he wouldn't notice. "I'm sorry, Matt," she murmured.

He put a finger under her chin and lifted her face to look at him again. "Effie, it's been three years since we fell in love. It's been wonderful. It still is for me. Tell me what's happened? Something has."

"I don't know," she whispered. But she did know. It was the diagnosis. She now knew that Lionel was sick. And a sick husband should have a loyal wife to look after him. A wife that doesn't two-time him. That's what marriage is all about.

In sickness and in health, till death us do part.

But especially *in sickness.*

CHAPTER 19

The Homecoming

The last leg of her journey. The taxi back from Heathrow. Effie was tired, both physically and emotionally. She wished she could have slept on the flight. At least her aisle seat had enabled her to pace up and down the plane without disturbing anyone.

England on a January morning.

Grey and cold. It was drizzling. But there was something about coming home, the fields, the trees, the hedgerows, that was essentially English. This was home and her heart lifted. It was another world from the one she had left behind, the one in which she had said goodbye to Matt. He would be home now, rejoining his own world in which she played no part. Though she was there inside his head. She knew that. As he was in hers.

The taxi turned into Larchfield Road.

"Yes, the house on the corner," she said. She looked up at it. No lights. Curtains closed. It was only nine o'clock. Lionel wouldn't be up yet.

The driver got her suitcase out of the car. She paid him, and retrieved her house keys from the bottom of her handbag and let herself in. The central heating was on and it was nice and warm. She looked around the house, switching on lights and checking things over.

The kitchen smelt stale. The dishwasher needed emptying and Lionel's dinner plate from yesterday, still thick with olive oil, was on top of it. The work surfaces were sticky, as was the floor, which glistened with patches of oil that had been spilt and trodden in. She put the kettle on. In the living room there were newspapers on the carpet by Lionel's table. Two used coffee mugs alongside more newspapers and envelopes of mail. Some were opened and some not. She'd go through them later.

In the dining room Lionel's laptop was in its usual place. But Effie could see that the screen was hanging crookedly from the keyboard. The hinges were broken, but the electrical connection appeared to be still intact.

She carried her suitcase upstairs and dumped it in her room. Then she opened Lionel's bedroom door and crept in. He was breathing softly, just as he'd been when she'd woken him to say goodbye two weeks ago. Not snoring. He was okay. She wouldn't wake him.

She checked the washing basket. It was nearly full. The washing machine couldn't have been run, but at least he must have changed his clothes in her absence. She opened her suitcase and added her own washing to the pile. Then she separated the dark from the light, and took a first load downstairs to put in the machine. She needed to shower. She needed to sleep. But the kettle had boiled so she made herself a coffee, took it into the living room and sat down.

When she'd finished her coffee, she picked up the old newspapers and put them in the recycling bin. It was tempting to scan through them to see what had happened to the world in her absence, but that would have taken all day. She'd check the mail later. More stuff for recycling. She emptied the dishwasher and wiped the work surfaces. The floor could wait, but she emptied the bins and rinsed them out. The smell, she decided, came from the fridge. Yellowed broccoli, old cheese. Dubious leftovers on saucers. She threw them all out.

She could hear movement from upstairs.

"Hello, love," she said as he came into the kitchen.

He was grinning broadly. "Hello, my flower," he said. He sounded so pleased. He always used to call her 'my flower' way back. Then there was a time when he'd make a joke of it and call her 'my flowerpot'. He put his arms around her and they hugged. She felt his shoulder blades, prominent under his shirt and jumper. He hadn't shaved for a while. He smelt stale. "My Effie," he said. "You came back to me."

"Of course I did," Effie said. "I always come back to you."

He made himself a coffee. Three heaped teaspoons of sugar and two of coffee. A little milk. Blue top. He only liked blue top milk. He carried it to the sitting room, slopping a little on the way. That was why the kitchen floor was so sticky. Presumably the carpets throughout the house were similarly grubby, but you didn't notice with carpets. Not at first anyway.

She followed him through.

"How's it been?" she asked.

"Fine," he said.

"Anyone call? Anyone phone?"

The answer was no.

"Any post of interest?"

"No." Then, "Yes!" he said brightly. "There was a letter about car insurance." He searched amidst the letters and papers on his table. "Where is it?" he muttered.

She came across and looked with him. "What did it say?"

"It was replying to your letter. Here it is!" he said triumphantly. "See, they're not bothered."

She read the letter. He was right. The insurance is still valid despite the diagnosis. "That's brilliant!" she said. What a relief! she thought.

She started tidying the table. Collecting together envelopes, dividing them into relevant and irrelevant. "Have you been out?" she asked.

He shrugged. "Just shopping. Basics. Had to buy fig rolls and stuff." Then he asked her a question. "Are you pleased to be back?"

She sat down next to him. "Yes," she said, though that wasn't entirely true. "Though the trip was very interesting."

"Good," he said.

"I've seen all sorts of wild life. Alligators, sloths, different types of birds," Effie said. "The Amazon is an amazing river."

"Very nice," he said. He picked up his Sudoku book.

"My cartouche was stolen," she said. "You know, the one we had made for me in Cairo. I've always worn it on chain round my neck".

She looked at him. "Remember?" she said. "You got stroppy with that slimy little salesman who wanted you to buy me a bigger one?"

No, he didn't remember, but she carried on with her story. "Someone ripped it from my neck. I was very upset. I'm going to try and get another one."

He clearly had no idea what she was talking about. Nor was he interested.

In the afternoon the phone rang.

"Is that Effie?" It was a voice she didn't recognise.

"Yes."

"It's Katy Crossland from the bridge club."

"Er... hello Katy."

"Is Lionel there?"

"He's asleep. He always has an afternoon nap. I'll tell him you called."

"I'm the secretary of the Disciplinary Committee and I'm just ringing to say I'm about to deliver a letter. I needed to check your address. Fifteen, Larchfield Road. Is that right?"

Oh no! Effie said to herself. A letter. Another letter? "What's it about?" she said.

"As he didn't respond to the third letter from the Conduct Committee his case has now been passed to the Disciplinary Committee which has a different, more specific role," said Katy. She was speaking rather fast, as though she'd rehearsed the sentence. Maybe she was reading it. "The letter explains Lionel's rights in the next stage of the investigation."

Good grief! An *Investigation!* Bridge is supposed to be a game. Does it really need a *Conduct Committee* as well as a *Disciplinary Committee*? Will there be a *Sentencing Committee* as the end of all this? Effie wondered.

"Look, Katy, why don't you and your committee addicts just give it a break? Lionel's partners have all dropped him, though some of them haven't had the decency to tell him so. He's not likely to play bridge again. What is the point of having more meetings and writing more letters?"

"I'm not a committee addict," protested Katy. "They talked me into being on this committee. And I'm only the secretary."

Effie took a big breath. "Lionel is mentally ill. That's been obvious for ages, but now, finally, after months of waiting, we have a diagnosis." She paused, waiting for Katy to say something. When she didn't, Effie continued, "He has a disease called frontotemporal dementia. His brain is being slowly destroyed. He can't help his behaviour. There is no point in you lot wasting your time having meetings. Unless you enjoy it, of course."

"I certainly don't. But I have to deliver the letter."

"Okay. Go ahead. But if it's anything like the last one he won't understand it. Look, the small bit of Lionel's brain that enables him to count the cards and work out bridge strategies is still working perfectly well. But other, far more important parts, are badly damaged. He's seriously ill, and now that we have a proper diagnosis I think the club should show some sympathy and stop attacking him."

"We're not attacking him."

Suddenly Effie felt the tears well. Her voice cracked. "Yes, you are. You don't know what it's like. Please stop hounding us."

"We're not hounding you. And I do understand."

"No, you don't. You have no idea." The tears were flowing freely now. "I'm sorry," she stuttered. "Do what you like with your stupid letter. It won't make any difference to anything. Goodbye." And she hung up.

Those committee members were like wild dogs tearing apart a dead rat. Why couldn't they just drop it?

The letter arrived. She watched Lionel open it, run his eyes quickly down the words on the two sheets of A4 paper, and put it aside. No way could he be taking it in, interpreting the content. Poor Lionel. If only he would talk to her. If only would tell her how he felt. Looking at all that had happened, he must have anxieties, disappointment, sorrows. Why wouldn't he share them with her? And what of the future? Did he think about what was going to happen to him? Or had his cognitive skills deteriorated to a level at which the concept of the future had no meaning?

She walked up to his table, put her hand on his shoulder and squeezed. He was so thin. She bent over him, kissed his forehead, and picked up the letter. "Another bridge club letter?" she asked.

He shrugged. "Fucking idiots," he said. "Nothing better to do than write stupid letters."

Effie was inclined to agree with him. "May I read it?" she asked.

He shrugged. "If you like," he said.

What she would have liked was to have screwed the letter up and stuffed it up Katy Crossland's backside. What she did, was reply to it. Another session in front of the computer.

Attention Committee DHBC
Copy to Charles Jones, Chairman.

Dear Katy,
Lionel showed me the letter you sent him yesterday.
He has frontotemporal dementia (FTD or Pick's Disease). He will not, as you suggest, remember Toby Mulligan's last letter. If it was written in the same style as yours, he would not have had the cognitive ability to interpret the complexity of the language. He has no recollection of 'personal misconduct' which I assume means 'rudeness'. As for making 'written representations' about his case, I doubt if he could write anything more complex than a shopping list. And to make a 'verbal representation' would require some level of discussion ability of which he has none.
His partners at the bridge club have all dropped him now, so he will not play again. I cannot see why you want to have meetings about him at this stage. The 'investigations of allegations...' you mention are pointless. His behaviour is due to a neurological disease. He can no more control it than a Parkinson's sufferer can stop shaking or a stammerer can stop stammering. There is no treatment, though he has been prescribed medication which may calm him.
It is clear to me that the Dalton Heath Bridge Club is going to hound us with hurtful letters either until this poor sick man resigns or until the various subcommittees complete whatever rigorous procedures that are required to formally throw him out.

Effie paused. This was going to go on and on and on. Enough was enough. She must make Lionel resign to shut them up. She saved the file, and then took a piece of A4 paper downstairs to the living room where Lionel was seated at his table looking at his Sudoku book.

"Lionel, I've been thinking."

"Yes?"

"The bridge club. They've got it in for you now. I think it would be best if you resigned."

"I have resigned. I phoned Toby and told him."

Oh. That was a surprise. Presumably a verbal resignation wasn't enough for these pernickety officials.

"I think they need it in writing. Otherwise they're going to keep hassling you with stupid letters."

He shrugged. He didn't seem that bothered.

"Look, you need to write a letter." She moved the Sudoku book away and put the piece of A4 paper in front of him. He already had his blue rollerball pen in his hand. "Now write our address in that corner."

She watched. He still knew their address. That was good. "And the date... OK. Well done."

"Now write, *Dear Charles Jones*. That's right. And now write, *I resign from the Dalton Heath Bridge Club*. Good." His writing was slow and shaky. "And now write, *yours, Lionel Butler*... That's fine. I'll get it in the post for you."

Tears were spilling down Effie's cheeks. They had been members of the Dalton Heath Bridge Club for over thirty years. In the early days, it had been fun. They had Christmas parties that were full of laughter. Lionel's amateur dramatic skills were called upon in that village hall to do silly sketches that sent the members into paroxysms of giggles – all fuelled by rather too much wine. He'd dressed up as a fairy once with a ballet dress made out of old net curtains. Another year someone had found him some size ten high-heeled shoes and he tottered around the stage as a pantomime queen of hearts. Happy days!

And it wasn't just his silly Christmas performances that his fellow bridge club members had appreciated. Many of them had bought tickets for his more serious performances with the Dalton Heath Amateur Dramatic Society. They'd seen him, and supported him, in roles created by playwrights ranging from Alan Bennett to George Bernard Shaw.

Effie's Lionel had been a popular man. Whoever could have foreseen that it would all end like this?

"What's the matter?" he said. "Don't cry."

"I'm not," she said, and she hurried back upstairs.

She reread her letter and deleted her last paragraph which was perhaps too aggressive. She replaced it with:

To avoid further distress to us, and inconvenience to the DHBC committee, I have persuaded Lionel to resign from the DHBC. I attach his resignation letter. Should the medication I mentioned above calm him in the manner intended, I would hope to bring him as my guest to the occasional club evening.
Regards
Effie Butler

Then she deleted the *Effie* and replaced it with *Frances*. Formality was how the DHBC operated.

She printed off three copies then sat there a while, wondering if she should resign too. It might best to put everything connected with this bridge club behind them.

She phoned Barbara to run the idea past her. Barbara knew her well and had been very understanding.

"Not yet," was her advice. "You don't want to cut off your nose to spite your face."

Barbara was a good friend and right now Effie needed all the friends she could get.

She took two copies of Lionel's handwritten resignation letter.

Then she stapled the original to the copy of her letter that was to go to the chairman, and a copy to the one for Katy. She addressed the envelopes, folded the letters and put them inside. She stuck stamps on them and walked down the road to post them.

She was still crying. At least they should stop writing to us, she thought.

That afternoon, when she checked her emails, there was one from Matt. He had arrived home safely and was missing her. Can we Skype later? he asked. She replied saying she was tired and jetlagged and, could we leave it a day or two? She didn't say that she couldn't stop crying.

She hadn't heard the last from the bridge club. A couple of days later she received a letter from the chairman. He thanked her for copying him in on her letter to Katy, and offered some suitable platitudes.

You have the sympathy of everyone at the club who knows what a tough time you've had, it said.

And who had contributed to that tough time? she thought. No mention of any sympathy being offered to poor sick Lionel.

And he didn't like her idea that if the medication worked she might bring Lionel as a guest. Before that could be permitted, the letter said, *the committee would have to receive compelling medical evidence that his mental condition has been cured.* What evidence? A letter from Dr Hazan? No. What it meant was there was no way anyone at that club ever wanted to set eyes on Lionel again. Well, who could blame them?

The final twist of the knife occurred a week or so later.

She was looking at the DHBC website, reading the minutes of committee meetings. Surprise, surprise – Lionel Butler's resignation was announced! And it was announced, not under the heading *Membership News*, but under the heading, *Disciplinary Matters*. She felt sick. Anyone in the world could read that.

She wondered if Lionel's brother had noticed it. Lionel and Michael had partnered each other at one time at the Dalton Heath Bridge Club. It was quite possible that Michael still followed the website.

CHAPTER 20

Cars

Effie didn't know what Lionel thought about his diagnosis. Nothing, perhaps? He remained in denial. There was nothing wrong with him, he said. It was the rest of the world that was mentally ill.

What did upset him was the loss of his car.

The DVLA took quite some time to write to him, and given that the insurance company hadn't been too concerned, the outcome was a shock.

That morning, as usual, Effie picked up the post from the doormat. Now that Christmas was over it was the season for direct mail from the holiday companies. Did they never give up? She took the pile of mail into the living room and sat down to open it. The Galapagos Islands. That had been her dream for years. Fat chance of it happening now. Burma. Iceland. So many places she had never seen. Did it matter? She'd been very lucky. She had happy memories of good holidays with Lionel, and these past three years of meeting Matt in far-flung places had been extraordinary. You have to count your blessings, she told herself. Again.

There was a bank statement addressed to them both and an electricity bill addressed to Lionel. He'd been leaving administrative matters to her for a while now, so perhaps it was time she put things into her own name. He never looked at the bills, and would never notice if something was wrong. And as for the various investments he had, should she implement the power of attorney that had been drawn up a while ago? She must talk to their solicitor and check that their wills were in order.

And there was a brown envelope addressed to Lionel.

Effie knew it was from the DVLA even before she saw the initials. She wanted to open it, but she placed it on the table beside Lionel's Sudoku book and in front of the chair he would occupy when he came down. What would be the verdict? Perhaps he would be required to take a driving test? That's what the Alzheimer's booklet had indicated. In which case he would have to prepare for it in some way. Would he be able to take instruction from anyone without reacting aggressively? Would he be able to take a test without telling someone to 'fuck off'? Effie couldn't see much wrong with Lionel's driving as such. His peripheral vision seemed fine. His reactions seemed in order. He could park his car accurately in a small space, albeit an illegal one. And swearing at people didn't make you a dangerous driver.

Or did it?

Lionel was later than usual. Should she go upstairs and check he was okay? Sometimes he slept so late it would cross Effie's mind that he might have died in his sleep. If he did, how would she feel? she wondered. Shock, undoubtedly. Horror? Relief? Panic? She didn't know. Some mornings she would creep into his room to check he was breathing. And she would retrieve his dirty clothes from the floor and replace them with clean ones.

Then she heard sounds from upstairs. His bed was creaking, so he wasn't dead. She heard sounds of shuffling. A door opening and closing. Footsteps on the stairs.

Effie listened to him go into the kitchen and put the kettle on. Then he came into the living room.

"Hello, my love," he said.

He was carrying a mug of coffee that she knew would have been made with two heaped teaspoons of instant coffee and three of sugar.

They gave each other a peck on the cheek and a bit of a hug. That was the routine.

"Sleep well?" he asked. Also the routine.

"Not too bad," she said.

He took his coffee to his table and sat down. He took a swig and then took a fig roll from a packet he kept on the window sill behind. He broke it in half and nibbled a bit. Then he arranged his bottles of pills in a line before him, took out one from each bottle, and swigged them down with his coffee.

Finally, he opened the envelope. He pulled out the letter and read it slowly. His mouth was hanging open sideways the way it often did. Then he put the letter aside and took another swig of his coffee.

"Anything in the post?" she asked. She was trying to sound casual.

"Yes," he said flatly. "I've got to hand in my driving licence."

Effie stood up and crossed over to him. "Just like that?" she asked. "I thought they'd ask you to take a driving test." She picked up the letter and read through. No apologies, no expression of regret, no good wishes for the future. A simple demand for the return of his driving licence, and the information that it would be illegal for him to drive from the given date, which was, she noticed, the day before yesterday. He had already been driving illegally for two days!

He didn't say anything.

Effie put her hand on his shoulder and squeezed. It was so unfair. He'd already had to give up playing bridge. Now he had to give up driving a car that he loved. And surrender his independence. What else was there for him? "I'm so sorry, love," she said.

Why was he so quiet? He ought to be ranting and raving. Swearing at these idiots who didn't know what they were talking about.

"So am I," he said.

She didn't know what else to say. She wanted to talk about it. The implications were enormous. And there were decisions that would have to be made.

If Effie were to be the only driver in the household they didn't need two cars. One of them would have to go. Maybe both.

"I'm going out," she said to him later. He was having his lunch in the dining room watching the BBC News as he always did. He was also playing bridge on his laptop that sat permanently on the dining room table. The hinges of the laptop lid were broken and the screen was propped up against two large Coca-Cola bottles. At some time that laptop must have been dropped. It was amazing that it still worked. She watched him click on the screen as slickly as ever.

"Where?" he asked.

"Just shopping." No need to tell him she was going shopping for a new car. Not yet.

"There!" he said. "I've made six no trumps!"

"Well done!" she said. And she squeezed his shoulder and kissed the top of his head.

Effie spent three days looking at cars. She needed to sell one two-seater fun car that was too small for practicality, and another five-seater luxury car that was too big for practicality. Neither of them was worth very much. What she needed was a small car with five doors and five seats that was easy to drive and easy to park. She wanted a boot big enough to take stuff to the dump, and she needed to be able to ferry the grandchildren around. And she wanted a car with a proper spare wheel. The one time her car had had a flat tyre the AA man had squirted horrid sticky stuff into it and sent her straight to a garage to get it sorted. Very inconvenient. She also fancied the idea of a car that had a parking bleeper. And one in a nice bright colour that was easy to find in car parks. Not much to ask, she thought.

She tried to talk to Lionel about it. "Do you want to come and look at cars with me?" she asked. She felt she should at least give him the opportunity to participate in what was a major family decision.

"No."

That was a relief. The last thing she wanted was him cracking snide one-liners about second-hand car salesmen to second-hand car salesmen.

At first she used Lionel's car to visit the various garages around town. She explained to each salesman in turn that she had two cars to sell and that this Jaguar was one of them. She test drove a Fiesta, a Micra, a Cleo, a Golf, a Corsa and something else with a name she couldn't remember. Then she went in her own car, repeated her circuit of the garages. And she chose a nearly new Corsa that almost fitted her requirements. It didn't have a spare wheel and it was white, not bright. But it did have a sunshine roof and very smart red and black upholstery. It had loads of gizmos but no parking bleeper. And the car salesman had loads of persuasive charm. He didn't give her a good price, but he did agree to have a parking bleeper fitted.

Then she went to talk to Gary at Barton Motors. He was in the office standing behind the counter, his eyes on his computer screen. He looked up and smiled. "Hello. How are you?" he said.

She told him about Lionel's diagnosis and about him having to give up driving.

"That's a bugger," he said. "He won't like that."

"You were the one who first told me that Lionel had dementia," she reminded him. And she explained about FTD.

"And it took that long to get the diagnosis?" he said.

They talked about cars. "I've found a Vauxhall Corsa I like," she said. "It's got a sunshine roof."

Gary laughed. "I get a lot of business repairing leaky sunshine roofs," he said. "And they're not much use these days, now that everything has air conditioning.

She looked down. "Well... I liked it," she said.

"And that's the best reason you can have for buying any car," he said. "How much are you getting for the other two?"

He balked at her reply. "You've been done," he said. "They're both low mileage cars, properly and regularly serviced. I'll sell them for you. I can get you a load more than that."

She felt stupid. Inadequate. What did she know about buying and selling cars? That was one of the things that she had always left to Lionel. "I should have talked to you first," she said.

"Yes, you should. Is the deal all signed and sealed?"

"I've paid a deposit. But I expect I can change things."

"You do that. I'll make a couple of calls. I know we can do better than that." He clicked on his keyboard and looked at his computer screen.

"I expect Lionel's gutted," he said.

Effie nodded. "He's very quiet. But he keeps looking out of the window at his car on the drive. I need to get rid of it quickly so he can take his mind off it."

"He might be tempted to drive it. Have you taken the keys away?"

"No. I thought about it, but I couldn't bring myself to do that."

"Bring it down here. You can park it out the back till it's sold. I'll come and get it if you like."

"Thank you so much," Effie said. "It's good to talk to someone who's not going to con me."

"Yeah... well... there are lot of sharks out there."

"Gary?" she asked tentatively.

"Yes."

"When Lionel was here, did you ever have problems with him?"

Gary shrugged. "He'd come up with odd remarks sometimes. I'd have a quick word with a customer and tell them he was bit batty but not to mind. It wasn't a problem. And his driving wasn't too bad, if you didn't mind the swearing. A whole lot better than some of those morons out there."

"Thanks Gary. It's good to talk to someone who remembers what Lionel used to be like."

"Yes. I always liked Lionel. I still do. He can't help what's happened to him."

When Effie got home she parked alongside the green Jaguar. She wondered for a moment if it had been moved, but she wasn't sure. Had Lionel been out in it? Ah well, if he had, it looked like he'd got back safely. But the sooner it was gone the better.

"Hello!" she called as she opened the front door.

He was sitting in his usual place. There was a cup of coffee and a packet of fig roll biscuits in front of him, along with an open newspaper and the Sudoku book.

"Where've you been?" he asked.

"Looking at cars. I've found one I quite like," she said.

"Oh," he said with studied lack of interest.

"Would you like to come and see it before I commit myself?"

"No."

"Okay. Then I went to chat to Gary Barton."

"Who?"

"You know. Barton's Garage. Where we get our cars fixed."

"Oh yes. I like him." Suddenly Lionel looked brighter.

"And he likes you too. He said so. He says he'll sell the cars for us. It'll be better than some rotten part exchange deal."

Lionel nodded sadly. He evidently didn't want to think about his car being sold. He changed the subject. "Can you drive me to the High Street?" he asked. "Please," he added.

This was a significant sentence. The first time Lionel had ever asked Effie to drive him anywhere. Life, as they knew it, was in for a big change.

"Of course I can," she said. "What for?"

"I need to pick a prescription from Boots."

Effie frowned. That was odd. Why were they sending his prescription to Boots? Ratigans, attached to the surgery and only five minutes' walk from home, was much more convenient.

"Shall we take your car?" she asked. It would be the last time. Gary was picking it up tomorrow.

"Don't know. Don't care."

So they did. It's a lovely car, Effie thought as they set off. So smooth. So comfortable. So quiet. All you had to do was point it. She asked herself, should she keep it for her to drive? But no. She wasn't a 'big car' sort of person.

"Why don't you get your pills from Ratigans Pharmacy?" Effie asked when she pulled up outside Boots. She noticed a traffic warden was watching them. Does he recognise the car? she wondered. Probably.

Lionel shrugged irritably and said something about those idiots at Ratigans being useless.

"Shall I wait for you?" Effie asked.

"No. I'll get a taxi back."

That was good. She couldn't park here anyway, not with that traffic warden watching. More importantly, she felt pleased that Lionel was ready and willing to use taxis. It was something he was going to need to do in his new life as non-driver.

As she drove home, she was thinking about Ratigans. What did Lionel have against them? She remembered all the trouble with Dunfords, and with the Leisure Centre.

And a curious thought formed in her mind.

I wonder? she thought.

CHAPTER 21

A Tale of Two Pharmacies

Effie walked up the road to the Park Health Centre. Ratigans Pharmacy was in the same building and you could access it either from the surgery's reception area or straight from the car park. This time she entered from the car park.

"Can I help you, Mrs Butler?" said an assistant from behind the counter.

She was surprised to be known by name. Did they recognise all their customers? It wasn't as if she came in that often.

"I hope so," she said. "I wanted to ask about my husband."

"Yes?"

"Lionel Butler."

"Yes, we know Mr Butler," said the assistant. There was tension in her voice and she stiffened a little.

Effie took a deep breath. "I wondered if you'd had any problems with him. Has he, by any chance, been banned from coming here?"

"Yes, he has." The assistant spoke in a clipped tone and pressed her lips tightly together.

"Could you tell me why, please?"

"Would you like to speak to the manageress?"

"Yes, please."

"I'll go and see if she's available."

Effie's pulse was racing. She felt her chest tighten. She'd thought all this was over. Since the diagnosis, Lionel had been on this new medication and his behaviour had improved. She couldn't see it herself, but Suzie had said she found him much less aggressive.

The manageress came through from the back of the shop. "Good afternoon, Mrs Butler. I'm Davina Wallace." They shook hands. "Would you like to come through to my office?"

She sat opposite the desk. It was a bit like being in a doctor's surgery, only smaller.

"You want to talk about your husband?"

"Yes. I understand he's been banned from coming here to get his medication."

"He has been banned from entering the premises unaccompanied."

"Can you tell me why?"

"No. I'm sorry, I can't do that. It would be breach of customer confidentiality."

Effie looked at her in astonishment. "Ms Wallace. I'm his wife. I'm his carer. He's mentally ill and I have to deal with it. I'm expected to pick up the pieces. How can I do that if I don't know what's going on?"

"I'm sorry, Mrs Butler. I'm not permitted to give you the details."

Effie felt as though she'd been punched in the stomach. She took a deep breath. "Are you allowed to tell me when whatever-it-was happened?"

The manageress opened a file and took out some letters.

Good grief – they'd got a whole file on him! Like he was some sort of criminal!

"Let me see, the first time was a couple of years ago. He was banned for two months..."

Effie's eyes widened. How many times had there been? "I know..." she began. She was remembering a stupid joke Lionel insisted on repeating. She'd been with him a couple of times when he did it. He'd be waiting for his prescription, and before the pharmacist would hand it over they always checked the address. It was a security precaution. Lionel would laugh and say something like, 'You know my address, it's written right there'. She continued. "He always joked about you asking for his address when you knew it already." It was stupid joke, but it wasn't offensive.

"No... we managed to deal with that," said the manageress.

"Okay," said Effie. She had to get to the bottom of this. "Has he done anything violent?"

"No."

"Has he done anything illegal?"

"No."

"Has he done anything indecent?"

"No."

"So he's been rude," said Effie. "He's probably sworn at people."

"We have to protect our staff and customers."

"He has frontotemporal dementia. You are refusing to serve a sick person because he exhibits the well-documented symptoms of his illness. You're refusing to provide him with the medication to treat those symptoms. It's... outrageous. You're discriminating against a man because he's sick!"

"We'll serve him if you accompany him."

Do they think her presence would stop him swearing? "It's a degenerative illness. It's good for him to do what he can on his own, while he still can."

"We have to protect our staff and customers," repeated the manageress.

Effie felt she wanted to explode. "Okay. When was the last letter?"

It was six month ago. So that was why Lionel had been driving to Boots all this time to get his pills.

"Look, he's now on medication which calms him down. Would you give him another chance?"

"I'm afraid I don't have the authority to do that. You'll have to write to our head office."

Effie gritted her teeth. So much for the so-called 'dementia-friendly society' this government was promoting!

"Please could you give me the name and address?" she asked.

She wrote it down.

As they shook hands, she had a sudden thought. If they wouldn't let him visit the pharmacy, maybe they'd deliver Lionel's pills.

"Do you deliver medication?" she asked.

Davina Wallace tightened her mouth. "Only to the housebound," she said.

Effie wondered what the definition of 'housebound' was.

Another session in front of the computer. Effie wrote and addressed the letter, as Davina Wallace had recommended, to the *Business Integrity Manager* at the company's head office in Derby. Her name was Jennifer Jarman. What, she wondered, did a *Business Integrity Manager* do?

She typed the letter:

Exclusion of Lionel Butler from Ratigans Pharmacy, Dalton Heath
Dear Jennifer Jarman,
I am writing on behalf of my husband, Lionel Butler, who has Frontotemporal Dementia and no longer has the cognitive skills to write a letter of this nature.
He has been banned from using Ratigans Pharmacy adjacent to the Park Health

Centre in Dalton Heath. I believe he was sent a number of warning letters and a final letter, but I have not seen them. I asked the pharmacy manager, Davina Wallace, to show me these letters but I was told that would be a breach of customer confidentiality. She did concede that he has done nothing illegal, nothing violent and nothing indecent.

I suspect he has used offensive remarks to staff and/or customers. Such behaviour is a symptom of FTD and he cannot help it. The disease has no cause, no cure and is not his fault.

However, in the last couple of months his psychiatrist, Dr Hazan, at the Larwood Mental Health Centre has prescribed medication to modify Lionel's behaviour. He is quieter and less rude to the public.

Because of the disease he had to surrender his driving licence and thus his car. In addition to dementia he also has chronic heart failure and a chronic lung condition so he cannot walk far. Ratigans is the only chemist near enough to our home for him to walk to pick up his medication. To visit other chemist shops he has to take a taxi or I have to take him, thereby reducing his independence.

I am appealing to you to lift the ban on him using Ratigans Pharmacy.

I refer you to a recent news item about a scheme in which the staff of Marks and Spencer, Argus, Homebase, Lloyds Bank and Lloyds Pharmacy will attend special sessions to enable them to support customers with dementia. Our Health Secretary visited Argus and publicised the plan. While Ratigans is not included in the scheme, I am sure the company will show sympathy for what is a cruel mental illness for both patient and carer. Society has grown more caring when it comes to physical illness or disability. With mental illness it is another matter.

Thank you for your attention. I look forward to hearing from you.

Kind regards

Frances Butler (Mrs)

She read the letter through, corrected some typos, and printed it. Then she put it in an envelope, and addressed it ready for posting.

"How long have you been going to Boots for prescriptions?" Effie asked Lionel later.

He was studying the *Radio Times* and marking, with his blue rollerball pen, programmes he might want to watch.

He shrugged. "Don't know. Don't care."

"What happened at Ratigans?" she asked.

"They're fucking idiots," he snarled.

Effie found herself wondering about Boots. Perhaps they were having problems with Lionel too?

Lionel frowned, picked up his magnifying glass and peered closely at the *Radio Times*.

"Are you seeing less well?" Effie asked.

"I need new glasses," he said.

She frowned. "You've only had those six months!"

"Well, they're useless at that place. I'll go to Specsavers next time."

That was interesting, Effie thought. Was it significant?

Her next task was to visit Boots.

She parked at the top of the High Street and walked down to the Boots. She walked through the automatic doors and headed for the pharmacy section.

There was an old lady talking to one of the pharmacy assistants. "He's ninety-three," she said, her voice brittle with anxiety. "And I'm eighty-seven. They think I can cope, but I can't."

"It must be very difficult," said the assistant as she handed across the packet of medication.

Poor dear, Effie thought. Will that be me in a few years' time?

Next to her stood a man in a dark suit with a badge that gave his name, Nicholas Cox, and his job title, Store Manager. That was lucky.

Effie wouldn't have to ask to see him. She looked at him and hesitated.

"Can I help you?" he asked.

"I don't know," she said. She was nervous. "My husband – his name's Lionel Butler – he comes here quite often. I was wondering..."

"Lionel Butler? Oh yes, we know him well!" The manager smiled.

"Oh dear," Effie said. "That sounds serious."

"Not at all. Don't worry about anything, Mrs Butler. We recognise the condition. We can deal with it."

Effie looked up at him. "Really? It's just that there's been so much trouble. He was banned from Dunfords, and now he's been banned from Ratigans Pharmacy."

"Ratigans?" said the manager. "I'd have thought they'd be more sympathetic. But don't worry; we do always keep an eye on him." He laughed. "He usually parks right outside the door on the double yellow lines. I think he's had a ticket or two in his time. It doesn't bother him one bit. He's quite a character, your husband. Certainly doesn't suffer fools gladly. Can't say I blame him."

Effie felt a lump rising in her throat. It was hard, like a pebble. It's people being nice to you that make you cry. People who are nasty just make you angry. "Well, he's had to give up driving now," she said. "So there'll be no more parking fines. He could walk to Ratigans, but to come here he'll be getting taxis. Unless I bring him, of course."

"Would you like us to deliver his medication?"

She paused and thought. It would be convenient. "That is so kind," she said. "But I'm not sure. His life is so limited now, and picking up his pills does give him an outing. Even if he has to do it by taxi."

"Well, just let me know," said the manager. "And don't worry about it. We do realise you are doing a very difficult job. And you're doing it very well indeed."

"Thank you," Effie managed. She struggled to suppress the tremor in her voice.

And by the time she reached the double glass doors there were tears streaming down her face.

She had to walk past Fairvue Opticians on the way back to her car. She paused and looked in the window. She would leave her visit there until tomorrow, she decided.

Right now, she was feeling far too tearful to talk to anyone.

CHAPTER 22

The Optician's Tale

The usual receptionist was behind the counter, and Philip Alvarez was seated at a side table fitting a pair of specs on a customer. "Does that feel okay?" he was saying. "At bit tight? Let's adjust them."

"Hello," Effie said to the receptionist. "I'd like to make an appointment for Lionel Butler." She was uncomfortably aware of Philip Alvarez glancing past his customer towards her. His dark looks revealed his Hispanic ancestry. He looked more like a film star than an optician.

The receptionist tensed slightly and looked at her bookings diary. "When would you like?" she asked tightly. She didn't look up.

"No hurry, but it needs to be in the middle of the morning, say about eleven o'clock?" Lionel rarely got up till after ten, and he always insisted on being back home in good time for his lunch at precisely one o'clock. So that left a fairly small window of opportunity to make any arrangements.

Effie settled on a date and time.

Philip handed his customer's spectacles to the receptionist for her to deal with the invoice and looked at Effie. "How is he now?" he asked Effie. She had told him a while ago that Lionel had a mental illness.

"He's had an MRI scan now, and we've finally got a diagnosis. He has a disease called frontotemporal dementia."

Philip nodded. "And that accounts for his behavioural problems?"

"You've heard of it?"

He nodded. "Yes. I've read about it. But I haven't come across it before."

"He's on medication that calms him down. He's not as aggressive as he was last time you saw him."

"That is good," said Philip with feeling. "At least... I don't mean that the diagnosis is good, but I'm glad that he's calmed down."

It was early last summer that Effie had last talked to Philip Alvarez. That had been pre-diagnosis. There was a line that divided her life into *pre-diagnosis* and *post-diagnosis*. She always saw life as divided into chunks like that. *Before leaving school* and *after leaving school. Before getting married* and *after getting married. Before having babies* and *after having babies.* There were many of these situations that marked points of change. And the *pre-diagnosis* and *post-diagnosis* was a recent one. Even more recent was, *before Lionel gave up driving* and *after Lionel gave up driving.* No doubt there would be others as the disease progressed.

Anyway, this last conversation with Philip Alvarez had been in the *pre-diagnosis* stage when Lionel had still been enjoying his green Jaguar, but when it was clear to Effie that something was wrong. He'd come home with new glasses one day.

"But you haven't had the last ones very long?" Effie had said to him.

"They weren't any good. They're useless at that place," he snapped.

"Why did you need new ones?" she asked.

"Because HE said so," snarled Lionel.

"HE? You mean Philip Alvarez?"

Lionel looked down the way he did when he was muddled. "I don't remember everyone's name," he reacted.

"Philip Alvarez is the optician. He used to be a friend of yours. Member of the drama group."

"Well he's bonkers!"

"Has your prescription changed much?" had been Effie's next question. Questioning Lionel was never easy. She'd since learned that you should avoid asking dementia sufferers direct questions. But she didn't know that then.

"I don't know, do I? Don't go on about it!"

She'd taken a deep breath and tried one more question. "Well, are the new ones any better than the old ones?"

He had shrugged. "I don't know, do I?" he'd muttered crossly.

So Effie had called in at Fairvue Optician's to find out what was going on. She knew what a slick salesman Philip Alvarez could be. He was quite showman with his pink shirts and skinny black jeans. And Lionel had known him years ago because they were both into amateur dramatics in big way. In fact, they'd acted together once or twice.

Philip was a good optician, but it was very hard to get out of the place without being talked into buying at least one pair of new glasses. Sometimes more.

"I'm Effie Butler," she had said to the receptionist behind the counter. "I'm Lionel Butler's wife. I wanted to ask about his glasses."

There'd been an uncomfortable silence and the receptionist had looked anxiously towards Philip.

He'd given her a little wave and called, "Nearly finished. I'll be right with you."

Effie'd felt that sinking feeling. "Has there been any trouble?" she'd asked when Philip had come across and joined her. "Has he been a problem?"

There had been an awkward pause that Effie felt obliged to fill. "He has some sort mental illness," she'd explained. "We're waiting for a diagnosis. He doesn't seem to have any idea how to behave."

Philip looked at the receptionist. "Valerie, can you get his file out?" Then, addressing Effie, "He's been impossible – he reduced Valerie here to tears. And as for the customers..." He crossed to take the file from Valerie. "It just doesn't make sense. He used to be such a nice bloke."

"It's been going on for ages," Effie'd said. "I couldn't get his GP to take it seriously."

"Last time he was here..." Philip had been flicking though the file.

Good grief! They'd kept records of it all! Just like Ratigans Pharmacy. Except that Philip Alvarez, who ran his own business in his own way, didn't worry about 'customer confidentiality'.

He had continued. "There was this customer with his two grandchildren. And Lionel said, very loudly, so everyone could hear, 'Look at him – he must be a paedophile!' Can you imagine the embarrassment? Then Lionel laughed and looked round like he was expecting everyone to applaud. I told him: 'Lionel! You can't say things like that!'"

"And then, I suppose," Effie had remarked, "he sniggered and said it was just a joke." She could imagine the scenario exactly. Lionel would have dismissed them all as lacking a sense of humour. "Well," she'd said, "he's been seen by the mental health people. We're waiting for a brain scan."

Shaking his head sadly, "I don't know how you cope," Philip had said.

"With difficulty."

Philip had put his hand on her arm. "I'm so glad you told me. I mean, what was I supposed to think? I didn't know what to do. I was thinking about asking him to go elsewhere for his specs, but he used to be a friend. I remember doing that Noel Coward play with him. Must have been twenty years ago now. He was so good. Such insight. Bit of a prima donna I suppose, but he was friendly and popular, and so good on the stage."

"I remember that play," Effie said. Lionel had been so handsome in that velvet smoking jacket. So smooth, so stylish. She had been so proud of him when he'd won that award for the best local actor of the year. Everyone wanted talk to him, and she had enjoyed the reflected glory. And there'd been that brilliant photo in the local paper. Now that pride had been replaced by embarrassment. She continually had to apologise for his behaviour. Always on edge about what he was going to say next.

"Now... he's like a different man," Philip said.

"I know," she agreed. "I keep looking for some glimmer, some tiny glimmer of the man he used to be..." Effie had stopped, her eyes filling with tears. She mustn't cry. She'd taken a deep breath and swallowed hard. She had come to discuss Lionel's spectacles, not his health.

"What about his eyesight?" she'd asked. "He hasn't had those specs very long."

Philip had looked at the file again. "His eyesight's changing quickly. And with all the medication he's on, it's probably unstable. If he's having problems that could be the reason."

That conversation had been *pre-diagnosis*.

Now it was *post-diagnosis*. Lionel was really confused about which specs he should be wearing. Effie had found several pairs lying around the house and he didn't know which were the newest and which the oldest. Nor did he know which were for distance, and which for reading. He couldn't see properly with any of them.

"I'll bring him myself this time," she said. "He's had to give up driving anyway. But you should find it easier now he's on this medication. And it's easier for me since we had the proper diagnosis. At least I can explain to people why he's like he is."

The appointment was early the following week and Effie took four pairs of Lionel's spectacles with her, in addition to the ones that he was actually wearing. She didn't know which had the most recent prescription. Apart from the usual difficulty of Lionel grumbling that she wouldn't park on a double yellow line outside the optician's and he had to walk a bit, they got there without mishap.

And they got through the appointment with minimal crises, though a few lightly spoken swear words were studiously ignored. A whispered comment about the fat receptionist was loud enough to be heard by the waiting customers.

"I'm so sorry," Effie said loudly to anyone who was listening. "My husband has dementia. He can't help being rude." She was getting more confident at dealing with the embarrassment.

"Speak properly!" said Lionel cheerily to the eye specialist who was of Asian origin. Then he proceeded to imitate the accent.

"Shhhh!" Effie hissed, but she found herself suppressing a smile. Lionel had always been a good mimic.

Afterwards Philip explained that the prescription had changed a lot.

"Would you like to choose some frames?" Philip asked him.

"No," said Lionel. "I'm just going outside for a moment," he said. "I'm bored with all this and I don't need new glasses."

"He'll have a cigarette and be back in minute," Effie said to Philip.

"I'll just browse a bit. And she tried on some of the newer styles of spectacles. Strong colours. Dramatic shapes.

"It's the new thing," said Philip. "Styles that make bold fashion statements. Much smarter. People are buying far more specs these days. Different colours for different outfits. That red would suit you. Go with that jacket. Though the blue would bring out your eye colour. And we'd do a good deal if you order yours at the same time as Lionel's."

Effie was tempted. She glanced out of the window. Lionel was leaning against the bus stop shelter, smoking.

"I'll keep an eye on him while Mahesh fits you. It won't take long."

"Where's Lionel?" she said when she'd made her choice and committed herself to a designer pair of spectacles that she didn't need, but that Philip said made her look a million dollars. There was no sign of Lionel through the window. "I'll have to go and look for him," she said. She ran up the road a hundred yards and down the road a hundred yards. No sign of Lionel. She felt panic tightening in her chest.

She hurried back inside, breathless. "I can't find him. "I'll have to go."

"He hasn't chosen his frames," said Philip.

That was the least of Effie's problems. "We'll have to leave it for now."

"Shall I put new lenses in two of the old pairs?" suggested Philip. "One for reading and one for distance? That'll make it cheaper for you anyway."

"Yes. That'll be fine." She gave him the bundle of old spectacles. "Pick the ones in better condition. I'll come back and pay you."

She hurried back to the car, then drove home keeping an eye open for Lionel en route. There was a hard knot of anxiety deep within her. If he wasn't at home, she'd have to call the police.

"Hello!" she called as she opened the front door.

Lionel was sitting in his usual place, looking at the *Radio Times*, a blue rollerball pen in his hand. Effie sighed with relief. Thank goodness!

"You got back quickly," she said.

He smiled. "I got a taxi," he said. "Where've you been?"

She was about to say, 'Well, you might have said,' but she stopped herself. "I ordered you some new specs," she said.

He frowned. "I don't need new specs." He adjusted the ones he was wearing and looked across the room. "I can see perfectly."

CHAPTER 23

No, He's Not My Loved One

Effie had discovered that when your spouse is diagnosed with dementia you become a carer. That's official. It isn't a job you applied for. It isn't a career move you would ever have planned, but a carer is what you are and you just have to make the best of it. You might become a carer of your mother or father or auntie or uncle, but in those cases there could be an element of choice. When it's your spouse, there isn't. It's back to *in sickness and health* and *till death us do part.* Even if you don't like your spouse very much. Effie found herself thinking quite a lot about *when death would them part.*

Despite all the medical research, there is not a lot the health services or the social services can actually do about dementia, but they do try to support you as a carer. For society, it's financially worthwhile keeping carers happy and healthy and thus keeping their *carees* out of care homes. Effie had invented the word *caree,* which wasn't in the dictionary. If she were a carer, then it was a reasonable word for the person for whom she cared. After all, you can have an employer and an employee, can't you? The word that all social workers, health workers and support workers used, and which appeared in all the self-help books, was *loved one,* which in Effie's opinion was an outrageously cosy euphemism. No way was she going to use it! Perhaps she could use *unloved one*.

She read a book called *A Selfish Pig's Guide to Caring*. The term the author used for a *caree* was *Piglet*. This stood for **P**erson to whom **I** **G**ive **L**ove and **E**ndless **T**herapy. Clever or what? thought Effie. What a pity it hadn't caught on.

Effie was reading everything about dementia that she could lay her hands on. In America, she learned, they used the word *caregiver*, instead of *carer*. So their word for *caree* should have been *caretaker*, which of course has an entirely different meaning. *Carereceiver* would have been ok, but no. *Loved one* was what the Americans used too.

After the diagnosis Effie's name found its way onto lists. Postal mailing lists and e-mailing lists. There were all sorts of organisations offering support. The Alzheimer's Society, Age UK, Care UK, Carers' Support and others. The names of these organisations were often very similar. Some of them were charities, but some financed or part-financed by the NHS. It was very muddling. In the beginning, she tried a number of different options.

She went to a Carers' Relaxation Day at the local town hall. There was coffee and cake to start and a talk from an elegant lady who told them all what a worthwhile job they were all doing and that they should be very proud of themselves. Local companies in the business of pampering were offering 'taster sessions'. Effie started with a foot massage that was very nice, and then she had her nails manicured. She realised that these organisations were looking for business.

At lunch, she sat with some really interesting people who were coping with appalling problems. There is always someone worse off than yourself, she reflected.

In the afternoon, she went to a taster session on *mindfulness* which was becoming very popular. She was told to close her eyes, relax, and focus on something she had done really well in the past. A great hole opened up inside her brain and she couldn't think of anything in the whole of her life that she had ever done really well. Nor even anything she had done quite well. What a failure she was! She started to cry.

"I'm sorry, I can't cope with this," she sobbed, and rushed from the room, leaving the mindfulness coach somewhat perplexed.

But it was a nice day out.

A while later she signed on for what was to be a six-session course on the early stages of dementia. It was in Haybourne and she got stuck in a traffic jam and then had trouble parking. So she arrived hot and bothered and slightly late. An Alzheimer's Society support worker and a volunteer were running the course. Eleven carers were seated around a rectangle of tables. Effie breathlessly apologised for her late arrival and took the twelfth seat.

The students were each asked to draw a penny coin on a piece of paper. Effie had a vague idea what a penny looked like. She knew it had to have the Queen's head on one side but she had no idea which way she faced. She knew it had to have the value written round the edge somewhere, and the date. But she didn't know where. The idea of this was to show what it might feel like to have dementia.

It worked.

She felt panicky at her inadequacy.

Then they were asked to talk to the person next to them and tell them about themselves and their *loved ones*. Effie turned to the man next to her, and he started telling her, in somewhat unnecessarily intimate detail, she thought, about the difficulties of helping his wife wash herself.

Effie didn't know what to say.

"And what about your loved one?" he asked.

"He's not my loved one!" she reacted. No! She couldn't talk to this complete stranger about Lionel!

Her heart was fluttering like a trapped bird and she was breathing too fast. "I can't do this!" she cried and she ran from the room, huge sobs overwhelming her. The volunteer worker ran after her and sat her down on a chair somewhere, fetched her a glass of water and tried to calm her.

"Don't worry," she kept saying. "It's all right."

But it wasn't all right. Effie knew that. It was never going to be all right. Why couldn't these people see that?

Eventually the tears subsided and she went to the cloakroom to wash her face. And she was led back to the room, by which time a PowerPoint lecture was underway. She could deal with that. It described how you might stick photos of the contents of your kitchen cupboards on the doors if your *loved one* couldn't remember what was inside. It explained that your *loved one* might be frightened of the person he or she kept seeing in the mirror, and how they might mistake a blue rug for a blue pool. The message was to get rid of mirrors and blue rugs.

She had a phone call from the Alzheimer's lady the next day. She told Effie there'd be another course running in Dalton Heath later in the year and maybe it would be easier for her to attend that one rather than driving all the way to Haybourne. Effie agreed.

She attended a social evening for carers and their demented carees. They called it a Dementia Café. She pressurised Lionel into coming to this because she thought it would be good for him to get out and it wouldn't interfere with his afternoon nap. A bearded folk singer played the guitar and led a singalong. Lionel positioned himself right in front of him in a squatting position and did a gorilla impression with accompanying grunting noises while playing an imaginary guitar. No one minded.

They were provided with tea and sandwiches. Lionel opened each sandwich to find out what the filling was, then closed it and put it back on the plate if it didn't appeal. It wasn't embarrassing because he wasn't the only one doing it.

What was embarrassing for Effie was the fact that it wasn't always one hundred percent obvious which member of a particular couple was the carer and which the caree. And you couldn't possibly ask, could you? In her and Lionel's case, she didn't think there could have been any doubt. She hoped not. After all, she didn't do gorilla impressions.

Anyway, Lionel hated it and they left after about twenty minutes.

"Not going to that fucking place again," he said.

Effie was too cross to cry.

Next, she tried an afternoon dementia support group run by the Alzheimer's Society on the second Tuesday of every month. The idea was to take your demented caree with you. The carees would be taken into one room to be entertained and stimulated by experts, while the carers went into another for support, discussion and exchange of information. It wasn't really suitable for Effie and Lionel because the timing of it coincided with Lionel's immovable afternoon nap. But she still went.

The first time she walked in she sat down in a vacant chair in a circle of occupied chairs. She looked across and recognised a face. Her mind searched for the name.

"Er... Sheila?" she said.

The woman stared across. "Effie!" she reacted. Her eyes widened and her mouth dropped open in astonishment. "What are you...? Your husband?" she asked.

Effie nodded. "Yours too?" she asked.

Sheila and Effie had both taught in the same school for the best part of fifteen years. Sheila had left first for another job and Effie had carried on for longer. They'd met up once or twice, but not for a while.

Sheila nodded.

"I've forgotten his name," Effie said. She remembered meeting Sheila's husband at a Christmas function.

"Andrew," she said. "He's got Alzheimer's," she said. "Diagnosed two years ago."

"Lionel has frontotemporal dementia," Effie said. "Diagnosed last year."

"FTD? That's really bad," said Sheila.

The convenor, an Alzheimer's support worker who had been handing round cups of tea, opened the meeting. She introduced herself and suggested they go round the circle, introducing themselves and saying something about their *loved ones*.

There was one with Vascular Dementia, one with Lewy Bodies Dementia, and the others all had Alzheimer's Disease. Lionel was the only one with FTD. She learned later that, as with FTD, you can abbreviate Alzheimer's Disease to AD. (You can't abbreviate Vascular Dementia as VD stands for something entirely different.)

The stories were all tragic. A TV presenter, a headmistress, a local builder, a professional golfer, a manageress of a travel agency. All struck down by mental illness.

Effie introduced herself and told them of the years leading up to Lionel's diagnosis. The five weeks he had spent in hospital with heart failure. How he nearly died in intensive care. She caught Sheila's eye.

"Do you think it might have been better if he had?" Sheila had never been one to mince her words. You could trust her to say what she thought. Effie liked that.

"Sometimes," Effie said.

She told them about the problems with his behaviour and the visits from the police. The way the matter had been handled – or rather mishandled – by Dunfords Supermarket, Ratigans Pharmacy, the Leisure Centre and the Dalton Heath Bridge Club.

These carers all had different problems. Effie, at least, could get out of the house without having to worry about Lionel. Home alone, he was safe. So far.

At the end they all, except Effie, collected their carees from the other meeting room and went home with them.

Effie just went home.

Her caree was, as expected, having his afternoon nap. She felt rather pleased with the afternoon. It had been interesting and she'd acquired some practical information. She'd learned that she must apply for a thing called an Attendance Allowance. And that she could get a reduction on her rates. She'd renewed an old acquaintance, and she'd got though the meeting without bursting into tears.

Then she put the kettle on and burst into tears.

CHAPTER 24

An AGM to Remember

"It's the AGM next week," said Barbara. "Are you going?"

"I don't know," Effie said.

"They'll get through the business as quickly as possible then we'll play bridge as usual, only not for so long. If you don't want to attend the meeting, you can just come along half an hour later."

Barbara and Effie were still playing bridge most weeks. When they played against the chairman of the bridge club or any of the other committee members who had been involved in implementing Lionel's resignation, Effie found them super-friendly, super-smiley. They were trying too hard to be nice to her. Not one of them had ever once asked how Lionel was. It was much the same with most of his ex-partners. A couple of them used to ask after him and tell her to wish him well, which she always did, and Lionel would be really pleased. But the others pretended he had never existed. Embarrassed, she supposed.

When she got home from each week's bridge session, Lionel would ask her how she and Barbara had done – were they bottom, or second-to-bottom? Then he would go upstairs to the study, check the results on the website and print out the results list. Sometimes the printer snarled up the paper and then she'd have to sort it out for him. If his ex-partners had done badly he'd be ever so pleased.

"Yes, I'll go to the AGM," Effie said to Barbara.

That week she explored the bridge club's website in greater detail. Yes, the announcement of Lionel's resignation under the heading, *Disciplinary Matters*, was still there. She clicked on minutes of previous committee meetings. There was a section under *Disciplinary Matters* every time! Lionel wasn't mentioned by name but it was clear that the committee, along with the conduct and disciplinary subcommittees (CC and DC) had been discussing his case for years. How could she have been so naive?

She looked at the agenda for next week's AGM. Someone should tell the club officially about Lionel's disease. It was right that members should know. She phoned Barbara. "I want to explain to the club about Lionel. I'm going to ask Charles if I could make a statement under *Any Other Business*."

Barbara knew her rather well. She knew how easily she could burst into tears. "It'll upset you," she said. "And Lionel won't know you've been through that for him. It could be very awkward."

"I'm going to write it in advance. All I'll have to do is speak up and read it out."

She spent a lot of time that week writing and rewriting what she wanted to say. Barbara made suggestions for a few cuts but in the end, she thought she'd got the right tone.

The committee were seated at one end of the room and the chairs were arranged facing them. She had a quick word with the Chairman before he opened the meeting.

"Would it be all right if I made a statement about Lionel's health? At the end under Any Other Business?" she asked.

Charles hesitated.

"I just want people to know what's wrong with him," she added. "That it wasn't his fault that he was so nasty."

"Er yes. That'll be fine," said the Chairman.

She sat at the side of the room with Barbara, her regular partner, and Sally, one of her occasional partners. They were both good friends and could both remember Lionel before this ghastly illness destroyed his personality. It felt good to have their support.

There was a Treasurer's Report and a Premises Report. Awards were presented. Committee members were elected and re-elected. Effie was on edge and found it hard to concentrate. When it came to Any Other Business there was a question about the provision of coffee and biscuits and another about whether evenings could end fifteen minutes earlier.

Then it was Effie's turn. She stood up and scanned the room. All eyes were turned to her. People she didn't know. People she had known for years. Many had enjoyed playing bridge with Lionel, and others had enjoyed his company at social occasions. She unfolded her script. She would have liked to have done this without a script, but that would have been far too difficult. As it was, her target was to get to the end without crying.

She began.

My husband, Lionel Butler, was a member of the Dalton Heath Bridge Club for over thirty years. I am very grateful that he was able to enjoy playing at such a nice club for so long.

She looked at her audience. She didn't actually think it was a very nice bridge club at all, but she felt she had to say something like that.

In recent years some of you found his rude behaviour and offensive language intolerable.

She paused.

Me too.

She took a deep breath.

Last September Lionel had a brain scan which led to a diagnosis of Frontotemporal Dementia – a deterioration of the frontal lobes of the brain which deal with communication, social skills, sympathy and empathy. FTD is a degenerative illness which has no cause and no cure. It has no connection with alcohol and Lionel would have developed it even if he had been a teetotaller all his life.

She'd thought she should get that in. She knew that some people had put everything down to drink. Which was entirely understandable.

FTD has many weird symptoms but the one which troubled the bridge club is this horrible behaviour. Sufferers lack insight into what is happening to them. Lionel never understood why he upset people. He thought he was being funny, or friendly.

She paused again.

An FTD sufferer can no more control his behaviour than a Parkinson's patient can control his trembling or a stammerer can stop stammering.

She had decided that was worth a mention. A couple of years ago there had been a player who had irritated some of his opponents with his inability to get his words out. At present, there was a Parkinson's sufferer who had great difficulty in sorting her cards. She was sitting at the end of the second row. As far as Effie knew, everyone had been kind and understanding.

The illness is less common than Alzheimer's, but starts younger. In the early stages memory loss is not a problem, so Lionel's skill with cards is as yet unaffected. I believe Lionel's personality change began about ten years ago. The long-term prognosis is total incapacity leading to death.

The bridge club's tortuous procedures for securing Lionel's resignation went on even after he had accepted that he could no longer play bridge here. The pressure on us was such that in December I stood over him while he wrote his resignation letter. In January the committee meeting minutes, which are published online for all the world to see, announced Lionel's resignation under the heading...

She paused and looked at the chairman.

...Disciplinary Matters.

She paused again and spoke slowly.

Dementia is a disease. No way is it a Disciplinary Matter. If only!

Society on the whole shows sympathy and tolerance of physical illness. With mental illness there is criticism, rejection and isolation.

Lionel is now on medication that has rendered him less objectionable. Because of the diagnosis he had to hand in his driving licence, and his car has been sold. He does crosswords and Sudoku puzzles, plays computer bridge, and watches TV. On the evenings after you've played bridge here, he prints the list of results from the website and studies it.

FTD is an evil disease. It has stolen my husband from me. It has stolen a friend and a bridge partner from some of you. I do hope that those of you who knew him years ago can remember the Lionel Butler that was. I'd like those of you who met him recently to know that you met a sick man.

I should like to thank his partners for continuing to play with him as long you did – I know it was difficult for you. I should also like to thank a few members for asking me about him since he resigned – I do appreciate your concern.

She swallowed. Don't cry, she told herself severely. She took another deep breath, put her hand on Barbara's shoulder and squeezed.

And my good friends, without whose support, my ability to count to thirteen would have deteriorated even further – thank you.

And thank you all for listening.

Effie sat down. She was trembling. She was blinking back tears. Then she realised that people were applauding. And some of them were standing up. It was extraordinary. She had done it, and without crying!

Afterwards people she had never met came and shook hands with her. One lady said, "I'm so glad you told us. We had no idea." Another told her she was very brave.

A retired psychiatrist spoke to her. "I suspected as much," he said.

Another man introduced himself. "Leo Fauvel. Pleased to meet you, Effie. Do give my best wishes to Lionel," he said. "He used to call me 'Le Frog'. He was kind to me when I first joined. I found some of the members were so intimidating."

A week or so later the DHBC AGM minutes were published online.

There was brief note under *Any Other Business*.

It said, *Frances Butler read a statement about her husband, ex-member, Lionel Butler*. It said nothing whatever about the content of the statement.

Was that it? Effie thought.

CHAPTER 25

Effie in FTD-Land

Effie had been to support groups. She had attended lectures and discussion groups on dementia. But she had not met people with similar problems to her own. She had never seen an FTD patient other than Lionel.

There was a small ad on the back of an Alzheimer's Society leaflet that drew her attention to an organisation that appeared to be relevant to her particular situation. What she didn't know was that it was going to set her life onto a new track. When she looked back later she wondered why none of the organisations like the Larwood Mental Health team, the Alzheimer's Society, Carers' Support, Age UK, or Social Services, who were supposed to be offering her advice, had told her about it.

It was an FTD Support Group and it was run by London University. She phoned the number in the ad and a woman with a bright, positive tone answered.

"Natalie Dryden," she said.

"My name's Effie Butler. I got your number from a leaflet," she said nervously. What was making nervous her these days was the fear that any moment she might burst into tears. "My husband's been diagnosed with FTD and..." Her voice trembled a bit but she kept going, "...and I'm not coping very well."

"I am so sorry," said Natalie. "You must feel terrible."

"Yes, I do. Quite a lot of the time."

Natalie encouraged her to look at the website and if possible come to the next meeting. "Can you get to London?"

"Yes. That's no problem," she said.

"You'll learn a lot about the disease and you'll meet other carers in the same situation as yourself. I think you'll find it helpful," said Natalie.

"Thank you. I'll do that."

"Great! I'll look forward to meeting you!" she said to her finally.

Effie always felt a frisson of excitement when she had an excuse for a day in London. Usually it was to meet friends for lunch, or maybe go to the theatre or an exhibition. This time it was different. She was anxious as she didn't know what to expect, and anxiety was her normal mode these days. She felt a curious thrill as she walked through the main entrance to the university. She looked across the quadrangle to the impressive facade of the central building with its classical pillars, its elaborate portico and its domed roof. It seemed to represent the very essence of education and knowledge, and she envied the youngsters who were sitting on the steps with their jeans and their iPhones and their easy familiarity. Had they even noticed the architecture? Did they have any idea how privileged they were?

She looked at the instructions and headed for a side door which led to the meeting room.

She was welcomed by Natalie Dryden who introduced her to a colleague and convenor who gave her a name badge and led her across to a small group of fellow attendees, who were, of course, fellow carers of FTD patients. "This is Effie," said the convenor.

"She's new to us and her husband has FTD, behavioural variant."

This was the first time Effie had met people in her situation and she felt she had, in a curious sort of way, come home. They all knew what *FTD, behavioural variant* meant.

"Nice to meet you, Effie," said a man with a sharply angled face and greying hair that curled down over his collar. "Welcome to FTD-Land," he smiled as he shook her hand. He had blue eyes and a friendly smile marred by slightly uneven teeth.

FTD-Land! Effie certainly knew she'd been living in a different world from everyone else she knew, and if you wanted to give it a name, FTD-Land would do nicely. Up until now she had felt she was the only one inhabiting this alien country. Now she knew she wasn't.

"I'm Dominic, and..." he turned to the woman next to him, "...and this is Eleanor."

"When was your husband diagnosed?" asked Eleanor.

This, Effie was to learn, was a standard question that FTD carers always asked each other. A bit like inhabitants of that other world who asked where you lived or what you did for a living. "How long ago did the symptoms start?" was another one. And, "How difficult was it to get the diagnosis?"

Effie thought back. "He had a brain scan in September. And we got the diagnosis in December."

"They took their time," remarked Dominic.

Effie laughed. "The report got sent to the wrong place, at first." She remembered phoning round trying to find out why things were taking so long.

They settled themselves in rows of chairs to listen to a presentation given by a young research neurologist who was working on the development of diagnostic methods in early stage FTD. It was wonderful to hear that all this excellent work was being done, but she had a feeling it was all too late for Lionel.

There was a break for coffee and an opportunity to talk further to fellow carers. Meanwhile, someone rearranged the chairs in a big circle to allow for general sharing of information and experiences.

"Come and sit here," said Dominic, indicating a place next to him. Effie sat down and counted. Twenty-six people whose lives were being ruined by this evil disease.

"Are you lonely?" asked Dominic.

Effie frowned. She was, in a way. "Yes. I mean, I go out, I have friends, things to do, but..." she began.

"Emotionally lonely, I mean?" prompted Dominic.

She didn't reply for a moment. She thought about Matt. She'd had over three years of love and romance with him. Meeting in exotic places for extraordinary experiences. She'd felt no guilt about the affair. Matt had lifted her out of an emotional desert. In the beginning, she hadn't known that Lionel was ill. She didn't know there was a medical reason for his personality change. All she knew, as did everyone else, was that Lionel had become thoroughly unpleasant. If it hadn't been for Matt making her feel loved for a while, making her feel good about herself, she might have left Lionel. Who knows? Maybe Lionel had Matt to thank for her continued caring services.

Now that she knew why Lionel was so horrible, everything was different. Not in practice, of course. He was still horrible, but she knew that it wasn't his fault. And that made an enormous difference. And now that it was all over with Matt, she did feel lonely. So she said, "Yes, I am."

"You're probably lonelier than if you lived on your own," said Dominic.

"Maybe." Enough of herself. "What about you? Your wife has FTD?"

He nodded.

"And are you lonely?"

He shrugged. "There's no emotional nourishment. No intellectual stimulation. No physical affection. Not even ordinary touching." Suddenly he put his hand on her forearm. "I mean, not even like this."

Effie froze. It was so unexpected.

"Welcome everybody!" announced Natalie.

Dominic removed his hand.

Natalie continued. "And an especial welcome to our new members, Effie Butler..."

Effie nodded and smiled.

"...Joseph Andrews and Stella Markham," completed Natalie. She asked if anyone would like to start the session by asking a question.

Effie raised a hand.

"Yes, Effie?" said Natalie.

"How does it end?" she asked. "How does an FTD patient actually die?" This was something she had tried to ask Lionel's psychiatrist, but Dr Hazan had avoided the issue. He had said the disease was degenerative. He had said there was no cure. He had prescribed medication that might improve the symptoms, but he said nothing about the future. And given that she had never seen Dr Hazan without Lionel being there, she had never been able to probe further. She had read about the disease, but she wanted someone to actually tell her face to face what was going to happen.

This time, she got a straight answer.

Natalie Dryden said that if the disease continued to its natural end, the long-term prognosis was total incapacity. The last thing to fail would be the brain's control of the swallowing mechanism, in which case the patient would starve to death unless fed artificially by a tube directly into the stomach. She said that many patients became so ill they died of other things before it got to that stage. Pneumonia, for example. Respiratory pneumonia, in particular.

"What's that?" asked someone.

"With the weakening of the swallowing mechanism, food can get sucked into the lungs and cause infection."

There were more questions. One woman was utterly exhausted dealing with her incontinent husband and was looking for a carer to spend the night occasionally and give her a few hours' respite.

"You need to insist that Social Services recommend a carer experienced with FTD," pointed out a man from across the room.

The woman's shoulders slumped. "Social Services!" she spluttered. "At the moment..." She was sobbing now and fishing a handkerchief from her bag. "...Sorry..."

The group waited patiently. They were evidently used to people crying.

The woman took a deep breath and continued. "The way things are going I just want to find any carer, of any kind, from anywhere, at any price. If I don't get a night's sleep I'm going to..." She sobbed again and blew her nose. "I don't know how it can go on like this."

There were further questions. Natalie invited a final comment.

Effie raised her hand. "I feel I have no status. I'm not married in the sense of having a partner with whom I can share a social life. The couples who used to invite us out have all dropped us because they can't cope with Lionel's rudeness. Not even his brother will see us. I don't blame them. Lionel is very unpleasant. I have other friends. I have a social life of my own. In many ways I lead the life of a widow or a divorcee, except I'm not."

A woman to Effie's left contributed. "I know exactly how you feel," she said. "Divorcees and widows might live on their own," she said, "but at least they know where they are in the scheme of things. People are nice to widows." She laughed. "I've a friend who's been recently widowed. Her neighbour came round and power-washed her patio for her. And another one mows her lawn. She's quite capable of mowing a lawn herself! Can you imagine anyone doing that for an FTD-wife?"

Dominic put in his view. "If I were a widower or a divorcee I could join singles groups, or go on singles holidays. But if I did that now I wouldn't fit in."

Another man had a point to make. "People avoid me because they're embarrassed. My wife's old friends don't like asking after her. And they feel guilty that they no longer have anything to do with her. Sometimes I spot one of them out in the street, shopping perhaps, but she'll avoid eye contact and hurry away. I don't blame them, but it hurts."

Yes, thought Effie. These people here understand. They live in the same world as me. It's called FTD-Land.

Natalie closed the meeting. "I've booked a table at La Trattoria for those of you who might like to go for lunch like you did last time. It's only a five-minute walk away."

Dominic turned to Effie. "Coming?" he said.

The table was downstairs in the restaurant, and of the twenty-six who were in the meeting fourteen took their places at a long table. Effie ended up opposite a young man who was attending the meeting because his father had the disease. "I'm not a full-time carer," he said, "but I move in from time to time to give Mum a chance to get away."

What a dutiful son! thought Effie.

"And it's good for me to come here to improve my understanding of the disease," he added.

Next to her was a man who introduced himself as Ivan. "Hello, Ivan," Effie said. "Do you care for your wife?" she checked.

"Well, I did, but she died five years ago."

"Oh... but..." began Effie, surprised. Why was he still attending the group meeting? she wondered.

He must have guessed her thoughts, because he said, "You're never free of it, you know. It's always with you."

Dominic was sitting on the opposite side of the table, a couple of seats down. There were women either side of him and women opposite. "What they never discuss at these meetings," he said, "is the effect it has on a marriage. They all assume that just because we're carers, we're dutiful and faithful spouses as well."

"And you're not!" laughed one of the women next to him.

"Yes, I am," he said. "But if I did... stray, I mean... it would have to be with someone who knew about FTD. No one normal could ever understand me."

He had a point, thought Effie. Her affair with Matt had been virtually ended by Lionel's diagnosis. Once she'd understood why Lionel was so impossible, her whole life had been taken over by it. She went to meetings about dementia, she read books about dementia and she watched films about dementia. She ploughed through stuff on the internet. It was as though her mind had been invaded by the subject and normal thought processes had been smothered. Lionel was unchanged by the diagnosis itself, but it had changed her. Her conversation, whatever that subject was, would always lead back to some aspect of Lionel's illness.

Boring!

She must be so boring.

That last time she saw Matt. That day in London, when he'd flown to

Europe for a whistle-stop meeting with a publisher, he'd still managed to find time for lunch with her. There were two things that had gone wrong.

One was that she had developed a new sense of guilt about infidelity. She knew that Lionel's unpleasantness was caused by sickness. And what do the marriage vows say about sickness? *In sickness and in health...* You are supposed to put up with it.

And the other thing was her conversation. She had told Matt about Lionel, at length. The doctor and the psychiatrist. The research initiatives and the protein changes in the brain. The short-term probabilities and the long-term prognosis. The obsessions and communication difficulties, and the incidents with the police.

Matt had made sympathetic noises, and then when she'd paused for breath he'd taken her hand and had said. "Effie, I've won a major U.S. literary prize for *Endless Wilderness*."

Effie had stared at him, suddenly ashamed. She had been so self-absorbed that she hadn't asked him a single thing about himself. She'd paused. Then, "Congratulations!" she'd said with a broad smile. "That's brilliant! What's it about?"

"I sent you a copy," he had said flatly. "Didn't you read it?"

And now, here in London, with Matt the other side of the world, this stranger, Dominic Darnfield, who was on his second glass of wine and was evidently utterly frustrated by a sick marriage and wanting to do something about it, was publicly admitting that an affair with a woman who was not an inhabitant of FTD-Land was not viable. He could see what Effie had discovered: that when it came to love and romance, no one normal could relate to an FTD Carer.

What had it all come to? Where were they all going?

Well, for the time being, they were all going home to their so-called *loved ones*. Their *carees*. Some of them left promptly in order to relieve paid carers. Dominic, who had been ignoring the bleeping of his smartphone during the course of the meal, finally responded to it. "Yes... Yes... A bus stop?" he said. "What bus stop?" He paused and listened. "Opposite Marks and Spencer's? Which Marks and Spencer's? OK, stay there, and I'll come and find you."

He closed the call.

He looked at his audience and shook his head despairingly. "She's lost again. I think she might have got on the right bus but in the wrong direction." He touched the screen, looked at it, and passed the phone across. "See, that blob is my wife. At least it's the person who used to be my wife. Now she's a blob."

Effie peered at the street map on the screen. The technology was amazing. "So you always know where she is?"

"She's got a GPS tracker in her handbag. So unless she loses her handbag, which does happen, then yes, I know where she is."

They picked up their coats and headed into the street.

"You taking the Northern Line?" he asked. Effie found herself hurrying to keep up with him as he ushered her across four lines of busy traffic. In the tube, she took the last available seat and he stood in front of her. He took a business card from his pocket and gave it her. "Email me," he said. "Keep in touch. We both need all the FTD pals we can get."

Effie's stop was first. She got up and extended her hand. "See you next time," he said as they shook hands.

CHAPTER 26

You Stink!

Lionel is looking for something. He has made his breakfast mug of coffee and has taken it to his usual place in the living room. But something is missing. He has gone back into the kitchen and is opening and closing things. The fridge door. A cupboard door. A cutlery drawer.

Effie has followed him. "Can I help?" she asks.

"No," he snaps. He doesn't like her interfering.

Then he changes his mind. "We need more bananas," he says.

Effie looks at him. "We?" she checks. "I don't. You should have said. I only went out this morning."

Lionel frowns. What is she getting at? "There aren't any," he says. Each morning he has half a banana with his breakfast mug of coffee and today there aren't any.

"I'll go out and get some," says Effie.

Lionel sighs. He'd like to go himself. He used to enjoy going out in his Jaguar to buy things he needed. Now he can't.

The phone rings and Effie picks it up. She listens. Then, "That's great," she says. "We'll be there at about eleven thirty. Bye now."

She puts the receiver back in its cradle and smiles at Lionel. "Your new specs are ready. I'll take you to pick them up."

Lionel looks at the phone. "It hasn't clicked," he says. She hasn't put it back properly. Again. He notices things like that.

She jiggles the receiver and it clicks into place.

"Who was that?" he asks.

"I told you. The optician. Your specs are ready. We can go and pick them up. And we can get some bananas while we're out."

Lionel looks at his watch. "Christ!" he said. "It's half past ten now!"

"That's okay. We've got plenty of time. And your watch is always fifteen minutes fast anyway."

Lionel frowns. He doesn't like being rushed. He likes things to be planned and put in his diary.

"I'll get the car out," says Effie.

Lionel gets ready. First, he changes his slippers for his shoes which he keeps next to the patio doors. Then he goes to check that the back door is locked. Then he picks up his keys off the right-hand hook by the front door. His money and credit cards are in his back pocket, his cigarettes and a lighter in his right-hand coat pocket, and his Ventolin puffer in his left-hand coat pocket.

Effie has picked up her own keys from the left-hand hook, and is getting her car out of the garage.

Lionel follows, carefully locking the front door. He opens the passenger door and levers himself in. "Fuck!" he says as he knocks his elbow. "Fucking stupid car you bought," he says. "We need a bigger one."

"Maybe we do," says Effie. She starts up and reverses into the road.

"You should go out forwards," he says. "Safer."

"Not necessarily," she says.

It isn't far. Effie slows down to park in a space at the top of the High Street. "Can't you drop me off?" Lionel asks. He doesn't want to walk all that way.

"I can't park nearer, and I need to go with you," Effie says.

"You could get a tank in there," he remarks as she struggles to get the car into the space.

He unfolds his legs, hauls himself out of the car and lights a cigarette. He feels a bit wobbly at first, but he soon settles. Effie takes his arm and hurries him down the road towards the pedestrian crossing.

"What's the hurry!" he says breathlessly.

They cross the road. "Just a minute," he says when they reach the opticians. He takes two more puffs of his cigarette, puts it out, then puts the unused half back in the box for later.

"Sit down," says the optician. "Would you like a coffee?"

"Yeah, okay," says Lionel.

Effie says, "No thank you. Not for me."

There is a plate of biscuits on the coffee table, a selection that doesn't include fig rolls. Lionel takes one and bites at it. He grimaces, puts it back, and takes another. Effie glares at him. Philip pulls up a chair and sits next to Lionel. "Now let's just take these off," he says, and he leans forward to remove Lionel's glasses. Then he takes another pair out of a packet, and is about to put them on Lionel. But Lionel doesn't want that. He snatches at them. "I'll do it!" he snaps, and puts them on. He looks around. He peers at all the different people in the shop.

"What are they like?" asks the optician.

"Load of idiots," says Lionel.

Philip suppresses a smile and says, "I meant the specs. Can you see all right?"

"Don't know."

"Look across through the window. Can you see the no parking sign? Does it look clear?" Then Philip hands him a card with large printing at the top and small at the bottom. "Can you read this?" he asks.

"'Course I can!" reacts Lionel. "I'm not stupid."

"Even the bottom?" checks Philip.

Lionel frowns. "No, 'course not! No one can read stuff that small! That's stupid!"

Effie leans across. "What about that paragraph?" she suggests, pointing.

Lionel follows her finger and reads some words aloud.

Philip nods. "That's probably as good as it gets," he says. "Now let's check the fit."

He leans closer and raises a hand to check the glasses.

Lionel can smell something. Sweet. Sickly. Cloying. Is it Philip? Suddenly pushes Philip's hand away from him. "Yuk! You stink!"

Philip leaps back like he's been slapped in the face.

Everyone in the shop turns away, pretending not to have heard.

"Lionel," Effie says gently. "Nothing smells. And you can't say things like that to anyone."

Philip frowns and looked at his hands. Sniffs at his hands. "It could only be soap," he says.

"It's not what he can smell, it's the way his brain perceives it," Effie says. "It's part of the illness."

Lionel glares at her. "I'm not ill," he says.

Philip raises his hand again to check the fit of the glasses.

"Get off!" says Lionel "They're fine. "I don't need you effing about with me."

Effie stands up. "I'm sure they're all right," she says in that especially calm voice of hers. "We'd better go. Thank you so much, Philip. I am so sorry."

"Bring him back in a year," says Philip.

Effie leans towards Philip and mutters something to him confidentially. "If he lasts that long," Lionel thinks she says.

CHAPTER 27

No Bananas

As they left Fairvue Opticians Effie took Lionel's arm again. "We need to get bananas and I need to post a parcel. It's Alicia's birthday."

"Who's Alicia?" said Lionel.

"Nigel's little girl! One of your granddaughters, Lionel. You don't have to remember their birthdays, but you could try and remember their names!" Even as she said it she realised she was breaking a golden rule of dementia caring. You should never comment on a dementia sufferer's failure to remember. Phrases such as 'I just told you' or, 'Can't you remember?' are absolute no-nos

"Oh, *that* Alicia," said Lionel.

They reached the Co-op. "We'll just pop in here. It won't take a minute," said Effie. Her hand was on his arm and she ushered him through the automatic doors.

The post office in Dalton Heath was inside the Co-op.

Lionel hesitated. "I don't like it in here," he said. "I'll wait outside."

"Don't be silly," she said, puzzled at his reluctance. "Look, I'll get in the post office queue. You buy some bananas." She picked up a wire shopping basket and put a bunch of bananas in it. "Now get in that queue. Have you got some money?

"Of course I have!" he reacted.

"Good. When you've paid for them wait for me right here. Understand? Don't go anywhere else."

Effie joined the post office queue. It was longer than she expected. She was on edge. 'You stink!' her mind echoed. How could he say such a thing? What had Lionel smelled? FTD had changed Lionel's sense of taste. Why not his sense of smell too? Philip Alvarez, with his crisply ironed shirt and his spotless white jeans, was more meticulous about personal hygiene than most men. Perhaps also more creative in his use of items such as deodorants and aftershave. Was it the perfume Lionel had perceived as so distasteful?

Effie reached the front of the queue. The cashier weighed her packages, stamped them and took them across the counter for posting.

"Thank you," she said, and headed for the entrance to the shop. Now, where was Lionel? He wasn't waiting where she'd told him. He'd probably gone out for a cigarette. She looked outside. No sign of him.

She went back inside to speak to the cashier. "I'm sorry to bother you," she said, "but I've lost my husband. He was buying some bananas and I told him to wait just there while I was in the post office. Have you seen him?"

There was an awkward silence.

"He's wearing a..."

Another of the cashiers spoke. It seemed to be the senior of the three on duty. "Yes, we have seen him, but we didn't serve him. We had to ask him to leave as he's been banned from entering the premises."

Effie's heart sunk. Oh no! Not another one! Would she never learn? She could have kicked herself. No way should she have tried to fit in posting that parcel in the same trip as picking up Lionel's specs. One thing at a time. And no way should she have let him out of her sight.

"Why? What has he done?" she asked. Effie remembered that a year or so ago he came home with one of their wire baskets. It was on the floor in the hall and he didn't know why it was there. That was pre-diagnosis, of course, but she'd taken back the basket, given the assistant manager their phone number and warned them about Lionel. Evidently the information hadn't been noted.

"He's been abusive to customers and staff. And he frightens children. He goes up close to them and... I don't know... makes faces... growling, roaring... snarling..."

"Hmmm," Effie said wryly. "Pretending to be a monster, I suppose, or a lion. His idea of a joke." She sighed. It was no joke. Not anymore. "Can you tell me how long ago he was banned?"

"I don't know. Would you like to see the manager? I'm sure it's all on file."

Yes, it would be. How many files in this town contained information about Lionel's behaviour? Effie hesitated. She needed to find Lionel. He might be getting into more trouble. "Could I phone when I get home? What's your manager's name?"

Lionel was at home. He was at his table doing a Sudoku and chewing a fig roll biscuit. Round and round his jaws went. There was biscuity dribble on his jumper. Why couldn't he just swallow it? Effie knew the answer, of course. His swallowing mechanism was weakening and it wasn't his fault.

"Hello love," Effie asked. "All right?"

He nodded. "Where've you been?" he demanded.

She carefully avoided saying, 'Don't you remember?' "We picked up your glasses," she said, "then I posted my parcel for Alicia."

She avoided asking him how he got back and said, "I expect you got a taxi, didn't you?"

He nodded.

"Very sensible," she said.

And then she made the mistake of asking a direct question. "Why didn't you wait for me?"

She knew the answer anyway. What was the point of asking?

He shrugged and grunted.

"Did you get the bananas?" Another stupid question. Why did she keep doing it?

"No," grunted Lionel.

She didn't ask why. There was no need. "Never mind," she said lightly. "I'll pick some up later." Bananas were one of Lionel's food obsessions and she tried to make sure they didn't run out.

What she did later was phone the manager of the Dalton Heath Co-op. "Can you tell me what happened?" she asked when she'd introduced herself. At least he didn't come up with banal excuses about customer confidentiality and the like. He described how he'd first seen Lionel walking aimlessly around the shop looked confused. "Can I help you?" he'd asked.

Lionel had replied with something like, "No. I'm not effing stupid." Only 'effing' wasn't the only expletive he used.

"That didn't bother me," said the manager, "but when he started abusing my staff and customers, I decided that enough was enough."

Effie explained about frontotemporal dementia. It was a speech she was getting used to delivering. "He can't help it," she finished. "It's not his fault." She could do with a tape recording of all this. Lionel did carry a card saying he had dementia, but it would never occur to him to show it to anyone. Perhaps he could wear a notice around his neck, or ring a warning bell like the lepers of mediaeval times.

"Thank you for explaining it to me," said the manager. "I don't know how you cope."

"With difficulty," she said. That had become her standard reply too. Then she asked, "Can you tell me when all this started?"

"Mmmm. Two or three months ago."

Effie sighed. "He's been on medication since before then. It doesn't seem to be working as well as I'd hoped." She paused. "Look Mr Matthews, I'll discourage him from using the store, but of course, I can't actually stop him. But do make a note of my number and if you have any problems you can call me and I'll come and get him. Or you can call the police. The community police officer who knows him is Mo Gorringe. You're not the first organisation in Dalton Heath to have problems with my husband."

"Yes, I know," said the manager.

When the call was over, Effie frowned, puzzled. How did he know?

Then she went out to buy some bananas.

CHAPTER 28

It Takes Two

Once you have a diagnosis of dementia, Effie discovered, although they couldn't offer a cure, or maybe *because* they couldn't offer a cure, they did try and keep an eye on you. All sorts of people started turning up at the house.

One day two nice firemen came to visit. Effie was impressed. Tall and hunky, which is how firemen should be. Joe was blonde with blue eyes and Mick was dark and swarthy with brown eyes. They told her that the two smoke alarms that she had fitted herself, were in the wrong place. So Mick fitted four more.

That made six. Does a house this size really need six smoke alarms? pondered Effie.

Then Joe gave Effie a lesson on how to avoid setting the house on fire. Things like not leaving hair dryers plugged in, and keeping all inside doors closed at night. She didn't tell him that her demented husband smoked regularly in his bedroom. That would have upset the poor man dreadfully.

He also suggested she plan her and Lionel's escape route should they fail to prevent the house burning down.

"Well, I suppose I could climb out of the bedroom window onto the garage roof," said Effie. "It'd be nice if someone big and strong could catch me," she smiled provocatively.

"And Lionel's escape route?" asked Joe flatly.

Effie shrugged. "I'd have to think about that," she said. "The thing is, is he really worth rescuing?"

Joe looked shocked. "I can't believe you really mean that, Mrs Butler," he said. There was a definite reproach in his tone.

Effie smiled, "Can't you?" she said. Her smile broadened to a grin. "That was a joke," she said. "I think."

A week later Effie set off the new fire alarm in the hall by burning the potatoes in the kitchen.

"What's that fucking noise?" shouted Lionel. "Turn it off!"

The other five alarms remained in virgin condition, but Effie's concern was that if Lionel did drop a cigarette and start a fire, he wouldn't realise what the offensively shrill bleeping was. He'd curse and swear at the noise but he wouldn't do anything.

Joe had said that they could, if she wished, be connected directly to the fire station. Would that mean calling a fire engine out every time she burned the potatoes? she'd wondered. She'd said she'd think about it.

A lady with a big power drill came to fit extra handrails on the stairs.

She loved her work, she said. So much variety. So many different people. The most important thing she'd learned from it, she told Effie, was that you never know what lies ahead and you must make the most of every day you've got. You must never say, 'There's always tomorrow.' There possibly isn't.

She'd also brought a step to make it easier for Lionel to get into the shower. She seemed to think that he'd have difficulty stepping over the rim of the shower tray.

"Thank you very much," said Effie, "but it's months since he had a shower."

The next person who visited wanted Lionel to wear a press-button rescue device around his neck.

"No thank you," Lionel said, quite politely.

There followed an explanation of how useful it would be if Lionel were to fall down the stairs when Effie was out. He'd be able to press the button and get help.

"No," said Lionel, this time without the 'thank you'. "I don't fall downstairs," he added.

"Now, what about a GPS tracker?" was the next suggestion. "You keep it in your pocket when you're out, so that your wife could find you if you got lost."

"I don't get lost," said Lionel, "but I wish you bloody well would!" he added.

Lionel was considered stable. The medication had calmed him a little and there was nothing further they could do for him. That meant Dr Hazan would see him every six months but in between they would send a community psychiatric nurse (CPN) to 'monitor progress'. Or maybe lack of progress. In due course, a CPN phoned.

"I can't get him up that early," Effie said when an appointment of half past nine the following Thursday was suggested. Two thirty was the next proposal, but Effie explained that that would interfere with Lionel's afternoon nap, which was sacrosanct. So they settled for eleven o'clock on Friday. That seemed a suitable window of availability.

When the CPN rang the doorbell, Lionel was already settled at his table at the end of the living room with his coffee and his banana and his fig rolls. He was looking at the daily paper. His Sudoku book was open. His blue rollerball pen was in his hand.

Effie opened the front door.

Her name, the CPN said, was Sheryl Basvar. She was of Asian origin, but her accent was estuary English.

"Come in," Effie said. "Did you find us all right?" She showed her through to the living room and introduced her to Lionel.

"Hello Mr Butler," she said as she shook hands with him. "May I call you Lionel?"

He shrugged. "Don't care," he said.

"How are you?" she asked.

A bad start, Effie noted. Sheryl Basvar was a qualified CPN so she was supposed to know that asking dementia patients direct questions was a mistake.

Effie made her a coffee, and initially Sheryl Basvar sat on the sofa from which she could see Lionel. She took a notebook from her bag.

Effie sat on the opposite sofa. "Come and sit with me," she called to Lionel. "You can't talk to Sheryl from over there." He shuffled across from his table and sat beside her.

"How are you feeling?" Sheryl asked him.

"Average," he said. His customary answer.

"And what does 'average' mean?" she asked.

"Oh for fuck's sake!" he reacted.

Effie was inclined to agree with him. "Lionel doesn't respond well to direct questions," she said.

She asked him another direct question. "How are you getting on with the medication Dr Hazan prescribed?"

He looked puzzled. Effie knew he wasn't aware of new medication. He looked at her to answer.

"The family find him calmer," Effie said.

Sheryl made notes. She had boxes to tick, Effie thought.

"How do you spend your time?" was the next unsuitable question.

He shrugged and grimaced and looked askance at Effie once more.

Effie patted him on the knee. "Lionel's very good at Sudoku puzzles," she said. "He's also an excellent bridge player but he only plays on a computer these days."

"Really?" Sheryl said. "Why's that?"

Effie glared at her, while Lionel said, "They fucking chucked me out."

"And he likes TV," continued Effie quickly. "He looks at the *Radio Times* every day and marks up programmes he's going to watch." Effie looked at him. "Crosswords?" she said. "You don't do them so much now, do you?"

"Do you go out much?" Sheryl asked.

"Of course I do," he said.

She wrote in her notebook. "Where do you go?" was the next question.

He shrugged. "Shopping."

"What sort of things do you buy?"

"This is so boring," Lionel said. He stood up and went back to his table and his Sudoku puzzle.

"He's not able to drive now," Effie explained. "So I take him to Boots to pick up his medication. I drop him off and he gets a taxi back. He could walk to Ratigans Chemists by the Parkside Health Centre, but he's been excluded from going there."

"Excluded!" she echoed. "Why's that?"

"You could ask them," Effie suggested. "They won't tell me. I'm only his wife and carer. Apparently it's none of my business." This woman was really winding her up.

Sheryl Basvar turned towards Lionel and said. "What about

Dunfords? It has a pharmacy, doesn't it? That's near you."

"He won't be able to hear you from there," said Effie. "You'd better go and sit at his table of you want to interrogate him."

That's was what she should have made her do at the beginning.

"I'm not interrogating him!" the CPN protested. But she crossed the room to sit at Lionel's table.

"He's been banned from Dunfords too," Effie said quietly as she walked past.

Sheryl pointed to a photo of the grandchildren on the window sill. "Who are they?" she asked Lionel.

Wrong again. She should have said something like, "They look nice."

"Isn't it time you left?" he said.

She forced a smile. "Nearly. I just want to get to know you a bit better."

Lionel was into the Sudoku now. Effie almost felt sorry for poor Sheryl. Except that she was supposed to understand how to communicate with FTD patients.

She made one more attempt. She leaned closer to him to look at his Sudoku book. "You must be very clever to do those," she said. "I think they're very difficult."

He screwed up his face at her. "When are you leaving?"

"I just need to talk to your wife for a few minutes." And she moved back to the sofa and wrote in her notebook. "It must be quite difficult for you," she said to Effie.

Effie didn't know whether that was an observation or a question. "You have no idea!" she said.

Sheryl looked up from her notebook as though waiting for Effie to elaborate, so she did. "Before the car was sold, I used to find little jobs for him. Go to the post office to post a parcel. Go to the bank to pay in a cheque. Take some garden rubbish to the dump. Now..."

"I mean personally," she said. "Your relationship?"

Effie laughed bitterly. "What relationship?"

"Well. Affection? Intimacy?"

Dear God! Did this woman have any concept of the effects of FTD? Did she have no idea of what revolting habits Lionel might have? "He moved into the spare room years ago."

"Why was that?" was the next question.

Effie's irritation with Sheryl Basvar was beginning to turn into distress. "I don't know." She felt that familiar lump in her throat. Her eyes were filling with tears.

Sheryl waited.

Effie had to say something. "I thought maybe he'd come back... from time to time..." she sobbed, "...maybe for a cuddle." She was crying now. "But he never did."

Her face was in her hands and she was weeping copiously. She didn't know why she was so upset, because the idea of sharing a bedroom, let alone a bed, with this person who used to be her husband, was utterly distasteful. Sharing a house was bad enough.

"It takes two, you know," said Sheryl Basvar.

"I know that..." Effie reacted.

Despite the tears, what she really felt was rage. How dare this woman talk to her like that! It takes two! Who did she think she was? An agony aunt with views about Effie's love life! A girl of that age! But all Effie could do was cry.

"That's right. Have a good cry," Sheryl said. "It's good to cry."

Lionel got up from his table and walked out. "I'm just going for a cigarette," he said.

Effie nodded through her tears, which he didn't appear to have noticed. Who said it was good to cry? she wondered. How patronising was that! They were wrong. Crying was horrible. Nothing about it was good.

Later, after Sheryl Basvar had gone, Lionel, unusually, sat beside Effie on the sofa. He took Effie's hand in his. "I didn't like her," he said.

"Neither did I," said Effie.

"She made you cry," he said.

Effie smiled. So he had noticed! She squeezed his hand.

He stroked Effie's shoulder. "My Effie," he said.

She gave him a hug. "My Lionel," she said. It takes two, she thought.

CHAPTER 29

Business Integrity

Ratigans Pharmacy, Effie noted crossly, had yet to reply to her letter. It must be the best part of a month now, she worked out. She opened her FTD file – it was getting very fat – and took out the copy of her letter.

Nine thirty should be a good time to phone. The office should be up and running and Lionel would still in bed so she could make her call in private. She dialled the number. She waited. There was a press-button menu and a lot of music, but finally she got to speak to a human being.

"Please may I speak to Janeene Jarman, your business integrity manager?" she asked.

"Who is it please?" asked the telephonist.

Effie was put through to Janeene Jarman's PA. The business integrity manager was in conference, she was told.

"My name is Frances Butler. I wrote a letter over month ago about my husband being excluded from Ratigans Pharmacy in Dalton Heath. I haven't had a reply and I wanted to find out if you had received the letter."

There was long pause. "Your husband is Lionel Butler?"

"Yes."

"Yes, we did receive your letter," said the PA. "We have replied to him about the matter."

"But the letter was from me. You should have replied to me! Please could I speak to Janeene Jarman?"

There was long pause, some hurried whispers, and a new managerial voice at end of the phone. "Good morning, Mrs Butler. Janeene Jarman speaking."

"I understand that you received my letter about my husband's exclusion from Ratigans Pharmacy, but that your reply has been sent to him."

"Yes. We cannot discuss your husband's affairs with you. That would be a breach of the Data Protection Act. We have explained the reasons for his exclusion to him."

"But... but... that's absurd... I'm his wife. I'm his carer!" protested Effie. "He can't read letters properly. He can't interpret them. He doesn't have the cognitive skills. There's no point in replying to him!"

"I'm sorry, Mrs Butler. It's a matter of confidentiality."

"What did he do?"

"I'm afraid I'm not permitted to tell you. Suffice it say that our staff are afraid of him. We have to protect them."

"And I have to protect him! How can I do that when I'm not allowed to know what he does?" Effie was allowing her voice to rise. Oh, how she wished she could remain calm and cool like these smooth manager types. "I have to deal with... everything... it's difficult enough to cope with a sick man without you people hiding behind your rules and regulations. I don't know how to..."

She felt that familiar lump in her throat. Damn, damn, damn! She was going to cry. She took a deep breath and swallowed hard but it didn't stop the tears coming.

"I understand your distress," was the oh-so-cool response.

"No, you don't!" Effie exploded. "Not unless you have a husband with FTD. Do you?" she demanded. "Do you have a husband with FTD?" She knew her voice was getting shriller. She was losing control. Breathe deeply, she said to herself. In through the nose, out through the mouth.

"No, but..."

"Then there is no way you could even begin to understand my distress," Effie reacted angrily. "How could you possibly? Nor could you understand how your ruthless and cruel attitude increases it. Or maybe you do. Maybe you just don't... care... I... I..."

The tears were flowing freely now. Effie couldn't speak any more. She hung up and she cried and she cried until she was all cried out.

When Lionel came downstairs she asked him if he'd received a letter from Ratigans Pharmacy.

"I don't go there anymore," he said. "Fucking idiots."

"I know, but did they write to you in the last few weeks?"

He frowned irritably. "No. Of course not!" he snapped.

She wrote another letter.

Lionel Butler : Exclusion from Ratigans Pharmacy

Dear Janeene Jarman

Further to our phone call I should like to inform you that my husband has no recollection of the letter you say you sent him. It may not have arrived or he may have received it and forgotten about it. As you know, he has Frontotemporal Dementia.

You say that the staff at the pharmacy are frightened of him. I find this beyond belief. They do not work alone. They work behind a shop counter which is reasonable protection. My husband is indeed very unpleasant, but that is not illegal. He does not carry a weapon. As the staff must know from his prescription list, in addition to FTD, he has chronic heart failure and lung disease which

renders him frail and thus unlikely to be violent. He has never hit anyone. Are
they frightened of a few rude words?

Ratigans is in the business of supplying sick people with medication. That is how
you make your money. When one sick patient's symptoms are not to your liking it
is discriminatory to refuse to serve him with the very medications that may help
relieve those symptoms. He has been prescribed something to calm him down.
Please would you give him another chance?

It would have been courteous of you to reply to my earlier letter and to address the
reply to me rather than him, given that the letter was signed by me. I hope you will
do that with this one.

Regards

Frances Butler (Mrs)

Writing the letter was curiously therapeutic. But it didn't stop her
being angry. The total lack of flexibility of Ratigans Pharmacy
disgusted her. Even if they relented now, she'd avoid going there
again. The whole thing had become a matter of principle. She
addressed an envelope and put the letter inside. She'd post it next
time she went out.

It was lunchtime and Effie looked into the dining room. Lionel was
seated at the dining room table eating his lunch. He was watching the
BBC News while looking at the *Radio Times* with a magnifying glass.
He was not, Effie noted, playing bridge on his laptop.

A small green light indicated that machine was on, but the blue
screensaver image was corrupted and the screen was no longer
propped up against the Coca-Cola bottle.

"What's happened to your computer?" Effie asked.

"It doesn't work," he said.

Effie leaned over the table and pressed a few keys. He was right. It
was hardly surprising. The screen had been connected to the

keyboard by a mere thread for ages. "When did it finally pack up?" she asked.

"I don't know!" he reacted irritably.

Effie unplugged it. "I'll see if I can get it repaired," she said brightly. If he couldn't play bridge on a computer, his already limited life would be restricted further.

He smiled at her and said three words that took her completely by surprise: "Thank you, Effie."

When he'd gone for his afternoon nap Effie put the whole lot, charger and all, into a shopping bag and drove into town. She took it to the laptop repair shop in the High Street to see if anything could resurrect it. "It's only used for one particular program," she explained. "My husband plays bridge on it. I can see it's just one electrical connection that's broken. He dropped it."

As Effie expected, it was far too old. "No way could we get the parts," said the sales assistant. "We've got a good deal on a new one. Much faster machine. Much better graphics. It's Internet ready."

It didn't need to be faster, or better, or Internet ready. It just needed to play bridge. Effie showed them the CD on which the bridge program had originally been supplied. "Would you be able to load this onto it? That's all I want it for."

The assistant considered the matter and went to consult his superior who did a lot of clicking and looking at stuff online. Not once did he make eye contact with Effie. "You could buy a more modern version of the program," was the conclusion. "They don't supply them on CDs anymore, but you could download it from the website."

"Could you do that for me?"

"It's easy," he said, "All you have to do is..."

"Good. In that case, please do it and I'll buy the machine, but I don't want to have to do any downloading myself."

Effie had a view that the first law of computing is that anything you try always takes ten times as long as you think it will. So if possible, get someone else to do it.

It took another twenty minutes for the sales assistant to get it ready. "Your licence allows you to install the program on three different computers," he said.

Effie smiled. One computer would be fine. "Now, can I see how it works?" she asked. She was not walking out of that shop without knowing that the computer had a working bridge program on it.

She clicked on the icon. Yes. It looked like the program Lionel used. Same colours. Same layout as far as she could remember. She played a clumsy hand of bridge, bid a contract and failed to make it, but that wasn't the point.

"Yes. That all seems okay," she said. "You can recycle the old one."

When she got home she put the new laptop on the dining room table.

"I've got a replacement bridge game for you," she said when Lionel woke up. "Come and see."

He looked suspicious. The laptop was smaller, a different colour, and the on-off switch was in a different place. Effie switched in on and they watched it power up.

"Look," Effie said. "You just click on there to start up."

The graphic images showed the dealing of the first hand. Effie watched Lionel consider it. "What do you think?" he said. "One spade to open?" His assessment of the hand was instant and he finished in three no trumps. He played that hand as slickly as ever and made an overtrick.

Then he stood up. "Aren't you going to play another hand?" Effie asked.

"Maybe later," he said.

"Is the program okay?" she asked.

"Yes, it's fine," he said.

He went back to the living room and settled down with his Sudoku book.

And as far as Effie knew he never touched that new laptop again.

The reply to her letter to Ratigans took over three weeks to arrive. By the time it did she had written three letters to the press about Ratigans' attitude to this country's so-called *Dementia-Friendly Society*. One to a national paper, one to a local paper, and one to the Alzheimer's Magazine. None was published.

The basic message from Janeene Jarman was that that unless Effie could accompany her husband, *the original Exclusion Order will remain in force*. This, apparently, was necessary to *provide a safe working environment for our staff and customers*.

Safe! Lionel wasn't a danger to anyone! If he were, he'd have been sectioned.

I trust this matter can be resolved for the benefit of both you and your husband in the near future.

No, it was not resolved! Lionel was going have to carry on getting taxis to Boots when he could have had a gentle walk up the road.

May I take this opportunity to thank you for your cooperation?

No, the bitch couldn't. No way would Effie cooperate. She went straight upstairs and wrote a reply.

Dear Janeene Jarman

Further to your letter of 19ᵗʰ May, I was only asking if my husband could be given a second chance now that he is on a medication that calms him.

As for your closing line thanking me for my cooperation – I am not cooperating. I am so upset that I am writing to everyone I can think of in order to publicise Ratigans' appalling attitude to the mentally ill.

Your manageress, Davina Wallace, told me that Ratigans Pharmacy only delivers to the housebound. I don't know your definition of 'housebound', but it's nice to know that as my husband's disease progresses we will have that to look forward to.

Regards

Frances Butler (Mrs)

CHAPTER 30

Crisis Time

Crisis time is here again... hummed Effie.

Another year over. *We wish you a merry crisis, we wish you a merry crisis... a disastrous new year...*

The only good thing about Christmas, thought Effie, was that it brought January just that bit nearer. And in January she had flights booked to Berlin. She was just longing to see Nigel and the children.

The end of a year is always a time to reflect on what has happened in the past twelve months and what might happen in the next. Who would be born and who would die? Maybe they were the only questions that really mattered.

As for the future, such as how she would cope if and when Lionel's condition deteriorated, she had no idea. The advice of the dementia course she'd attended was to 'be prepared'. Don't wait for a crisis, they said. Learn about available support services *before* you need them. So she'd visited a number of the local care homes and tried to imagine if Lionel could ever fit into such establishments. The crunch, she'd decided, would be the smoking situation. The significance of this hit her when she was visiting Highgrove Manor, a residential home that was said to specialise in dementia. While the manageress, who reminded her of Hattie Jacques in the Carry On films, was showing Effie around the establishment and explaining its merits, her sales pitch was momentarily interrupted. A stooped and shrivelled little man sidled anxiously up to her. His hands were shaking and pulling at her sleeve. His mouth was drooping and unable to form the words he needed.

"Yes, Harry?" smiled the manageress with benign magnificence. "I'll get you your two cigarettes in a minute." She took a small breath and made a minimal pause. "And this is our day room," she continued to Effie. "Lovely room, isn't it?"

What a way to treat an adult! thought Effie. Perhaps that was what ageing was about. A reversion to childhood.

To smoke a cigarette, residents had to ask permission and go outside into the garden under supervision. Effie could understand the health and safety difficulties of allowing demented residents (*inmates*, Effie was tempted to think) loose with matches and lighters. But where did it leave those poor residents?

A Fundamental Truth: A smoker is always waiting for his or her next cigarette.

When a smoker has a cigarette, he is content for twenty minutes or so. Then he starts thinking about the next cigarette. Or worse, worrying about whether he will have the opportunity to smoke it. That worry is a permanent source of stress. There's nothing you can do about it. Okay, so he shouldn't be a smoker. But he is. That's the way it is.

No way would Effie send Lionel to one of those places.

What Effie was prepared to do, was to use a care company to check up on Lionel when she went away. Her visits to Berlin a couple of times a year. The house in Spain from time to time. And hopefully there would be other opportunities to travel. Who knew? But she did know that from now on she couldn't risk leaving Lionel totally on his own. So she arranged for the manager of Primacare to come and assess him.

"Please to meet you," said the manager to Lionel. "I'm Andrew Hoskins, but most people called me Andy."

"Andy Pandy," said Lionel. "Where's Looby Loo!"

Andy Hoskins was a short, slightly overweight gentleman with a perfectly smooth bald head that looked as though it had been polished.

They shook hands.

The manager went through a questionnaire about Lionel's needs and medication, all of which Effie answered. At one point Lionel got up to walk out of the room, but as he passed Andy Hoskins he stopped, grinned, and ran his left hand gently over the shiny bald head. "Humpty Dumpty sat on a wall..." he began.

Andy, totally unfazed, smiled benignly and continued with, "Humpty Dumpty had a great fall."

Lionel laughed. "All the king's horses..." he recited. Then he stopped and shrugged. "Can't remember the rest," he said cheerfully.

The dreaded C-word crept up on them. Effie sent and received fewer Christmas cards than in the past, but she didn't mind. There were fewer to hang on ribbons and trail untidily on the door frames and banisters. She got out their artificial Christmas tree from the cupboard under the stairs. She had bought it when both Suzie and Nigel had first left home, and she had put it away ready-decorated with lights in place, so there was nothing whatsoever to do but put it on a table and plug it in. Very convenient, but she couldn't help but miss the delight of children dressing a Christmas tree. She remembered painting holly and sticking glitter on egg boxes. Joyful, but messy. Perhaps, though, she was reminiscing through rose-tinted glasses.

"That's nice," said Lionel when she switched the lights on. She hadn't expected him to notice and she felt a surge of pleasure that was almost Christmassy. He took her hand. "My Effie," he said. She wondered if he were reminiscing too, but she had no way of knowing.

They spent Christmas Day with Suzie and family again. Only this time they went in one car and nobody got lost. They went a little later than Effie would have chosen and they left considerably earlier to get back in time for Lionel's afternoon nap. But Effie felt curiously relaxed about the compromise. Nothing mattered very much, she had grown used to thinking. Most things don't matter at all.

Lionel's appetite was reduced and his ability to eat properly had deteriorated in the past twelve months. Suzie sat him on the same side of the table as her, but separated by two children. Effie suspected that was so Suzie wouldn't have to watch her father eat, which was not a pretty sight. One of the side effects, or perhaps symptoms, of FTD is a loss in efficiency of the swallowing mechanism. That does nothing for table manners. At one point Lionel got up from the table. "I'm just going to talk to the chickens," he said.

"He's gone for a cigarette," said Effie. He'd be standing in the garden by the chicken run having a smoke. At least it wasn't raining.

"Grampa likes the chickens," remarked Cameron.

So Christmas was okay. There were no crises. Effie realised she'd reached a time in her life when if there were no crises she was having a good time.

She had a Christmas card from Matt together with a copy of his latest book, hot off the press. A travel book that included a chapter about the River Amazon. She recognised a photo of the alligator that had lurked between the lily pads and she wondered if it was still alive. Maybe it had grown.

The card's message was *A Merry Christmas and Happy New Year* and it was signed, *Matt x.*

She felt curiously unemotional. They had shared so much and she'd have liked him to say more, but why should he? On the inside of the book, he wrote, *To Effie. Hope you enjoy it. Matt x.*

Effie also had a Christmas card from Dominic. He had written, *Hoping you get through Christmas with no crises.*

No crises, Effie reflected. Was that all she could hope for?

Then he said, *Keep well enough and strong enough to deal with whatever the New Year might bring.*

That said it all.

It was on New Year's Day that the crisis did occur. Effie was thinking about what to pack for Berlin when she noticed that Lionel looked unwell. Or given that unwell was the norm, he looked more unwell than usual. She watched him sitting at his table doing his Sudoku and nibbling on a fig roll biscuit. Trails of biscuity saliva were dripping on his jumper. That was also the norm. But what was different was that she could hear him breathing. A troubled rasping sound. She could also see him breathing. She could see his chest rising and falling with every breath, almost as though he were panting. As a healthy person might pant after running for bus. But Lionel wasn't running anywhere. Lionel was never going to run anywhere.

Suddenly he was a sick. Not much, but a pool of dark mucous lay on the carpet.

"Don't worry," Effie said, leaping up to fetch a bowl of hot water and a cloth. "Why don't you go and lie down?" she suggested while she mopped up the mess.

He looked at his watch. "Not now," he said.

It wasn't the correct time for his afternoon nap. It wasn't part of his routine.

"But you're not well," she said. "You'd be better off in bed."

"I'm fine. Everyone's a bit sick sometimes."

Denial. He was always in denial. He had never ever admitted that anything was wrong.

As she carried out the bowl of dirty water there was a crash. She didn't see it happen, but by the time she got back to him he was sitting in his usual chair at his table.

"What happened?" she asked.

"I think I fainted," he said. "I'm fine now."

She remembered the last time she had taken him to A&E.

"Maybe I'd better call a doctor," she said.

"I'm fine," he repeated. He stood up. "I'm just going to make myself a coffee."

And he did. And he was fine.

But the next day, it happened again.

Again, she didn't see it, but she heard the crash and she found him on the floor between his table and the window. She knelt beside him. She didn't know whether he had blacked out, but if he had, he came round very quickly.

"What happened?" she said.

"Nothing. Here, help me up?" He held his hands up and she managed to pull him into a sitting position. "Pull me up," he said.

Effie pulled. He came up a bit, but fell back.

"Pull me," he repeated.

She tried again. "I can't. I'm not strong enough." She didn't want to risk damaging her back. "Lie down and rest for a bit," she said.

He grabbed the arm of a chair and tried to pull himself up on that. But it tipped over with a crash. "Fuck, fuck, fuck!" he snarled.

"No, Lionel!" she cried as she pulled the chair upright. "Just lie down for a while!"

He stretched up and grabbed the edge of the table. There wasn't enough grip. The velvet cloth that protected it slid off, accompanied by his belongings. His Sudoku book, the *Radio Times,* the daily paper, a couple of half-eaten fig roll biscuits, a coffee mug that was unfortunately half full, and two blue rollerball pens. All fell on the floor.

He grabbed at the edge of the table again.

"No, Lionel, you'll pull it over," Effie reacted. Why did he have to be so stupid?

He turned and pulled at one of the curtains. He managed to get a grip on that and tried again to pull himself up.

"No Lionel, you'll..."

And he fell back as the curtains tumbled in folds all over him, followed by the curtain pole. The Rawlplugs and their screws left dark holes in the plaster.

"Lionel!" Effie cried. "How can you be so stupid?" She lifted the curtain fabric off him and put the pole to one side.

He was flat on his back. "Pull me up," he said.

She took his hands and once more pulled him back into a sitting position. That was all she could do. There was a moment that would have been silent if it weren't for the rasping of his breath.

"I can't pull you up," she repeated. "I'll get you some water. Have a rest and you might feel better."

She came back with a glass of water, but he pushed it crossly out of her hands. "I'm not thirsty," he said. "I want to get up."

"Well you can't!" she shouted. "Now lie back and relax!"

At last he stopped struggling. He must have exhausted himself. Effie tucked a pillow under his head. "Now lie still," she said. "Don't move. I'll get help."

She dialled 111, explained what had happened and they put her through to 999. If someone collapses that was regarded as an emergency, she was told, and they'd get someone out to help as soon as possible. "Thank you," she said as she put the phone down.

She knelt beside him and stroked his forehead. "They're sending someone to help." She took his hand and squeezed.

"My Effie," he said. And he began to try and get up.

"Lie still!" she shouted.

He did, and she said more gently, "They won't be long." She stroked his forehead again, but he pushed her hand away.

He raised his arm and looked at his watch. "It's nearly supper time," he said.

He couldn't be hungry, Effie thought. He couldn't be well enough to feel hungry.

"What's for supper?" he asked.

"Close your eyes," Effie said.

Then he wanted a cigarette. She lit one and held it for him while he puffed on it.

The doorbell rang. Thank goodness! She hurried to the front door and let in a big burley uniformed paramedic, whose name, according to his badge was Jason.

"That was quick!" she said, leading him towards into the living room. She stopped before showing him in. "My husband has frontotemporal dementia. FTD. I should warn you that he can't help the way he behaves."

"Fronto-what?" he said.

"It's an aggressive form of dementia. Quite rare. He's inclined to make..." Effie was about to say 'inappropriate remarks', but she stopped herself. That euphemism, 'inappropriate' was utterly inappropriate. She mustn't allow herself to use it. "He can't help being rude," she said.

"Yeah. OK. I can deal with that," Jason remarked as she led him through.

"Lionel, this is Jason," Effie said. "He's come to help you."

Jason was strong enough to have no problem yanking Lionel onto his feet. He got him upright and standing and then, holding his arm, walked him around the room.

"I can manage!" said Lionel. "I'm okay." He yanked his arm crossly away from Jason.

Jason smiled. "Now sit and down and let me take your blood pressure."

Lionel curled his lip. "Nothing wrong with my blood pressure," he said. But he sat and allowed Jason to take his arm and push up his sleeve.

"Fuck!" shouted Lionel. "Does it have to be that tight?"

"It won't be a moment." Jason filled in some figures on a form. "Now for your temperature."

More fiddling. "His temperature is up." He made more notes. "I ought to take him into A&E."

Oh, no! Effie thought. Not again. Not like last time. "Do you have to?" she asked. "He'll find it very stressful. What with his mental condition."

Jason paused thoughtfully. "Yes, he will," he said. "It's very busy there. They're under a lot of pressure. It's this time of year."

"I've read about it," Effie said. There'd been a lot of criticism in the press about A&E waiting times and the stretched service over the

Christmas period.

"Look," said Jason. "I'll leave him be, but you must call your doctor first thing in the morning. Tell them what's happened and tell them you must see someone. If they fob you off, tell them that I said so."

So that's what Effie did. More or less. She knew that phoning the Park Health Centre first thing in the morning would be a dead loss. The line was almost always continuously engaged and you just had to keep dialling. So just before eight, long before Lionel was awake, Effie got in the car, drove there, spoke to the receptionist and made an appointment for ten-fifty. She should be able to get Lionel up and dressed in time for that.

She was wrong.

She opened his bedroom door and as usual, reacted to the pungent smell of cigarettes, stale sweat and urine. "Lionel," she said.

"What?" came a mumbled response from beneath the duvet.

His feet were sticking out at one side of the duvet. They looked gross. Blue veins, white flaky patches, a couple of scabby sores and long yellow toenails. They needed treatment.

"Just checking you're still alive," she said cheerfully. "Time to get up!" she added. She crossed to his window, pulled back the curtains and opened the window.

"Why?"

"You've got a doctor's appointment at eleven."

"What for?"

"To be checked over after your fall. The ambulance man said."

He frowned. "What ambulance man?"

Effie took a deep breath. "The one who picked you up after your fall."

He frowned. "What fall?" he asked.

"Just get dressed. We'll be late."

He got dressed and came downstairs. He was looking very wobbly, Effie thought. And he was wearing yesterday's clothes stained with the biscuity dribble that was now set hard like plaster of Paris. Should she make him change? No. Too much hassle.

"I'll just make myself a coffee," he said.

Effie didn't think he could function without his morning fix of caffeine and sugar, but they were running late. "I'll do it," she said.

"No," he reacted crossly. "I'll do it. You don't know how I like it."

She did know how he liked it. Too strong and too sweet. And he'd probably learned that if he left it to her he'd be getting a healthier option.

Finally, he was changing his slippers for his shoes and putting on his coat. He checked he'd got his cigarettes his lighter and his blue puffer in one pocket. House keys, money and credit card in another.

"Okay," Effie said. "Let's go."

But they couldn't and they didn't. He wasn't strong enough to get himself into the car. He couldn't bend. He couldn't stretch. Effie held the door open for him. "Sit sideways," she said, "and I'll move your legs round." But he was too weak. He grabbed the door frame and pulled, but to no effect. He could just perch on the side of the seat, but he didn't have the strength to move his bottom back into a proper sitting position ready for Effie to help him swivel round.

"Fuck, fuck, fuck!" he said.

Effie felt her pulse racing. A tight panic gripped her chest. She deliberately tried to slow her breathing down. In through the nose. Out through the mouth. It was no good. They had to give up. Somehow she got him back into the house and sat him, wheezing and panting and cursing, in his usual chair.

She phoned the surgery and this time, halfway through the morning, they answered reasonably quickly. She explained that she couldn't get him to the appointment because she couldn't get him into in the car.

"We'll arrange a home visit," said the receptionist. "Expect the doctor after midday."

And sure enough, there was a ring on the doorbell and a lady doctor was standing expectantly on the doorstep. She introduced herself as Dr Fayed.

"Do come in," Effie said. "I'm so sorry you've had to come out. He couldn't get into the car and I wasn't strong enough to lift him."

Dr Fayed sat on the sofa next to Lionel. "How are you feeling?" she asked.

"Average," he said. "A lot of fuss about nothing."

"I understand you had a fall last night?"

"No. I'm fine. I never fall."

"Perhaps I could listen to your chest?" asked the doctor, getting her stethoscope out of her bag. "Could we just lift the back of your jumper up?"

Lionel grimaced. "If you must!" he grumbled. "Fuck! It's cold!"

She tapped and listened. Listened and tapped. "A bit crackly," she said.

"A chest infection?" Effie asked.

The doctor finished and allowed him to pull his shirt down.

"About bloody time!" he said.

"I'll prescribe an antibiotic," said the doctor, "but if it doesn't clear up..." She looked at Effie. "He ought to be in hospital, but that would be very stressful for him." Effie didn't know whether she was asking a question or making a statement.

It would also be very stressful for the medical staff who would have to deal with him, Effie thought. "Yes, it would," she agreed.

"We'll see how he responds to the antibiotic," said the doctor.

CHAPTER 31

Admission Avoided

Effie got the car out and took the antibiotic prescription to Boots. No way was she ever going to use Ratigans again, even though it was only walking distance. Not that she wanted to walk anywhere in this wind and the rain. The weather was the pits.

"How is he?" asked the pharmacist on duty. They all knew him, and now they all knew Effie.

"Not very well," she said. "He collapsed yesterday. The doctor came out to see him," she added. "He's got a chest infection. That why he needs the antibiotic."

The pharmacist smiled. "It isn't easy for you, is it?" he remarked. "How do you cope?"

Effie took a deep breath. "With difficulty," she said. That was becoming her standard reply to a question she was being asked with increasing frequency.

Lionel was getting his lunch by the time she arrived home with the antibiotic pills. He seemed back to normal.

"You need to take two of these a day and you might as well have the first one now," she said. Adding this to his elaborate programme of medication was going to require as she watched him swallow the first pill with a swig of his usual tonic. She shook her head. How much of this fizzy junk was he getting through? she wondered. She was always loading up her Dunford trolley with all the bottles. He must be addicted to aspartame. Still, that had to be safer than alcohol. And he kept his sugar intake up with three heaped spoonfuls in every cup of coffee he drank. Of which there were many. He must be addicted to caffeine too.

At three o'clock precisely he headed upstairs for his afternoon sleep. "Just going for my kip," he said.

He had put his lunch plate on top of the dishwasher, but not before slopping surplus olive oil on the kitchen floor. Effie suppressed her irritation and got out the mop and bucket to clean up. Again. It should be dry before Lionel awoke from his afternoon nap. She emptied the bucket of dirty water in the sink and rinsed out the mop. It would be easier if he didn't insist on getting his own lunch, she thought.

Effie sighed. Mopping the kitchen floor had become a rather more regular task than it used to be and Effie usually tried to do it when Lionel went for his afternoon nap at three o'clock.

January. It was cold and it was wet and it was windy. Just looking at it was enough to drive you into a depression. And Effie had a tickly feeling in her throat. She was going to get a cold. When you got that feeling you know there is no way out. She made a cup of tea and wished she had something sweet and comforting in the house to eat with it. Chocolate biscuits, iced carrot cake, anything. On the whole, she avoided buying sweet things. It was a matter of discipline. But sometimes, like today, she regretted her good intentions. She opened and closed some kitchen cupboards. She took down a tin of golden syrup and helped herself to a spoonful. Very nice. She had another. Maybe she could make some fudge, or some flapjacks, she thought.

Then somehow, she just didn't have the energy.

She carried her tea into the living room and settled down on the sofa to relax with the Sunday paper that she still hadn't got around to reading. She took one of Lionel's fig rolls, but it didn't do anything for her. What's the point of biscuit that isn't chocolate? she asked herself. She was so tired. She'd hardly slept at all last night. She was too tired to read. She switched on the TV and flicked between channels. Then she looked at the list of programmes she'd recorded in recent months. There were so many that she hadn't yet viewed. Perhaps this afternoon was a good time to catch up.

It was after six when Effie woke up.

The TV was still on but she hadn't a clue what she was watching. She switched off. Where was Lionel? He was normally up from his afternoon nap by half past five. She'd go and check on him in a minute. Her sore throat was worse. Was there a lemon in the fridge? A hot drink of honey and lemon would be nice. She stood up and went back to the kitchen. The floor was dry now except for the puddle in the corner where the water collected because the floor wasn't flat. She mopped it with a dry floor cloth. That was better. She switched on the kettle, cut a couple of thick slices of lemon and scrunched it up with some honey in a mug. Then she added the hot water. She stirred and tasted it. More honey? And maybe a splash of brandy.

She took the mug back into the living room. Lionel was sleeping very late. She'd better check on him. But not till she finished her hot toddy.

She pushed at his bedroom door and realised that something was stopping it opening fully. She peered round the door into the semi-darkness. The room was lit by the streetlight outside. She looked down and realised that it was Lionel, or maybe Lionel's dead body, that was stopping it. She felt curiously calm. She squeezed through the gap, putting the light on as she went in. She stepped over Lionel. He was on the floor, but he didn't look dead. His trousers were half on. He must have got out of bed, started to get dressed and collapsed. She knelt down and listened to him. He was alive, breathing gently. She'd had no feeling of panic at the possibility of him being dead, and now no relief that he wasn't. There was a damp patch on the carpet where he'd wet himself.

She stroked his face and kissed his cheek. "Lionel, it's me, are you all right?" she asked. Which was a stupid question because he evidently wasn't all right. "Lionel," she said a bit louder. He responded with grunt. "Wake up!" she said, giving him a bit of a push. He opened his eyes a bit, muttered something, then closed them. He looked okay, just sleepy, comfortable. It seemed a pity to disturb him. She tucked a pillow under his head and covered him in a blanket. How long would she have to wait, she wondered, for something to happen? He might recover and get up. Or he might die. How long would that take?

She went downstairs to think about what to do. There was no hurry. She made another hot toddy and looked at the paperwork that the paramedic had left with her yesterday. She switched the TV back on to the ITV news, but the only thing she took in was the item about the overstretched NHS and the chaos in A&E this winter. She'd been right not to let them take Lionel in yesterday. Another half hour went by. She picked up the phone and carried it upstairs. Lionel was just the same. Peaceful, sleepy, but alive. She couldn't leave him there. It wouldn't be right. She'd have to call emergency services again. She keyed in 999 and waited. Then she explained the situation, just as she had yesterday.

Then she went to brush her hair and put some lipstick on. She looked in the mirror. What a wreck!

The first paramedic was there in a couple of minutes.

"That was quick," Effie said.

The name on his badge was Joe.

"I was just driving past."

But he couldn't move Lionel, who had now come round and was sufficiently conscious to tell the poor man to fuck off.

"Lionel! He's doing his best to help you!" Effie protested. She turned to the paramedic. "I'm sorry. He has frontotemporal dementia. He can't help being rude to people."

"I can't get him up on my own. I'll call for help," he said. "I'm about to come off duty anyway."

Further help came in the form of Eric, a beefy man with a shaved head and with tattoos on his forearms, and Lucy, a slender young woman with a sympathetic smile and wispy fair hair tied back in a single plait. They managed to get Lionel out of his wet pants and into a dry pair. Effie fetched a clean pair of trousers for him too. Then they eased Lionel onto an inflatable pillow. They pumped the air in, and up he came!

"That's clever," Effie said.

"Yeah. Usually does the trick," said Eric.

Lionel seemed bemused. "Who are they?" he said.

"They're here to help you," Effie explained.

Eric pulled Lionel into a standing position.

"I'm fine," said Lionel. "You can piss off now."

Eric laughed. "Let's see if you can get downstairs safely."

"'Course I can," said Lionel.

And he could.

They supervised him down the stairs and onto the sofa. Lucy knelt in front of him to check his blood pressure, tightening the device on his left arm. She had removed her jacket and was wearing a short-sleeved paramedic's uniform shirt that revealed smooth, lightly tanned arms coated with soft downy hairs. No freckles, no imperfections. Suddenly Lionel leaned forwards and smiled at her. Then he stretched his right hand forward and stroked the length of her arm. "Nice," he said, with a smile. The girl froze a moment, then relaxed and noted the blood pressure reading.

Eric was starting his paperwork, and Effie handed him the report that yesterday's paramedic had left with her. "You can get some of it off here," she suggested.

"Would you both like a cup of something? Tea? Coffee?"

By the time she returned with the coffees, Lionel had slumped back on the sofa and was fast asleep, and Lucy was looking up FTD on her smartphone. "I haven't come across it before," she said. "It's very interesting."

Eric looked up from his notes. "You don't want him admitted?" he checked.

Effie nodded. "It'd be so stressful for him. He'd be so confused."

"I'll call Admissions Avoidance," he said, clicking on his phone.

Effie frowned. "Whatever's that?"

"A team that try to keep people out of hospital." He grinned. "It's not publicised at all, and you can't call them yourself. They'll send a carer to spend the night with him, and someone else will be here to look after him in the morning. We need to be off." He looked at Lionel slouched back into the sofa. "Sleeping like a baby," he said.

She looked at Lionel's crumpled face and hanging jaw. "My babies were rather prettier than that when they slept," she remarked.

Eric packed his bag and handed her a copy of his notes. "The carer will be here in a few minutes. The idea is that you can go to bed and get some sleep. He smiled. "I can see you need it."

She did need it. She rarely slept well, but with a strange man called

Yusri, who came from somewhere in the Far East, sitting in the lounge to keep an eye on her sleeping husband, how could she possibly relax? What would Lionel think if he woke up to find a stranger with him? What would he do? she asked herself. Apart from imitate the man's accent and crack an inappropriate slit-eyed joke.

She set her alarm for five thirty because Yusri had told her he was leaving at six. She wanted to be up and dressed to say goodbye to him.

She lay there waiting for sleep. She lay there listening. It's an odd thing about insomnia. Her rational mind told her that she had a comfortable mattress, but insomnia filled it with lumps and bumps that felt utterly real. She knew she didn't have a skin disorder, but one bit of her after another itched, crying out to be scratched. Her hands wouldn't stay still. Her fingers locked and interlocked and she fidgeted with her nails. And on top of that, her sore throat was getting worse. She was wide awake thinking about that man downstairs. The front door keys and her car keys were hanging on their hook by the front door. Easily available. Maybe she should have hidden them. Okay, so Admissions Avoidance was enabling Lionel to avoid the stress of being admitted to hospital. But it was doing nothing to enable Effie to avoid the stress of keeping him at home.

She switched on her light and tried to read, but her eyes were too tired, too sore, for reading. She got up and went to the loo even though she didn't need to. She tried again to sleep and realised she felt hungry. Had she eaten tonight? Not properly. When had she last had a decent meal? She crept downstairs as though she were a burglar in her own home. The last thing she wanted was a conversation with Yusri. She put some cereal and some milk in a bowl and carried it upstairs. But she forgot a spoon, so, rather than creep downstairs again, she managed to scoop the cereal into her mouth with an emery board. She turned the light off again but she knew there was no way she was ever going to get to sleep.

A moment later the beeping of the alarm clock blasted through to her brain.

CHAPTER 32

Admission Arranged

Lionel shifts uncomfortably. His back hurts. His throat is dry and he has a nasty taste in his mouth. He opens his eyes. Where is he? It is dark, but a trapezium of light from an open door falls on the carpet. It is the living room carpet. He can tell because he can see the pattern. He is not in his bed. Why not? He needs a pee. He sits up. He is on the sofa in the living room. He must have dozed off instead of going up for his kip. Must stand up. Must get to the doorway. Must get to the loo. Then someone is standing beside him holding his arm.

He snatches his arm away. "Who the fuck are you?" he snarls. He can't see the man properly in the semi-darkness. Is it a burglar?

"My name is Yusri. I am here to look after you."

The man has a foreign accent. "I don't need looking after," says Lionel. "Get out of my fucking way." He pushes the man's arm away and steps towards the door to flick the light switch on. He blinks a moment in the brightness then stares at the man. A stranger. Slanting eyes. Yellow skin. "What the...?"

"Your wife called the emergency services. You collapsed. She was very worried about you."

Lionel frowns. Effie fussing again. He looks at his watch. It is nearly six o'clock. He doesn't normally wake up this late. And why is he downstairs? "I'm going for a pee," he said. "Go back to fucking China."

The man smiles. "I am not from China," he says.

"Then go... wherever."

Lionel has his pee and goes into the kitchen. It's late. He wants his coffee. He fills the kettle and puts in on. The man is following him. He says to the man. "Would you like a coffee?"

"No. Thank you very much, but I need to leave soon."

Lionel hesitates. He suddenly feels dizzy. It's like the kitchen is going round and round.

"Here," says the man again, taking his arm. "Sit down." And he eases him onto a kitchen chair.

Lionel feels sick. He slumps forward, his face in his hands.

"Lionel, are you all right?" calls a voice. Effie's voice. He hears her feet on the stairs. He looks up.

Effie is wearing a dressing gown. Why is she wearing a dressing gown at this time of day? "Of course I'm all right!" he snaps.

"We must get him back on the sofa," says the man. They each take one arm and walk Lionel back to the living room.

"Now sit down," says Effie sharply as he slumps back on the sofa. "And stay put."

The man speaks to Effie. "I've checked with the office. They'll be here in about an hour."

They? Who are they? And are they coming to get him? Lionel is worried.

The man continues. "He has been fine. He slept all night." He hands her a piece of paper. "This is my report."

After Effie has shown the man out, she sits by Lionel and strokes his forehead. "How d'you feel?"

"Average," he says. "Below average."

She smiles. "I'll just go make myself a coffee."

Lionel is puzzled. Effie never has coffee in the afternoon. "Coffee?" he queries. He looks at his watch. It's half past six which is too late for tea. Sometimes she has a sherry at half past six.

"Yes," she says. "It's a bit early, but I'm going to have some breakfast. Then I'll shower and get dressed. Do you want anything?"

Lionel is more puzzled. What is happening? What is going on? He looks at his watch but it's hard to see the time. His eyelids feel heavy. "What day is it?" he asks. Then he closes his eyes.

When he wakes Effie has two visitors. The curtains are open and bright sunshine streams in.

"Hello, Lionel," says one of the visitors. "I'm Mary. I'm a nurse working for the Admission Avoidance Team. Yusri told me you had a very good night's sleep." She sounds very bright and cheery.

Yusri? What's she on about? Who's Yusri?

She continues. "We want to keep you well enough for your wife to look after you at home."

Mary has a badge. He thinks it says Mary, but it's a bit blurred. Mary is putting one of those blood pressure things on his arm. "Fuck!" he says when it gets tight. It hurts.

"Won't be a minute," she says. She is makes notes. "Now for your temperature."

She holds something in his ear. He remembers doctors used to have glass thermometers that they shook, but he can't remember why. They used to put them in your mouth. Now they go in your ear. Doesn't matter. The nurse writes something down.

He stands. "I need to get a coffee," he says. But he feels dizzy.

"Sit down," says Effie. "I'll get it." And he slumps back on to the sofa. He breathes deeply. It's hard to get enough air.

Effie brings him a coffee then sits on the other sofa to talk to Mary. He can hear some of what they are saying but he can't follow it. "It'll confuse him. He'd hate it," Effie is saying.

Mary says that they don't have any choice. Then Mary takes a phone out of her pocket and walks into the hall to call someone. There's a lot of discussion but he can't follow what they're on about.

Then she comes back to speak to him. "I'm sorry, Lionel, you're not well enough for Effie to look after you at home. I've called for an ambulance to take you into hospital."

"That's stupid!" he says. "I'm fine."

"It'll be for the best. And Effie can go with you."

Lionel is not sure what is happening. He is in a wheelchair wrapped in a blanket. Someone pushes the wheelchair down the drive and up a ramp into a van. It doesn't take long but it's windy and the rain is very cold.

"It's okay," says Effie. She sits on a bench next to his wheelchair and holds his hand. "We're both going to the hospital."

And now he's on a trolley with curtains either side. He has been here before, but he can't remember when or why. Someone else comes to do the blood pressure thing on his arm. Why do they keep doing that? A girl in a white coat talks to Effie, making notes. Effie tells her, FTD, COPD, AF and so on. Effie tells her that he was admitted before, over five years ago, and they should have records of him. He hears something about resuscitation. It is hard to follow those long words, but Effie seems to know what the girl is talking about. "Yes, I entirely agree," he hears Effie say. "There's no point."

The girl is gone and Effie bends closer to his trolley, "We'll have to wait for you to be admitted," she says. "They have to find you a bed."

"I need a cigarette," he says.

Effie goes to find a wheelchair and someone to help him into it. Then she wheels him outside.

He light ups and looks around. What a load of decrepit-looking idiots smoking cigarettes. Most of them are fat and ugly. There's a bit of a canopy but it's not much use against the wind and rain. But he breathes deeply of his cigarette and it all seems a whole lot better.

He's hungry after that, and Effie gets someone to get him a sandwich, but he doesn't like it. He eats a bit and Effie eats the rest.

Other things happen but it all merges together. He's taken on a trolley along a corridor to the X-ray department. Then he's brought back. He looks around. "Where's Effie?" he wonders. Then he's taken along another corridor and up in a lift. Another corridor and finally someone helps him into a bed. And Effie is there again. She has a bag with pyjamas and washing things. His cigarettes must be in his coat pocket.

And another nurse tries to do that blood pressure thing. "Fuck off!" he says. He pulls his arm away.

Effie says to the nurse. "He's getting agitated. He's going to need some nicotine patches very soon."

Somehow there is a tube attached to a bottle of something going into his arm. He looks at it and pushes at the place on his arm with his forefinger. It itches.

"Don't touch it," says Effie.

Then she says. "I'm going home, now, Lionel."

"Yes," he says eagerly, pushing his sheet down. "Let's go home."

"No, Lionel. Don't be stupid!" she says, her voice raised. "You're ill, you can't go home yet."

She puts his clothes into a bag, and kisses him on the forehead. "I'll be back in the morning," she says. "Don't try and get out of bed, and don't touch that drip in your arm."

CHAPTER 33

Gone Walkabout

Effie had scrambled eggs on toast for supper. There was something comforting about scrambled eggs on toast. She remembered her mother making it and bashing the crusts of the toast with a wooden rolling pin. Modern cut bread doesn't have such hard crusts, she supposed.

Then she phoned Nigel.

"Hello, Mum," he said. "How's things?"

"Not so good really. What about you? How was your New Year party?"

"Pretty good. I think they enjoyed themselves. You're sounding croaky."

"I've got a sore throat, but it's your dad who's not well. He's in hospital. Looks like it's pneumonia. He kept collapsing. An ambulance took him in."

"Oh... that's rough. I'm so sorry, Mum."

"Look, Nigel. I won't be able to come. I'll have to cancel my visit."

There was a pause. "Are you okay?" he said.

Effie felt suddenly tearful. "Not really," she said.

She took a sleeping pill, two paracetamol capsules, and went to bed sucking a throat pastille. Her throat felt really raw now. But it was a relief to be on her own, to have Lionel out of the house. Someone else's responsibility. But her mind was filled with thoughts that buzzed round and round like angry wasps on a window pane. If she swatted one, another would pop up demanding attention.

She remembered that first time she'd taken Lionel into A&E. Four and a half years ago now. Back then no one had mentioned dementia and she'd never even heard of FTD. Nor, unfortunately, had Lionel's GP.

Heart failure, Chronic Obstructive Pulmonary Disease, and Atrial Fibrillation were the things that had combined to cause Lionel's collapse that time. But looking back, his behaviour must have been caused by the FTD. He'd been lying there in A&E wired up to monitors and a drip in his arm, grumbling and cursing at the hospital staff. Effie had gone off to the hospital cafeteria, partly to have something to eat – a cup of tea and a Mars bar — but mainly to get away from him. When she'd got back, he was standing up, facing a nurse.

"I've had enough of this fucking place," he was shouting. "I'm going home." He'd disconnected himself from the monitors and pulled out his cannula, splattering blood everywhere. Someone was already scooping up the bloodied sheets.

Three nurses had approached Effie. Like a deputation. The one in the middle said to her, "Mrs Butler?"

"Yes."

"Is Mr Butler discharging himself?"

"Yes, I am," he'd said. "I want to get the hell out of here. Effie, take me home!"

Effie put on her most persuasive tone. "Lionel, you collapsed. You need to give them a chance to find out why. Now they'll have to start all over again."

He hesitated.

The nurse spoke to Effie carefully and calmly, "Mr Butler does of course have every right to discharge himself. But if he does, he could well die."

Lionel laughed. That laugh of his that was part snigger, part put-down. "I'm just going out for a moment," he said.

"Lionel!" Effie reacted. "You can't just..."

"I'll be back," he said.

"He's gone for a cigarette," Effie told the nurse. "I think he'll come back. I've got the car keys."

He had come back, calmer after his cigarette. They'd got him wired up again and settled, then finally admitted to a ward. Just like today. And Effie had left him to go and get some pyjamas for him.

When she'd come back, his bed was empty.

"I'm terribly sorry, Mrs Butler," the nurse had said. "He's gone."

"What!" Gone where? Home?

"We've called security. They should find him, but if they don't we'll have to call the police. But I'm sure they will find him. Try not to worry."

Effie had sat down on the bed that should have been Lionel's. Should she go and look for him? Maybe he would find his way home. He didn't have any car keys, and he wouldn't know where she'd parked, but he was still capable of getting a taxi.

At which point he'd appeared again, walking cheerfully down the ward. "I went to the garage to get cigarettes," he'd said brightly. "But I'm feeling fine now. We might as well go." At which point he'd suddenly paled, sat down on the edge of the bed and thrown up.

The nurse had spoken quietly to Effie. "Could you check he didn't buy anything alcoholic? He's on an alcohol detox medication, and if he drinks anything now it could be lethal."

"Er... yes, of course," she had said. How had they known? she'd wondered.

That time it had been five weeks before he was well enough to come home. There had been two weeks in intensive care. "We might be able to save his life," one of the junior doctors had said to her, "but we won't be able to make him better."

It had been a long time before she understood what that meant.

But this time they'd asked her about whether she'd thought he should be resuscitated should his heart stop. Last time they hadn't asked anything about that. Last time they'd been determined to keep him alive. Regardless. This time... presumably they were wondering if it was worth it.

So was Effie.

The sleeping pill did its job and the wasps finally stopped buzzing inside her head. When she got up next morning her throat was still sore and although she was calm, she felt very shaky. She phoned for a taxi to take her to the hospital. No way did she feel well enough to drive.

How long would he be there this time? she wondered as she walked along the familiar corridor, took the stairs to the next floor, and headed for the ward. Long enough to give her a break? She rang the bell and someone released the door catch. Lionel's bed, when she left last night, had been in the third bay on the left. In the corner by the window. Hadn't it? Only he wasn't in it. That bed was empty. It was his, though. She could tell that from the open Sudoku book on the table. His blue rollerball pen was beside it. She sat on the chair by the bed. Maybe he had gone to the loo.

"He's gone walkabout," offered the patient in the opposite bed.

"What?" Effie said.

"He's escaped."

Effie gave a wry smile. Not again! They'd been here before.

The patient continued, apparently enjoying the drama. "There's been a right panic round here. They've gone to look for him." He sounded very pleased. Lionel and his behaviour were evidently providing some excellent in-ward entertainment.

Effie stood up. She had better find out what was going on.

A nurse approached her. "Mrs Butler?"

"Yes?"

"We're very sorry. We don't how it happened, but he's got out of the ward. The door locks when it closes but he must have slipped out when someone came in."

Effie laughed. "I'm... sorry..." she spluttered. "I... know it's not really funny, but..." She took a deep breath to calm herself. To think that they had told her that Lionel would be safer here than at home! "But I took his clothes back with me. He's only got pyjamas."

"We think he's taken someone's coat. Don't worry. We've called security. He's not well enough to get far. He won't get out of the building."

Effie felt that curious calmness that seemed to come to her in a crisis. It was the little things that sent her into a panic. Losing her glasses or her car keys could trigger floods of tears, but big things like someone mislaying her husband was no problem. Whatever happened, it wouldn't be her fault. There was nothing she could do. No decision she had to make. That let her off the hook.

She wandered into the day room and found a magazine to read. From here she could keep an eye on the entrance to the ward. She would see when Lionel came back.

If Lionel came back.

CHAPTER 34

The Great Escape

Lionel buttons up the coat. It's a bit tight, but it's a nice long winter coat with a hood. Not quite long enough to cover the bottoms of his pyjamas, or his slippers, but no one will notice. He's lucky to have found it hanging in there. *Staff cloakroom* it said on the door. It's not really a cloakroom. More of a cupboard really. He's only borrowing it for a bit. After all, he can't go home in just pyjamas! Effie would be hopping mad if he did that. When he gets home he'll get Effie to bring back the coat and apologise. Say thank you to whoever owns it.

He stands near the doorway of the ward. It's locked. Like you're in prison. But he's worked out that when people get in, you can slip out quickly before the door clicks shut. No one notices. Good. Like now.

He's out of the ward now but he doesn't know how to get out of the hospital. He walks down the corridor. It's big and wide. How do you escape from this place? He needs to find the front entrance. He'll be able to find a taxi there. And the taxi will take him home. He's feeling wobbly. He leans against the wall to steady himself. Christ, he needs a cigarette. He's got to get out of here and find some cigarettes.

There is a glass door. There's a sign on it but it's hard to read. He feels in his pocket for his specs, but they're not there. That's because it's not his pocket. It's a strange pocket and it doesn't feel right. He feels inside. Some loose change. That might be useful. He peers at it. Not enough for a taxi. A set of keys. No good if you don't what they're for. He pushes open the glass door. Christ, it's cold out here! There is a ramp with handrails on a walkway that leads down into a parking area with delivery vans. And boxes and crates of stuff stacked up in front of wide double doors. And it's bloody cold. Maybe there's a taxi down there. Effie will pay the driver when he gets home. He gets his keys out of his pocket ready, but they aren't his keys. Whose are they? It doesn't matter very much. It doesn't matter at all. He holds the handrail tight as he makes his way down the ramp. It's cold and he wishes he had gloves. Not far now. He's nearly at the bottom.

"Hey!" comes a voice from somewhere. "You all right, mate? Where yer goin'?"

He looks back and peers. Someone is following him through the glass door.

"I'm fine!" he calls and hurries down the ramp. He holds the hand rail. Wet and cold. He needs gloves. And a scarf. And some proper shoes and socks. His slippers are getting wet and his feet are cold. There is an icy wind swirling around him. His hands are cold on the handrails, so cold he can't grip them. And the ramp is slippery in the rain.

"You sure?"

He is being followed. He's nearly at the bottom. He'll be able to find a taxi. "You shouldn't be out in this weather, mate."

"Fuck off! I'm going home!" he snarls. And suddenly he is slipping on the wet walkway. He hangs onto the rail, but his fingers are cold and wet and his feet are sliding from under him. And he is falling sideways and rolling... and rolling... He's got to stop. How is he going to stop?

"What the... I'm just..."

And Lionel is jammed up against a something hard. His legs are twisted under him and he can feel something warm trickling down his chin.

There's this bloke kneeling beside him. "Hang on there, mate... I'll get help..." And he speaks into a radio thing. "Patient had a fall outside loading bay two. Can you send a wheelchair? Over... Yes, yes... over and out."

And then there are more people fussing around, and Lionel is being lifted into a wheelchair and covered in a blanket. He realises he is being pushed back up the ramp. "I want to go home. Get me a fucking taxi!" he shouts.

"Sorry mate. Need to get you back to where you're supposed to be. They'll check you over."

Effie has arrived. "Lionel!" she cries when his wheelchair is finally pushed back into the ward. "What did you think you were doing?"

She leans over the wheelchair and hugs him. She shakes her head. "Just look at you, Lionel! Grazed knees! Bleeding elbows! You're all wet and filthy. What on earth...?

"We think he's all right," says the staff nurse. "We don't think he hit his head. No concussion."

He did hit his head, remembers Lionel. On that railing when he fell over. It would all have been ok if that bloke hadn't been bothering him.

"Well that is a blessing!" says Effie. She sounds sarcastic. It's not like Effie to be sarcastic. Lionel can tell she's cross. But he doesn't think it's with him, which is unusual.

"He's only here, because they said I couldn't look after him properly at home!" she protests. She sounds cross. "When he fell over at home, at least it was on a carpet, and in the warm." She pauses. "And they also said he'd be on an antibiotic drip. No sign of that is there?"

"We tried, but he kept pulling it out," says a nurse.

Effie continues her diatribe. She's very good, thinks Lionel. He's impressed.

"And now he's cold, wet, and bleeding, but we're all supposed to be pleased that at least he hasn't been bounced on the head. So his brain's no worse than usual. That's brilliant!"

"I'm so sorry, Mrs Butler," says the nurse. "We'll discuss it later."

"Now," she says to Lionel. "We'd best get those knees and elbows cleaned up. And you'll need a nice clean, dry pair of pyjamas before we settle you down."

"What about handcuffing him to the bedstead?" suggests Effie. "Or maybe put him in a straitjacket? Isn't that what you lot used to do with people like Lionel?"

"I'm so sorry Mrs Butler," says the nurse again. "Somebody must have left the door open. We can't keep an eye on everyone all of the time. But we're moving him up to the dementia ward. It's quieter with more staff, and it's more secure."

"And the antibiotic drip?" asks Effie.

"We'll try again."

Effie nods. And suddenly she groans and puts her hands over her face. "I... I... can't..." She's sobbing now. Lionel hates it when Effie cries. Tears falling down her face and her nose all runny. And it's a horrible noise. He puts his hand over his ears. He hates noise.

"I'm sorry I get like this," Effie splutters to the nurse. "I do know what he's like. I know it isn't your fault."

And then Lionel, with bed, bedding and belongings, is wheeled out of the ward, along the corridor and up in the lift. Effie accompanies him and holds his hand all the way. "Are we going home now?" he says to her.

"I'm sorry, love," she says. "We have to wait till you're better."

The new ward is much the same, except it has funny notices and pictures pinned up all over the place.

There are pictures of toilets on the toilet doors. There are pictures of baths on the bathroom doors. There are pictures of a TV, a piano and a cup of coffee on another door. Can't people work out things for themselves? thinks Lionel. Bloody hell! What sort of nutters do they have in this ward?

There is a list of activities, and now that Lionel had got his glasses back, he can read them. There is a singalong on Monday, jigsaws on Tuesday, bend-and-stretch on Wednesday. What, Lionel wonders, does 'pat-a-dog' entail? The room that has a TV and a piano also has lots of books and magazines. There are books about the Royal Family from way back, books on thrifty wartime cookery, and books on the film stars of yesteryear. On the piano is sheet music of Vera Lynn songs. How old, Lionel wonders, are most of these patients? This isn't for Lionel's generation. It's for his mother's.

The consultant and his team are doing their rounds, pausing at each bed, checking records and discussing things.

"I'm fine. I want to go home," says Lionel. He looks at Effie. "Effie, take me home. Please."

"You have pneumonia," says the doctor to him.

"What?" he says.

"Pneumonia. But don't worry, you'll be fine."

"Of course, I will!" responds Lionel. But his voice comes out slurred and he thinks he might be dribbling. He isn't sure that anyone but Effie can understand him.

CHAPTER 35

Hospital Visiting

Effie's cold had developed and she felt she was running a temperature. She was coughing too. Maybe it was flu. She decided she wasn't going to visit today. She really didn't feel well enough, but Suzie and the grandchildren were going instead. So at least poor Lionel would have visitors. Whether he would notice, let alone remember, was another matter.

She ought to tell Michael and Joanna about it all. She didn't really want to talk to them, but Michael should be made aware that his brother was in hospital. She didn't think they'd visit him. After all, when they'd visited that last time Lionel's 'goodbye' to them was a 'fuck off'. Meant in jokey way of course, but they didn't like it very much.

She dialled the number and Michael answered.

"I thought I should tell you that Lionel is in hospital," she said. She'd wondered momentarily about saying something on the lines of, 'Did you have a nice Christmas?' or, 'A happy new year to you,' but small talk had never been Michael's strong point, and after all this time, it didn't seem worth the effort.

"Oh," said Michael. There was a pause and Effie wondered if he was going to add anything at all to his, 'Oh'. She had no intention of helping out.

"Why's that?" he asked eventually.

"He's got pneumonia," she said.

"Oh," said Michael.

"And... he's so confused..." That infuriating lump was rising in her throat. She swallowed hard. "He doesn't understand why he's there and..." The tears were coming and she wasn't going to be able to hold back. "...I thought you should know," she managed. "Goodbye." And she put the phone down.

She was sobbing copiously. Why had she bothered? They didn't want to know.

The days were merging together. So were the doctors and the nurses and the psychiatrists and the occupational therapists and the nutrition advisors and the dementia support workers.

Most days Nigel phoned from Berlin to see how his dad was getting on. Yesterday, or maybe it was the day before yesterday, he said he'd booked a flight to visit at the weekend. "Thank you," she said. "Thank you so much."

Lionel had responded to the antibiotic and was, she was informed, well enough to come home. If she felt she was able to cope, that is.

She didn't.

"Don't worry," said the dementia crisis advisor in response to her weeping. "You'll have support. You won't be on your own."

Lionel appeared to have devised his own routine within the constraints of the ward structure. Each morning he made his way to the day room and selected the most comfortable armchair opposite the TV. With him, he had his Sudoku book and his *Radio Times*. With his blue rollerball pen he'd mark up the programmes he planned to watch. He didn't know how to switch the TV on. Nor did he know how to change channels if it were on. And he certainly didn't know how to formulate a sentence in order to ask someone for help. But that didn't seem to trouble him.

It was the eighth day. Effie was over the worst of her cold and just about to go to the hospital for her second visit of the day when there was a ring at the doorbell.

It was Lionel's nephew, Michael's son.

"Steve!" she cried delightedly. "How lovely! Come on in."

And he gave her a big hug. God knows, she needed a hug from someone.

"How's things?" he said.

She shook her head. Don't cry, she told herself. "Not good," she said. "Come on in." She led him through to the living room. "It's great to see you. Would you like a drink?" she began. Then she remembered that Steve was a recovered alcoholic and didn't drink. "Cup of tea?" she asked.

"No thanks, I'm ok," he said. "Dad told me you phoned. How's the lad?" Steve, since his late teenage years, had always referred to his Uncle Lionel as 'the lad'. They had a lot in common. Football, cricket, a jokey attitude to life, and unfortunately a weakness for drink. In fact, Steve had more in common with his uncle that he did with his father. Even looked a bit like him.

"I was just about to go to the hospital to find out. D'you want to come with me? Have you got time? I don't usually stay long."

"Of course. Shall I drive? I'll drop you home after."

"That'd be great. I'm so tired. I don't think I'm safe driving."

As Effie settled into the passenger seat of Steve's car, she felt irrationally happy that Michael had taken the trouble to phone Steve and tell him that Lionel was ill. And even more delighted that Steve had decided to call. Maybe the Butlers weren't quite as disinterested as she thought.

Lionel was in his chair in the dayroom doing a Sudoku in front of the TV that was switched on at full volume. He looked up and smiled. "About bloody time," he said to Effie. "Are we going home?" he asked. "I hate it here."

"Sorry love, not for a day or two," said Effie as she kissed him on the forehead. "I brought Steve to see you." Lionel was chewing, a biscuit presumably, and biscuity saliva was dribbling down his cheek onto his shirt. Effie quickly mopped it away with a tissue then stepped aside.

"You remember Steve, don't you?" she said as she picked up the remote control of the TV and turned the sound down.

Lionel, still chewing, looked at Steve and his smile broadened in recognition. "Yeah. Yeah. 'Course I do."

Steve stepped forward, shook Lionel's hand and clapped him on the shoulder. Man to man style. "How yer doing, mate?"

Lionel shrugged. "Rubbish. Got to get out of this place."

Steve asked Lionel what he was watching on the box, and when he didn't appear to know, he suggested they change channels and watch the football.

"If you want," said Lionel.

Effie felt a surge of satisfaction. This was the sort of company Lionel needed. No way would she have thought of that.

"Still supporting Arsenal?" asked Steve.

Lionel frowned and his mouth dropped open. "Yeah... yeah," he said.

"You must have been chuffed when they beat Chelsea," offered Steve.

"Yeah," he said. But he seemed a bit puzzled when Steve started going on about the finer points of the premier league results.

The minutes dragged until Effie said, "Well, we'd best be off. Steve has to get to work tomorrow."

Steve grinned. "Some of us are still gainfully employed," he remarked.

He shook hands with Lionel, told him to keep his hands off those nurses, and headed for the door.

Then Effie gave Lionel a hug and said, "I'll be back tomorrow."

Lionel was frowning. "Steve," he said thoughtfully. "Nice bloke, that Steve. How do we know him?"

Effie sighed. "Steve!" she said, forcing a cheery tone into her voice. "Steven Butler is your nephew. You know, Michael and Joanna's son."

"Oh yes," he said. But his eyes were back on his Sudoku.

Effie gave him a kiss and hurried after Steve, who evidently couldn't wait to get out of the place.

"What did you think?" she asked him as they headed for the exit.

"Christ!" Steve said, and shook his head.

"A bit of a shock?"

"Yeah. You could say that."

Effie took his arm and squeezed. "Thank you so much for coming," she said. "I'm sure it meant a lot to him."

Steve grunted. "How can you tell?" he said flatly.

"Well... it means a lot to me. Thank you."

CHAPTER 36

Pat-a-Dog Day

They're a load of bloody nutters in here, thinks Lionel. He is sitting in his armchair in the TV room. He always comes in here after breakfast. He has his Sudoku and the *Radio Times* with him, and the box of fig roll biscuits that Effie brought in yesterday. Someone has brought him a cup of coffee. He'd prefer a mug to a cup and he'd prefer to make it himself, the way he likes it, but they think he's too sick – or too thick – to do it himself. There you go. He's dressed today and he doesn't feel so decrepit. Effie brought him some clothes. Trousers, pants, shirt, socks and jumper. "That doesn't mean you're going home yet," she said. "No wandering!"

He's dribbled some stuff down his jumper and that's going to annoy her.

This morning is Pat-a-Dog day. Every day there is an event to entertain these nutters. A quiz. An exercise class. A singsong. A painting class. Today the event is Pat-a-Dog. A woman has been taking a dog on a lead round the ward, stopping at every bed and chatting. Some of those idiots look like it's their birthday. "Nice doggy! Come to Uncle Benny!" says the guy in the corner. What the fuck's going on? Lionel didn't think dogs were allowed in hospitals. Fucking well shouldn't be. You're not allowed a nice relaxing cigarette, but you can bring some mangy old animal in here with its germs and its fleas and its big teeth. Anyway, he's in the day room now, in peace and on his own.

The door opens.

"Hello," says the woman with the dog. She has a round, pink, smiley face and bright blue eyes. She looks fit and suntanned and healthy, but is definitely overweight.

"Hello, Fatty," says Lionel. "You haven't by any amazing chance got a cigarette on you?" he asks.

The woman smiles, unfazed. "I'm Sally," she says, "and sorry, I don't have a cigarette. This is Honey. She's a golden retriever. Honey, this is Lionel."

Lionel glares at the dog. "Mr Butler to you!" he says.

It looks up at him with big brown eyes and wags its tail. It seems to wag its whole body as though it's brimming with delight. It has a shiny brown coat and soft floppy ears. It looks pleased to see him. Lionel smiles. Not many people look pleased to see him these days. Not even Effie. She smiles when she arrives and she sounds bright and cheerful, but he can tell it's forced. He's not as dumb as they all think he is.

"Hello Honey," he says, and he leans forward and extends an arm to the dog. Honey snuffles at him and licks his fingers. He strokes the top of her head. "Nice doggy," he says. "Come to your Uncle Lionel." He laughs. "I mean Mr Butler!" He breaks off a bit of fig roll biscuit, and offers it to the dog. The dog takes it, gulps it down, and wags its tail with pleasure. Then it lays its head in Lionel's lap and looks at him adoringly with its shiny wet eyes. "She's lovely," he says, stroking her head between her ears.

"She'll be back to see you next week," says Sally. "Honey, say bye-bye to Mr Butler!"

Next week! thinks Lionel. I've got to get out of this fucking place before next week!

Pity about the dog going. You can talk to a dog and it doesn't get all uptight about what you say.

He settles down to marking up the *Radio Times* with his blue rollerball pen. He circles each programme he might want to watch. Trouble is, he's not sure what day it is. Every day's the same when you're stuck in a place like this. Except when it's Pat-a-Dog Day, of course. How long has he been here? It feels like forever. Christ, he needs a ciggie. He needs to know. He pulls himself out of the armchair and heads back to the ward. "Nurse!" he calls. He likes that little nurse with the slitty eyes.

"Hello, Lionel," she says.

"Hello, Suzie Wong," he says.

She smiles. "I'm Sarah Walters."

He peers at her. Slitty eyes and smooth, straight hair. Skin looks soft and golden. Chinesey. He puts a hand forward and strokes the side of her hair. "You don't look like a Sarah Walters," he says.

She smiles. "Sorry about that. Can I help you with something?"

"Yes." He pauses. What was he going to ask her? He's forgotten. "I don't think so."

"Well, I'll see you later, Lionel. Have you filled in your lunch order?"

"Not yet."

"Well don't forget."

As he watches her neat little bum sway the length of the ward in time to her neat little steps, he remembers what he needs to know. "What day is it, Susie Wong?" he calls.

She stops and turns around. "I'm Sarah, and it's Thursday."

He looks at his *Radio Times* and flicks the pages until he gets to

Thursday. He frowns. "Thursday the second of January?" he checks.

"No," she says. She comes back and looks at his *Radio Times*. "That's last week's," she says. "You need this week's."

"Bugger!" he says. Has Effie brought in the wrong one? Had she thrown out the right one? She does that sometimes when she gets into one of her tidying up moods. "Look, I have to have the *Radio Times*. Can you get me one?"

Susie Wong frowns. "Not right now, but maybe later. Maybe someone else..."

"Look I need this week's *Radio Times*. For Chrissake, I'd go down to the hospital shop and buy one myself if they'd let me! He heads down the ward and shouts, "Anyone gotta *Radio Times*?" There's a guy in that corner bed with a pile of magazines on his table. "You gonna sleep all day?" he asks. The man lies there, mouth open, his breath rasping. Lionel grins and imitates the rasping sound, only louder. He looks about him to see who might be listening. "Only joking," he says to the guy in the next bed.

There's a nurse in a darker uniform holding up a magazine. "Mr Butler. Is this what you want?"

He takes the magazine and looks. "Yeah. That's the one. Where d'ya get it?"

"It was on the table by your bed, Mr Butler. I believe your wife brought it in for you last night."

"Yeah. Well, about bloody time!" he says as he snatches it. He flicks through pages, frowning. Just for the moment he has forgotten what he is looking for. Then he remembers. At least he thinks he does.

"What day is it?" he asks.

CHAPTER 37

A.R.M

Effie took her usual seat between Ewan and Georgina. Funny how they all tended to sit in the same places each week. Something to do with security and familiarity. All human beings need that, but this particular group of damaged souls needed it more than most. Sometimes a new patient joined the group and there had to be a change of positioning. Some found that more difficult than others.

Can you get addicted to self-help? Effie wondered. She looked back at the meetings she had attended. It had started with Al-Anon. Then there had been Dementia Support. FTD Support had come later, as had the two dementia courses she had attended. She had been coming to these Applied Relaxation and Meditation classes for the best part of a year now. And she wouldn't be without them for anything.

"Hello Ewan," Effie said. Ewan was a thin, scraggy man of indeterminate age and with flyaway hair that was neither grey nor blond. It floated untidily around his neck. He wore a T-shirt with an Iron Maiden symbol on the front, and frayed black jeans. His right upper arm was tattooed, but, what was more significant, were the scars that that striped his left forearm from the inside of his wrist right up to his inner elbow. They had never been mentioned in the group, but at some time in his life he must have self-harmed.

He smiled and nodded. He rarely spoke.

"Hello, Effie," said Georgina. "How's your cough?"

"Much better, thanks," Effie said.

"And your husband?"

"Also better. He's coming home soon."

"That's good," said Georgina.

"Is it?" said Effie. She was dreading Lionel's return. "I'm not so sure," she said with a wry smile. "But my son's coming for the weekend." Tomorrow, Nigel was flying over from Berlin to be with her. At least she had that to look forward to.

"That'll be nice," said Georgina.

Other members of the group settled down in the circle of plastic green chairs, and finally the instructor, Jack, a community psychiatric nurse (CPN), completed the circle.

"Good evening, everyone," he said. He grinned. "This is a good turnout!"

He looked round at the group. "I wondered how many would manage to get here in this awful weather. You've done well."

"It's the weather that makes us feel we need even more support than usual," remarked Judy. Judy was a teacher who'd taken early retirement due to ill health. Effie didn't know what form of ill health that was, but it had to be a psychiatric disorder rather than a physical one.

Jack smiled. "It's a bad time of year," he said. "Cold and miserable, Christmas hype over. Spring on the way, but not here yet. How are you all coping?" He looked around the circle of faces. He needed to pick on one to get started. "Sadie, how are you?" he asked.

Sadie looked down at her hands that were linked in her lap. Her fingers were locking and interlocking. She picked at the skin around the edge of a thumb nail. "I'm fine," she said. "Yes, absolutely fine."

That was untrue. No way was Sadie fine. None of them were fine. They were here because they'd been referred. And the NHS wouldn't waste its valuable resources referring happy, healthy, well-adjusted people to a group like this.

Effie had been referred by a CPN called Stan at the Larwood Mental Health Centre. He was cheery chap – whose cheerfulness might have been connected with the fact that he was shortly to retire. During Effie's first appointment with him he'd given her a questionnaire to complete. For each question, you had to tick boxes according to whether you did something, or felt something, *never, rarely, sometimes, frequently, always*. The questions included:

Do you take as much care over your appearance as you used to do?

Do you enjoy doing the things you used to do as much as before?

Do you ever have feelings of panic?

Do you ever have feelings that something terrible is about to happen?

Do you ever think about killing yourself?

There'd been no questions about whether you ever thought about killing anyone else, Effie had noted. Such as your caree. Nor about how often you cry. Nor what makes you cry. Nor questions about how well or how badly you slept. Effie had felt that if she could only have a proper night's sleep she would be able to cope. If her brain would only stop buzzing with anxieties about Lionel and his health and his behaviour then maybe she'd be able lay her head on her pillow, close her eyes and drift off into welcome oblivion.

Stan had marked her questionnaire and pronounced that she got three out of twenty-five for depression and twenty-two out of twenty-five for anxiety. So his diagnosis had been that she was anxious but not depressed.

She'd talked to Stan about Lionel and all the things that had happened over the years. It had seemed a bit silly telling him all this stuff when she'd already told most of it to Lionel's CPN who worked in the same building. Wouldn't it be better for the two of them to have the same CPN, given that they were part of the same problem? It would have saved all this duplication of information.

Each time she'd had an appointment, she'd talked and Stan had listened. She'd even told him about Matt. Stan didn't actually suggest anything. Then, on the last occasion, she'd asked him if he thought that meditation might help her relax, help her sleep.

"You could try that," he'd said.

And he mentioned a weekly class in what was called Applied Meditation and Relaxation. (A.R.M.) "Would you like me to refer you?" he'd asked.

"Yes, please," she'd said. What had she got to lose?

So that was how she'd ended up coming here.

"That's great," said Jack. He looked at the next person in the circle. "What about Drax? Haven't seen you for a while. How was Christmas?"

Drax had a long story about driving up North, getting involved in car crash and visiting a whole string of relations, most of whom he couldn't stand.

"So you're glad to be back?" said Jack. "That's good."

It was Effie's turn. "I'm picking up Lionel on Friday," she said. "He's been well enough to come home – physically I mean, for three days now. But they said they wouldn't discharge him until I felt well enough to cope."

"And do you," asked Jack, "feel well enough to cope?"

"I know they want to discharge him. I couldn't expect them to keep him there any longer. He hates it, and they need the beds, don't they?"

"You didn't answer my question."

"I had a session with a woman from the Dementia Crisis Team. I... er... cried quite a bit. She said I was at the end of my tether and I ought to be on an antidepressant. But she said I wouldn't be on my own. I'd have plenty of support." Effie frowned. No one had said what sort of support this would be. "I expect it'll be okay." It wouldn't be okay. Effie knew that. How could anything ever be okay?

"Mmmm," said Jack.

Then he turned to Ewan. "How've you been, Ewan?"

"Fine," said Ewan. "Absolutely fine."

When every member of the group had been given an opportunity to unload their problems, it was time for the next part of the session.

"Okay," Jack said. "Everyone sitting comfortably, feet flat on the floor about eight inches apart. Back straight, hands relaxed on knees. Eyes closed."

He paused while the group shuffled and made themselves comfortable.

"Breathing in, breathing out. Nice and even. Just normally. In through the nose, out through the mouth. Relaxed breathing... A slightly deeper breath. Hold it just a little longer. In through the nose, out through the mouth..."

The next phase was what Jack called the Body Scan. "Clench your toes, then relax them. Tense your ankles and relax. Calves... thighs... buttocks..." He continued all the way up... "Ribcage... the top of the head. Fingers, arms, neck. Tense and relax.

"Think about being in some special place where you feel happy and safe. Beside a cool stream... lie back in the soft grass... listen to the water burbling over the pebbles..."

Effie thought about their house in Frigiliana that she'd bought the year after Mum and Dad died. The roof terrace there. Watching the sun go down. That was her special place.

"And now for the final stage – check everything is relaxed. Breathing in and breathing out... My right arm is heavy... my right arm *is* heavy... my right arm is *very* heavy."

In through the nose, out through the mouth.

"My left arm is heavy... my left arm *is* heavy..."

Each week Jack summed up by saying that the twenty-minute meditation exercise should be done if possible three times a day. "We all think about keep our bodies fit," he said. "We go the gym, play sports, or attend exercise classes. We should be doing the same with our minds."

Effie was highly sceptical. But she did almost as she was told. Twenty minutes' meditation in the morning, twenty in the evening. She couldn't quite manage it in the middle of the day too, but she did try. After all, the NHS was financing her attendance of this group so it was her duty to make the most of it.

The first time Effie tried meditation at home was a failure. She closed her eyes, but with her eyes closed she couldn't tell the time, so she had no way of knowing when the twenty minutes was up. She tried setting a timer, but she was so tense waiting for the time to ring she couldn't relax at all. And the last thing she wanted was to be blasted awake from a peaceful meditation by a nasty noise, whether it be a raucous bell or a shrill bleep. She tried guessing, but when she opened her eyes she found she'd only done a couple of minutes. So she decided to use some low-level relaxation music. If she listened to three tracks of the CD, she'd have done twenty minutes. This worked. She did it once in the morning and once before going to bed most days. After a couple of months of she started sleeping a bit better at night. Not every night, but enough to feel almost like a normal human being.

She'd been a member of this group for a while now, and although she was never quite sure exactly what it achieved, she knew that it made a difference.

"Now for the cancellation procedure," said Jack, breaking across the fragile calm that had fallen on the group. "Clench your fists, cross your arms, and... stretch!"

Effie kept her eyes closed. Oh, that felt so good.

They put the chairs away and said goodbye to each other, goodbye to Jack.

"Thank you. See you next week," Effie said to him.

"Good luck with Lionel!" he responded.

CHAPTER 38

Another Homecoming

Lionel sits on his hospital bed. He is ready. He is dressed. His things – some clothes, his washing stuff, his Sudoku, his *Radio Times*, are in two plastic bags. He doesn't have his house keys or his cigarettes or a lighter. But there is a bag of pills that he must take home with him. Where is Effie? He needs to get out of this place. Away from all these nutters. He wants to be in his own home.

There she is. Effie is approaching.

"Hello, love," she says, and she gives him a hug.

"About bloody time," he says. He stands up, holding carefully on to the back of a chair for support.

"How are you?" she asks.

"Fine," he says. "Let's go."

"I'd better talk to them," she says.

He follows her to the desk. "I've come to take Lionel Butler home," she says. "He's being discharged today. Is that right?"

"Yes," says the nurse on duty. "It's all done."

"Don't I have to speak to a doctor?" Effie asks.

"No. He was seen this morning and his medication is all ready."

"Oh," says Effie. "Don't we have to..." she hesitates, "...sign out or something?"

"No, it's all done."

"Let's go," says Lionel.

"I'll just get your bits and pieces," she says.

He watches her walk back into the bay where his bed is. She picks up the plastic bags and checks under the bed and inside the drawer of his bedside cabinet. Then she comes back to the desk. "Okay then," she says. She smiles at the nurse on duty. "Thank you so much," she says.

"A pleasure," is the response. "Goodbye Mrs Butler. Goodbye Mr Butler," they all say.

"Thank you," Effie repeats as they move off.

"Thank you for what?" he asks her.

She shrugs. "Putting up with you. Saving your life, I suppose."

"I wasn't dying," he reacts.

"You had pneumonia."

"Did I?"

"Yes. You might have died."

She opens the door to the ward and holds it for him. "It's along here to the lift," she says.

When they reach the main entrance, Effie tells him to sit on a chair while she goes to fetch the car from the car park. "Don't wander off." She is speaking slowly, like she thinks he's an idiot. "I'll be a few minutes, Lionel. I'll fetch the car. Then I'll drive up and stop the car right there." She points outside. Then she turns to him. "And I'll come back in here and get you. Don't go away."

Lionel sits and waits. He needs a cigarette. He'll have to go outside to smoke a cigarette. He gets up from his seat, goes through the double glass doors and looks up and down the road. Christ, it's cold. Nasty wind. He turns his coat collar up. He'd like to do it up, but that's too difficult. There's a bench there. He sits on it and feels in his pockets for his cigarettes. He must have left them somewhere. He stands up. He's needs a cigarette. He'd better go and buy some. He remembers there's a garage just across the roundabout outside the hospital. They'll have some cigarettes.

It's further than he thinks. He leans against a lamp post to get his breath back. He can see the roundabout now.

"You all right, mate?" comes a voice. It's a young guy with torn jeans and leather jacket. He's got a scarf wound a couple of times round his neck.

"Yes. Just having a rest."

The guy frowns. "Where're you going?"

Lionel isn't sure. "Buy cigarettes," he says.

"Blimey," says the guy. "This is a hospital. You can't buy cigarettes here! Here..." He fishes a packet from his jacket pocket. "Want a couple to be going on with?" He takes two cigarettes from the pack and sticks one in Lionel's mouth and the other in Lionel's jacket pocket.

"Wanna light?" He flicks a cigarette lighter and holds the flame to Lionel's cigarette.

It takes a couple of tries to get it alight. "Effing wind," mutters Lionel. He puffs on it for a moment then takes a long deep inhalation. Christ, that's good! "Fuck it," he says as he exhales. "Thanks."

"Here – take the lighter too," says the guy. "Just in case." He tucks it in Lionel's pocket alongside the spare cigarette.

"That's my first for..." How long was he in that place? It isn't that he can't remember. He just doesn't know.

"You been in the hospital?" says the guy.

Lionel nods. "Going home now."

The guy looks puzzled. "Don't look to me like they shoulda let you out. You got someone at home?"

Effie? Where's Effie? "Wife," he says. "Picking me up."

"Here. Let's get you back into the hospital. I'll get someone to call her. What's your name?"

"Lionel. Lionel Butler."

"Yeah, well, pleased to meet you, Lionel. I'm Jason, Jason Cartwright. Lionel is feeling very shaky.

"Here, Lionel, hang on to my arm," says Jason Cartwright.

And they walk slowly back towards the hospital entrance. Lionel feels very wobbly.

There is a white car parked outside double glass doors, where it says *pick and drop off only*. "That's her car," says Lionel. "Where the fuck's she gone?"

And Effie comes running out of the double glass doors. "Lionel! Where've you been? I told you to stay put! They've just called security." She's looking very cross.

"This your missis?" says Jason Cartwright. He gives Effie a broad grin. "He was looking for a fag," he says to her. Then he pats Lionel on the back. "You'll be all right now, mate. You've got a good one there – quite a looker, in't she? You hang on to her." Then he turns to Effie. "Good luck, Mrs Butler," he says.

"Got a nice surprise for you," says Effie.

"What that?"

"Nigel's at home. He's come over from Berlin."

"Oh." Lionel smiles. "That's good. What for?"

"To see us of course! I've left him putting up the curtain rail you pulled down."

"Curtain rail! What curtain rail?"

Effie smiles at him and takes her hand off the steering wheel to pat his knee. "Looking forward to being home?"

"You bet!"

The car turns into the drive. It all looks very green. The trees, the grass, the hedges. Effie gets out and comes round to his side to open the passenger door for him. "I can manage!" he snaps as she takes his arm. She stands back.

He makes his way to the front door, and as he waits for Effie, it opens.

"Hi Dad," says Nigel. "How are you?"

They shake hands and hug.

"Average," says Lionel. "What are you doing here?"

He looks around. He walks around. The sitting room, the dining room the kitchen. He heads up the stairs, hanging on to the banisters. "Don't watch me," he says to Effie.

His room looks different. Effie has done something to it. He comes downstairs. He opens and closes cupboards in the kitchen. The chest of drawers in the dining room. The drinks cabinet in the lounge.

"What are you looking for?" Effie asks.

"Cigarettes."

"Lionel, you've been on nicotine patches for nearly a fortnight," says Effie. "You shouldn't need cigarettes. This would be a very good time to try and give up smoking."

Lionel glares and puts up two fingers at her.

Effie sighs. She goes upstairs and comes down with a wrapped package of five packs of his usual brand. Should be a hundred cigarettes, thinks Lionel. Except it's only ninety-five, because there are only nineteen in every box. And five times nineteen is ninety-five. A bit of a con really.

Lionel sits at his table. He rips open the package and takes out a pack. He'll go upstairs in a minute, but first he needs a cup of coffee.

He stands up.

"Can I get you anything?" asks Effie.

"No. I'm going to have a coffee," he says.

"Shall I get it for you?" she asks.

"No." He goes back to the kitchen and makes his coffee the way he likes it. "Don't slop it," says Effie as he carries it back to his table. She's still watching him.

Effie hands him his *Radio Times* and his Sudoku.

"What's for supper?" he asks.

"Shepherd's pie," she says.

He nods.

"Everything all right?" she asks.

He nods. Everything is fine.

CHAPTER 39

Inappropriate Remarks

Effie was accustomed to Lionel making what were euphemistically called *inappropriate remarks*. The tendency to make such remarks, she had learned, was a well-documented symptom of FTD. As was *challenging behaviour*. For inappropriate, read rude, Effie thought. And for *challenging*, read *nasty*.

Sometimes Effie made *inappropriate remarks* herself.

There was a call from Lionel's GP to find out how he was since he'd come home from hospital.

"He's fine," said Effie, almost automatically. Then she corrected herself. "At least, I don't mean he's fine, he's an absolute wreck. Just like he was before he was taken ill."

"So he recovered from the pneumonia," remarked the doctor.

"Yes, unfortunately," said Effie.

There was an awkward space that Effie decided to fill. "Someone told me that pneumonia used to be called the 'old man's friend'," she said. "That was in the days before penicillin, I suppose."

"I believe so," said the doctor tightly.

"Isn't anyone allowed to die of it anymore?" Effie asked.

The GP didn't reply, but Effie changed the subject. "I've just remembered something else," she said.

"Oh yes?"

"It's Lionel's feet. They're flaking. They're splitting. There are sores that look infected. They smell infected. I asked the doctor in the hospital about them, but... well... he was busy saving Lionel's life, wasn't he? It was hardly a priority. But Lionel needs to see a podiatrist."

"I'll email you a list of ones that do home visits," said the GP.

"Thank you," said Effie. "And thank you so much for taking the time to phone us. I'm sorry I made that remark about... the old man's friend. I do know you're all doing your best."

Dr Dauncey was very nice, she reflected. Lionel's previous GP, Dr Andrews, wouldn't have bothered to phone. He'd always thought Lionel was a waste of space. Which was possibly right. Definitely right.

Then there was another phone call.

"Please could I speak to Mrs Butler?" came a voice.

"Speaking," said Effie.

"My name is Becky Braman. I'm a senior social worker, specialising in problems with dementia patients."

"The Dementia Crisis Team? That's great," said Effie. "I was expecting you to call. I'm at my wit's end. I really don't know how I'm going to cope with him now."

"Er... no... I'm actually on the county Safeguarding Team. I'm ringing about a report made in connection with the CDIC course that I believe you attended in November and December."

"Ye-es..." said Effie cautiously. She could guess what this was about.

"The course tutor put in a report about something you said that he felt indicated a need for safeguarding."

"Really?" said Effie with carefully contrived innocence. "And what might that be?" she asked. As if she didn't already know.

Effie had attended the Carers' Dementia Information Course, Stage 2 (*CDIC2*), shortly before Christmas. It had run for one morning a week for six weeks, and part of the reason she'd signed on for it was that she knew a few others who would be attending. Sheila, her ex-colleague, whose friendship she had renewed in those carers' group meetings. Laura, whom she met at the CDIC Part 1 course she'd attended earlier in the year. Laura was the only FTD carer she'd met locally. The carers were a mixed bunch, as presumably were their carees.

Mary, a single, retired college lecturer, had been looking after her mother, Gladys, who was eighty-six and had trouble washing herself properly. Mary had complained that the poor dear could no longer understand that you are supposed to use one flannel for your face and neck, and another for your nether regions.

Dear God, Effie had thought. Is that all Mary had to worry about?

"Lionel doesn't wash at all," she'd said. "So it's easy for me."

Laura had said that her husband was too frightened of the noise of water to go into the shower cubicle. She'd tried going in with him, but he'd pushed her out of the way so she'd fallen, bruised her bum, grazed her elbow and broken the shower door. "So I've given up," she'd said.

"I'm lucky," Effie'd said. "Lionel hasn't been near a shower for months."

The course tutor had advised on the importance of drying your *loved one* properly, especially in the creases and folds of sagging bellies and the like. "For women," he said, "fungal infections under the breasts can be a problem."

Effie found herself getting more and more irritated. "In the unlikely event of my so-called *loved one* having a wash or a shower," she said, "no way would he let anyone dry him!" Then she added, "Not that my *loved one* is loved by anyone. Do you think I should call him my *unloved one?*"

Another carer called Arthur, had spoken of his wife's personality change. "What you have to do," he'd advised, "is accept it. Stop looking for that person you used to know. Try and think of your loved one as a well-loved family pet. Like a cat or dog."

If Lionel were a dog, Effie had thought, she'd have him put down. But what she'd said was: "I think my husband should be painlessly put to sleep."

There'd been a silence and Effie'd known that this time she had gone too far. She'd smiled at the course tutor. "You did say, that everything said in this room, was confidential, didn't you?"

The tutor had looked down at his notes. "It is, providing we feel that no risk is indicated to any of the concerned parties."

Well, that's all right then, Effie had thought at the time.

But it was not all right, as Effie was about to discover. Effie's remark had been considered so *inappropriate*, so *unacceptable*, that Lionel might be considered to be *at risk*.

Becky Braman continued her account of what was contained in the course tutor's report. "He said, that you said, that your husband should be..."

Effie sat back on the sofa, the handset at her right ear. She found herself grinning. "...painlessly put to sleep," she completed. "Is that what you're ringing about?"

"Er... yes..." came the voice.

There was a silence, which Effie broke with, "Well he hasn't," she said.

"Hasn't what?"

Effie stood up and walked to the window. It was foul day. Light drizzle that you could barely see against the greyness of it all. "He hasn't been put to sleep. Painlessly or otherwise." She could hear Lionel shuffling in from the kitchen, pushing open the living room door, a cup of coffee in his hand.

Effie smiled at him. "In fact, he is very much awake." Then she lowered her voice. "Were you afraid I'd kill him?"

"No... no... it's just that we have to follow up..."

"It's been weeks!" she protested. "If you really thought I was going to... do him in... don't you think you should have followed it up before now? Like on the same day!"

"Well, we didn't really think... It's just that we are obliged to..."

"Tick boxes?"

"No. Follow procedures."

Effie pressed her lips tightly together. "So what about Dementia Crisis? Are they going to follow a procedure and come and see us? I was promised I wouldn't have to cope on my own."

"I don't know anything about Dementia Crisis," said Becky Braman.

I bet you don't! thought Effie. But she didn't say so. "Did you know he's been in hospital?" she asked.

"No, I didn't. Why?"

"Pneumonia." Effie left the living room, the handset still held to her right ear.

"Oh." Becky seemed thrown. "I'm sorry. Is he..."

"He didn't die. But he is more demented."

"You mean his dementia appears to have progressed further?"

"I mean he is more demented," repeated Effie. *Demented* was another inappropriate word.

There was long pause. "I wonder if I could arrange to pay you a visit?" asked Becky.

"To check on Lionel's safety?" asked Effie.

"To safeguard his well-being," said Becky.

Effie shrugged, "If you like," she said. "How about carrying out a Social Services Assessment on him?"

"Hasn't Mr Butler had one?" asked Becky.

"No. They said it wasn't necessary." Effie had asked for a Social Services Assessment of Lionel ages ago, but in her view she had been fobbed off.

"Really? There should have been a Social Services Assessment."

"Of Lionel, you mean?"

"Yes, of course."

"Not of me?"

"No. That would be a Carer's Assessment."

"So could you arrange that too?" Effie had asked. Then, "Great! Shall we fix the dates?"

And they did. Nearly a whole month later.

"Do come in," Effie said. She showed Becky into the living room and suggested she join Lionel at his table. She would sit the other end of the room and try not to participate. It was Lionel's Assessment after all. Nothing to do with her.

But when Becky asked Lionel if he had any problems with washing, showering, or bathing, he answered. "No. I like a daily shower."

Effie pressed he lips tightly together and tried not to say anything. But she couldn't stop herself. "That's nonsense," she said. "He hasn't had a shower for months!"

Effie's last inappropriate remark was made to the matron employed by the Dementia Action Team. These were the people who'd organised the handrails, the smoke alarms and the key safe.

The team matron phoned. "I wondered if I could come and talk to you to about how to recognise the signs of heart failure," she said.

Effie was slow to reply. She was tired of talking to people who told her things. None of them told her how to cope with living with this impossible man for an indeterminate length of time. What was the point?

"I'd rather not," she said.

"Oh. Is there any particular reason?"

"Well..." Effie hesitated. She took a deep breath. "Well, I don't want to know. I think that the best thing that could possibly happen to Lionel, would be for him to die of a massive heart attack."

CHAPTER 40

The Podiatrist's Tale

"Let me see your feet," says Effie.

Lionel grimaces. Why is she always fussing about his feet? "Not now," he says.

"Why not now?" says Effie. "Are you busy? Have you got a date with anyone?"

"Oh, all right, then!" concedes Lionel.

She kneels in front of him and he reluctantly lets her ease off his slippers. She begins to peel off his right sock.

"I'll do it!" he snaps. He leans down and takes off the sock.

"And the other one," she says.

His toenails need cutting. He can see that. They are thick and long and yellow.

Effie runs her fingers over his foot and flakes of skin fall off like confetti. "They're very dry," she says. She scratches with the nail of her index finger.

"Aagh!" he says and jerks it away.

"Does it hurt?" she says.

"No. 'Course not." But it does tickle. It's a horrible feeling.

She pushes at the side of his foot.

"Fuck!" That does hurt.

Effie peers closely at the foot. "It's cracked and swollen. I think it's infected," she says. "You need proper treatment. But we'll cream them for the moment."

And she squeezes a big dollop of stuff from a plastic bottle and rubs it into his feet. All over, toes, soles, ankles. It's not so bad. After a bit, it feels quite nice.

"You used to love having your feet stroked," she says wistfully.

"Did I?" he says. He can't remember that.

She smiles. "Other things too," she says. It's a sort of secret smile.

She pushes up his trouser legs and creams his shins and calves. There's a sore here," she says, pushing at something. "Does it hurt?"

He jerks his leg away. She's fussing again.

She kneels back. "I've made an appointment for a podiatrist to come to the house to give you a pedicure."

Lionel frowns. "I can go to Harriet's. She'll cut my toenails." Harriet's nice. She lives opposite and she's a chiropodist. She's been cutting his toenails ever since they got too thick for him to cut.

Effie gets up off her knees and sits down on a chair beside him. "I think Harriet's retiring," she says.

"Retiring? She can't be old enough!"

"Well... I phoned her."

Effie is hiding something. His brain might be scrambled, but Lionel can tell when Effie's hiding something. He's not so green as he's cabbage looking. "What for?"

"Well... I asked her if she could do rather more than cut your toenails, and treat this cracked skin. But she made excuses. She doesn't want to. I don't think she likes you swearing at her."

"I don't swear at her!"

"Well... maybe... but she said it would be best if we found someone else."

Lionel puts his socks back on. And then his slippers. "This pod... thing?"

"Podiatrist. Same as Chiropodist. He's fully qualified and recommended by the surgery. And, as it happens, he used to be a psychiatric nurse, but he retrained. So he knows about FTD.

What's Effie on about? Lionel wonders. "STD?" he queries.

"No. FTD. Frontotemporal dementia. It's the name of the brain disease you've got."

Lionel laughs. He doesn't have a disease. He's fine.

Effie continues. "He's trained to cope with difficult patients. He's coming tomorrow morning. His name's Finn O'Donnell."

Effie introduces the podiatrist. She puts on that pseudo cheery voice of hers. "Lionel, this is Finn O'Donnell."

"Good morning, Mr Butler," says Finn O'Donnell in a soft Irish accent. He puts down his black bag and shakes hands with Lionel.

Imitating Irish is a doddle, thinks Lionel. "And the top o' the morning to you too, Mr O'Donnell!" he says.

Finn grins and glances out the window. The sky is blue and the sun is streaming in. "It's a grand old day, isn't it?" he responds, exaggerating the lilt of the dialect.

Effie smiles. "And Finn is going to sort your feet out."

"Finn?" says Lionel, puzzled. "What sort of a name is that?"

Finn shrugs. "It's my name," he says.

"Named after a fish finger, are you?"

"I don't think so. Maybe *Finnegan's Wake*."

Lionel frowns. "That's a book, isn't it? I think we read that at school."

Finn laughs. "So did we. We had to read all that James Joyce stuff." He paused. "So how are your feet, Lionel?"

Lionel glares at Finn O'Donnell. "My feet are fine," he says.

"Well, let's take a little peek, shall we? Just to see."

"Where would you like Lionel to sit?" Effie asks Finn.

Finn considers the layout of the room. "He can sit on the sofa here, put his feet up on one of those chairs. We can put it there…"

Lionel sits and they put a dining chair in front of him. Finn puts a paper cloth on the chair and Effie says, "There you are Lionel. Put your feet up."

And he does. Then Finn pulls out another chair for himself ready to work on Lionel's feet. He puts on a white plastic pinafore, and slips his hands into thin plastic gloves.

Finn's black bag is a treasure chest of what look to Lionel, like instruments of torture. Files, clippers, scalpels.

He starts on Lionel's right foot, clipping and scraping at each nail in turn.

"Ouch!" yelps Lionel. "Fuck!"

"Now that can't hurt, Lionel," says Finn softly. "There are no nerves in a dead toenail."

How the fuck does he know? thinks Lionel. "That's enough!" he says. "You must have finished."

"Be patient, Lionel. Be nice. We've only just started. There's a lot of work to be done." He takes out a file. "We need to reduce the thickness," he says.

Every stroke of the file makes Lionel cringe. "Fuck!"

"Now, keep still, Lionel. This is sharp."

And Finn lifts Lionel's right foot and starts cutting away peelings of dead skin with a scalpel. Heels, soles, and each side of the foot are all attended to.

"That's enough. Surely you've finished now?" says Lionel. He can't stand much more of this.

"Nearly... nearly..." says Finn. Finally, he puts Lionel's left foot down on the plastic-covered dining chair and massages some cream into it.

"Now let's start on the other foot," says Finn.

"The other foot! Are you doing it to both?"

Finn laughs. "It is usual for a podiatrist to treat two feet," he says.

And the process starts all over again. "Fuck!!" says Lionel. "Isn't it finished?"

"Just a bit more," says Finn. "Don't move. This is sharp."

And finally, "There! Bob's your uncle!" he says.

"No, he isn't," says Lionel. "I haven't got any uncles, not live ones, anyway."

Finn addresses Effie. "You need to soak his feet in warm water with disinfectant, or vinegar or salt if you prefer. Every day. That infection will soon clear up."

"You don't think he should have an antibiotic?" asks Effie.

Finn shakes his head. "Basic hygiene is all it needs. A good soak will get rid of the dry skin. And moisturising them afterwards will help. Any moisturising cream will do. It's when the skin dries out that it splits and infection can get in. And if there are cracks, vitamin D pills will help the healing."

"I see," says Effie. "I'll try... but he doesn't make it easy for me."

"I can imagine," says Finn. He is putting away his equipment and untying his apron. He folds up the piece of plastic on the chair, collecting together all the nail trimmings and skin remnants that now litter it. Then he wraps the whole thing in his plastic apron. "A bin?" he says to Effie. "Have you a bin?"

She points to the waste paper basket. "That'll do."

Effie writes him a cheque and gets out her diary. "Should we make an appointment for a second visit?"

Effie shows Finn O'Donnell to the door, Lionel hears him say to her in his soft Irish lilt, "And what about you, Mrs Butler? Are you coping all right?"

Effie pauses a moment. Then, "It isn't easy," she says.

"No. I can see that. Don't forget to look after yourself."

What was all that about? thinks Lionel.

Effie tried to follow the podiatrist's instructions. She really did. What can be so unpleasant about someone bringing you a nice bowl of warm water in which to soak your feet? she wondered. Afterwards, she would kneel before Lionel and gently pat those size ten blotchy clod-hoppers with a soft fluffy towel.

"Ouch!" Lionel sometimes reacted. "Careful!"

Then she'd massage the newly washed feet with moisturising cream. Wasn't that one of the services that Mary Magdalene offered Jesus? Presumably he must have liked it. Why couldn't Lionel?

Well, he didn't. He'd grunt and grumble and curse and swear.

"There," she said after few weeks of regular and unappreciated effort. "They're looking much better."

"Have you finished?" he demanded.

It had been worth it. The infected lesions were almost healed. "Finn will be impressed," she remarked.

"Finn?" said Lionel.

"The podiatrist. He's coming tomorrow."

"Oh," said Lionel. "I don't like him!"

"Well, try and be polite. He just does his job."

Next day Effie realised she'd slipped up with her diary. Finn was booked for five o'clock so as not to interfere with Lionel's afternoon nap. But she needed to leave just after five-thirty for her A.R.M session that began at six o'clock. It was a bit tight, but it shouldn't matter too much, she thought. After all, Finn knew Lionel now, and with his past experience of mental illness, he shouldn't have any problem coping with Lionel on his own if she had to leave before he finished.

She was wrong.

It just happened that Finn was running late, the traffic was bad, and Effie had to leave before he arrived.

"Finn'll be here in a minute," she said to Lionel. "You might offer him a cup of tea or coffee." She wrote a cheque for the fee and put it in an envelope. "And don't forget to pay him."

She picked up her handbag. "Byeee. Be nice to him."

What happened after she'd left, led to Effie writing a letter to Dr Hazan.

Lionel Butler : FTD Patient

Dear Dr Hazan

Lionel and I have an appointment with you next week. As I will be unable to talk privately during the appointment, I am writing in advance.

In January, I found a podiatrist for Lionel. Finn O'Donnell is a retired psychiatric nurse. He did excellent work on Lionel's feet, tolerating the extreme behaviour with stoic patience.

Last Wednesday Mr O'Donnell came for a second visit. Unfortunately he was running late and I had to go out. I thought that Mr O'Donnell, with his psychiatric background, would be able to deal with Lionel in my absence.

I was wrong.

When I arrived home Lionel told me that the podiatrist had come, but left without doing anything.

I phoned Mr O'Donnell the next morning and learned that Lionel's aggression had forced him to leave. He asked if I realised how much my presence calms Lionel down. How could I? Then Mr O'Donnell asked me if you, as his psychiatrist, have ever seen Lionel alone, because, if not, you would have no idea what he is really like.

So I think it would be best if you talked to each of us separately. You will find out what Lionel is like without me, and I will be able to speak to you without being inhibited by him.

I look forward to seeing you next Thursday.

Yours sincerely

Frances Butler (Mrs)

The next week Effie and Lionel went to the Larwood Mental Health Centre for an appointment with Dr Hazan. First, he invited her into his office alone to discuss matters.

Then he phoned the receptionist and asked her to bring Lionel along.

"But aren't you going to see him on his own?" Effie asked.

Dr Hazan smiled. "I don't need to. I know what he's like."

CHAPTER 41

Texts, Calls and Emails

Effie looked at her smartphone screen and keyed in the words.

Hi Dominic. Can we chat some time? Effie.

Dominic Darnfield had made it clear that he did not want Effie to ring him without warning. He needed to be sure that his wife wouldn't overhear the conversation. It wasn't that there was anything to hide, but one of Kerry's FTD obsessions was an excessive interest in his acquaintances, especially the female ones. Her cross-questioning could be intense, irrational, and utterly exhausting, Dominic had explained. Sometimes she'd rant and rave, like a mad woman. Which is what she was, of course, reflected Effie. Though 'mad' was one of those words that mustn't be used to describe people with dementia. Effie wondered if there had been grounds for Kerry's extreme suspicion at some stage in the couple's marriage, but there was certainly no reason for the poor woman to suspect Effie's motives. What Effie needed was a chat with an FTD pal. As Dominic had said, you can't have too many FTD pals.

The reply arrived a minute later: *After 8.00pm.*

Effie keyed in: *OK.*

At exactly 8.00pm, another text bleeped its arrival. *Now OK.*

And she pressed the call button.

"Hello, Effie," he responded. "Is something up? How's Lionel?"

"Fine. I mean... he's not fine... He can't ever be fine, can he? But he's totally recovered from that pneumonia."

"That's good," said Dominic evenly.

"Is it?" said Effie.

"Well... maybe not," said Dominic.

Effie smiled to herself. Dominic understood.

"You know," she continued, "Lionel has no recollection of being in hospital. Within one day of getting home it was completely gone. Weird, isn't it? How's Kerry?"

"Getting worse. She's using all the wrong words for things and then gets angry when I don't know what she's talking about. And she goes out shopping and buys loads of stuff she can't possibly want. Sometimes I take things back and sometimes I just give up. We have seven tea cosies."

Effie laughed. "One for every day of the week!"

"We don't need any at all – she smashed the teapot in one of our rows."

There was a pause and Effie said, "The reason I rang... apart from wanting to keep in touch, of course... is that I was wondering if you knew anything about Admiral Nurses? It seems I'm to have a visit from one."

"That's brilliant!" said Dominic. "How did you fix that?"

"I didn't. I don't know who did. Maybe it was that social worker who came here on a 'safeguarding' mission. She thought I wanted Lionel to be painlessly put to sleep."

Dominic laughed. "Is that what you said?"

"I didn't mean it."

"I bet you did. That's what I like about you, Effie. You say what the rest of us only think." There was a pause. One that wouldn't have been noticed in a face to face conversation, but was obvious in a phone call. "I know how to do it, you know," he said.

"Do what?"

"Painlessly put someone to sleep."

Effie felt uncomfortable. Dominic had taken early retirement from the medical profession in order to care for Kerry. He presumably had knowledge and skills that most people knew nothing about.

He continued, "Without being caught, I mean... at least, I don't think they'd find out... but if they did, I'd end up in prison. Though maybe not for very long."

"Mmmm," Effie said. "Aren't you effectively in prison anyway?"

He agreed. "True. We all are, aren't we?"

It was time to get back to the subject. "Anyway, this Admiral Nurse rang up and made an appointment to come and see me. It's next week but I don't know what it's about." Effie sighed, "I wonder if there's any point. So many people have seen Lionel now. They all pontificate about this and that, and rabbit on about all that's happened, but no one can actually do anything."

"But an Admiral Nurse is for you!" protested Dominic. "She's not for Lionel. Her job will to be to look after you."

"But I don't need looking after."

"Yes, you do. You're an FTD carer, and that makes you vulnerable. You're more likely to suffer from other illnesses compared with the rest of the population. Even more than Alzheimer's carers. Psychiatric disorders, obviously, such as anxiety or depression. But because of the stress you've a higher probability of contracting cancer, heart disease, and all sorts of horrible things."

"Really?" Presumably Dominic knew what he was talking about.

He continued. "There aren't very many of these nurses and you're lucky to have one assigned to you."

"Oh. It's a good thing then?"

"Absolutely! Have you read John Suchet's book?

"John Suchet. The actor?"

"No. His brother. News reporter. His wife had dementia and he's written a book about his experiences. I'll lend it to you. I'll bring it next time we meet. It's a love story, really, though his wife's died now, and he's found someone else. But my point is that he had an Admiral Nurse and he's done a lot to develop the service since."

Effie's brow puckered. "He's found someone else?"

"So I read. He met her in the care home. A fellow carer, I suppose."

"Very romantic," Effie remarked wryly.

Dominic laughed. "I suppose sharing problems can bring you together."

"I imagine so." The fact that she and Dominic shared similar problems was certainly the reason for their somewhat tenuous friendship. She wondered if they had anything else in common. Was being a dementia carer a strong enough link to build a relationship? And when the demented partners died, would there be anything left?

"Are you going to the next meeting?" he asked.

"Yes. I expect so."

"Well... let me know how you get on with the Admiral Nurse. And I'll bring that book to the meeting."

"Thanks, Dominic. I'll look forward to it."

Effie checked her emails. There was one from Home Angels, the company which, for some years now, had been supplying two cleaning ladies to clean the house once a fortnight.

Effie, in the beginning, had always gone out when the cleaning ladies arrived, to give them some space. She couldn't stand them hoovering around her. Lionel, too had often been out. But since those early days, things had changed. Lionel never went out, and anything that interfered with his routine caused conflict. He wouldn't get up for the ladies to clean his room. Or if he were up he always wanted to make a coffee just when they were washing the kitchen floor, or he'd settle with his Sudoku in the living room, just as they began to hoover in there. And then there had been that complaint from the manageress that Lionel had teased one of the ladies about her obesity, and another about her accent. Effie had apologised and explained that it was Lionel's dementia that was to blame for his rudeness. "He can't help the things he says," she'd said.

"Hmmm!" the manageress had said.

Effie opened the email.

Dear Mrs Butler

We have decided, given the circumstances of Mr Butler's ill health, that for the safety and comfort of our employees, we can only continue to send cleaning ladies if you yourself can undertake to supervise Mr Butler at all times while they are in your home.

Effie sighed. Presumably, as Finn O'Donnell had pointed out, Lionel's behaviour was worse in her absence. She thought for a moment or two. No, she couldn't undertake to supervise Lionel. Not at all times. Not at any time. And if she did, what difference would it make? He never did anything she told him.

She replied and thanked *the company for their help over the years*, but said she felt that, *given the circumstances of Mr Butler's ill health*, it would be easier for her to do the housework herself.

As the email was sent another arrived. This was from Justin

Collins from Effie's German conversation group. When Nigel had married and moved to Berlin, Effie had started German classes. After three years, she had given up lessons and joined an informal German conversation group. Justin Collins sometimes sent out group emails to the class about proposed topics of discussion or suggested reading matter. This one was a suggestion of a group outing.

Hallo Deutschegruppe
Ich habe eine Idee. Eine Deutschegruppe Ausflug! Nächste Woche das Film, **Das Leben der Anderen** *kommt zum Picture House. Gehen wir zu es sehen? Donnerstag oder Freitag ist besser fur mich.*
What do you think? Let me know if you'd like to go. I'm happy to drive, but if we're more than five we'll need another driver.
Tschuss!
Justin.

Justin usually sat next to Effie in the conversation group. He was one of three men in the group of eight... or was it nine? They were never all present. Justin's German was somewhat better than Effie's. Like her, he attended diligently and he always prepared something to talk about, or brought something to read aloud. She didn't know much about him. There'd been no mention of *eine Frau*. He'd spoken of holidays he'd taken, but had never mentioned *eine Freundin*. Stilted German conversation didn't lend itself to personal matters, but Justin didn't come across as a bachelor. He must be widowed or divorced.

The idea of an outing to see a German film appealed to Effie. She replied.

Hallo Justin
Vielen Danke. Eine Exzellente Idee!

Ich das Kino mag. Donnerstag is besser für mich.

Tschuss!

Effie

PS. I don't mind driving if another car's needed.

Another car was not needed. It transpired that none of the others wanted to go. So it was just the two of them. Well, why not? Justin said he'd pick her up.

"Where are you going?" Lionel asked Effie.

"The Picture House, to see a German film. With a friend from the German conversation group." She didn't say whether it was a woman friend or a man friend. English is useful like that. You don't have to reveal the gender as you do in other languages.

When she saw Justin's car pull up outside the house, she called out a quick, "Goodbye!" to Lionel, then hurried down the drive to open Justin's passenger door and step in. The last thing she wanted to do was to have to introduce him to Lionel, who would undoubtedly come up with the old Monty Python German joke, *Don't mention the war!* Not that it would matter if the two met. It wasn't as though it were a date.

Except, in a way, it turned out like a date. Justin insisted on paying for the tickets, and then he suggested going for a drink afterwards to discuss the film.

"*Auf Deutsch?*" you mean, asked Effie with questioning smile.

He looked at her. "Not necessarily," he said.

They did discuss the film, but they moved on to other things.

Effie told Justin about her life with Lionel. The personality change. Her role as a carer. The things that had happened. She didn't tell him about Matt.

Justin told Effie about his life as a long-established and confirmed divorcee. Undoubtedly he left gaps. But they said things about their hopes and their anxieties that they could not possibly have said in German.

"It's been a lovely evening," she said when he dropped her off outside the house. "Thank you so much."

There was pause. "I'm going away for a couple of months," he said.

"Oh. Where?" Effie felt curiously disappointed.

"I'm visiting my son in New Zealand. I'm leaving on Monday."

"That's nice," Effie said. He'd told her about the son, but not about the fact that he was off to see him so soon.

"Effie, can I email you when I'm away?" he said.

Effie laughed. "Only if it's in German," she said lightly.

"*Natürlich*," he said looking intently at her. For a moment she thought he was going to kiss her. He put his hand on her forearm. "I'll email you whenever I can, and I'll see you when I get back. *Gute nacht!*"

And she was pushing open the car door to get out. She had to get away. "Thank you," she said again. She slammed the door behind her, then hurried up the drive to the house without looking back. She heard Justin's light goodbye beep on his car horn as he pulled away.

No! No! No! Effie was saying to herself as she turned the key.

CHAPTER 42

Sharing the Journey

Effie approached the imposing columns of the classically designed main entrance. Since that first visit she had never missed a meeting, though once every three months was not enough. Coming here was like coming home. It was only here that she met people who could understand what she'd been experiencing, people who would understand where her journey might be going. These were the people she could share it with. They were like a second family. And they were a whole lot more supportive than her first family.

She entered through a side door, and headed for the ladies' cloakroom. She went to the loo, washed her hands, then stood before the mirror to brush her hair and renew her lipstick. Not too bad. She took a deep breath, closed her eyes and slowly breathed out. Relax, she told herself.

In the conference room, Natalie was handing out name badges. "Hello, Effie! Lovely to see you," she said in that cheery, positive tone of hers. "Now, come this way. I want to introduce you to a couple of new members."

And a few moments later, "Now, Effie, this is Dave, whose brother's just been diagnosed, and Alice, whose husband's symptoms sound very much like Lionel's."

313

Effie shook hands with the two newcomers. "Welcome to FTD-Land," she smiled. Dave, a thickset man probably in his mid-fifties, was here to support his brother who'd been recently diagnosed. She couldn't imagine Lionel's brother taking such an interest. In fact, Michael had shown no interest at all. The link between Alice's husband and Lionel, they soon discovered, was the alcoholic background, which they had both been told had nothing whatever to do with FTD.

Effie told them what to expect at the meeting. It wasn't long since she'd been a first-timer. It was good to think that she was now accepted almost as an old hand. She was always learning, but she knew enough to sympathise with someone who'd recently experienced the trauma of the events leading up to a family member's diagnosis.

"Hello Effie," came a familiar voice.

She turned. "Dominic!" she said. "Good to see you. How are things?"

He grimaced. "Dire. Tell you later." Then he smiled for her to introduce the two new members.

"When I started coming here," he said, "I almost felt like a fraud. My problems were so much simpler than everyone else's."

"And now?" asked Dave.

He shook his head. "I could never have foreseen..." Then he smiled at them all. "...but it's good to be back." He looked at Effie. "And great to see you. You're looking well. Have you been away again?"

"Only to our place in Spain. I get a care company to send a carer twice a day to check on Lionel. Just for quarter of an hour."

"Is that all?" interjected Dave. "Surely they can't do much in that time?"

"It's only to see that Lionel's okay. Sometimes he won't let them in. Sometimes he tells them to eff off."

Dominic laughed. "Which means he's fine!"

"So can you leave him safely?" asked Alice. She sounded dubious.

Effie paused thoughtfully. "There's always a risk. At the moment, I can. He can find food in the fridge, providing it's in the front of the fridge where he can see it. He can dress himself, though he wouldn't think of ever putting on clean clothes. He's not incontinent. I don't know how long it'll be like this, but..."

"Make the most of it while it is!" put in Dominic.

"I am," Effie said. "I've booked to go again in the autumn."

"Mmmm," said Dominic. "Wish I could get away somewhere."

Effie gave a small smile. "It would do you good," she said. The poor man deserved a chance to escape from the nightmare that had become his home life.

It was time for the lecture. Dominic steered the two newcomers into vacant seats while Effie found herself in a seat between him and a woman she had talked to last time. "Hello. Sally, isn't it?" she checked.

The woman nodded, but didn't say anything.

"How are you getting on?" prompted Effie.

Sally pressed her lips tightly together. "William passed away six weeks ago," she said.

"Oh... I'm sorry," said Effie.

Sally shrugged. "It was for the best."

"How was he... at the end?"

"Awful. His legs went black. They wanted to amputate them, but... well they didn't, but... he was in pain..."

"I'm so very sorry..." Effie began. She felt utterly inadequate. She wasn't sorry. The death of an FTD patient should be grounds for celebration.

But Natalie stepped up to the front, ready to welcome them officially and introduce the speaker. A Professor Rose Darwell. How could someone so young and pretty be a professor? Effie wondered.

Effie got out her notebook. The PowerPoint presentation showed images of different brains. Diseased ones and healthy ones. Effie was fascinated. You could actually see the difference! What would Lionel's look like? she wondered.

At the end, she turned and checked the rows behind. Twenty-five, twenty-six, twenty-seven people. Most of them frightened carers who didn't know how to cope with the present and were shit-scared of the future. And Sally, of course, for whom it was all over. Only it wasn't. There were others like her. After years of caring you didn't revert to the person you used to be. FTD changed you, infected you, scarred you. Effie realised that FTD would always be with her, no matter what happened to Lionel. There is no such thing as closure.

After a sandwich lunch, they were divided into four groups small enough for discussion purposes. This time Effie ended up in a different group from Dominic. She felt slightly disappointed, but it was no big deal, she told herself.

Afterwards she had a word with Natalie. "I noticed on the website you don't have a regional contact for my part of the world?" she asked.

"No," said Natalie. "Margot was going to do it, but her husband died last year and... it didn't happen."

"I was wondering," asked Effie, "if you'd like me to take over the role? Unless someone else wants to, of course."

Natalie gave a delighted smile. "That would be fantastic! I'll put your name on the website and include the information in the next newsletter."

It was all over and people were saying goodbye and drifting away.

"Have you got to rush off?" asked Dominic.

Effie shrugged. "Not especially."

"Care for a drink somewhere?" he said. "We haven't caught up properly, have we?"

He led her down a side street to a pub that he evidently knew quite well.

"What'll you have?" he asked.

She hesitated. "It's really tea time," she remarked doubtfully.

"Don't be so rigid about time! That's a well-known FTD symptom and I don't like it!" he said with mock severity.

Effie smiled. "In that case, I'll have a glass of white wine."

He ordered and they settled at a corner table.

"So," Effie said. "What's so especially dire?"

Dominic raised his glass and took a sip. "Kerry's getting worse," he said. "She can't be left unsupervised. I'm going to have to get a carer in permanently."

"Who's with her now?" asked Effie.

"My sister." He glanced at his watch. "But it isn't easy for her. She stayed for a few days to give me a chance to get away. God knows I needed it! But it drove her to distraction and she won't do it again. I don't blame her."

"Where did you go?"

"The Gower Peninsular. A cosy little hotel. We walked along the cliffs. Had a few nice meals, but..."

"We?" asked Effie.

He took a deep breath. "I have... I mean I had... a girlfriend... a lover... but it's over now. She's ended it."

"I'm sorry."

"So am I, but I can't blame her. I would have married her... if things had been different. But how long can I keep her waiting? It's been years already. She's met someone else. She says she's not in love with him, but she wants a normal relationship."

"And she's not going to hang around waiting for Kerry to die?"

He smiled. "You get to the point, don't you?"

Effie shrugged and took a slug of her wine. "I can't stand all these euphemisms."

"The thing is... I don't know when my marriage started going wrong, and how much of it was due to Kerry's FTD personality change. I wanted a divorce. I saw a solicitor the month before she was diagnosed. And then..."

"You knew you were stuck," said Effie.

He nodded. "It's beyond the marriage vows, isn't it? They hadn't heard of FTD when they wrote the wedding service. *In sickness and in health.* Sixteenth century, wasn't it? Sickness meant smallpox, or TB... or various infections that could kill you off very conveniently. They didn't hang about dying for years."

Effie laughed.

He shrugged. "I want to get out, but I have to see it through."

Effie nodded. "We all do."

Dominic frowned. "It's a wicked irony, isn't it?"

"What?"

"If you live with a healthy spouse you can't stand, you can leave. But if your spouse is sick, then you can't."

Effie paused to think that through.

Then he said, "Oh, I brought John Suchet's book for you." He took the book from his bag and put it on the table. "Not FTD, of course, but still interesting. How was the Admiral Nurse?"

"Good, very good indeed. She's been to see me a couple of times now. I send Lionel to sit in the dining room and I make it quite clear to him that it's my health she's looking after. She talks to me for...

maybe a couple of hours. There's no hurry like there is in a doctor's surgery, and I feel there is someone there for me. She can liaise with doctors about things, find out about nursing homes when the time comes. It's a sort of safety net, I suppose." Effie smiled. "I feel I can say anything." She lowered her lashes. "I even told her that I have a new gentleman friend."

"Have you indeed? That's good," said Dominic.

"Well, I don't really know him yet. We met, then he went off to New Zealand for a couple of months, but he's keeping touch, and I'm pretty sure that when he gets back..."

"...You'll welcome him with open arms!" completed Dominic with a smile.

Effie laughed. "I'm not sure about that. But I'm glad he's not around at the moment. It gives me a bit of space to think about things."

"What things?"

Effie shrugged. "He's straightforward, I think. Divorced. Doesn't see his ex-wife. Has his own home. No commitments."

"Sound's fine."

Effie looked into her glass. "I think what attracted him to me is my lack of availability."

"What do you mean?"

"He likes living alone. He doesn't want a woman taking over his life. A widow or a divorcee might be too demanding. Might want to move in, rearrange the furniture, as it were. He knows I can't do that, and it'll probably suit him very nicely."

"Mmmm," said Dominic. "I wouldn't count on that. I don't suppose he's that devious. I expect he just fancies you."

Effie decided to change the subject. "I've offered myself as a regional contact for the FTD Support Group. Natalie will put my details on the website. I'll see if I can start a local group in Dalton Heath."

"Good for you! Maybe I could come as guest from time to time?"

"That'd be great!" said Effie.

CHAPTER 43

A Gorilla Impression

Lionel is troubled. Effie says she's got to have an operation. He doesn't understand what it's all about. She'd drawn him a picture of her insides, but he still doesn't understand. Not that he wants to. It's one of these women things that men don't need to know.

"I'll only be in hospital for a day," she tells him, "but I'd like some peace and quiet to recuperate."

"That's okay," he says. "I can be quiet."

"I'll need to rest. I can't do that when you're here."

He doesn't see why not.

"I think you should have a week's respite care," she says.

Lionel doesn't understand. "What? Respite care? What's that?"

"You can go into a residential home for a week while I get better."

He frowns. "What? Where?" He likes it here, at home.

"It'll be like a hotel. They'll get your food, make your bed. Coffee whenever you like. You can take your Sudoku book and your fig roll biscuits. It'll be like a home from home."

No it won't, he thinks.

She continues, "I've looked at a place quite near here called Greenfield Haven. They're used to residents like you, who have FTD."

"STD?"

"EffTD. Frontotemporal dementia. That's the disease you've got."
Lionel laughs.

"And if I'm well enough after the operation I'll be able to visit you. I won't be able to drive, but I'll get a taxi there."

Lionel doesn't like this idea. "I don't know them. I won't know my way around. Not like I do here." Lionel is feeling anxious.

"I'd thought of that. So I've booked you in for what they call a 'day care' session. That's for the day after tomorrow. So it'll be familiar when you go there for the week." She crosses over to him and squeezes his shoulder. "I'll need to be on my own to convalesce," she says. "I'll need to get better, Lionel. I know you won't like it, but I don't know what else to do. I'm sorry, love."

Effie has put his stuff in a shopping bag. His Sudoku book, his blue rollerball pens, his cigarettes, his lighter, his puffers and a box of fig roll biscuits. They get into the car and she drives until they get to the place. It is a big old house and there is a decrepit old man with one leg in a wheelchair by the front porch. He is smoking a cigarette.

A woman answers the door. She's very smiley with a great big bosom. "Hello Mrs Butler," she says. "And you must be Lionel." She offers him her hand. He doesn't want to, but he shakes it. "I'm Melanie, the manageress here. Do come on in. We hope you'll be happy with us.

He looks at her bosom. "Melanie Melons?" he says. He laughs.

There is a row of people lined up. They wear blue. One of the girls puts her hand over her mouth to hide her smile.

"This is the care team, all ready to look after you. Aren't you lucky? Floella and Tina and Jason and Debbie. And this is Tim and Chakri and Valentino."

"I don't need looking after," growls Lionel. He knows he can't remember any of those names. He doesn't even want to remember those names.

One of the carers in the row is a short, thickset black man with a round smiley face. It looks like it's been polished.

Lionel grins at him. Then, "Ughh, ughh, ughh!" says Lionel. He pushes his shoulders forwards and curves his arms, fingers spread beneath his armpits. He bends at the knees in a squat. Then he pushes his lips forward and goes, "Ooghh, ooghh, ooghh!" That's better, he thinks. That's more like a gorilla.

"Lionel!" says Effie. "Stop it!"

But the girls in the row are giggling a bit and the black shiny gorilla man is laughing. They like his gorilla impression. Lionel feels pleased. He has made them all happy. Why does Effie put a dampener on everything he does?

"Perhaps Lionel would like to start by bringing his things into the sun lounge," says Mrs Melons. She isn't laughing. Miserable old cow.

"Moo!" he says to her.

"Lionel likes to sit at a table to do his Sudokus," says Effie. "But he'll need to go outside for a cigarette from time to time."

"That'll be fine," says Mrs Melons.

"Bye-bye, Lionel," says Effie. "I'll be back after supper."

She kisses the top of his head and leaves without looking back. He goes to the window and watches her car drive away. It's not nice here, he thinks. He goes back to his table and gets on with his Sudoku.

He wants a cigarette. He'll have to go outside for a cigarette. He gets up from his table and walks back through the lounge past all the old people sitting in chairs. Some of them are asleep. He bends down to an old lady who is snoring with her mouth wide open. "Stop snoring!" he shouts into her ear. She starts in surprise. There is a TV on but they aren't watching. It's hard to get past all the chairs. "Don't stare!" he snarls at an old man who is staring. An old lady waves at him and he claps his hands. She laughs. She likes that.

He gets to the hallway and pushes at the front door. It won't open. He jiggles at the lock.

"Lionel, you're not allowed outside unsupervised," says a pretty Scottish girl in a white overall that done up tight across her belly. He looks. Is she pregnant?

"Och aye, lassie," he says, "but I need to smoke a wee cigarette."

"I'll call someone to come with you," she says.

"Canna ye come, lassie?" he asks. He points at her belly. "Whatya got in there, lassie?" She's very pretty.

She presses a bell and the gorilla man appears.

"Tim, can you take Lionel into the garden for a cigarette?" she says.

"Oogh, oogh, oogh!" says Lionel.

They stand outside and Lionel sits at a garden table. It's fucking cold out here. "Want one?" he asks the gorilla man, offering him a cigarette.

"I don't smoke," he says.

Lionel sighs. Pity. It's nice when you can offer someone a cigarette. Then the front door opens and the man with one leg is pushed outside in his wheelchair. He wears tracksuit bottoms and the right leg is pinned up over the empty space. "Cigarette?" offers Lionel. The man nods and takes it.

"Why did they cut off your leg?" asks Lionel as he bends to give the man a light.

The man frowns. "It rotted," he says. "Too many cigarettes, they told me."

"That's a load of rubbish!" says Lionel. "I've smoked all my life and my legs are fine." He coughs.

They show him the activity room and they ask him if he'd like to play a game.

"Bridge," he says. "Anyone here play bridge?" But no one knows what he's talking about.

Then it's lunch in the dining room. He has to share a table with the man with one leg and two old women. Lunch is horrible and he spits most of it out. He looks around the room and sees that some of these idiots have to be fed like babies.

"No, I don't want any pudding, thank you. I don't eat pudding."

"Perhaps just a little ice cream?" asks the waitress.

"I told you," he shouts. "I... DON'T... EAT... PUDDING!"

Later he is invited to take an afternoon nap. He checks his watch. Yes, it's time.

He is escorted to a bedroom. That's better. It's away from all those awful old people. He takes off his shoes and trousers and climbs into bed. That's good, he thinks. And he sleeps.

It's tea time when he comes downstairs. There is an old lady in a wheelchair coming towards him through the doorway from the living room to the hall. Why can't the silly bitch look where she's going? "Get out of my effing way!" he shouts at her, and she starts to cry. He pushes her wheelchair roughly back and it crashes into an armchair.

"What the dickens!" shouts the man in the armchair.

Lionel has a coffee, but it's in a little cup with a saucer. He likes his coffee in a proper mug. And no, he doesn't want any cake. "I... DON'T... EAT... CAKE," he shouts. He speaks to a carer. "I want to go home," he says. "Please will you phone my wife, and tell her to come and fetch me?"

And at last Effie comes. "It's horrible here," he tells her.

She sighs and says to one of the carers, "How's he been?"

The girl doesn't say anything. She lowers her eyes and shuffles.

"Challenging?" suggests Effie.

The girl smiles and nods.

They all go out to the car to say goodbye to him. They seem to want to shake hands with him. That's part of the job, he supposes. "Oogh, oogh, oogh!" he says to the black man, who claps him on the shoulder like an old friend.

Effie shakes hands with Mrs Melons. "You'll send me the bill, will you?" she says.

The old cow nods.

"I'll phone you tomorrow morning to talk about how Lionel got on." Effie scans the sea of faces. "It'll be easier than talking here."

He gets into the passenger seat of Effie's car and does up his seat belt. "Christ, I'm glad to get out of that fucking place," he says as Effie puts the car in gear and she pulls away. Then he notices that Effie is crying.

"What's the matter?" he says.

"Nothing."

"Then stop crying. Concentrate on your driving."

CHAPTER 44

The Admiral Nurse

Effie had never been more pleased to see her Admiral Nurse. She watched through the hall window. Amanda Jackson got out of her car, hunched her shoulders against the driving rain and hurried up to the front door.

"Hello, Amanda. Come on in," said Effie. "Filthy day. Were the roads all right?"

"Hello Effie. Not too bad. It's always worse in the rain." Amanda took off her jacket which was already wet from the few seconds of downpour between her car and the front door.

Effie took the jacket, shook it out and hung it up.

She showed Amanda into the living room and let her take her usual seat. Lionel was seated in his customary chair at the table at the far end.

"Coffee?" she offered Amanda.

"If you're having one."

She went to the kitchen and brought back two coffees.

"Lionel, this is Amanda. Remember?"

Lionel looked blank.

"She's a nurse and she's come to see me about my health. Me. My health. Please will you take your things into the dining room so that she and I can talk privately?"

Lionel grumpily picked up his Sudoku book, his blue rollerball pen and his packet of fig roll biscuits. Then he shuffled off.

Effie sat on the sofa opposite Amanda and smiled.

"So, how are you? You look rather pale," said Amanda.

"I'm really pleased to see you, but I don't feel too good." She paused. "Lots has happened."

"Tell me." Amanda got out her notebook and looked attentively at Effie.

"Well, I had the operation."

Amanda wrote. "A success?"

"I'm not sure yet. I think so, but it's early days."

"And how did Lionel get on in respite care?"

"He didn't," Effie said flatly. "They wouldn't have him."

Amanda's eyes widened. "Greenfields Haven wouldn't have him?"

Effie nodded. "I'd booked him in for a week's respite from the day before the operation, but I took him for a day care session the previous week. So he'd know the place." Effie sighed. "I picked him up at the end of the day and..." She shook her head. "...I could feel an awkward atmosphere when we said goodbye to the staff." Effie leaned forward and picked up her coffee mug. She took a sip. "I hadn't paid for the day care at that point. So I said to the manageress I'd ring her the next day about paying the invoice and to discuss any problems. I was expecting to confirm the respite booking."

Amanda was making notes.

"So I phoned her next morning. I said I could tell he'd been difficult and she agreed. She said they have some very frail residents there and that he'd frightened them. They'd done their best, but they couldn't get him to settle."

"But didn't Greenfields Haven say they understood about FTD?"

"They didn't understand about Lionel. The manageress said that, for the sake of their patients, they couldn't have him back. I... I couldn't believe it. I asked if she knew of anywhere that would take him and she suggested I got in touch with Social Services. How useful is that? It was Social Services who recommended them! I asked her to write me a letter saying exactly what happened so that I could show it to Dr Hazan and put it on file. He has no idea what Lionel is really like. She said she would, but I never heard another word!"

Amanda frowned. "That's dreadful."

"I didn't get an invoice either. So at least I saved a hundred pounds. But what really worries me is..." Effie took a deep breath. "All this time I have assumed that when things get even worse, when I can no longer cope, there will be someone who can. I'm not sure there is now."

Amanda was taking copious notes. "Okay Effie. Just because Greenfields can't cope, it doesn't mean there isn't somewhere that can," she said. "I suspect," she added thoughtfully, "that Greenfields won't put things in writing because it would mean officially admitting their failure."

Effie nodded. "I suppose so."

"But... you've had the operation. What did you do?"

"I arranged for my daughter to pick me up from the hospital and I stayed with her for three nights. Primacare sent carers to check on Lionel twice a day. I've used them when I've been away. It was okay. Except Lionel was such a pain – he kept phoning Suzie telling her to bring me home. And he didn't once ask how I was."

"It's a thankless task, isn't it? Literally."

Effie nodded. "I tried to rest when I did get home, but it wasn't easy. I'd been so looking forward to being on my own, in my own home, for a few days." She smiled sadly. "It would have been such a luxury."

"And how are you? Is the operation a success?"

"Yes, I thought it was at first... I was very pleased. But I haven't been so good this week. I don't feel at all well."

Amanda asked Effie some specific medical questions. Then she said, "I think you might have a urinary infection. You need to see a doctor, today."

"What? I'll never get an appointment."

"Phone now, and I'll talk to someone if necessary."

Effie picked up the phone and keyed in the number. Why did you have to listen to all this recorded rigmarole before you could speak to a human being? She finally did, and she asked to make an appointment. She was offered one in two weeks' time. "My Admiral Nurse, Amanda Jackson, is with me now," she said. "She says I need to see someone straight away."

Grinning, she put down the phone. "Those magic words, *Admiral Nurse!* Better than *Abracadabra!* I've got to be there in ten minutes. I'm sorry, Amanda, do you mind if I go?"

Amanda smiled. "Of course not. I'll just write up a few notes if I may, and then I'll be off too."

Effie grabbed her coat and put her head round the dining room door to speak to Lionel. "I've got to go to the doctor's," she said. "Amanda will be off in a few minutes."

"Why?" asked Lionel.

Effie shook her head. "Don't worry. I won't be long," she said.

She picked up her car keys, and ran to her car. Would this rain ever stop? She reversed out past Amanda's parked car and into the street, wipers swishing at full speed. And in ten minutes she was in the surgery waiting room, waiting.

She had to wait nearly an hour, but she didn't mind. She did some deep breathing exercises, the way she'd learned at the A.R.M. group, and then she found a magazine to read.

The diagnosis was yes. She did have a urinary infection, which required an antibiotic. She took the prescription through doorway from the surgery into Ratigans Pharmacy. She didn't really like going there, since Lionel's exclusion, but she wasn't going anywhere else in this weather.

"Good morning, Mrs Butler," said the pharmacy assistant, who was being super-smiley, super-friendly. Maybe the staff here felt guilty about the way they'd treated Lionel. "How are you?" asked the assistant.

"Not too good," Effie said. "That's why I'm here."

When Effie arrived home she was astonished to see Amanda's car was still in the drive. And Amanda was sitting in it!

Effie parked her own car and got out.

Amanda wound down her driver's window sufficiently far for Effie to speak to her. She was eating a sandwich.

"What's happened?" asked Effie.

"The car wouldn't start," said Amanda, swallowing hurriedly. "I've called the AA. They should be here soon."

"But you could have waited inside, in the warm."

"I'm fine. Lionel wouldn't let me wait."

"What!"

"Well, he let me back in to go to the loo, but he wasn't going to let me stay."

Effie shook her head despairingly. She was getting wetter and wetter just standing there. "Well come in now."

"Don't worry about me," said Amanda. "The AA will be here in a minute. What did the doctor say?"

"You were right. I've got an infection and they prescribed me an antibiotic." She hesitated. Amanda probably preferred the isolated cold of her own car to Lionel's company in a warm house. But before she could say anything else an AA van pulled up. She gave a quick thumbs-up sign to Amanda and hurried into the warm and dry.

Lionel glared at her. "Where've you been?" he demanded.

CHAPTER 45

Pills, Panics, and Primacare

Effie had never been one of those lucky people who could sleep easily. On long-haul flights she'd gaze with envy at those passengers who could push the seat back, put on an eye mask and simply doze off. How lucky is that! On night flights, when she'd come home across the Atlantic after travelling with Matt, she'd always made sure she had an aisle seat so she could get up and wander up and down the aisles in the dimmed light without having to disturb anyone.

She'd taken sleeping pills from time to time for years, and it gave her a feeling of security to know that she had some available just in case. She used to stock up every time she and Lionel went to Spain. That was after they bought the house there. At that time you could get them over the counter in the Frigiliana *Farmacia,* and each time they visited, Effie bought a couple of packs to have in reserve. That way she didn't have to see a doctor and admit what she felt was a weakness. Then, quite rightly, the Spanish had put a stop to it. The rules changed and you had to have a prescription, like at home. Effie knew these pills were addictive and she tried not to take them too often. But on holidays they helped her deal with strange beds, difficult situations, and different time zones. It was all part and parcel of travel.

They'd also stocked up on cigarettes for Lionel. In those days if you bought a thousand cigarettes from the *Tabac* in Frigiliana you saved enough money on British prices to pay for your flights, your car hire and whole lot more besides.

Effie remembered those first few visits. Retiring to bed in the heat of the afternoon sun to rest, make love, and renew those feelings that got lost in the routine of life at home. Then, sitting on the roof terrace with an early evening drink. Watching the sun go down turning the whiteness of the village houses to rosy hues of pink and gold. The moon following the sun to some magic rendezvous below the horizon. And the deepening dusk revealing a starry, starry sky. Orion was her favourite. He seemed to be up there in the heavens watching over her. No wonder the ancients had assigned such meaning to those celestial worlds!

She and Lionel had been happy then. Hopeful? Definitely. Still in love? Probably. Then Lionel had lost interest in going there. He'd lost interest so many things. Apathy had set in. Effie hadn't known then that apathy was one of the early symptoms of FTD.

It was a good thing that he no longer wanted to travel. That last trip to Frigiliana before he'd been taken ill had been tortuous. He'd made such stupid remarks to the security staff at the airport, that she'd thought they were going to arrest him. "Want to see the gun in my pocket?" he'd asked. "There's a bomb in there!" he said pointing at Effie's handbag. The officer had taken them aside and searched their hand luggage thoroughly. Lionel's bottle of ready mixed gin and tonic that he'd intended to drink on the plane had already been confiscated. What had he been thinking of? The whole experience had been excruciatingly embarrassing.

Since Lionel's diagnosis, Effie's sleep patterns had worsened. She took forever to get off to sleep. She'd get up and pass the early hours doing things like tidying up, washing the kitchen floor, and eating. Breakfast muesli was what she wanted in the early hours. And then, maybe, she could drop off for an hour or so. But she'd still wake at the normal time, exhausted and weepy.

Each morning, when the reality of Lionel's future, which was her future too, came back to her, she would start to cry. She would shake so much with all-consuming sobs that she could barely hold her toothbrush. Then she would shower and dress and struggle downstairs for a coffee and something to eat. Maybe it was the caffeine fix or the sugar surge, but that was when she would stop crying. The all-enveloping grief would subside and she would feel ready to face the day. Face Lionel getting up and coming downstairs. "Good morning!" she would say cheerfully to him as though she were absolutely fine and all was well with the world.

And through the day, the most trivial things could creep up on her and turn on her tears. The most minor problems would cause her to shake with panic. Failing to find a parking place, getting paper stuck in the computer printer, or losing her car keys would all bring on the weeping and reduce her to a crumbling wreck. She dreaded new situations. She dreaded having to talk to normal people about normal things. There were times when she turned down invitations to potentially enjoyable occasions, simply because she'd become nervous of talking to new people, and terrified of having a panic attack in public.

She'd told her Admiral Nurse about this.

"You could try an antidepressant?" suggested Amanda.

Her GP prescribed one that sounded promising. It wasn't addictive. You had to build up gradually and it should help her cope, she was told.

"Will it help me sleep?" she asked.

"Yes, because you'll feel more relaxed. But it'll take a while for you to settle down with it. You could feel worse before you feel better."

Effie was planning a trip to Frigiliana with her friend, Nicki. She'd met Nicki on an organised touring holiday a couple of years earlier. Nicki had been recently widowed after years of being a carer, and had some understanding of the life that Effie had been forced to take on. They teamed up, had a good time and kept in touch.

"How about coming to stay in our Spanish house?" suggested Effie.

The dates were fixed. Effie had booked the flights and reserved a hire car, just as she had done many times before. But this time was different. Lionel's health was deteriorating. So Effie had contacted Primacare and arranged for a carer to visit Lionel each day to check that he was okay. Just fifteen minutes would be enough. They'd see how things went.

She told Suzie about it. "It'll be fine," Suzie said. "I'll come and visit him mid-week. See if he wants any shopping. Don't worry."

But she did worry. She worried about Lionel. She worried about Primacare. She worried about the Spanish house and whether she should sell it. She worried about whether Nicki would enjoy herself. And she worried about driving in Spain. Why? It was nothing new. You got off the aeroplane, you went to the car hire desk and you picked up a car. They were very efficient. She'd done it often enough before. She knew the way out of the airport, round a couple of roundabouts, over the flyover and onto the motorway. And given that Lionel wouldn't be with her telling her how to drive it would be easy. But the very thought of it made her shake. Were the antidepressants working? Not yet.

Two days to go. She'd showered, she'd cleaned her teeth and she'd had her coffee and muesli. But the panic didn't subside. It was a knot inside her chest that was pressing on her lungs, making it hard to breathe. I can't do it, she thought. She couldn't do it. She couldn't go away, leave Lionel, drive a foreign car on foreign roads and look after her guest. It was all too much.

She phoned Suzie. "I can't go..." but the sobs engulfed her and she couldn't say anything else. She put the phone down.

She phoned Nicki. "I'm so sorry," she sobbed. "I can't go... it's all too much... I'm so sorry to let you down, but it's so awful... I'll pay for the flights of course..."

"Don't worry," said Nicki calmly. "Especially about me. If you can't come, I'll go on my own. It'll be all right. Now, why don't you pour yourself a drink and sit down and listen to some nice relaxing music? I'll phone you later."

She phoned Primacare. "I'm sorry," she sobbed. "I've realised I'm not well enough to cope with going away. I'll have to cancel. I'll pay of course."

"That's all right, Mrs Butler. We don't charge for this sort of cancellation. Are you all right?"

"Not... not really..." At which point there was a ring on the doorbell.

"I'm sorry – there's someone at the door. I'll have to go." And she hung up.

Effie stood there a moment or two before answering. Deep breaths, she told herself. In through the nose, out through the mouth. Keep calm. Think calm. Think rosy sunsets and burbling streams and golden beaches. Think, Orion and his starry, starry sky.

It was Suzie. "Mum!" she said.

"Hello, love," said Effie. All her calming strategies collapsed as

Suzie hugged her. Deep pervading sobs re-established themselves. "I'm sorry... shouldn't you be at work...?" Effie stuttered through her tears.

"One of the team is covering for me. Where's Dad? Not up yet? Now you sit down while I make us some tea."

Effie sat at the kitchen table while Suzie put the kettle on.

"Mum. Now what's all this about?" Suzie said as she put a mug of tea in front of Effie.

"Thanks, love," said Effie. "It's just that..." Her voice shook.

"Take your time," said Suzie evenly. "What's the problem?"

"I can't leave him." Effie looked into her tea and took a sip. It was weak and milky, the way Suzie always made it.

"Yes you can. He'll be fine. Primacare will check on him, and I'll call as well." Suzie spooned sugar into her own tea and stirred.

"Well I've cancelled everything. I can't go now anyway."

"Everything? You've cancelled the flights?"

"No. I don't think you can. But I've told Nicki, and I've cancelled Primacare."

Suzie took a swig of her tea. She looked thoughtful. "Are you taking the tablets?" she asked. "The antidepressants?"

Effie nodded.

"Hmm. They don't seem to be working very well do they?"

Effie shrugged.

Suzie continued. "Is anything worrying you besides Dad?"

"It's just that... I'm not coping... I've got to pick up a car... you know what that's like in Malaga... I've booked one... but I'm in no state to drive on those motorways... I'm so panicky... I never know when these awful feelings are going to take over... and what if we had an accident...? I couldn't deal with it..."

"Well, I agree with that, Mum." Suzie got up from her chair and fetched the biscuit tin from the cupboard. It had a scratched picture of the Prince of Wales with Lady Diana Spencer on its top. Suzie pulled the lid off, peered inside, and grimaced. "Is this all you've got?" she said, looking at the somewhat limited selection of broken biscuits. She took one.

"I don't buy biscuits any more, except for Dad's fig rolls of course, and they're in the dining room if you want one."

"No thanks. But I agree that you shouldn't drive. Not in the state you've been in recently. Even without panic attacks your concentration's dire."

"There's nothing wrong with my concentration..." Effie began to protest.

"Have you paid for the car hire?" asked Suzie.

Effie frowned. "I don't think so. I think I paid a higher rate with a cancellation option. Just in case."

Suzie threw out the stale contents of the biscuit tin and put the tin back where it had been since she was at school. Then she laughed. "Must have been meant," she said. "Cancel the car, and you and Nicki can get a taxi. You can have a relaxing week in the sun without any driving. You can get a bus down to the beach if you want to, and you won't have to worry about parking. I don't suppose there's much difference in the price of car hire for week and an airport taxi each way."

This was all true. "But I've told Nicki... and I've cancelled Primacare... and..."

"You can call Nicki. I expect she knows you're just having a bit of a wobbly. And I'll call Primacare and explain. God knows, they'll understand you need to get away."

"But..."

"But nothing. It'll be fine." She picked up the phone. "Nicki's number?" She looked on Effie's phone list and dialled. She listened a moment then, "It's ringing. Speak to her." She passed the handset over.

Later Effie sent Nicki an email:

Hi Nicki,
So sorry about all the fuss
See you at the departure gate, as arranged.
Effie x

There was an email from Justin. These emails were coming almost daily now. He'd left his son's home and was touring New Zealand on his own. At the moment, he said, he was lying on a sun bed on a beach. *Das Himmel ist blau. Der Sand ist golden,* he wrote. *Wish you were with me*, he added.

Then:
Enjoy your trip to Spain. See you when we're both home.
Justin x

Effie smiled. She was beginning to realise that she was going to do a whole lot more than just see him when they both got home.

Three days later she was sitting on that roof terrace looking at the stars. She and Nicki had been out for dinner, been chatted up by a couple of aging Spaniards with terrible teeth, and were having one more drink before turning in for the night.

A cat padded across the roof of the adjacent house, jumped up on to the terrace and settled on Effie's lap, purring contentedly. She stroked it. Physical contact is so nice, she thought. Even if it's only an animal.

"This is the life," said Nicki. "I can't imagine why you ever thought of selling up."

"Neither can I," said Effie. Orion was up there watching over her. But something was troubling her. Not the usual, not just Lionel. Not the fact that Justin had sent her two more emails and, reading between the lines, was coming on just a bit too strong considering she could hardly remember what he looked like.

No, what was troubling her was more practical. Her face. It felt hot and itchy. Had she been bitten by something? Had she had too much sun? It was a strange feeling, tight and dry, but when she looked in the mirror when she went to bed, there was nothing to see.

But next morning it felt worse and there was plenty to see. Her cheeks were red and itchy and on fire.

"Look," she said to Nicki over breakfast. "What do think could have caused that?"

Nicki peered at her. "An allergy? What did you eat last night? Those prawns? Hey, it couldn't be that cat, could it? Bet it's got fleas."

Effie shook her head. "It was starting before then." She sighed. "I've been taking some tablets... antidepressants... I wonder if it's a side effect."

Nicki frowned. "Effie, you shouldn't be on antidepressants. There's nothing wrong with you. You've got problems. But they're... external ones... you can't solve the Lionel situation by taking pills."

Effie was inclined to agree. Especially as they didn't seem to be working. Could she contact her doctor from here? It wouldn't be easy. She'd have to phone the surgery on her mobile, get through all the recorded junk, and arrange for a telephone appointment at some specified time. Then she remembered Dominic. He was a medical man. He might know.

She sent him a text saying what she was taking and describing the rash.

The reply was instant.

Rare side effect.
Stop taking the tablets
See you when you get home. D

When she did get home, she unpacked her bag and tipped out her dirty washing ready to go in the washing machine. Then she looked in the dirty clothes basket to add Lionel's to the pile. It was just as she had left it – empty. She realised that Lionel must have been wearing the same clothes for the whole of her week away. Probably both day and night.

CHAPTER 46

A Regional Contact

Lionel gets up from his Sudoku to pick up the phone. It won't be for him, he thinks. It's never for him.

"Hello," he says. He carries the handset across from the little side table where it usually sits, to the place at his table where he usually sits.

"Hello. Could I speak to Frances Butler?" comes a man's voice.

For a moment Lionel is puzzled. Then he remembers that Frances is Effie's proper name. "You mean Effie?"

"Er... yes... I expect so."

"Effie Butler is my wife," says Lionel. He is disappointed. It would be so nice if someone phoned wanting to speak to him, but they never did. He sits down.

"Can you hear me?" asks the caller.

"Yes. Of course I can hear you," reacts Lionel. Why do people keep thinking he's deaf? He's not deaf. Or stupid. "What do you want?" he asks.

"Frances Butler, or Effie Butler, if that's what she's called. If that's possible."

Not many people call her Frances, but it is her name. "She's not here at the moment," says Lionel.

"Okay, right," says the caller.

"She's gone out," says Lionel.

"Okay, right. Do you know when she'll be back?"

Lionel tries to remember where Effie said she was going. "She went shopping," he says. "Or maybe she's playing tennis."

"Okay, right," comes the voice again.

"Shall I get her to ring you back?" asks Lionel.

There's a pause.

"Just say yes or no," says Lionel.

"Er... yes... if that's possible."

"Of course it's possible!" says Lionel.

"Then, yes, please."

"Hold on a minute. I need to find a pen." Where is his blue rollerball pen? He had it a minute ago. He shifts the newspaper and his Sudoku book across his table, muttering under his breath. The pen rolls on the floor and he has to bend stiffly to pick it up. Yes, here it is. "Right. Name?" he asks. His pen is poised over his yellow post-it notepad.

"My name is John."

"John," repeats Lionel as he writes it down. "Do you have a surname?"

"Don't worry about that. It'll be easier. I'll just..."

"We know more than one John. Effie knows lots. There's one she plays tennis with. Another she pays golf with. You must have another name."

"It's John Goodbody."

"Goodbody," Lionel repeats as he writes it down. "Not Badbody?" he suggests. And he gives a little laugh to show he's making a joke.

There's another of those silences.

"Say yes or no?" says Lionel.

"No, not Badbody. At least not very bad, and only sometimes when I'm under severe pressure." He also gives a little laugh. "I'm John Goodbody."

Lionel writes *Goodbody*. "John Goodbody. I'll get her to phone you."

"Thank you. Shall I give you my phone number?"

"Doesn't she have your number?"

"No, she doesn't have my number."

Lionel is suspicious. "Does she know you?"

"No, she doesn't know me. I've got her name off a website. It's about her carers' FTD support group meetings. She's a regional contact for FTD."

"STD?" echoes Lionel. "What's that?"

"No. *Eff*TD."

Lionel raises his blue rollerball pen. "*Eff* for *fuckoff*?" he asks. And he laughs to show he's just joking again.

"No," says John Goodbody. "*Eff* is for *fronto*. FTD stands for *frontotemporal dementia*."

"Oh. Is that what I've got?"

"I don't know. You sound fine to me."

"Of course I'm fine. Effie thinks I'm a nutter but I'm fine."

"Shall I give you my number?"

John Goodbody says the number slowly and clearly as Lionel writes it down. Then Lionel reads it back to him.

"That's right."

"I'll get her to call you when she gets in."

"Thank you very much."

Lionel is about to say goodbye, when he hears the front door open and then click shut.

"Hold on," he says. "I think she's back... don't hang up." He calls out. "Effie! There's a phone call for you. It's a man called John

Badbody and he's ringing about an STD meeting." As he stands up, he puts the handset back down on its cradle and hurries to the front door.

CHAPTER 47

Doing Her Bit

Since Effie's name had been listed on the website as the regional contact, she'd received a number of phone calls and emails from anxious, even desperate FTD carers. One young man, whose father had just been diagnosed, told her he'd already had a long, entertaining telephone conversation with Lionel. "He's not a bit like my dad," John Goodbody said to Effie when she returned his call.

"Why's that?" Effie asked.

"My dad," he said, "can't answer the phone properly. He picks up when it rings and then he just says what the time is. He thinks he's the speaking clock. And he wants my mum around the whole time. Gets very stressed when she goes out. It's very difficult for her."

"Sounds like I'm lucky," remarked Effie.

Usually the phone calls or emails were from the partner or spouse of a newly diagnosed patient. Sometimes, as in the case of John Goodbody, they were from the son or daughter wanting to help a shocked family prepare for a daunting future.

There was, of course, no solution to this ghastly disease. Effie remembered her Al-Anon experience when she'd learned that there was no solution to alcoholism. There were ways of approaching the problems, and strategies for coping with the pressures. But there were no rules. Every FTD patient was different. As was every FTD carer. And learning how other people coped, or failed to cope, was worthwhile.

It was time she started up a local FTD support group. She wanted to meet carers like herself who lived locally. She wanted to share their problems and learn from their experiences. Her visits to London were fine, but once every three months was not often enough. Her contact with Dominic Darnley was helpful and she wished he lived nearer. Surely Lionel couldn't be the only FTD sufferer in the area?

She told Justin about her plans to start a local support group.

"Good idea," he said. "You need to unload on other people in the same situation." What he meant was that he had enough of her unloading on him.

"Mmmm. I'm not sure how to start."

"Just decide when and where and let them all know. See what happens."

So she did. There was a Harvester restaurant on the main road coming into Dalton Heath. That should do. It had a car park and a big sign that you couldn't miss. She went there to consider the layout. Eleven o'clock in the morning was as good a time as any. They could meet and have coffee in the comfortable armchairs near the entrance. Perhaps some of them would like to stay on and have lunch there. She prepared a flyer: -

DALTON HEATH & DISTRICT FTD SUPPORT GROUP

This is an informal support group for carers, family, and friends of people affected by **Frontotemporal Dementia** *(FTD) in the Dalton Heath area. The aim is to offer mutual support, exchange of information, and an opportunity to share problems in a friendly and relaxed environment. Occasionally professional experts might attend the group to offer specific advice.*

FTD is a rare disease, but it is nevertheless the commonest early onset dementia. It is very different from other forms of dementia. Carers can feel sadly isolated. The first meeting will be at the Dalton Heath Harvester restaurant where members can chat over a morning coffee. Those who wish might like to stay on for lunch.

She added a date and time for the inaugural meeting, directions, and contact details. Then she emailed it to all those FTD carers who had contacted her, but copied everyone she knew who had anything to do with dementia, be they dementia workers, social workers, or mental health workers.

There! It was done. All she had to do now was wait and see.

The big day arrived. Justin sent her a text message. *Good luck*, it said. *I'm so proud of you. Jxx*

Effie smiled. Since Justin had got back from his trip to New Zealand they had seen each other a couple of times a week. Sometimes they would go out. That had been easy enough. "I'm going to the cinema," she would say to Lionel.

"Who with?" Lionel would always ask.

"A friend from the German class," she might say. Or she'd invent someone. "Hermione Smith from the tennis club," could be another lie.

Sometimes, in the afternoons, she would go to Justin's home. She had to think of other lies to tell Lionel. She didn't feel good about that.

Justin would offer her a glass of wine and they'd start off by talking about films and books and travel and all the ordinary things that normal people talk about. But through it all, Effie could never clear her mind of Lionel and FTD. Nor could she stop herself from steering the conversation back to the subject. Justin was sympathetic but it must have bored him rigid. Surely there must be rules of *Etiquette for Adultery*? she reflected. And one of those rules, probably clicking in at something like *Rule Number 27*, might be: Do *not give your lover unnecessary information about your demented husband.*

Justin would offer her a second glass of wine and invite her upstairs to his bed. He'd undress her slowly and sensuously, and he'd make her feel young and happy and sexy. It was so good to be with a man. He made her feel valued. He made her feel beautiful. He even made her feel loved, though that wasn't what she was looking for. She knew right from the beginning that the affair had no future. How could it when her destiny was to care for Lionel to the end? *Till death us do part.*

She made it clear to Justin that there was no future for him with her. "You should find someone who's free," she said.

"I want you," he said, "even if I can't have all of you."

Her awareness of the situation was not going to stop her enjoying the pleasure of his company and his bed.

Afterwards she'd get dressed and drive home, warm and tingling with echoes of sensual pleasure, but feeling like a prostitute going home from a client. She'd push open the front door, stand in the hall and pause, laden with guilt. She was an adulterous wife and she still carried the taste and smell of Justin Collins with her. Would Lionel notice?

As far she knew he never did.

"Hello, all ok?" she'd ask brightly as she walked into the living room. Lionel would look up from his Sudoku.

"Where've you been?" he'd demand crossly, looking at his watch.

And she'd repeat whatever lie she'd told earlier. Though she doubted if Lionel would notice if it were a different lie. "Any phone calls?" she'd ask.

"No. What's for supper?" was the usual response.

Effie arrived half an hour early for the inaugural meeting of the Dalton Heath & District FTD Support Group. She took her FTD file with her and spread some leaflets on the coffee tables where she hoped the group would sit. Then she went up to the bar to get a coffee.

Much to her surprise and delight, the first arrival was Dominic Darnley. "Dominic!" she cried, standing up to welcome him. They hugged and kissed cheek to cheek. "I didn't know you'd be coming."

"I saw it on the website," he said, "and I thought you might need some moral support."

She smiled. "You bet I do," she said. "I have this fear that no one will turn up and I'll be sitting here the whole morning looking and feeling like a dummy." She sat down and picked up her mug of coffee. "At least I know I've got you."

Dominic sat in the chair opposite her.

"But it's a long way for you," continued Effie. "How come you can get away? I thought you could only leave Kerry for a while."

"I've just taken on a live-in carer for her. The carer told me to get out of the house so that she and Kerry could get on with things."

"Charming!" Effie said.

"Well, she didn't put quite like that, but I'm sure she'll find Kerry more co-operative when I'm not around. If it works out with her I should have a bit more freedom." He paused and smiled. "A lot more freedom."

Effie smiled. "That would be nice," she said.

"Yeah. Fingers crossed." He stood up again.

"Full time care. That must be expensive?" asked Effie.

He raised a brow. "Don't go there! I'll just go and get a coffee."

By the time he returned two others had arrived and introduced themselves. Jodie arrived together with Gerald. Jodie's husband had been in a care home for nearly fifteen years, while Gerald's wife had died in a different care home a year ago.

"We both met at the support group in London," said Jodie. She glanced sideways at him. "That was over ten years ago now."

Gerald put his hand on Jodie's forearm. "It's through FTD that we got to know each other," he elaborated. "And now…"

"Now we live together," completed Jodie.

Effie looked at them and across to Dominic. Two people who had shared traumatic experiences, who had supported each through the cold darkness, had somehow turned it into something positive, maybe even love.

"Good luck to you both!" said Dominic.

What will happen when Jodie's husband dies? wondered Effie. Would they find that sharing the experience of FTD was not enough? FTD had brought them together. Was it enough to keep them together?

The next arrival was Craig, closely followed by Ellen and Fay.

"Shall we all tell each other something about ourselves, about our journey?" Effie suggested when they were all seated. She was doubtful about the word *journey*. A journey should have a positive end, and they all knew that an FTD journey never could.

They nodded in assent.

"As you know, my name is Effie Butler. My husband, Lionel, was diagnosed two and half years ago with behavioural variant FTD." She told them about the symptoms, the diagnosis and a few of the crises that had happened along the way. She finished by telling them how lucky she was. She could still go out and leave him unsupervised.

"And you can still get away, on holiday," prompted Dominic.

She nodded. "I arrange for a company called Primacare to send someone twice a day for fifteen minutes. I'm going next week. With a friend to our place in Spain." She didn't tell them her friend was a man called Justin and what they shared was a whole lot more than mere friendship.

"Just fifteen minutes?" queried Craig. "Is that all?"

"Lionel can feed himself. He's not incontinent. It's just to check up. Sometimes he won't let them in. Sometimes he tells them to eff off. But then they know he's ok, don't they?"

There was a laugh of agreement.

Effie continued. "Fortunately, Lionel is very lazy. He doesn't wander. Providing I stock the house with all the things he needs – cigarettes in particular – he'll stay put."

Craig nodded. His journey, they all learned, had been appalling. His wife, who suffered from semantic FTD, was totally incapacitated and needed full-time care. She couldn't speak, couldn't walk, and couldn't feed herself. He had carers there in the mornings, which was why he was able to be here now, but the rest of the time he managed on his own. "It isn't easy," he said.

"Have you thought about a care home?" asked Gerald.

He shook his head. "No. She needs to be with me."

Craig was a saint, thought Effie.

Ellen, on the other hand, had just arranged for her husband to move into a care home. "I couldn't cope anymore," she explained. He'd become violent and had taken to wandering around the town at night in his pyjamas. Once he'd been brought back in a police van, handcuffed and clad in nothing but a blanket. She'd finally realised she had no option, she said, but that didn't stop her feeling guilty about depriving the man she still loved of his home.

Fay's husband was in the early stages, newly diagnosed. She just wanted to listen and learn. And she was so glad, she said, so grateful to meet others who understood.

Craig, Fay and Dominic stayed on with Effie for lunch and some of the conversation did touch on things that had nothing to do with FTD. They chatted, laughed and learned a little about each other as human beings, not just as FTD carers.

"Thank you so much for starting this up," Fay said to Effie. "It's so good of you."

Effie glowed and smiled smugly. "It's a pleasure," she said. She was glad to be doing her bit. But she knew it was more for her than for them.

CHAPTER 48

Passports and Boarding Passes

It was five-thirty in the morning and still dark. Effie was sitting on the sofa, her hands gripped tightly together to stop them shaking. Her small suitcase was in the porch. Her handbag was on her lap. She opened the side pocket to check her passport and her boarding pass. Not that she had to worry about the boarding pass as Justin would have printed off a copy anyway. Her chest felt tight and her breathing was fast. She was going to spend a whole week away with Justin. Up until now they'd not been together for more than a few hours on any one occasion. Did he snore? She wondered. Would she sleep?

Everything was ready for Lionel. Primacare had her mobile number, Suzie's phone number and the PIN number of the key safe. If Lionel didn't answer the door, the carers could let themselves in. If anything happened she could be contacted. She had booked for a carer to call twice a day, once late morning when there was good chance of Lionel being up, and once in the evening after eight o'clock. That was so that he would have finished his supper and they could check he'd turned off the cooker. She asked the manager of Primacare if it would be a good idea for them to come for longer than fifteen minutes.

"Not really," he said. "That would annoy him even more!"

She'd stocked the fridge with meals she'd made especially. They had to be in the front of the fridge where Lionel could see them easily. Small pots of chicken casserole, mini shepherd's pies and fish cakes. Things that he liked, things that he could warm up in the oven. He never used the microwave. He'd probably forgotten what it was, thought Effie. There was more food in the freezer, but he wouldn't think of that. She'd bought cauliflower, broccoli and leeks. They were the only vegetables that Lionel would eat these days and he liked to overcook them in a saucepan of very salty boiling water.

So when Suzie called to see him in the middle of next week she would check the fridge, throw out anything that looked dodgy and get fresh stuff from the freezer if it was needed. It was all fine, Effie told herself.

"Dad'll be fine," Suzie had assured her.

A couple of months ago Effie had taken Suzie out to lunch. It was good to have the occasional mother-daughter outing. Effie had admitted, somewhat self-consciously during the second glass of wine, that she had a 'gentleman friend'.

Suzie was delighted. "About time too, Mum! Perhaps you'll cheer up a bit now!"

"I'm not in love," Effie had said thoughtfully, "but we get on well, and enjoy lots of the same interests. We've read the same books, we've been up to London for museums and theatre trips. He's very interesting." Then she added. "And I'm enjoying the sex, which is pretty good at my age."

Suzie had grimaced. "Too much information, Mum," she said.

Effie grinned. "Sorry." Children, even grown-up ones, could never imagine their parents having sex.

"You need to be cautious, Mum. You're very vulnerable."

"Why?"

"You've been with Dad so long, and he's been so nasty to you, you've probably lost your ability to judge men. You're likely to think that someone who's merely quite nice is absolutely wonderful."

Effie had nodded. "I'm just enjoying it," she had said.

Justin was quite nice, but he wasn't wonderful. But it did feel wonderful to have someone being nice to her. And now he was going to be nice to her for a whole week.

She'd written a note for Lionel and left it on the kitchen table.

Gone to Spain. Take care.
Lots of love
Effie xx.

On the table in the living room, next to Lionel's Sudoku book, he kept a page-a-day spiral calendar that Effie had bought from the Alzheimer's Society online shop. It had the day and the date in large letters and a space for notes on every page. Each day you had to turn the page over and, much to Effie's surprise, Lionel usually did. Effie had written in when the carers would be calling, when Suzie would be visiting and when she herself was coming home.

She had called Nigel in Berlin to say she was going to Spain and ask him to phone his dad while she was away. Effie knew that no one else would. Those people she had once thought of as friends had disappeared into the ether.

There was no point in telling Lionel's brother that Lionel would be on his own. Last time she had called them to catch up on news, Joanna had said, "I expect you think we should have been to see him."

"Yes," Effie had said tightly.

"Well, we want to remember him the way he used to be."

"So do I," Effie had said. What she'd thought was: What a copout!

On the coffee table by the window Effie put the Primacare file. Each time a carer called they would make a note of how Lionel was and whether they were any problems. There was a pen tucked inside it.

Yes. All was ready. Effie felt sick and faint. She didn't want to go, but it was too late to back out.

She went upstairs to have a last look at Lionel. Fast asleep. His feet stuck out at the bottom of the duvet. His toenails needed cutting. The skin was flaking badly and there was a split on one heel that looked as though it might be infected. She must ring the podiatrist when she got home. Poor Lionel. How had it come to this? She straightened the duvet, then leaned over the bed and kissed his forehead. "Bye-bye, love," she whispered. He stirred a little but he didn't wake.

As she walked downstairs she heard a car pull up. She opened the front door and watched a taxi reverse into the drive. Justin was getting out.

"Good morning, Effie," he called brightly. He came up to the front door. Then, "All right?"

She didn't answer. She was afraid that if she spoke she would cry.

He picked up her suitcase and took it down to the taxi.

"All aboard?" checked the taxi driver as they set off.

"That's right," said Justin. Then, "All right?" he said to her again.

"Not really," she said. Her hands were trembling.

"Got your passport?" Justin asked.

She took it out of her handbag.

"Shall I put it with mine?" he asked.

She nodded. "Yes, please."

He took it from her and tucked it in the inside pocket of his jacket.

Then he took her hand. "I'll look after you," he said.

That was she wanted – someone to look after her. She hadn't had that in a very long time. "Thank you," she said.

The cabin staff were making their way down the aisle with the catering trolley. "Right," said Justin. "What do you want for breakfast?"

"I'm not very hungry," she said.

Justin ignored her. "We'll have bacon baguettes, coffee and orange juice," he said to the stewardess.

Effie smiled. It was good to have someone making decisions.

"And we'll have two of those little bottles of Cava," he added.

"Cava!" Effie protested. "We can't drink Cava at breakfast."

"We're on holiday. We can do anything we like!"

And he turned to kiss her.

She squeezed his hand.

"Don't worry about anything," he said. "It's going to be all right."

CHAPTER 49

Mrs Ginger Pubes

Lionel is wrapped in that comfy place between sleep and wakefulness. He is in his home. He is in his bed. And even though his eyes are still closed he knows that there is light slanting through the gap in the curtains. Soft sounds of daytime activity slip-slide into his consciousness. A car going past the house. The distant hum of a hedge trimmer somewhere down the road. Voices of pedestrians chattering as they walk by. All familiar sounds that don't intrude. He turns over and adjusts the duvet around his shoulders. He is half listening for Effie busying herself about the house. Sometimes she hoovers, and that's horrible.

He is jerked awake by another sound. One that he doesn't like. The doorbell! Bugger! It is a new doorbell that Effie bought not so long ago. It is designed especially for the 'hard of hearing' and it has a nasty electronic bleep that would suit an emergency fire alarm rather than a home that should be a haven of peacefulness.

He opens his eyes. "Effie!" he calls. "Effie! Door! Get the door!"

There is no response. She must be out. He frowns as he tries to remember what she said she was doing today. Shopping? Playing tennis? He doesn't know.

The doorbell rings again. He buries his head under the duvet.

They'll soon give up and go away.

The next thing he hears is a knock on his bedroom door. He emerges from under his duvet and watches it open.

"Good morning, Mr Butler," comes a voice. A female voice that is not Effie's. The door opens further and, "Or should I say good afternoon?"

Lionel sits up. What the fuck...?

She has a round smiley face and ginger wispy hair that is tied back in an elastic band.

Lionel has never liked redheads. He points at her head. "Ginger hair," he says.

She nods.

She wears a blue overall thing that is tight across her boobs, and she has a name badge hanging from a ribbon around her neck. He can't read it. The print is too small. She has a soft pasty face with oodles of freckles.

"I'm Maggie, remember?" she says. "From Primacare. We met before. Just checking up you're okay?"

He points at her crotch. "Ginger pubes too?" he asks.

She purses her lips. "Now, Mr Butler," she says, wagging her finger at him. "That's none of your business, is it? Would you like me to make you a cup of tea?"

"No. Just fuck off, Mrs Ginger Pubes!" he snarls.

"Now, Mr Butler, that isn't very nice!" She bends to pick up a few crumpled tissues from the floor and drops them in the waste paper basket.

He pats her lightly on the bum. It's a very big bum. "Fancy a shag?" he says. Then he laughs. "That was a joke," he adds.

She stands up and smiles. "I should hope so. I'll go and put the kettle on anyway," she says.

"Wasser time?" he grunts.

She checks her watch. "A quarter past twelve," she says. "Nearly lunch time!"

"Oh Christ!" groans Lionel. "I'd better get up."

"That's a good idea. Would you like some help getting dressed?"

"No!" he reacts. Who does she think he is? A bloody cripple!

"Okay, Mr Butler. I'll see you downstairs in a few minutes. I'll tidy up a bit and empty the bins." She picks up his waste paper basket and carries it from the room.

Lionel puts on yesterday's trousers, jumper and socks. He always sleeps in his shirt and pants so he doesn't have to put those on. He opens the bedroom window and lights a cigarette. Where's Effie? he wonders.

He finishes the cigarette and goes downstairs. On the kitchen table is a message. Fuck it! He remembers now. She's gone away. She's always going away. He picks it up and peers at it. She's got god-awful handwriting.

Gone to Spain. Take care.
Lots of love
Effie xx.

He shuffles along the hallway. What day is it? He needs to check his page-a-day diary. The living room door is open and Mrs Ginger Pubes is coming towards him carrying a full waste paper basket. She steps to one side to let him pass. But he steps to the same side. Stupid woman!

"Get out of my effing way!" he snarls. And he clenches his fist and punches in the direction of her midriff.

She drops the waste paper basket, and falls against the wall, clutching her stomach as though she's been winded. "Mr Butler!" she says, "You frightened me."

"It was joke," he says. And he laughs.

"Well, it wasn't very funny," she says, getting awkwardly to her feet. And she stoops to refill the waste paper basket.

CHAPTER 50

One Day at a Time

Effie was seated on the roof terrace. This was her favourite place in the world, and this was her favourite time of day. The sun was dipping behind the purple hills and a white crescent moon hung over a darkening sea. The clouds were edged with a rosy glow and there was a faint sound of dogs barking in the distance. And she was here, with a man, who, for the moment, was her friend, her lover and her favourite companion.

Justin came through the doorway carrying a tray with two glasses of white wine and a bowl of local olives. Later they would go out to eat, but for now they would enjoy the view.

"Happy?" he asked her as he put the tray down on the patio table and sat beside her.

She nodded, took an olive, and put it in her mouth.

If you are an FTD carer, she thought, you have learn to live in the moment. There is an underlying sadness running through your life. True happiness is not an option, but there is pleasure and there is joy. You have to live one day at a time and savour whatever gems it has to offer. That was what she was doing now. Today was perfect. This moment was perfect. There would be other moments that were sad, some unimaginably sad, but she mustn't think of those moments now. She had learned a lot in the last three years, and one of those things was that she could cope with what life threw at her. She raised her glass. "Cheers!" she said, and took a sip.

Justin did the same. He put his hand on her arm. "I don't want to break the magic," he said, "But have you phoned Lionel this evening?"

"Thank you for reminding me," she said. Let's get it over with, she thought. She didn't want to phone Lionel because she knew he would have nothing to say. A telephone conversation with someone of so few words was almost impossible.

She smiled at Justin. He was a divorcee. One day he would tire of this stilted relationship that enabled him to see Effie only at her convenience. He should be with a woman who was available. She had told him that many times, but he always shook his head. "You don't choose who you fall in love with," he said.

Effie wasn't sure about that. She thought she had chosen not to fall in love with Justin. She'd reined in her emotions. She had to protect the stability of the life she was destined to lead with Lionel. Whatever happened, she had to see it through.

She picked up her mobile phone and called the home landline. It rang.

"Hello," said Lionel.

"Hello. It's me," she said.

"Mrs Me?" he asked.

"Yes."

"Hello Mrs Me," he joked, as he always did.

"Is that Mr Me?"

He laughed. "Yes."

"How's things?" she asked.

"Fine."

"What's the weather like?"

"Horrible."

"It's nice here," she said.

"Oh."

He wasn't going to ask her about anything. He couldn't. His poor depleted brain no longer had the ability to formulate a question more complex than what was for supper. That part of his brain that once exhibited curiosity and interest was destroyed by the disease. He didn't want to know, didn't need to know about anything. At least she didn't have to field questions about what she was doing and with whom.

"Any phone calls?" she asked.

"No."

"Did the carer come?"

There was a pause, almost as though he didn't, in that moment, understand her question. Then, "Yes," he said.

"Which one? What was her name?"

"How should I know?" he snapped.

"What did she do?"

"Oh... I don't know," he said irritably.

"Have you had your supper?" was Effie's next question.

"Yes."

"What did you have?"

"Oh... I don't remember," he said, his irritation increasing.

She realised she was asking too many questions. She must stop. "Well, take care, I'll phone you tomorrow, love. Bye now."

"Bye."

She ended the call. There, duty done, she thought. Now she could relax.

She shivered. The sun had dipped below the horizon and the temperature was dropping fast. The evening star had appeared, hanging like a jewel below the crescent moon.

"All right?" asked Justin. He stretched an arm across the table and took her hand in his.

"Yes," she said. She squeezed his hand. "More than all right." And so it was.

It was so good have him there for her.

Three years ago, she had felt alone. She had felt she was the only person in the world with these problems. Now she knew she wasn't. Amanda, the Admiral Nurse, was there in the background, ready to offer support when she needed it. There were the other FTD carers. They were ready to talk and listen and share. Natalie and the team in London. They understood her as none of her old friends, nor even her family, ever could. And for now, she had Justin. She was so lucky.

And no one, but no one, had criticised her for breaking those marriage vows.

Her phone bleeped with the arrival of a text message. It was from Suzie. She smiled an apology at Justin and tapped the screen.

Hi Mum. Primacare phoned. Dad was aggressive. They want to send two carers together from now on. I said it would be fine. Doubles the price, but so be it. Don't worry about anything. Love Suzie xx

Oh no! thought Effie. Another problem.

"What's the matter?" asked Justin. He must have seen her face fall.

Effie deleted the text and forced a smile. "Message from my daughter. She says, *Have fun, Mum. Don't do anything I wouldn't do!*"

Justin laughed. "Is that going to limit our activities?"

Effie lowered her lashes and stretched her arm across the table to take Justin's hand again. "I don't think so."

She smiled happily. Live in the moment. This moment was as good as it was ever going to get.

EPILOGUE

The End of the Beginning

In the beginning there were words. Lot and lots of words. In the beginning there was a man called Lionel. He had good friends and loyal colleagues. He married a girl called Effie who loved him.

FTD has stolen his brain cells. It has stolen his friends. It has stolen his world.

Lionel isn't the only one. There are many Lionels in this world of ours, and not many people understand.

Now is the end of the beginning. There are still a few words that slip through the spaces in Lionel's brain. One day there will be no words at all.

All Effie can do is wait. She is, she knows, a Widow-in-Waiting.

THE END

25484307R00213

Printed in Poland
by Amazon Fulfillment
Poland Sp. z o.o., Wrocław